Get a Feel for English !

喚醒你的英文語感！

Get a Feel for English !

喚醒你的英文語感 ！

New TOEIC

多益新鮮人
一定要有的奪分筆記

輕鬆超越650分，熱門職缺搶著要你！

作者 大賀理惠、Bill Benfield、Ann Gleason、Terry Browning

貝塔語言出版
Beta Multimedia Publishing

IRT 語言測驗中心
Language Testing Center

本書對於參加 TOEIC 測驗經驗尚淺、想開始努力奠定實力的人特別有效。它是專以 650 分門檻為基準，排除過難題目，聚焦收錄基本及常見考型，來確實幫助考生衝刺、提高分數。

過去 20 年來，筆者在一系列專為 TOEIC 設計的特殊培訓課程，指導了數千名學生，並編寫了許多以提高 TOEIC 分數為本的輔助教材。許多考生在此課程的訓練後，分數顯著提升；因為好口碑，此課程從原本的一個班級，在短時間內暴增為八個班級，甚至每次都有許多人列名等待候補。目前您手中的這本書，正是筆者這數十年來的教學經驗；提供您最精華、最有效的學習指標。

首先，讀者可利用本書的「Pre Test」（前測驗）來評估自身實力、找出弱點。請讀者切勿跳過「自我評估」這項重要的程序；唯有先了解弱點，才能對症下藥。即使「Pre Test」的分數不盡理想，也別氣餒，在閱讀過「Pre Test」中提供的各項學習要點及建議後，請依「Half Test」（準測驗）和「Full Test」（全測驗）中的說明持續學習。

另外，建議讀者在閱讀「全題型奪分攻略」篇中的「奧格的悲劇」（奧格〔Ooga〕為筆者的英文名字）時能同時想像測驗情境，祝福讀者在實際考試時，能避免筆者當時所犯下的錯誤。

本書與市面上其他多益學習書最大的不同在於，筆者特別著重於編寫自然、生活化的情境，讓讀者在學習時覺得輕鬆、容易吸收且進入狀況。建議讀者可將書中所附 MP3 的語音內容複製到 iPod 等裝置中，出門時隨身攜帶，以便隨時隨地跟讀練習。如此，即可達成 （1）記住實際語調與發音 ；（2）充分吸收英文 ；（3）TOEIC 測驗得分大幅提升，以上一石三鳥的學習效果。

即使一開始參加 TOEIC 測驗時無法考出理想分數，也別灰心，可以多應試幾次（每次間隔以不超過一至三個月較為理想。）不論是誰，多練習幾次之後，分數定會出現 50 到 200 分左右的大躍進；持續挑戰，必可突破 650 分門檻。每次的得分就像在攀岩，緊緊攀附的同時，也朝頂峰彈跳躍升。

最後，在此要對 ASK 出版社的編輯影山洋子小姐獻上由衷的感謝之意，她不僅為本書犧牲了無數個週末，也提供了眾多寶貴建議。

大賀 Rie

目錄

Section 1 ✏ 全題型奪分攻略

Section 2 ✏ 漸進式模擬試題完整解析

✏ 漸進式模擬試題本 （別冊）

本書 特色與使用方式

✎ 本書架構

本書包含 Pre Test（100 題）、兩組 Half Test（各 100 題）與一組 Full Test（200 題）。為了幫助以 650 分為目標之讀者有效率地學習，故所收錄題目都以 400 ～ 600 分程度為主。若想達到 650 分，最好能正確解答本書七成五以上的問題。每次答題完畢後，請再複習一次全部題目，以增加答對題數。本書共有完整解析與模擬試題各一冊，方便讀者對照使用；模擬試題最後附有 Answer Sheet（答案卡），方便讀者以正式測驗的方式畫卡作答。

✎ 關於 MP3

收錄 Pre Test、Half Test 1、Half Test 2 與 Full Test 之聽力試題音檔。

✎ 使用步驟

Step 1 閱讀「全題型奪分攻略」：掌握得分先機

此章節將為讀者說明 TOEIC 測驗各部分的出題形式與出題要點。無論是否已參加過 TOEIC 測驗，建議在進行本書所有測驗前，先熟讀「全題型奪分攻略」，以透析 TOEIC 測驗的解題要領、出題方向，並掌握得分訣竅。讀者更可藉由筆者親身應考的慘痛經驗──「奧格的悲劇」，吸取教訓，免於重蹈覆轍。以下為您簡介此章節的功能標題：

> 🔑 **解題要領**
> 細說出題方式，如：命題題數、方向、方式；為考生規劃作答時間。
>
> ⚓ **出題要點及趨勢**
> 進一步詳列出題種類，如：命題主題、句型，破題關鍵及技巧。
>
> 😲 **奧格的悲劇**
> 真實闡述測驗當下會遇到的最遭情況，以予前車之鑑。
>
> 😊 **超越 650 分的訣竅**
> 各大題型考題攻略結束後，再次重點歸納答題訣竅。

Step 2 **實戰「Pre Test」： 小試身手掌握弱點，延伸學習累積實力**

1. 首先進行 Pre Test。將聽力測驗用的 MP3 準備就緒，並嚴守 Reading Test 的時間限制，建議您可事先設定好馬錶或鬧鐘。

2. 做完 Pre Test 後，將您的答案抄到 p.40 的解答一覽表中，再算出各大題的答對題數與答對率。只要算出各大題答對率，便能看出您自身的弱點分布。

3. 以自己答錯的題目為主，閱讀其完整解析。文中除了有中譯和各答案選項為何正確或錯誤的詳細說明外，也包括有助增加得分的各種資訊：

> 🕐 **小心陷阱**
> 針對誘餌類選項進行重點解說，以免誤入陷阱。
>
> ✓ **這樣練習最有效**
> 傳授可快速提高得分的簡易練習法。
>
> 💡 **奪分祕笈**
> 依據各出題要點，介紹出現頻率最高的片語及例句。除了學習時使用外，也適合當做考前的衝刺維他命。

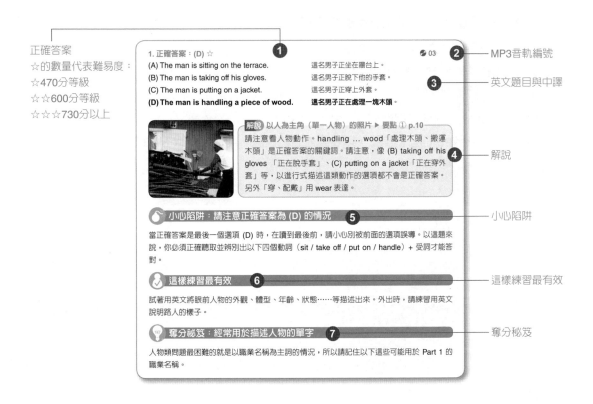

正確答案
☆的數量代表難易度：
☆470分等級
☆☆600分等級
☆☆☆730分以上

❶

1. 正確答案：(D) ☆ ❷ 🔊 03 ──── MP3音軌編號

❸ ──── 英文題目與中譯

(A) The man is sitting on the terrace. 這名男子正坐在陽台上。
(B) The man is taking off his gloves. 這名男子正脫下他的手套。
(C) The man is putting on a jacket. 這名男子正穿上外套。
(D) The man is handling a piece of wood. **這名男子正在處理一塊木頭。**

解說 以人為主角（單一人物）的照片 ▶ 要點 ① p.10
請注意看人物動作。handling ... wood「處理木頭、搬運木頭」是正確答案的關鍵詞。請注意，像 (B) taking off his gloves「正在脫手套」、(C) putting on a jacket「正在穿外套」等，以進行式描述這類動作的選項都不會是正確答案。另外「穿、配戴」用 wear 表達。 ❹ ──── 解說

🕐 **小心陷阱：請注意正確答案為 (D) 的情況** ❺ ──── 小心陷阱
當正確答案是最後一個選項 (D) 時，在讀到最後前，請小心別被前面的選項誤導。以這題來說，你必須正確聽取並辨別出以下四個動詞（sit / take off / put on / handle）+ 受詞才能答對。

✓ **這樣練習最有效** ❻ ──── 這樣練習最有效
試著用英文將眼前人物的外觀、體型、年齡、狀態……等描述出來。外出時，請練習用英文說明路人的樣子。

💡 **奪分祕笈：經常用於描述人物的單字** ❼ ──── 奪分祕笈
人物類問題最困難的就是以職業名稱為主詞的情況，所以請記住以下這些可能用於 Part 1 的職業名稱。

Step 3 勤做 「Half Test 1 & Half Test 2」：針對常見重點再做練習

詳讀 Pre test 的解說，先複習、弄懂自己答錯的題目，然後繼續挑戰各 100 題的兩組測驗。這兩組準測驗的答題方式和 Pre Test 相同。請準備好 Answer Sheet 與馬錶，在時間限制內答完所有題目後，將自己的答案抄進解答一覽表（Half Test 1 的解答在 p.148，Half Test 2 的在 p.200），再算出各部分的答對題數與答對率。在 Half Test 的解答與解說裡，也都清楚列出了出題要點，而如「 ⊃ Pre 15」這類標記則代表須參照 Pre Test 的題目編號。對於自己特別不懂的題目，請依據該編號翻回 Pre Test 中對應的解答與解說處，再次複習。

Step 4 迎戰「Full Test」：利用和正式測驗相同的題數驗收學習成效

請以面對正式測驗的態度來做 Full Test。針對閱讀測驗，請事先計算並分配好各部分的時間，一邊注意時鐘或馬錶，一邊注意時間運用狀況，務必及時答完全部題目。

做完 Full Test 後，就和做 Pre Test 及 Half Test 時一樣，把自己的答案抄進解答一覽表，在比對後，算出各部分的答對題數與答對率。其解答與解說也都已清楚列出了出題要點，與 Half Test 同，請針對自己特別不懂的題目，回頭翻閱參考 Pre Test 或 Half Test 中對應題目的解說內容。

Step 5 擅用「附錄」：方便預習及複習的小補丸

1. 節錄重要單字及片語（p. 348 ~ 353）

   將出現在本書各題目、解說中的重要單字、片語及其意義、詞性列出。若想複習相關例句時，則可參照所列頁碼。

2. 各題目的 MP3 音軌編號與腔調（p. 354 ~ 355）

   列出 MP3 中各題目的音軌編號，以及講述者的腔調，可供您聽取 MP3 複習時參考。

關於 TOEIC® 測驗

- ▶ TOEIC（多益）是用來評估各方面英語溝通能力的世界性測驗。
- ▶ 由美國非營利測驗開發機構 ETS（Educational Testing Service）所開發，實施於全世界共約 90 個國家，每年受測人數約 500 萬人。
- ▶ TOEIC 測驗分為給一般個人參加的 National Program（公開測驗），還有以學校、公司為單位的 Institutional Program（團體測驗制度）。在台灣每年會舉辦 12 次公開測驗。
- ▶ 除了用於個人測驗外，TOEIC 也廣為各企業、政府機關、學校單位所採用，因此不僅可驗收自我能力，也能作用為升遷、加薪的標準，或是推薦入學的門檻。

● 測驗形式

TOEIC 包括聽力測驗（45 分鐘，100 題）與閱讀測驗（75 分鐘，100 題）兩大部分，需在 2 小時內以答案卡作答 200 題。測驗內容全為英文，沒有英翻中、中翻英等題目，各部分內容可細分如下。

聽力測驗	45 分鐘	共 100 題
Part 1　照片題 Photographs		10 題
Part 2　應答題 Question-Response		30 題
Part 3　簡短對話題 Short Conversations		30 題
Part 4　簡短獨白題 Short Talks		30 題
閱讀測驗	75 分鐘	共 100 題
Part 5　單句填空題 Incomplete Sentences		40 題
Part 6　短文填空題 Text Completion		12 題
Part 7　文章理解題 Reading Comprehension 單篇文章 Single passage 雙篇文章 Double passages		28 題 20 題

● 測驗結果

TOEIC 測驗不像全民英檢等有合格與否的結果判定，只以聽力、閱讀測驗各 5 ~ 495 分，總共 10 ~ 990 分，以 5 分為一單位的分數做為評估結果。

▶ 各種分數等級所代表的意義
關於 TOEIC 測驗的分數與英語能力及實際應用狀況的關聯性，存在各式各樣的不同見解，而筆者以過去 20 年來所主講之 TOEIC 課程的學生為範本，自訂出如下表的標準，供讀者參考。

得分水準	英語能力	與工作、留學之關聯
Level 1 200 ~ 350	▶ 聽力方面雖可聽出最基本的單字，但須經過練習才能完整辨識一個句子。	
Level 2 355 ~ 450	▶ 對於日常生活的一般問候、詢問，能以 Yes、No 表達意思。 ▶ 仍須經過一些練習才能聽出完整句子（尤其是否定句等）並做出回應。	
Level 3 455 ~ 550	▶ 能運用 and、but、or、then 等連接詞說出簡短句子。 ▶ 能依需要，做到某個程度的意思表達。 ▶ 能運用所知單字拼湊出英文電子郵件內容，以便與朋友往來溝通。	
Level 4 555 ~ 650	▶ 能充分掌握如購物等日常生活及辦公室固定用語的表達。 ▶ 若身為某些專業領域人士，即使知道該領域的特殊詞彙與知識，仍需經過一些練習才能進行相關討論。 ▶ 即使在商務領域中，也能進行某個程度的英文電子郵件溝通。 ▶ 能處理辦公室內簡單的英文文件（帳單、收據等）。	
Level 5 655 ~ 750	▶ 可進行日常會話溝通，也相當能表達自我意見。只要經過事先練習，就能發表演說。但在討論事情時，需經過一些練習，才能有效表達自身意見。 ▶ 在商務方面，能撰寫固定形式的信件。	
Level 6 755 ~ 850	▶ 在日常生活及自身專業上的閱讀能力與聽力方面，都沒什麼問題。 ▶ 能聽懂對方所說的，並繼續對話。而從此等級開始，口說與書寫能力的個人差異會越來越大。	
Level 7 855 ~ 990	▶ 能夠相當自在隨興地以口語或書寫方式表達本身意見。 ▶ 能夠順利執行專業領域的工作。 ▶ 若要與英語為母語者平等爭辯，可能還有一小段距離。	

與工作、留學之關聯：

- 新進員工：200 ~ 450
- 不考慮就業／留學：200 ~ 450
- 技術部門：450 ~ 600
- 業務部門／具備外語留學能力：500 ~ 700
- 海外部門／外派人員／具大學留學能力：550 ~ 750
- 國內金融機構／外商公司：600 ~ 800、800 ~ 990

Section 1

全題型奪分攻略
Strategies

TOEIC →→→

Part Photographs 照片題

 解題要領★題數：10 題

此部分題目會針對 1 張照片提供 (A)、(B)、(C)、(D) 四個選項，你必須選出你認為最能正確描述照片情境的句子。正如下列**出題要點** ① 所述，這些照片的主題可能是人物、東西，或景觀……等。Part 1 和 Part 2 一樣，都是習慣其會話語速之後就能輕易得分的部分。如果想在 TOEIC 測驗中拿到 650 分以上的成績，請持續練習，直到 100% 答對本書所有題目為止。

⚓ 出題要點

Part 1 的出題趨勢可分為以下 5 點：

① 以人為主角的照片佔 80%

Part 1 照片描述題的照片有 80% 都是人物照。如果能養成看過照片，就分析出該主題的習慣，那麼實際參加測驗時，便能自然而然將內容分類，並在最短時間內找出正確答案。絕大多數的題目問的都是「誰」、「在哪裡」、「做什麼」……等，**時態則為現在式或現在進行式**。請訓練自己能在聽取問題陳述前，先快速看出人物「性別」、「姿勢」、「服裝」、「背景」……等要素。此外，在這類人物照的題目中，四個答案選項的主詞多半都會相同（the man / the woman、she / he、the girl / the boy、they 等），所以只要把注意力集中在述語的動詞與受詞等部分即可。與人物相關的題目很容易拿分，每一題都要好好把握。例如：

▶ 單一人物：呈現「誰」、「做什麼」、「在哪裡」、「穿著怎樣的服裝」

  例 <u>The boy</u> <u>is running</u> <u>along the river</u>.（男孩正沿著河邊跑步。）
     現在進行式

▶ 人＋人：呈現「誰和誰」、「在做什麼」、「兩人的位置關係如何」

  例 <u>Two men</u> <u>are sitting</u> <u>face to face</u>.（兩個男人面對面坐著。）
     現在進行式

▶ 人＋物：呈現「人與物」、「在……的地方」、「有著……的關係」

  例 <u>The man</u> <u>is standing</u> <u>next to a tall tree</u>.（這個男人站在一棵高大的樹旁邊。）
     現在進行式

  <u>There's</u> <u>a tall tree</u> <u>next to the man</u>.（這個男人旁邊有一棵高大的樹。）
     現在式

② 以多個物體為主題

人物照的正確答案通常是現在進行式，但是事物或景觀類的照片（例如：詢問「什麼東西」、「在哪裡」、「有著……的位置關係」等題目）所呈現的是拍攝時的狀態，因此答案幾乎都為「描述狀態的**現在式**」或「**被動式**」。所以可將以**進行式**描述物品的句子視為**錯誤選項**，例如：

▶ 物或景觀

○ The cars <u>are parked</u> in a row.
（汽車被停放成一排。）

✕ The cars <u>are moving</u> fast.
（汽車正在快速移動。）

▶ 物＋物或景觀

○ The telephone <u>is next</u> to the bed.
（電話在床旁邊。）

✕ The telephone <u>is ringing</u>.
（電話正在響。）

另外，以「物體或景觀」為主題的照片題，其四個選項的主詞、述語往往各自不同，所以較難拿分。這時，勝負關鍵就在於能否正確聽取事物的英文名稱，及表示位置的介系詞片語。

③ 掌握動詞時態

照片所呈現的是拍照瞬間的狀況，因此「選出表示目前狀況之動詞」通常就能答對。反之，包含代表未來的 will 或 be going to 等選項肯定都是錯的，例如：

▶ 現在進行式

○ The man <u>is riding</u> a bicycle.
（這個男人正在騎一輛腳踏車。）

✕ The man <u>will ride</u> a bicycle.
（這個男人將騎一輛腳踏車。）

▶ 現在式

○ The lamp <u>is</u> on.
（燈是亮的。）

✕ The lamp <u>is going to</u> be turned on.
（燈將會被打開。）

▶ 現在完成式＋被動式

○ The car tires <u>have been removed</u>.
（車子的輪胎已被拆除。）

✕ The tires <u>will be</u> removed.
（車胎將被拆除。）

---

④ 代表物體狀態變化的「現在完成式」+「被動式」

代表物體狀態變化的現在完成式，出現頻率雖然不高，但仍偶爾會出現。舉凡物體所發生的「明顯變化」或「平常理所當然會產生的變化現象」都會以完成式描述，例如：

> ▶ 完成式

All the leaves <u>have fallen</u>. （所有葉子都已落下。）
The car tires <u>have been removed</u>. （車子輪胎已被拆除。）

請記住「輪胎已被拆除」這樣的被動式特性。

另外，與物體有關的描述通常會使用「說明靜態狀態的」現在式，例如：

> ▶ 現在式

Leaves <u>are piled up</u> on the ground. （葉子堆在地上。）

⑤ 想像、推測、故事性的描述都不列入答案

照片題的正確答案，一定都是描述拍攝當時狀態的句子，因此「他很開心」和「幾位女性正要去餐廳吃午餐」等情況雖有可能，但都屬於推測，不會是正確答案，例如：

> ▶ 描述句

○ The man is smiling.　　　　　　　○ The women are going into a restaurant.
　（這個男人正在微笑。）　　　　　　　（這個女人正要進餐廳。）

> ▶ 推測句

× The man is happy.　　　　　　　　× The women are going to have lunch
　（這個男人很開心。）　　　　　　　　　at the restaurant.
　　　　　　　　　　　　　　　　　　　（幾位女性正要去餐廳吃午餐。）

奧格的悲劇 Part 1

幾十年前我初次參加 TOEIC 測驗，當 Listening Comprehension 開始，一播放起 Part 1 的 directions 時，我立刻努力聽並用鉛筆塗答案。就在我突然意識到那只是說明範例時，「Look at the Picture No.1 (A) ... 」的語音已經響起……。於是悲劇就此上演。接下來的第 2、3 題，我都在不小心超前了一步的震驚情緒中亂了陣腳。因此對於照片題部分，請一定要仔細確認目前進行的是否為範例說明還是正式考題。

超越 650 分的訣竅

(1) 播放 directions 說明範例時（範例永遠是同一個），可利用這段時間快速瀏覽下列有那些照片題。光是這簡單的瀏覽動作，就能讓你在測驗一開始，逐一讀出題目、遊刃有餘輕鬆應答。

(2) 各題目的間隔約為 5 秒。一聽到覺得正確的句子，就立刻畫在答案卡上。若一直都沒聽出答案，在聽到最後一句後，就應立即在答案卡畫上你推測的答案。測驗中的 5 秒間隔最完美的安排是能像這樣運用：前 3 秒用來畫答案卡，後 2 秒用來觀察下一張照片。

Part ② Question – Response 應答題

 解題要領 ★題數：30 題

語音首先會唸出一個問題或一段評論，然後再接續讀出對應的 (A)、(B)、(C) 三句選項。你必須選出你認為最合適的句子，並畫在答案卡上。此部分和 Part 1 相當不同，其問題與對應選項都只有語音，測驗卷上只印了 Mark your answer on your answer sheet. 的字樣，完全沒有任何可幫助理解的線索。但是相較於 Part 3 & 4，Part 2 仍屬於容易得分的部分，請至少把握 80% 的答對率。

⚓ 出題要點

這部分測試的是在日常生活及商務環境中，正確回應問題及評論的能力。Part 2 常出現令人意料之外的答案，不只是「How are you?」、「Fine, thank you.」這種制式化的應答，這正是令考生頭疼的地方，你必須聽懂問題或評論內容，選出合理的回應。

Part 2 的出題趨勢主要可分為下列**出題要點之** ①、②、③ 等三大類，而列在下一頁**要點** ④ 中的則為另一種趨勢。

現在，繼續為您介紹 Part 2 的出題要點。

① Statement-Response（陳述與反應）

Statement-Response 類型的題目在 Part 2 的 30 題中約佔了5 題，比例為 16% 左右。這類題目要求考生必須了解對方所說的話，並當場判斷該怎麼回應。例如：

 你會聽到

Arthur wasn't in the office, so I gave the report to Marie.
（亞瑟不在辦公室，所以我把報告交給了瑪莉。）
(A) O.K. Marie will write a report. （好，瑪莉會寫報告。）
(B) O.K. Marie will give it to Arthur. （好，瑪莉會把它交給亞瑟。）
(C) Arthur isn't here. （亞瑟不在這裡。）

正確答案：(B)

針對「由於亞瑟本人不在，所以我把報告交給了瑪莉」這句話，「瑪莉會把報告交給亞瑟」是最合適的回應。像這樣的應答，一般人雖能以中文輕鬆反應過來，可是一旦換成英文，好不容易擠出一個 Yes 或 No 之後，恐怕就再也吐不出更妥當的回應了。若想突破這種窘境並培養自然的應答能力，可多練習 Statement-Response 類型的題目。這是 2006 年修訂題目時才新增至 TOEIC 測驗的新出題趨勢。

② 以 Yes-No 回答的疑問句

Yes-No Question 在 Part 2 的 30 題中佔了約 11 題，比例為 36% 左右。例如：

> 在 Yes-No Question 中，包含肯定疑問、否定疑問及附加疑問等句型。
>
> ▶ 肯定　　　Are you going to watch the game?　　　（你要看比賽嗎？）
> ▶ 否定　　　Aren't you going to watch the game?　　（你不看比賽嗎？）
> ▶ 附加疑問　You're going to watch the game,　　　　（你要看比賽，不是嗎？）
> 　　　　　　aren't you?
>
> 英語的 Yes / No 並不完全等於中文的「是」、「否」。在英文中，不論聽到肯定或否定句，回答方式都一樣。尤其在遇到否定疑問句時，請千萬小心別弄錯了。例如：
>
> ┌ 問1　Are you hungry?　　　　　　　　　（你餓了嗎？）
> └ 答1　Yes, I am. / No, I'm not.　　　　（是的，我餓了。／不，我不餓。）
> ┌ 問2　Aren't you hungry?　　　　　　　（你不餓嗎？）
> └ 答2　Yes, I am. / No, I'm not.　　　　（是的，我餓了。／不，我不餓。）

如上，英文的回答方式都一致，只考慮述語中 hungry 的部分，若是如此就用 Yes, ... ，若非如此就用 No, ... 回答。而被用中文問到「你不餓嗎？」時，則應回答「是的，我不餓」，或「不，我餓了」，也就是會有「是」與「否」相反的組合出現，這點是使用中文的人在會話時很容易弄錯的部分，請多注意。

③ Wh-Questions（Wh- 疑問句）

Wh-Questions 在 Part 2 的 30 題中佔了約 12 題，比例為 40% 左右。
疑問詞包括 What / Who / Which / When / Where / Why / How（How much、How far 等）及相關變化用詞。這些疑問詞一定會出現在句首，很容易一不小心就可能漏聽。因此**你的第一要務就是別漏聽疑問詞**。例如：

Where did you go last night?　　　（你昨晚去哪裡了？）
(A) I went there at 9 p.m.　　　（我晚上 9 點去了那兒。）
(B) I went there by bicycle.　　　（我是騎腳踏車去那兒的。）
(C) I went to see a movie.　　　（我去看了電影。）

正確答案：(C)

如果你漏聽了疑問詞 Where，而選 (A) 或 (B)，就落入了陷阱選項：(A) 是 When did you go? 的答案，(B) 是 How did you go? 的答案。因此，若要避免落入陷阱，就必須正確聽取疑問詞才行。（相關說明請參考下一頁「超越 650 分的訣竅」中的第（2）項。）

④ 請小心同音異字、多義詞，以及發音相似的詞彙

依據以下要素設計的陷阱選項（distracters）也相當常見。

▶ 發音相同但意義不同的詞彙（同音異義字）	heal	[hil]	動 治療
	heel	[hil]	名 腳後跟
▶ 擁有多種不同意義的詞彙（多義詞）	file	[faɪl]	名 文件檔案；銼刀
▶ 發音相似的詞	button	[ˋbʌtn̩]	名 釦子
	bottom	[ˋbɑtəm]	名 底部

包含與題目中關鍵字相同詞彙的選項，幾乎都是錯的。事實上，在正確答案中，該詞彙多半會被「改述」(paraphrase) 成其他詞句。如下列題目裡的關鍵字 fixed 在正確答案 (B) 中就被改述為 treated。此類題目考的不是你能否聽出詞彙發音，而是要確認你是否真的理解其意義，所以才要求必須選出改述後的詞彙。例如：

fix　[fɪks]　動 修理、調整、固定、治療（疾病）
　　　　　　　　名 修理、定位、受操縱的事、困境

🔊 你會聽到

I'm going to the dentist to get my tooth fixed.　（我要去牙醫那兒看牙齒。）
(A) You're in a real fix.　　　（你真的身陷困境。）
(B) I got mine treated last week.　　　（我上週也去看了我的牙。）
(C) I have a fixation on dentists.　　　（我對牙醫有種刻板印象。）

正確答案是用了 fixed 之同義詞 treated 的 (B)。另外兩個選項所包含的是 fix 和 fixation（同形異義詞和衍生詞），皆為牛頭不對馬嘴的陷阱選項。

奧格的悲劇 Part 2

在我第一次考 TOEIC 時，還沒有出現針對敘述句做回應的題型。不過問與答也不如 Part 2 directions 的例題 How are you? Fine, thank you.（你好嗎？我很好，謝謝。）那麼單純，而是有許多類似 How are you? If I didn't have this nasty cold, I'd be fine.（你好嗎？若沒這討人厭的感冒的話，還挺好的。）這樣有些拐彎抹角的題目；這其實讓我很慌亂，而且測驗卷上沒任何線索可循，即使我的聽力已相當接近以英語為母語者， Part 2 仍讓我感覺困難。不過， Part 2 在某個程度上是靠熟悉度決勝負的，所以只要多累積考試經驗，就能快速提高得分。

 超越 650 分的訣竅

(1)　當測驗卷上不存在任何可靠的文字資訊時，就表示須徹底專注聆聽語音，因此只要習慣了，你就能在 Part 2 輕鬆得分。從一題結束至下一題開始前，會有 5 秒的空檔。請利用這 5 秒內的 3 秒決定答案並畫記好答案。即使不知道答案，也務必養成在下一題播放前就畫好答案的習慣。

(2)　在 Part 2 的 30 題中，約有 12 題是以 What / When 等 Wh- 疑問詞起頭的題目。為了在這部分獲得滿分，你絕不能漏聽任一個句首疑問詞。從一題結束到下一題開始之間的 5 秒鐘內，依照上述第 (1) 點的時間分配，畫記好答案後，請務必屏住呼吸，在下一句播放前持續集中注意力，以免漏聽了任何疑問詞或主詞。例如：句首的 Wh- 疑問詞為何、是否為否定（Didn't you、Aren't you 等），還有主詞為何……等等。

Part Short Conversations 簡短對話題

 解題要領★題數：30 題

總共有 10 段不同主題的對話，每一段對話各出三個題目，每題有四個選項。兩個人以 A-B-A 或 A-B-A-B 的形式進行對話。除了對話外，每一題組的三個題目也會被唸出來，且問題與選項都會印在測驗卷上。選項不會被唸出來，請快速瀏覽並選出你認為最正確的答案。

 出題趨勢

會話內容以日常生活及辦公室中的對話為主，例如：購物、約定會議時間、調整行程……等。在台灣，即使是平日經常「閱讀英文」的人也少有機會熟悉英語會話，因此 Part 3 算是很不容易拿分的；而且，有些人在 Part 3 的得分甚至會比 Part 4 的 Short Talks 還低。若想超越 650 分，請把握這部分 80% 以上的答對率；若想提高分數，請在做完本書 Pre Test 的題目後，反覆聆聽語音並進行 shadowing 練習[註]，藉此習慣聽取語音及該類會話形式。

註 shadowing（跟讀）：聆聽 MP3 語音並立即跟著唸出英文發音的練習方式。這種練習法不僅有利於學習發音、語調，也能幫助理解詞彙和句子結構。練習時絕不可暫停播放，務必反覆練習直到能跟上 MP3 語音的速度為止。務必以即使「不看書也能跟著讀」為終極目標。

出題要點

Part 3 的出題趨勢可分為以下 3 大類。接著就以如下會話為例，介紹題目分類：

🔊 **你會聽到**

Man: Excuse me, how much are the silk flowers?
Woman: They range from $27 up to $49. The price is on the bottom of the flower pot.
Man: That's pretty expensive. I can get real flowers for much less.
Woman: Yes, but the silk ones last forever. This arrangement is $32, but I can give you 20% off.

男子： 請問，這些絲花要賣多少錢？
女子： 27 美元到 49 美元之間，價格就標示在花盆盆底。
男子： 相當貴耶，買真花比這便宜多了。
女子： 是，不過絲花永不凋謝。這組插花賣 32 美元，但是我可以給你打八折。

① 較大範圍的問題

所謂的大範圍問題，就是與會話整體的主題、概要有關的問題。通常會從第一個說話者的台詞找關鍵字提問，上述例子的關鍵字是 silk flower，而題目可能會這樣問：

🔊 **你會聽到、看到** ──────

What are the speakers talking about?　　　（談話者在談論些什麼？）

👁 **你會看到** ──────

(A) Fresh flowers　　　　　　　　　（鮮花）
(B) Potted plants　　　　　　　　　（盆栽）
(C) Dry flowers　　　　　　　　　　（乾燥花）
(D) Artificial flowers　　　　　　　（人造花）

正確答案：(D)

會話中的關鍵字 silk flowers 可改述為 artificial flowers，故（D）「人造花」是正確答案。即使不了解男子所說的 silk flowers 為何，只要聽到第 2 句 I can get real flowers for much less.「買真花比這便宜多了」，就知道此對話的主題是人造花。而若能回答「在談論些什麼？」這類宏觀問題，第 1 題就過關了。

② 較小範圍的問題

所謂的小範圍問題，就是測試你對會話細節理解程度的問題。例如題目可能會這樣問：

🔊 **你會聽到、看到** ──────

What does the salesclerk say about silk flowers?　　（對於絲花，店員說了些什麼？）

👁 **你會看到** ──────

(A) Silk flowers never die.　　　　　　　　　（絲花永不枯萎。）
(B) Silk flowers are more beautiful.　　　　　（絲花比較美。）
(C) Silk flowers tend to get diseased.　　　　（絲花容易生病。）
(D) Silk flowers don't require any care.　　　（絲花不須照顧。）

正確答案：(A)

Strategies / Pre Test / Half Test 1 / Half Test 2 / Full Test

這是考驗你是否理解細節的問題。當客人說「相當貴」的時候，店員回應了 ... but the silk ones last forever.，而這正是此題正確答案 (A) 的關鍵。像這種枝微末節型的問題，其答案多半在會話的中段或最後的部分，跟 ① 的宏觀型題目相比，此題型較難找出答案。不過若先讀過題目，應該就能注意到女子在第 2 句 the silk ones ... 中對絲花的評論。只要牢記此要點並「反覆練習」，很快就能達到迅速接收資訊的程度。

③ 與數字有關的問題

在 Part 3 中經常出現（1）日期時間、（2）人數、（3）商品價格、（4）商品數量等這 4 種與數值有關的問題。而這類問題正是 Part 3 中最容易答錯的，因此一定要在聽會話前先瀏覽題目，答對機率才高。為了讓你盡可能多多練習，本書的 Part 3 都包含了與數值相關的題目。例如題目可能會這樣問：

🔊 **你會聽到、看到**

How much was the customer probably expecting to spend?（客人大約打算花多少錢呢？）

👁 **你會看到**

(A) Over $20　　　　　　　　　　　　　（20 美元以上）

(B) Over $49　　　　　　　　　　　　　（49 美元以上）

(C) Under $27　　　　　　　　　　　　（27 美元以下）

(D) About $32　　　　　　　　　　　　（大約 32 美元）

正確答案：(C)

在會話中店員說了 They range from $27 up to $49.，針對這句話客人的回應是 That's pretty expensive.，可推測客人並不想花到 27 美元這麼多。因此除了 (C) 的「27 美元以下」，其他選項都是陷阱。

奧格的悲劇 Part 3

我第一次考 TOEIC 時,在 Part 3 連一半的分數都沒拿到,
簡直是徹底慘敗!我不是聽不懂英文,而是參加考試時過度
緊張。(1) 當試題進入第 2、3 題時就開始跟不上試題的語
速,而且當下一段會話都已經開始的時候,還留戀地想著上
一題題目,(2) 更糟的是我還畫錯答案卡……。

(嘆氣)所謂「捨得、捨得,有捨才有得」這
句話,我一直到做了好多練習題之後,才終於
體會其深意。

超越 650 分的訣竅

(1) 實際參加 TOEIC 測驗前,請先利用本書的題目進行shadowing(跟
讀)及聽取關鍵詞的訓練。應付 Part 3 時,是否能完整想像會話場
景,且同時掌握整體狀況非常重要。

(2) 在考試中,請利用 Part 3 的 directions 播放的時間,盡量多預先瀏覽
正式考題及選項,以便掌握大方向、小細節等關鍵詞。

(3) 每段會話的每個問題之間,都有約 8 秒間隔,所以 3 題就有共約 24
秒的時間。**在對話語音播放出來前,一定要先讀完題目。**若有某些問
題無法在對話開始前讀完,那就一邊聽對話,一邊利用各問題間的 8
秒時間來回答。

(4) 不知道答案時,尤其是較小範圍類問題的相關資訊很容易漏聽,這時
的補救方法就是:依靠你的「直覺」,在答案卡上猜一個答案。有些
心理學家認為,「直覺」就是一種經驗累積的結果,故請信賴你的學
習成果,勇敢猜出答案;「不要過度堅持追究答案」,正是增加答對
題數的秘訣之一;若是死不放棄地回頭研究,很容易在不知不覺中連
續答錯一題、甚至三題,要是再畫錯答案,那就得不償失了。

(5) 就如 Part 3 出題要點 ③ 所提到的,數字型問題實際考試很常出現。
雖說 Part 3 的選項不會以語音播放出來,但是在練習本書題目時,
請你將問題和選項全都讀出來。然後將生活中常用的數字
(時間、價格、人數、電話號碼)等也都反覆唸出聲練
習。另外,上網搜尋英文廣告,並練習將廣告中的數
量、價格等唸出來,都是很不錯的練習方式。

Part 4 Short Talks 簡短獨白題

解題要領 ★題數：30 題

此部分有各種不同主題的語音說明，約十個段落，而每段說明都有三個題目，每題各有四個選項。說明文與其問題都會以語音播放，但是選項不會。測驗卷上則同時印有問題及選項。你必須選出你認為最正確的答案。

出題趨勢

由於在台灣接觸到 Part 4 形式說明文的機會多於 Part 3 的對話形式，所以對於平常有聽英語、閱讀英文文件習慣的人來說，Part 4 可能反而比 Part 3 更容易拿分。不過 Part 4 畢竟是 LISTENING SECTION 中困難詞彙最多的部分，其語音讀出的速度也屬於自然語度，因此若沒有經常聆聽文章口述，將很難獲得高分。所以在正式參加測驗前請多用本書題目進行 shadowing 練習，以努力獲得 60% 的分數。

出題要點

Part 4 也和 Part 3 一樣有較大範圍的問題（與主題概要有關）和較小範圍的問題（與細節相關），以下將為讀者分類題目形式，請參考：

① 較大範圍的問題（與主題概要有關）

> ▶ What is the advertisement / announcement / news report / message about?
> 這是關於什麼的廣告／聲明／新聞／訊息？
>
> | | |
> |---|---|
> | What is the purpose of this message? | 這段訊息的目的為何？ |
> | What is the problem? | 問題是什麼？ |
> | What does the speaker say? | 講者說了些什麼？ |
> | What is the occasion? | 這是什麼場合？ |
> | What kind of weather is predicted? | 天氣預測會如何？ |
> | What will take place on July 4th? | 7 月 4 日會發生什麼事？ |
> | How did this problem occur? | 這問題是怎麼發生的？ |

② 較小範圍的問題（與細節相關）

▶ 與講者有關的問題

Who is the speaker?	講者是誰？
Who is involved in this incident?	誰涉及了此事件？
Who is this message for?	這段訊息是給誰的？
Who should listen to this announcement?	誰應該聽這段聲明？

▶ 與地點有關的問題

What is the destination?	目的地在哪裡？
Where is this announcement being made?	這段聲明是在哪裡公布的？
Where is the meeting taking place?	會議將在哪裡舉行？
Where is the hotel located?	飯店位於何處？

▶ 與數字有關的問題（分機號碼、時間、種類、價格、人數等）

What number should you press to get ... ?	欲接通……你應該撥幾號？
What are the business hours?	營業時間為何？
What is the price of the product?	此產品的售價是多少？
What day / date[註] will be the concert?	演唱會將在星期幾／哪一天舉行？
How long will it take to get to the destination?	到達目的地要花多少時間？
How many different kinds of workshops are offered?	有幾種研討會？
How many people are going?	有多少人會去？
How much does the shipping cost?	運費是多少錢？
How much refund can the customer expect?	預計將退還給顧客多少錢？

註 day 是指星期幾，date 則是指幾月幾日。

奧格的悲劇 Part 4

和 Part 3 不同的是，Part 4 說明文中的各句子間幾乎沒有「空檔」。雖說是以自然速度讀出，但對於初次參加 TOEIC 測驗的我來說，實在跟不上。另外，就像稍後「超越 650 分的訣竅」之（3）所提到的，說明文裡的關鍵詞在問題選項中往往都會被「改述」成其他詞彙，因此這部分也讓人聽得很辛苦。儘管我對於自己的字彙能力信心滿滿，而且萬分謹慎，不過因為是初次應考、練習經驗也不足，最後因為趕不上速度而徹底失敗。

超越 650 分的訣竅

(1) 快速瀏覽問題中的關鍵詞：在說明文語音開始播放前，由上而下迅速掃描並掌握三個問題裡的關鍵詞。由於問題順序和說明文中，關鍵詞的出現順序通常會一致，所以只要事先掃瞄一下問題裡的關鍵詞，基本上就能連結至說明文內的關鍵詞，並找到正確答案。例如：

Q 1. <u>What</u> is this announcement about? （這是關於什麼的說明？）
　　　關鍵詞是 What ... about
Q 2. <u>How soon</u> is the bus coming? （公車多快會到？）
　　　關鍵詞是 How soon

(2) 與 Part 3 一樣，問題間隔為 8 秒，3 題就共有 24 秒時間可以利用。對於語音開始播放前沒能掃描到的問題，請邊聽邊作答。

(3) 和 Part 3 相同，Part 4 的選項內容常是關鍵詞之總結、改述或換句話說後的結果。如果想順利解答 Part 4 的問題，請牢記以下三個步驟。
step 1：找出問題裡的關鍵詞。
step 2：邊聽語音邊找出相當於問題中關鍵詞答案的詞彙或片語。
step 3：同時在選項 (A)、(B)、(C)、(D) 中選出與該詞彙或片語同義的答案。由於選項裡的詞彙及片語往往會經過改述轉換，所以你必須迅速從四個選項中選出同義詞才行。而這正是 Part 4 不易得分的主要理由之一。
例如：語音 ▶ We would appreciate if you could <u>update</u> us.
　　　（若您將最新情況告知我們，我們將感激不盡。）
　　　經改述後的正確選項 ▶ Let us know about the <u>present status</u>.
　　　（請讓我們了解目前狀況。）
　　　▶ update 被換成了 present status

(4) 在 LISTENING SECTION 結束之後即進入 READING SECTION，此時最大的改變就是你必須自行掌控並分配 75 分鐘的作答時間。以本書進行練習時，也請務必手持馬錶並設好時間再開始作答。以 TOEIC 來說，最重要的單位是「秒」而不是「分」。若能養成用馬錶練習的習慣，你的大腦便能自然記住時間長度，例如 10 秒到底有多長……等。這將有助於使實際參加 TOEIC 測驗時不至於手忙腳亂。

Part  Incomplete Sentences 單句填空題

 解題要領 ★題數：40 題／答題時間：約 12 分鐘

此種題目會在簡短句子中留下空白部分，例如："-----"。參加測驗者須填入最適當字詞以完成整個句子。由於這類題目和**文法及詞彙**有關，所以對於一路以「閱讀和文法」方式學習的人來說，READING SECTION 是最容易得分的部分。READING SECTION 包含 Part 5、6、7，共 75 分鐘時間，但是你必須一邊自行考慮時間分配、一邊作答，因此不能將大多時間浪費在 Part 5。

為了保留足夠時間給 Part 7 的文章理解題，這 75 分鐘裡**最多只能撥出 12 分鐘**給 Part 5 使用。也就是說，1 題只能用 20 秒作答。

Part 5 的設計目的，是要測試考生是否有快速且正確理解文法及詞彙的能力。這類題目中的空白部分除了 so that ... 或 according to ... 之類的常用片語外，幾乎都是一個單字作為選項。

 出題趨勢

此部分問題句的長度約在 12 ~ 25 個字之間，70 ~ 80% 內容都與商務相關，其餘則與公共事件、個人日常生活有關。正如以下**出題要點** ① 所述，很多題目都不必從頭到尾讀完就能答對，另外只要練習一邊選擇一邊維持穩定節奏，快速作答也非難事。

 出題要點

Part 5 考的是文法與詞彙，其出題趨勢可分為以下 3 點。

① 不必從頭到尾讀完也能作答的問題

為了以每題 20 秒的速度正確答題，就要練習快速辨別出不須完整讀完的句子，然後只看空白處的前後部分就直接作答。在 Part 5 的 40 題中，約有 15 ~ 20 題是不須讀完的問題。選擇介系詞、動詞、副詞、形容詞等詞性的問題。例如：

Strategies

Pre Test

Half Test 1

Half Test 2

Full Test

▶ 介系詞

The convention building is ----- the corner of 55th Street and West End Avenue.

（會議大廈位在第 55 街與西區大道的轉角。）

(A) in (B) on (C) beside (D) by

正確答案：(B)　　　　在室外轉角處要用介系詞 on 或 at。

▶ 動詞

Don't ----- to talk to your boss whenever you have a question.

（有問題時別猶豫，請隨時與你的上司商量。）

(A) hesitant (B) hesitation (C) hesitated (D) hesitate

正確答案：(D)　　　　Don't 之後應接動詞原形。

▶ 副詞、形容詞

I attached a map to this e-mail so that you can ----- find my place.

（我隨此電子郵件附上了地圖，以便你輕鬆找到我家。）

(A) easily (B) easy (C) ease (D) easier

正確答案：(A)　　　　修飾動詞 find 的應為副詞。

▶ 出現在名詞前之限定詞

例如：every、each、all、almost all of、both A and B、either A or B

----- person on the project team should come up with a new idea.

（此專案團隊中的每個人都該提出一個新構想。）

(A) All (B) Whole (C) Every (D) One of

正確答案：(C)　　　　person 為單數形，故只能用 every。

② 不看上下文就無法作答的問題（與連接詞、慣用說法、時態有關的問題）

▶ 連接詞

------- the road was crowded, I got to the meeting in time.

（雖然一路壅塞，但我還是及時趕上會議了。）

(A) Because (B) So (C) Due to (D) Although

正確答案：(D)　　　　只有 (D) 有逆接的意思。

Strategies

Pre Test

Half Test 1

Half Test 2

Full Test

▶ 常用片語

My boss wants me to turn in the monthly report ----- I can.

（我老闆要我儘快交出月報。）

(A) as much as (B) as soon as (C) as far as (D) as long as

正確答案：(B)　　表示「儘快」之意的 (B) 為正確答案。

▶ 時態

For the past ten years, T&T Company ----- buying from us.

（過去 10 年間，T&T 公司一直都向我們採購。）

(A) having (B) had (C) has been (D) will be

正確答案：(C)　　表示持續性的現在完成進行式。

③ 不知道詞彙意義就無法作答的問題（與詞彙、常用片語有關的問題）

面對以詞彙含意為主的問題，答對的關鍵就在於能否從選項中找出符合句意的字詞。注意，即使是簡單的詞彙也可能具有多種不同意義，故背單字時請勿偷懶。例如：

Bert is in charge of taking ----- at the meeting.

（伯特負責做會議記錄。）

(A) work (B) space (C) minutes (D) time

正確答案：(C)　　minutes^註 有「會議記錄」之意。

註 一般都把 minutes 記成「分」對吧？但複數形有「會議記錄」的意思，在商務相關題目中多半用來表示此意義。

📌 奧格的悲劇 Part 5

第一次參加 TOEIC 測驗時，我最有自信的就是 Part 5 了。當時有關 TOEIC 測驗的資料還相當貧乏，LISTENING SECTION 等幾乎都無法事前演練，只能在考試時直接迎戰，而 Part 5 是其中唯一可先行練習的。那時的相關考試用書雖不像今日豐富，但是坊間還是有不少選擇。我就靠著那些參考書拼命練習，一心想著要在 Part 5 拿到滿分，但不幸的是，這部分我也出了紕漏。嚴格來說這不是我的錯，是那些充滿奇怪英文例句的參考書的錯。那時候的考試用書 Chinese English 相當嚴重，使得我對 TOEIC 實用簡潔但卻陷阱重重的出題方式苦惱不已。之後到美國留學時最讓我痛苦的，也是矯正那中式英語的過程。時至今日，市面上的教科書及參考書裡還是存在不少中式英語。因此你最好多多閱讀道地的英語雜誌及網路資訊，以學習道地的英語表達。

 **超越 650 分的訣竅**

(1) 請先瀏覽選項，以判斷是否須讀完全句：

  a. 當選項為介系詞、不同詞性、形容詞、副詞、動詞的常用片語時，那只需看克漏字的前後，不必讀完整句。在 Part 5，平均每題可有 18 秒作答時間，若可不讀完整句作答，大約一題只需花 10 秒鐘。利用機會，省時間留給較難的題目。

  b. 若選項為連接兩個句子的連接詞，就必須了解全句意義才能作答，所以可先大致判斷其意義應為順接（順接型的連接詞：→且→），還是逆接（逆接型的連接詞：←但→）。掌握連接詞所連接的前後句或片語的方向後，再決定選項。例如：

    ▶ 順接型的連接詞：

    Our business is turning upward and <u>therefore</u>, we should expand.
    （我們的業務在增長，<u>因此</u>我們應該要擴張才對。）

    ▶ 逆接型的連接詞：

    Our business is turning upward; <u>however</u>, we should be careful not to overspend.
    （我們的業務在增長，<u>但是</u>應該小心不要花太多錢。）

(2) 打好基礎文法：

作為題目的詞彙通常不難，考出來的文法大多也都很基本。然而最忌諱的就是一知半解。舉例來說，你能立刻區分出以下兩個例句的意思嗎？TOEIC 500 分以下的人多半無法明確區分出兩者意義。別忘了，你的弱點就是出題者的最愛，請務必打好基礎。

  a. She is embarrassed.^註
  b. She is embarrassing.^註

正如前面「奧格的悲劇」提到的，記住詞彙之細微差異與正確、道地的用法非常重要。首先從接觸真正的英文句子開始，你可以閱讀 *Newsweek*、*Reader's Digest* 等讀物。其中 *Reader's Digest* 所用的詞彙相對簡單，有趣的文章又多，在此大力推薦。另外上網搜尋 *Newsweek* 並下載短篇文章來閱讀也是不錯的辦法。而閱讀時請注意下列事項：

a. 第一次讀時，別查字典。

  先瀏覽一下 *Newsweek* 的 Society、The Arts 等專欄，然後選個你有興趣且似乎讀得下去的文章，在不查字典的情況下讀一遍。遇到不懂的詞彙就打個勾。讀過一遍後，應該就能大致了解文章內容了。

b. 讀過一遍後，再以查字典的方式將已打勾詞彙弄懂。

c. 選定喜歡的專欄，並定期閱讀。

d. 先快速讀一遍台灣有報導性的、你覺得熟悉的新聞。掌握了大意後，再把該則新聞的英語表達方式學起來。

註　前面例句的答案：a. 她覺得很尷尬。　b. 她令人覺得尷尬。

 全題型奪分攻略

Part 6 Text Completion 短文填空題

 解題要領 ★題數：12題／答題時間：約 6 分鐘（剩下 63～51 分鐘）

共 4 段文章，合計 12 題，在一小段文章裡約有三個與詞彙、文法相關的問題。填入空白部分的答案通常為一個單字或 1 組詞句。雖然只有 12 題，但最好把 Part 6 的答題時間估算為 6 分鐘左右。約花 30 秒時間了解文章內容，每題花 15 秒作答。

 出題趨勢

Part 5 和 Part 6 的差異不只是單句和短文之別而已，兩者的出題內容也不太一樣。Part 6 中的短文包括電子郵件、信件、文件、說明、指示、廣告……等等，商務及日常生活上常見的內容。

 出題要點

Part 6 的出題趨勢可分為以下 4 點。

① 詞彙問題：6～7 題（連接詞除外）

> 名詞（包含代名詞）

If I could be of any -------, please do not hesitate to let me know.
（如果我能幫得上什麼忙，請告訴我，別客氣。）

(A) assistance (B) kindness (C) instruction (D) friendship

正確答案：(A) 援助、幫助

> 形容詞

Special appreciation is in order to the doctors who provided their ------- time and service.
（特別感謝提供了寶貴時間和服務的醫師們。）

(A) busy (B) leisurely (C) precious (D) rare

正確答案：(C) 寶貴的

▶ 動詞

The woman was ------- for the mail fraud.

（該名女子因郵件詐欺罪被捕。）

(A) admitted (B) inspired (C) invited (D) arrested

正確答案：(D) (被)逮捕

▶ 介系詞

Due to the snowstorm, today's game will be postponed ------- next Monday.

（由於暴風雪之故，今天的比賽將延至下週一舉行。）

(A) over (B) when (C) until (D) on

正確答案：(C) 至……為止

▶ 常用片語

出現頻率較高的常用片語題包括動詞片語（例如：take off 起飛；脫掉）及慣用句（例如：to tell the truth 老實說）等。

a. 動詞片語

I have to take my son to the doctor, so may I ------- the appointment for lunch today?

（我得帶我兒子去看醫生，所以我可以取消今天的午餐之約嗎？）

(A) give out (B) call off (C) put out (D) hand in

正確答案：(B) 取消

b. 慣用句

If you wish to attend the Auto-manufacturers' convention, please apply ------- .

（如果你想參加汽車製造商大會，請事先申請。）

(A) in the end (B) as a result (C) as soon as (D) in advance

正確答案：(D) 事先

② 詞性問題：1～2 題

此類問題不需讀完全句，只須看空白的前後部分就能作答，請有效運用時間。例如：

It was quite ----- to be able to attend your science seminar.

（能參加你們的科學研討會實在是獲益良多。）

(A) inspiring (B) inspire (C) inspiration (D) inspired

正確答案：(A) 激勵人心的

③ 時態問題：1～2 題

同 ② 類問題，大部分時態問題也都只看空白的前後部分即可作答。例如：

> As soon as you ------- filling out your application form, please give it to me.
> （填完申請表後，請交給我。）
> (A) have finished (B) will finish (C) had finished (D) are finishing
>
> 正確答案：(A) 已經完成

④ 連接兩個句子的連接詞：1～2 題

Part 6 的特色之一，就是會出現較進階的連接詞問題。而其目的是要測試考生能否理解文章脈絡。另外請記得，連接詞大致可分為順接（因此、然後）與逆接（但是、反之）這兩種：

> ▶ 與整體文章相關的「順接型」連接詞有：
>
> | therefore | 因此、所以 | subsequently | 隨後、接著 |
> |---|---|---|---|
> | consequently | 結果、因此 | accordingly | 依此、因此 |
> | as a result | 結果、所以 | additionally | 此外、另外 |
> | specifically | 確切地、具體地 | moreover | 而且、還有 |
>
> ▶ 與整體文章相關的「逆接型」連接詞有：
>
> | although | 雖然 | however | 然而 |
> |---|---|---|---|
> | in contrast to | 相對於 | on the contrary | 相反地 |
> | on the other hand | 另一方面 | otherwise | 否則 |
> | despite | 儘管 | | |

奧格的悲劇 Part 6

Part 6 在 2006 年時改成了現在的新格式。為了研究新的測驗內容，我一直持續參加 TOEIC 考試，因為已歷盡艱辛成為英語專業人士良久，每次總能獲得滿分或至少接近滿分[註]，所以在 Part 6 並無可供各位參考的悲劇發生。不過就初學者來說，Part 6 最大的困難可能在於：「有些人會試圖，或是忍不住要完整讀完占滿了一整頁的文章」。關於這問題，請參考緊接著的「超越 650 分的訣竅」之說明。

註 為了統一各測驗的難易度，TOEIC 提出了所謂的 EQUATION SCORE（標準平均值），因此即使在某次測驗中獲得滿分，成績單上未必會出現 990 分。

超越 650 分的訣竅

(1) **由上而下快速瀏覽並找出關鍵詞**

每段短文各有 3 題，而短文共有 4 段，總計 12 題，但分配給 Part 6 的答題時間只有 6 分鐘。首先應由上而下概略看過整體文章並找出關鍵詞（收件人、寄件人、職位、主旨等）。約花 30 秒時間了解文章內容，這樣一來每題約有 15 秒時間可作答。請睜大眼睛掃描整頁內容，由上而下地瀏覽文章。

(2) **每題花 15 秒作答**

看到 Part 6 中佔滿整頁的文章就嚇得魂不附體的人可能不在少數。不過沒關係。雖是文章，但也沒必要鉅細靡遺地讀，而且實際上也沒那個閒工夫。請在 15 秒內閱讀空白部分的前後內容並作答就好。

(3) **較具挑戰性的連接詞問題，12 題中佔 2 題**

連接詞問題的設計，是為了測試考生能否確實理解文章脈絡，但是對參加測驗的人來說，這種與文章整體相關的連接詞很可能令人望而生畏。不過只要把這些當成 and、but 的變形就沒問題了。因此應快速檢視空白部分的前後文，並判斷是順接型連接詞 and 的同類，還是逆接型連接詞 but 的同類。

(4) **與詞彙意義有關的問題佔壓倒性多數**

雖然這部分對 TOEIC 初級程度的人來說相當痛苦，不過做完本書練習題後請務必回頭再多加複習，以增強你的詞彙能力。

Part 7 Reading Comprehension 文章理解題

解題要領 ★題數：48 題／答題時間：剩下 57 分鐘（第 63 ~ 120 分鐘）

Part 7 又分為以下兩部分：

▶ **單篇文章** ➡ 題數：28 題／第 153 ~ 180 題

各篇文章的題目數分別為 2、3、4 或 5 題不等，而每題都有四個選項。**可花在這「單篇文章」部分的時間約為 26 分鐘左右。**首先快速掃描問題中的關鍵詞，接著瀏覽文章，這兩個動作共花約 2 分鐘，如此一來，每題可分配到 20 秒的答題時間。

▶ **雙篇文章** ➡ 題數：20 題／第 181 ~ 200 題

兩篇文章或一篇文章加一個圖表的組合，共會有 4 組，考生須讀完整組內容後再作答。每組各有 5 題題目，每題有四個選項。**可花在「雙篇文章」共 20 題的時間約為 31 分鐘。**首先應掃描問題中的關鍵詞，接著瀏覽兩篇文章，每組花費 3 ~ 5 分鐘（視文章長度而定），如此一來，每題可分配到 20 秒的答題時間。

出題趨勢

此部分文章包括電子郵件、商務信函、廣告、公家機關相關通知、公告、日常生活中的留言訊息、新聞，以及圖表等。而雙篇文章會組合這些不同內容來出題。

(1) 電子郵件（3 題）

電子郵件可分為 3 大類：① 公司內部或給客戶的信、② 廣告宣傳用文章、③ 私人信件。務必先讀過「收件人」、「寄件人」、「主旨」部分後，再掃描題目內容。

(2) 商務信函（2 ~ 3 題）

主要是與「會談」、「請託」、「要求」、「工作程序」、「會議日期」等有關的信件。而這和一般電子郵件有 2 項差異：

a. 表達方式較正式，句子也較長。

b. 文章分成多個段落，通常每個段落就是一個問題。

請先注意看信頭處公司名、地址等資訊，接著閱讀所提及內容，之後再掃描問題。

（3）廣告（2～3 題）

有商品廣告也有求才廣告等類型，而其特徵有三：

a. 商品名稱以大型字體呈現。

b. 用字遣詞極為誇張，例如：

never before「前所未有」、innovative「創新的」、epoch-making「劃時代的」、revolutionary「革命性的」。

c. 題目多半與商品的「特性」、「賣點」、「價格」、「訂購方式」、「付款方式」、「銷售截止日」等有關。

（4）公司或公家機關的通知、指示（1～2 題）

此類型的出題頻率不高，所以一般考生不太熟悉，而答題時最重要的是要找出關鍵詞，並在腦海中想像該情境。較常出現的主題包括以下兩種：

a. 與公司設備有關的「維修」、「改建」通知。

b. 與都市中「道路工程相關公告」、「因災情及交通堵塞而須改道」等有關的內容。

（5）一般的公司內部文件或內部備忘錄、留言訊息（1 題）

此類文章會包含「由誰」、「給誰」、「主旨」等簡潔資訊。通常不出現於單篇文章部分，而會做為雙篇文章組合中的一篇來出題。雖說內容多半簡潔，但在同時閱讀兩篇文章又要答題的情況下，也很可能出現容易令人混淆的資訊。此外，寄件人、主旨等欄位內容也會出陷阱題。

（6）新聞報導（1 題）

新聞報導的特徵就在於第 1 段落會是該篇報導的摘要，因此請先將該部分瀏覽一遍後，再掃描題目。較常出現的報導主題包括「自然災害」、「交通事故」、「經濟」、「地方新聞」等，有時也會出現「戰爭、恐怖攻擊」等相關文章。

（7）表格或分項清單（1～2 題）

包括時刻表、行事曆、商品與價格清單、帳單、意見調查表、天氣預報等內容，會出現於雙篇文章中的一篇。

① 與主題概要有關的大範圍問題

題目通常會依據文章段落順序排列，也就是第 1 題的答案就在第 1 段落裡，而且問的多半是與該段落主旨有關的大範圍問題。但是有時也會例外，例如第 1 題可能會問收件人、寄件人或標題主旨……等內容。

② 與細節資訊有關的小範圍問題

在英文裡，原則上一個段落只能有一個主題，撰寫英文文章時若新起一段落，表示要轉換話題或擴展情境。只要習慣了，難題就變少了。當選項裡包含與文章段落中一致或簡化的詞彙時，通常就是正確答案。另外，選項內容也經常使用改述後的詞彙，所以須特別注意。

③ 包含 NOT 的問題

Part 7 中會有如下包含 NOT 的問題。其中的 NOT 以大寫強調。由於作答時必須確認文章裡是否不含該項資訊，所以免不了會花費較多時間。例如：

> In this passage, what is NOT mentioned as a treatment of a cold?
> （在這段文章中，並「未」提到哪種感冒治療方式？）

④ 與詞彙意義有關的問題

Part 7 中必定會出現與詞彙意義有關的問題。例如：

> The word "participate" in paragraph 1, line 3 is closest in meaning to
> （與第 1 段第 3 行中的 participate 意義最接近的是）
> (A) leave 離開　(B) buy 購買　(C) join 參加　(D) work 工作

奧格的悲劇 Part 7

在應付 Part 7 時最重要的就是時間分配，以確保答完所有題目。但是，「知易行難」，我自己初次參加測驗時也沒來得及詳讀最後幾題，測驗就在監考老師說出「好了，請停筆」時匆忙亂猜的窘境中結束。正因本身有過這種悲慘經驗，所以誠心希望各位能徹底牢記 READING SECTION 的時間分配策略。請各位加油囉！

超越 650 分的訣竅

(1) 有效運用時間

　　在本節開頭處我就已提出了時間的分配方式。在本書 Pre Test 的 READING SECTION 部分，若能於作答前先決定各題的時間分配，並盡力於決定的時間內答完，這練習才會有效果。TOEIC 是靠速度和正確性取勝的測驗，若要熟悉它就不能浪費時間。因此，第一次挑戰本書的 Pre Test 時，請嚴守時間分配，務必準備好馬錶。

　　a. 「單篇文章」部分可花約 26 分鐘。首先快速瀏覽所有問題，接著掃描文章內容。這兩個動作共使用 2 分鐘，每題可分配到 20 秒的答題時間。

　　b. 「雙篇文章」部分可花約 31 分鐘。用 3 ~ 4 分鐘掃描文章內容，每題便能有 20 秒的時間作答。

(2) 徹底記住作答程序

　　a. 若為信件或電子郵件，請檢視收件人、寄件人及主旨等內容。各個人物的職位也不能漏掉。至於說明介紹與廣告類內容，則務必確認標題和店名等資訊。

　　b. 快速掃描題目。

　　c. 邊瞄問題中的關鍵詞邊瀏覽文章，在整篇文章中尋找與答案相關的資訊。

　　d. 一旦找出答案，別猶豫，請立刻畫入答案卡。

(3) 多閱讀 NEWSWEEK、Herald Tribune、U.S.A. TODAY 等刊物，進行尋找關鍵詞的練習。（U.S.A. TODAY 的詞彙較簡單，讀起來會比較輕鬆。）

　　a. 一定要在開始計時後才閱讀。請將馬錶設成你自認所需時間的一半長度，以便掌握速讀的感覺。

　　b. 閱讀時不要查字典（但事後回頭複習時則一定要查字典）。

　　c. 在各段落中你認為是關鍵詞的詞彙上打勾。一開始時每個段落裡你可能只打了一個勾，一旦熟練後每個段落一定都會有好幾個勾。

Section 2

漸進式模擬試題本

Answer Keys

- Pre Test
- Half Test 1
- Half Test 2
- Full Test

TOEIC →→→

漸進式模擬試題 完整分析

Pre Test

解答與出題要點一覽表

Listening Section

Part	No.	正解	你的答案	出題要點
Part 1	1	D		以人為主角（單一人物）的照片
	2	A		以多個物體為主題
	3	B		確實聽取動詞
	4	A		代表物體狀態變化的現在完成式 + 被動式
	5	B		包含多個人物的照片
Part 2	6	A		陳述與反應
	7	C		Yes-No 疑問句（尤其是否定疑問句的回答）
	8	B		用了 What 的問題
	9	A		用了 Who / Whose 的問題
	10	B		Who ... for? 形式的問題
	11	B		用了 Which 的問題
	12	A		用了 Where 的問題
	13	B		用了 Why 的問題
	14	B		用了 How 的問題
	15	C		包含兩個疑問詞的疑問句
	16	C		附加疑問句
	17	A		表達提議、建議
	18	A		Shall we ... ? / Let's ...（提議、建議句型）
	19	A		感嘆、強調、諷刺
	20	C		表達拜託、請求之意
Part 3	21	B		與機械、汽車故障有關的問題
	22	B		↓
	23	D		↓
	24	C		與提案、發表有關的問題
	25	B		↓
	26	C		↓
	27	D		與飛機及旅館的預約有關的問題
	28	A		↓
	29	A		↓
	30	B		與請求協助、給予建議等有關的問題
	31	C		↓
	32	A		↓
	33	A		與抱怨、投訴有關的問題
	34	B		↓
	35	D		↓
Part 4	36	D		錄音訊息
	37	B		↓
	38	A		↓
	39	C		天氣預報
	40	B		↓
	41	D		↓
	42	A		新聞
	43	C		↓
	44	D		↓
	45	A		廣告
	46	D		↓
	47	B		↓
	48	B		公告
	49	C		↓
	50	C		↓

請記下 Pre Test 的成績。

Listening Section

	答對題數	答對率	目標答對率
Part 1	/ 5	%	90%
Part 2	/ 15	%	80%
Part 3	/ 15	%	70%
Part 4	/ 15	%	70%
合計	/ 50	%	75%

※ 務必針對自己答錯的問題，仔細閱讀出題要點中的說明。

Reading Section

Part	No.	正解	你的答案	出題要點
Part 5	51	A		詞性（Word Form）
	52	C		詞彙、文法（區別意義近似的單字等）
	53	B		使役動詞
	54	D		時態的一致與完成式
	55	B		被動式
	56	B		助動詞
	57	A		數量形容詞 few / little 與可數名詞、不可數名詞
	58	D		有多種含意的 as ... as
	59	A		both / either / neither
	60	C		no matter how / what / when
	61	D		介系詞與連接詞（during / while 等）
	62	B		具有副詞功能的介系詞片語
	63	B		be used to + ...ing、look forward to + ...ing
	64	C		表示頻率的否定型副詞
	65	A		less / fewer / more ... than any other + 單數形
	66	B		關係詞
	67	C		間接疑問句
	68	A		過去假設式、過去完成假設式
	69	D		使用 do、make 的常用片語
	70	A		動詞片語
Part 6	71	B		廣告 詞彙
	72	C		↓ 詞彙
	73	C		↓ 逆接型的連接詞
	74	A		商務信函 詞彙
	75	D		↓ 詞彙
	76	B		↓ 順接型的連接詞
Part 7	77	C		廣告
	78	B		↓
	79	B		信件
	80	D		↓
	81	A		申請表
	82	D		↓
	83	D		↓
	84	B		↓
	85	C		指示說明
	86	A		↓
	87	C		↓
	88	B		電子郵件（行程變更）
	89	A		↓
	90	B		↓
	91	C		廣告與電子郵件（客訴郵件）
	92	D		↓
	93	B		↓
	94	A		↓
	95	D		↓
	96	D		2 封商務信函
	97	C		↓
	98	B		↓
	99	A		↓
	100	C		↓

請記下 Pre Test 的成績。

Reading Section

	答對題數	答對率	目標答對率
Part 5	/ 20	%	70%
Part 6	/ 6	%	70%
Part 7	/ 24	%	70%
合計	/ 50	%	70%

☆470 分等級 ☆☆600 分等級 ☆☆☆730 分以上

1. 正確答案：(D) ☆　　　　　　　　　　　　　　　　　　　🔘 03

(A) The man is sitting on the terrace.　　　這名男子正坐在陽台上。

(B) The man is taking off his gloves.　　　這名男子正脫下他的手套。

(C) The man is putting on a jacket.　　　這名男子正穿上外套。

(D) The man is handling a piece of wood.　　**這名男子正在處理一塊木頭。**

> **解說** 以人為主角（單一人物）的照片 ▶ 要點 ① p.10
> 請注意看人物動作。handling … wood「處理木頭、搬運木頭」是正確答案的關鍵詞。請注意，像 (B) taking off his gloves「正在脫手套」、(C) putting on a jacket「正在穿外套」等，以進行式描述這類動作的選項都不會是正確答案。另外「穿、配戴」用 wear 表達。

💣 小心陷阱：請注意正確答案為 (D) 的情況

當正確答案是最後一個選項 (D) 時，在讀到最後前，請小心別被前面的選項誤導。以這題來說，你必須正確聽取並辨別出以下四個動詞（sit / take off / put on / handle）+ 受詞才能答對。

✅ 這樣練習最有效

試著用英文將眼前人物的外觀、體型、年齡、狀態……等描述出來。外出時，請練習用英文說明路人的樣子。

💡 奪分祕笈：經常用於描述人物的單字

人物類問題最困難的就是以職業名稱為主詞的情況，所以請記住以下這些可能用於 Part 1 的職業名稱。

Word List

- ☐ dentist [ˈdɛntɪst] 名 牙醫
- ☐ veterinarian [ˌvɛtərəˈnɛrɪən] 名 獸醫
- ☐ architect [ˈarkəˌtɛkt] 名 建築師
- ☐ painter [ˈpentə] 名 畫家
- ☐ carpenter [ˈkarpəntə] 名 木匠
- ☐ office clerk [ˈɔfɪs klɝk] 辦事員
- ☐ computer engineer
　　[kəmˈpjutə ɛndʒəˈnɪr] 電腦工程師

- ☐ nurse [nɝs] 名 護士
- ☐ politician [ˌpaləˈtɪʃən] 名 政治家
- ☐ photographer [fəˈtagrəfə] 名 攝影師
- ☐ craftsman [ˈkræftsmən] 名 工匠
- ☐ plumber [ˈplʌmə] 名 水管工
- ☐ programmer [ˈprogræmə] 名 程式設計師
- ☐ sales clerk / representative
　　[selz klɝk / rɛprɪˈzɛntətɪv] 銷售人員／代表

☐ front clerk [frʌnt klɜk] 櫃台接待人員　　☐ concierge [kɑnsɪˋɛrʒ] 图 門房

☐ hairdresser [ˋhɛrˌdrɛsə] 图 美髮師　　☐ assistant [əˋsɪstənt] 图 助理

☐ (cabin) attendant [(ˋkæbɪn) əˋtɛndənt]
　客艙乘務員、空服員

2. 正確答案：(A) ☆☆

(A) There are low buildings on both sides of the street.　　街道兩側有低矮的建築物。

(B) The street is very narrow.　　街道很狹窄。

(C) The intersection is crowded with cars.　　**十字路口擠滿了車。**

(D) The buildings on the right are very tall.　　右側的建築物很高。

解說 以多個物體為主題 ▶ 要點 ② p.11

請注意看街道與建築物。(A) low buildings 「低矮的建築物」、on both sides of the street「在街道兩側」為正確答案之關鍵詞。(D) on the right 「右側的」建築物並不高，所以不是正確答案。

Word List

☐ intersection [ˌɪntəˋsɛkʃən] 图 十字路口、道路交叉點

☐ be crowded with ... 擠滿了……

💣 **小心陷阱：正確答案為第一個選項時也要特別小心**

當正確答案為最早播放的 (A) 時，有可能一不小心就漏聽了。漏聽的人會慌忙地誤以為答案在 (B)、(C)、(D) 之中，而造成雙重悲劇。一般人尤其容易被包含較難詞彙 intersection 的 (C) 給引誘。「不知不覺地恍神了」在英語裡就說成 space out，請注意別 space out 而漏聽了第一句喔。

✓ **這樣練習最有效**

你可運用各種介系詞片語，觀察出「什麼」、「在哪裡」、「如何地」等狀況，並練習用英文描述出來。例如：一邊看著照片或風景，一邊練習說出 A 物和 B 物的相對位置關係。與位置關係有關的句子很容易弄錯，因此建議你平常就要多練習使用下面「奪分祕笈」所列的介系詞片語。

請好好練習運用下列常見的介系詞片語吧！

Word List

☐ across the street 在對街
☐ at / on the corner 在轉角處
☐ behind / in the back of the house
　 在房子後面
☐ in front of the station 在車站前
☐ opposite the street [`ɑpəzɪt] 在街道另一側
☐ street below（從較高樓層看）下方街道

☐ above the door 在門的上方
☐ at the top of the shelf 在架子頂部
☐ by the window 在窗戶旁、靠窗
☐ close to the house 在房子附近
☐ to the right / left 往右／左
☐ over the fence [fɛns] 在柵欄的另一頭
☐ under the desk 在桌子下面

3. 正確答案：(B) ☆☆

(A) The woman is walking away. 　　　這名女子正步行離開。
(B) The woman is folding her arms. 　**這名女子正雙臂交疊。**
(C) The woman is holding her hands. 　這名女子正雙手緊握。
(D) The woman is looking to the right. 這名女子正看向右方。

解說 確實聽取動詞

此題問的是女子的動作。 (C) ... holding her hands「兩手緊握」和正解 (B) ... folding her arms「雙臂交疊」類似，所以很容易聽錯。這是陷阱選項，你必須仔細聆聽發音才行。

奪分祕笈：拼字或發音很像的動詞

以下各基本動詞的發音都很相似，請利用下列單字做練習，在寫下音標前先遮住答案，答題後再對照右欄解答，把不熟悉的發音釐清並出聲練習。

單字	寫下你的音標	音標正解
collect 收集／correct 改正	_____	[kə`lɛkt]／[kə`rɛkt]
lead 帶領／read 閱讀	_____	[lid]／[rid]
put 擺放／putt（高爾夫球）推球入洞	_____	[pʊt]／[pʌt]
shut 關閉／shot（開槍）射擊	_____	[ʃʌt]／[ʃat]
walk 走路／work 工作	_____	[wɔk]／[wɝk]
glow 發光／grow 成長	_____	[glo]／[gro]
live 生活／leave 離開	_____	[lɪv]／[liv]
saw 鋸開／sew 縫合	_____	[sɔ]／[so]
sip 啜飲／ship 運送	_____	[sɪp]／[ʃɪp]
write 書寫／ride 乘坐	_____	[raɪt]／[raɪd]
hold 握住／fold 摺疊	_____	[hold]／[fold]
play 玩／pray 祈禱	_____	[ple]／[pre]
think 思考／sink 下沉	_____	[θɪŋk]／[sɪŋk]

4. 正確答案：(A) ☆☆☆

(A) The bed has already been made.　床已經鋪好了。

(B) The bed is small and compact.　床又窄又小。

(C) There're lamps next to the bed.　床的旁邊有燈。

(D) There's a telephone by the lamp.　燈的旁邊有個電話。

解說 代表物體狀態變化的「現在完成式」＋「被動式」——
▶ 要點 ④ p.12

由於照片裡的床鋪已鋪好，所以正確答案為 (A)。(B) 錯，由圖所示，此為雙人大床；(C) 錯，因為只有一個燈在床右側，(D) 也不對，因為電話在床的另一側，和燈不同邊。

小心陷阱

表示物體狀態的句子其主詞通常不一致，因此聽取這些選項時得特別用心才行！現在完成式

Strategies　Pre Test　Half Test 1　Half Test 2　Full Test

的句子本來就較不容易聽懂，再加上主詞又不一致，所以可算是 Part 1 測驗中最難答對的一題。另外，若漏聽了 (A)，便很可能會落入 (C) lamps 複數形（實際上只有一盞燈）的陷阱。

奪分祕笈：抓住現在完成式的感覺

現在完成式這種時態很難以中文的觀念來理解，所以可說是最難拿分的類型。請反覆練習，好記住下列常用現在完成式表達的句型。

▶ 現在完成式為正確答案的情況

TOEIC 測驗中的現在完成式句子只在兩種狀況下成立：
(1) 物體狀態本來就會規則地變化的情況、(2) 發生緊急狀況而臨時產生變化的情況。
請閱讀接下來的句子以培養語感。

○ (1) The sun has come up.　　　　太陽已升起。
　　　（太陽每天都會升起，當太陽出現在剛好超出地平線處時，此句便成立）

○ (2) The area has been roped off.　　該地區已拉起封鎖線禁止進入。
　　　（由於是臨時性的變化，所以可推斷是最近發生的事）

▶ 現在完成式不是正確答案的情況

無從知道照片中狀態的產生時間，卻自行推斷、編造出的句子就不會是正確答案。

× The light has been turned on.　　　　→ ○ The light is on / is turned on.
　　燈剛剛已被點亮。　　　　　　　　　　　　燈亮著／是點亮的。
　　（也許燈一直都是亮著的）

× The plane has just arrived at　　　　→ ○ The plane is parked at
　　the gate.　　　　　　　　　　　　　　　the gate.
　　飛機剛剛已抵達登機門。　　　　　　　　飛機停在登機門處。
　　（也許飛機一直都停在那兒）

× The door has been shut.　　　　　→ ○ The door is shut.
　　門已經被關上了。　　　　　　　　　　　門是關著的。
　　（也許一直都是關著的）

× The sea has become calm.　　　　→ ○ The sea is calm.
　　海已變得平靜。　　　　　　　　　　　海是平靜的。
　　（也許一直都很平靜）

5. 正確答案：(B) ☆☆

(A) They're fond of each other. 　　　他們互有好感。

(B) They're talking to each other. 　**他們正在對話。**

(C) They're working together. 　　　他們正在一起工作。

(D) They're sitting down. 　　　　　他們坐下來。

解說 包含多個人物的照片 ▶ 要點 ① p.10

請掌握「誰」→ they，「正在做什麼」→ talking 這兩個關鍵。正確描述兩個人物狀態的只有 (B)，而 (A)、(C)、(D) 都未正確說明拍照瞬間的情況，因此都不是正確答案。

小心陷阱：別選具有不確定性的想像式描述

「一男一女」→「互相」喜歡這種推論太浪漫，很容易讓人陷進去，但終究只是想像，非正解，要格外小心。

這樣練習最有效

你可一邊看照片一邊練習以英語描述照片中人物的「服裝」、「姿勢」、「動作」、「狀態」等。筆者就經常在坐電車時一邊觀察其他乘客，一邊進行英語描述練習。這種方式相當有趣又有效，可大幅提升與人物有關的表達能力。如果有同伴，還可進行看照片說英文並讓對方依描述畫出照片的內容。

奪分祕笈：常見動詞

請記住常出現於 Part 1 的動詞／動詞片語及其用法。而以下動詞均為需要受詞的及物動詞。

Word List

☐ arrange a meeting 安排一場會議

☐ discuss something 討論某事

☐ look over the window 從窗戶望出去

☐ pack a suitcase 打包行李

☐ put away something 收拾東西

☐ straighten up the desk 整理桌子

☐ board a plane 登機

☐ do the laundry [`lɔndrɪ] 洗衣服

☐ climb a ladder [`lædə] 爬梯子

☐ examine a patient 檢查病人

☐ make the bed 鋪床

☐ pick out a sweater 挑選一件毛衣

☐ stack the chairs 堆疊椅子

☐ take a picture 拍照

☐ direct the traffic 指揮交通

☐ lean against the wall 靠在牆上

- [ ] make copies 影印、複印
- [ ] pay for the merchandise [`mɝtʃənˌdaɪz] 支付商品款項
- [ ] set up a computer 安裝電腦
- [ ] watch the house 看家
- [ ] move a desk 移動一張桌子
- [ ] prepare a meal 準備餐點
- [ ] remove the broken glass 清除碎玻璃
- [ ] sweep the floor 掃地

Memo:

Part ② Question–Response 應答題

 ☆470 分等級 ☆☆600 分等級 ☆☆☆730 分以上

6. 正確答案：(A) ☆   🔊 05

Since Mr. Richardson became the manager, the business has really improved.
自從理查森先生成為經理後，公司業務真的改善了。

(A) It's going much better now.   **現在變得好多了。**

(B) We need a new manager.   我們需要新的經理。

(C) The office is clean.   辦公室很乾淨。

解說

... has really improved 在正確答案 (A) 中被改述成 ... going much better。

 小心陷阱

題目中的 has improved 是指工作狀況，不是指清潔度，所以要小心別被 (C) 誤導。

 奪分祕笈：Statement-Response（陳述與反應）型問題

正如 Part 2 出題要點 ① 介紹過的，「Statement-Response 陳述與反應」型問題和 Yes-No 型的問題不一樣，其可能的回答方式五花八門，所以只能選擇你認為最妥當的答案。但亞洲人最不擅長的幾乎都是這類情境對話的題目，所以請一定要完整理解陳述句（一開始的題目句）的意思，而不只是其中各單字的意義，接著才能判斷用怎樣的英語回答對話才恰當。

▶ **請練習下列生活中常見情境的對話應答**

a. 被稱讚時

  A: I really like your tie!
    我很喜歡你的領帶！

  B: Thanks. It's a gift from my daughter on Father's day.
    謝謝。這是我女兒在父親節送我的禮物。

b. 被別人抱怨時

  A: Please be sure to turn off the lights when you go out last.
    最後離開時請務必記得關燈。

  B: Oh sorry, I'm so absent-minded sometimes.
    喔，抱歉。我有時很心不在焉。

c. 對他人意見的回應

  A: I think our new guy, Sam, is a bit slow in learning the office procedure.
    我想我們的新人山姆學習辦公室流程學得有點慢。

  B: I've noticed that, too. I'll have a talk with him.
    我也注意到了。我會跟他談談。

7. 正確答案：(C) ☆☆

Isn't it a shame that Bob had to miss the game because of the meeting?

鮑伯因會議而必須錯過比賽不是很令人遺憾嗎？

(A) No, it's a shame.　　　　　　　不，很遺憾。

(B) Yes, I miss Bob.　　　　　　　是啊，我很想念鮑伯。

(C) Yes, it is.　　　　　　　　沒錯，的確如此。

> **解說** ▶ 要點 ② 以 Yes - No 回答的疑問句 p.15
>
> 選項A的No 之後又用 it's a shame 來肯定對方的話，顯然是自相矛盾。即使是否定疑問句。要回答「不是這樣」，並同意對方的論點時，仍須用 Yes 回應才行。故 (C) 才正確。

小心陷阱：與問題包含相同關鍵詞的選項多半都是錯的

選項 (B) 的 miss 是「想念」之意，和問題中的「錯過」意義不同，必須依據使用時的狀況來判斷其意義。

奪分祕笈：Yes-No 疑問句（否定疑問句的回答）

千萬別忘了在英文裡，Yes 永遠接著肯定句，而 No 則永遠接著否定句。另外還要注意在某些情況下是不能只答 Yes 或 No 就好的。請看看以下這些例句並好好學起來。

A: Aren't you working today?	你今天不用工作嗎？
B: Well, actually I'm off today but just came in for a few hours.	嗯，其實我今天休假，只是進來幾小時。
A: Don't you like onions?	你不喜歡洋蔥嗎？
B: Well, Yes and No. I like it when it's cooked.	嗯，看情況。我喜歡煮過的洋蔥。
A: Don't you remember where you left your wallet?	你不記得把錢包掉在哪兒了嗎？
B: I think I left in the bathroom, but I'm not sure.	我想是掉在廁所了，但是我不太確定。

8. 正確答案：(B) ☆

What was the name of the restaurant on the corner we used to go to?

我們以前常去在轉角處的那間餐廳叫什麼名字？

(A) We used to go there once a week. 　　　我們以前每週會去一次。

(B) Wasn't it The Golden Peacock? 　　　**不是叫「金孔雀」嗎？**

(C) Let's go there again. 　　　咱們再去一次吧。

解說

只要沒漏聽疑問詞 What，就會知道這題問的是餐廳名稱。注意，正解 (B) 稍微拐了個彎，用「不是⋯⋯嗎？」的問句做為回答。

💣 **小心陷阱**

選項 (A) 是給漏聽了疑問詞 What 的人的陷阱，以 When 或 How often 起頭的問句才會用這類答案來回應。另外也要小心，別只因為聽到以前曾經去過的資訊，而選 (C)。

💡 **奪分祕笈：用了 What 的問題**

使用 What 的問題經常會問到「人或物的名稱」、「職業」、「事物種類」或「某人的意見」等。請記住下列常見說法。

---

a. 名稱

What is the name of the woman? 　　　這名女子的名字為何？

b. 職業

What is the man's occupation? 　　　這名男子的職業是什麼？

What does the man do? 　　　這名男子從事什麼工作？

c. 職位

What is Ms. Wilson's present position? 　　　威爾森小姐目前擔任什麼職位？

d. 種類

What kind of job is available? 　　　哪種工作有職缺？

What type of work does the woman do? 　　　這名女子做的是哪類工作？

e. 意見

What do you think about the new employee? 　　　你覺得新員工怎麼樣？

What do you want to do after work? 　　　下班後你想做什麼？

Strategies　Pre Test　Half Test 1　Half Test 2　Full Test

9. 正確答案：(A) ☆☆

Who will volunteer to chair our next committee meeting?

誰要自願擔任我們下一屆委員會的主席？

(A) I think I will.	**我想我願意。**
(B) This meeting is for volunteers.	這是義工會議。
(C) The meeting will start in a few minutes.	會議將在幾分鐘內開始。

解說

連結到正確答案 (A) 的關鍵為 Who will volunteer?「誰要自願？」這三個字。

小心陷阱

別因為抓到了 chair the meeting「擔任會議主席」的意思就忘掉好不容易才聽出來的關鍵詞 who 和 volunteer。

 奪分祕笈：用了 Who / Whose 的問題

▶ **Who 可當主詞或受詞使用：**

只要將直述句改成疑問句，便能充分了解其構造。以下我們試著分別造出詢問主詞、受詞的句子：

Berny told Tom about the plan. 　　伯尼告訴了湯姆該項計畫。
主詞　　　受詞

a. 只將主詞 Berny 替換成 Who

Who told Tom about the plan? 　　是誰告訴了湯姆該計畫？

b. 先將 Tom 替換為 who註**，再把 who 移到句首做成疑問句形式**

Berny told who about the plan.
Who did Berny tell about the plan? 　　伯尼告訴了誰該項計畫？

註 做為受詞的 who 原本應該用受格 whom，但在會話中則使用 who。

▶ **詢問 Whose「誰的」**

這種疑問句同樣只要從直述句變化而來，就能輕易看出其句型結構：

This is Vic's umbrella. 　　這是維克的傘。

將 Vic's 替換為 whose

Whose umbrella is this? 　　這是誰的傘？

這樣練習最有效

請練習將直述句改成疑問句。

▶ 直述句

I'm going to see my client this afternoon.　　我今天下午要去見客戶。

▶ 疑問句

Who are you going to see this afternoon?　　你今天下午要和誰見面？
What are you going to do this afternoon?　　你今天下午要做什麼？
When are you going to see your client?　　你何時要去見客戶？

---

10. 正確答案：(B) ☆☆　　　　　　　　　　　　　　　　06

Who are they remodeling the corner office for?
他們正在為誰改裝轉角處的辦公室？

(A) Their office is on the corner.　　他們的辦公室在轉角處。
(B) We are getting a new branch manager.　　**我們將會有新的分公司經理。**
(C) The office is being redecorated.　　該辦公室正在重新裝潢。

解說

針對 Who ... for?「為誰？」這樣的疑問，(B) 中出現了關鍵詞 new branch manager，為
正解。至於 (A) 和 (C) 都不包含回答 who 應有的人名或職務名稱等資訊，因此不可能為
正解。

💣 小心陷阱

由於被問到 Who ... for?，所以若有包含 for a new branch manager 的選項那就再明白不過
了，但此處提供的卻是 We are getting a new branch manager. 這樣稍微拐了個彎的說法。另
外疑問句中的 remodel 和 (C) 選項的 redecorate 近乎同義詞，因此很容易引人上鉤，請特別
注意。

奪分祕笈：Who ... for? 型問句

在第 9 題中我們做了主詞與受詞的 who 使用練習，在此則要記憶一下帶有介系詞（at、for、to、with、like 等）的疑問詞（who、what、which 等）用法。

▶ **將受詞前帶有介系詞的直述句改成疑問句時**

其介系詞還是會留著，因此一定要專心聽取句子的最後部分。

Larry is looking at Mary.	賴瑞正看著瑪莉。
× Who is Larry looking?	賴瑞正看著誰？
○ Who is Larry looking at?	

▶ **這類疑問句也一樣只要從直述句變化而來，就能輕易理解：**

Kenny is waiting for his girlfriend.	肯尼正在等他的朋友
將 his girlfriend 替換成 who	
Who is Kenny waiting for?	肯尼正在等誰？

▶ **請看看以下各種「疑問詞 + 介系詞」的組合：**

What ... for [註]

What are you studying English for?	你為了什麼學英文？

Who ... for

Who are you working for?	你為誰工作？

Which ... for

Which plan will you go for?	你會支持哪個計畫？

Who ... to

Who is Jim talking to?	吉姆正在和誰說話？

Which ... to

Which exit is Annie walking to?	安妮正朝著哪個出口走去？

Who ... with

Who did Vicky go to the exhibit with?	維琪和誰一起去看了展覽？

What ... like

What's the climate in Melbourne like?	墨爾本的氣候如何？

目的

○ Why do you need a map?　　　　　　　　你要地圖做什麼用？

○ What do you need a map for?

原因

○ Why was he late?　　　　　　　　　　　他為什麼遲到？

✕ What was he late for?

註 What ... for 也可用 Why 替換。但與 Why 不同，What ... for 只能用於詢問目的，不能用來問原因。

11. 正確答案：(B) ☆☆

Which hotel might be suitable for the writers' conference, Hotel Reinier or The Park?

哪間飯店較適合舉辦作家會議，雷尼爾飯店還是公園酒店？

(A) We are staying at the Reinier.　　　　　我們住在雷尼爾飯店。

(B) The Park has a large conference room.　　**公園酒店有大型會議室。**

(C) Three hundred people will attend.　　　　將會有 300 人出席。

解說

疑問關鍵字為 Which，所以可知這是與選擇有關的問題。而問的是 writers' conference 的
地點，所以提到了 large conference room 的 (B) 選項就是正確答案。

小心陷阱

(A) 提到的是目前住宿飯店名稱，不見得就是會議地點。請小心別過度簡化，將住宿地點直
接連結到會議地點。

奪分祕笈：用了 Which 的問題

以 Which 出題的題目在每次測驗中通常只會出現一題，為了在 Part 2 達成 80% 的答對率，
這種煮熟的鴨子絕不能讓它飛了。

▶ 使用 Which 的問題可分為以下 2 種基本類型：

a. 在 A、B、C ... 等多個項目裡中選擇一個

　　Which do you like the most?　　　　　　你最喜歡哪個？

b. 在 A、B 兩個項目中選一個

　　Which do you prefer, the blue jeans　　　你比較喜歡哪個，藍色牛仔褲

　　or the black pants?　　　　　　　　　　還是黑色褲子？

a. 最高級

- I think plan B is the best of all. 　我認為 B 計畫是最理想的。
- Our section has the most employees in the company. 　我們這個課的員工人數是全公司中最多的。
- That tree is taller than any other trees in the forest. 　那棵樹比森林中的其他樹都高。

b. 比較級

- New Orleans had more rain than Toronto had. 　紐澳良的降雨量比多倫多要多。

c. 原級

- My office is half as large as this room. 　我的辦公室是這個房間的一半大。

d. 其他

- Your car is twice as big as mine. 　你的車是我的車的兩倍大。
- I prefer plan A to B. 　我較喜歡 A 計畫，較不喜歡 B 計畫。

這樣練習最有效

Which 是與比較和選擇有關的提問，請參考前述「奪分祕笈」中 2. 所列之常見表達方式，進行與人、物有關的「大小」、「形狀」、「顏色」等的比較描述。

12. 正確答案：(A) ☆☆

Hey, Mel. Where are you off to in such a hurry?
嘿，梅爾，你匆匆忙忙地要去哪兒？

(A) I'm already late to pick up June. 　**我要去接瓊恩但已經遲到了。**
(B) I still have plenty of time. 　我的時間還很充裕。
(C) I'm sorry. I can't go with you today. 　抱歉，我今天沒辦法跟你去。

解說

可回應疑問詞 Where ... to 的，只有 (A) 選項中的 to pick up June。雖然 (A) 選項中的 I'm already late 與問題裡的 such a hurry 相呼應，但卻不足以成為答案資訊。由於通往正確解答的關鍵詞 to pick up June 位於句子後半段，這題不太容易答對。

Strategies

Pre Test

Half Test 1

Half Test 2

Full Test

 小心陷阱

(C) 那樣的回答在現實生活中也不是完全不可能出現。但是別忘了測驗一開始 directions 說明中所指示的 Select the best response to the question.。「或許」、「可能」的答案是稱不上 best response 的。

 奪分祕笈：用了 Where 的問題

Where 算是用途相當廣泛的疑問詞，請牢記如下與 Where 有關的兩個要點。

▶ 使用了 Where 的疑問句情境

使用了 Where 的疑問句多半和「人或物的所在位置」、「事件發生地點」、「目的地」等相關。不過偶爾也會用於「詢問理由」、「詢問出生地」等情境：

所在位置

物 ▶ A: Where is the city hall located? 市政府位於哪兒？
B: It's on the corner of 14th and Canal. 在第 14 街和卡納爾街口。

人 ▶ A: Where does Patty live? 派蒂住在哪兒？
B: She lives at 111 Bond Ave. 她住在邦德大道 111 號。

地點 ▶ A: Where was the farmers' convention held? 農民大會在哪裡舉辦？
B: It was held at the Milton Hotel. 在米爾頓飯店舉辦。目的地

▶ A: Where are you headed? 你要去哪兒？
B: I'm picking up a client at O'Hare. 我要去奧黑爾機場接一個客戶。

詢問 ▶ A: Where did you get that idea? 你怎麼會有這個想法的？
理由 B: My mother taught me. 我媽教的。

▶ 注意 Where 之後若有介系詞 to、from 時的答法：

A: Where are you off to? 你要去哪兒？
B: To the drugstore. 去藥房。
A: Where does this information come from? 這資訊是從哪兒來的？
B: I looked up some old records. 我查閱了一些舊記錄。

 這樣練習最有效

Which 是與比較和選擇有關的提問，請參考前述「奪分祕笈」中 2. 所列之常見表達方式，進行與人、物有關的「大小」、「形狀」、「顏色」等的比較描述。

有助於聽懂實際考試的內容。由於不是隨時隨地都有會講英語的人做伴,因此你可以打開地圖,練習以 Where is ... located? / where does ... live?這類的句型來自問自答:

A: Where does Ms. Loris live?　　　　勞瑞斯小姐住在哪兒?

B: Ms. Loris's apartment is located　　勞瑞斯小姐的公寓位於紐約皇后區。
　 in Queens, New York.

以下替換地點部分

a. Ms. Loris's apartment is located on Flatbush Avenue.

b. Ms. Loris's apartment is located at 1112 Flatbush Avenue, Queens, New York.

▶ 請利用與自己相關或有興趣的話題來練習:

例如:上網搜尋娛樂資訊,看看有哪些活動在哪些地點舉辦,然後以 Where is ... being held? / Where will ... be held? 這類句型來自問自答:

A: Where will Professor Takehisa's concert be held?
　 竹久教授的演唱會將在哪裡舉辦?

B: His concert is going to be held at Suginami Public Hall.
　 他的演唱會將在杉並公會堂舉辦。

---

13. 正確答案:(B) ☆☆

Why is Alan wearing a suit and tie today instead of a T-shirt and jeans?
艾倫今天為何穿西裝、打領帶而不是 T 恤加牛仔褲?

(A) He always wears the suit.　　　　　　　　　他總是穿西裝。

(B) He has to work today.　　　　　　　　　**他今天必須工作。**

(C) Because casual clothes are more comfortable.　因為休閒服比較舒適。

解說

(B) has to work 與問句中的 a suit and tie 直接相關,是正確答案。 (A) 若是作為反對意見,表示「你在說什麼啊,他一直都是穿西裝的呀」的意思時,也是可能成立的選項,但是該句完全沒針對「為何」這項疑問做回應,因此不能算是 best response。

小心陷阱

若輕率斷定 Why ...？這種詢問理由的問題一定要用 Because ... 回答的話，就會直接選 (C) 而答錯。另外 suit and tie 並非 casual clothes，請小心別上當。

 奪分祕笈：用了 Why 的問題

Why 做為詢問理由的疑問詞時，可分為「問目的」和「問原因」這兩種情況。請分別牢記這兩種問題形式的基本說法。

▶ 問目的：為了什麼、目的是什麼

Why did Danny call you?	丹尼為何打電話給你？
Why did Danny go to Chicago?	丹尼為何去芝加哥？
Why does Danny need a car?	丹尼為何需要汽車？
Why does Danny need the information?	丹尼為何需要這項資訊？

▶ 問原因：因為什麼理由

Why was there a delay?	為什麼延誤了？
Why did the machine break down so easily?	那部機器為什麼這麼容易壞？
Why didn't you go by train?	你為什麼沒坐火車去？
Why are the polar bears dying out?	北極熊為何正走向滅絕？

這樣練習最有效

筆者在學生時代曾試驗過一種練習方法，還蠻有趣的。這原本不是什麼英文學習法，而是了解自我心理狀態所用的一種方法，不過一但用了英文的 Why ...？問句進行，就能成為有效的英語訓練法。

首先將一整天，從起床開始的一連串行動依序記錄下來。接著只要一有空，便針對各項日常作息，用 Why 問句來自問自答。

A: Why did I get up early this morning?	我今早為何早起？
B: I had to attend English 100 class at 9:00.	我必須去上 9 點的 English 100 課程。
A: Why didn't I have breakfast?	我為何沒吃早餐？
B: There was no cereal because I forgot to buy some.	沒有玉米片了因為我忘記買。

Strategies · Pre Test · Half Test 1 · Half Test 2 · Full Test

A: Why did I miss the 8:10 train?	我為什麼錯過了 8:10 的火車？
A: Why did I move to the next car on the train?	我為什麼要移動到隔壁車廂？
B: There was Tony, who(m) I didn't care to talk to.	東尼在那個車廂，我不想和他講話。

14. 正確答案：(B) ☆☆   🔊 07

How are you going to spend your last vacation before you start your job?

就業前你打算如何運用最後的假期？

(A) My last vacation was great!   我最近一次的假期棒透了！

(B) I'm going on a cycling tour in Sicily.   **我要去西西里島騎單車旅遊。**

(C) I hope my vacation lasts forever.   真希望我的假期永不結束。

解說

How ... last vacation before you start your job?「就業前你如何……最後的假期？」為問題關鍵詞，所以談到預定計畫的 (B) 是正確答案。

💣 小心陷阱：小心多義詞

此題的選項以問句中的 last vacation 的 last 當誘餌。last 本身有三種意思。選項 (A) 表示「最近一次的」休假，選項 (C) 表示「延續」當動詞用。唯獨 (B) 選項切合題意。

💡 奪分祕笈：用了 How 的問題

以 How 為首的疑問句分為兩種：(1) 只用 How 的問句、(2) 如 How many 之類和其他形容詞或副詞組合起來運用的問句。

a. 問狀態

A: How is your mother?   您母親的狀況如何？

B: She's feeling better. Thanks.   她覺得好多了，謝謝。

b. 問方法

A: How did you find out?   你是怎麼發現的？

B: I just looked into the past records.   我只是查了過去的記錄。

c. 與數量有關

A: How much snow is there? 　　　　　　　　有多少雪？

B: There's about 1 meter. 　　　　　　　　　有 1 公尺左右。

A: How many books does the library carry? 　該圖書館有多少本藏書？

B: There are about 800,000. 　　　　　　　　約有 80 萬本。

d. 與價格有關

A: How much are those digital cameras? 　　那些數位相機要多少錢？

B: They start at 150 dollars and up. 　　　它們都在 150 美元以上。

e. 與時間有關

A: How much time do you need? 　　　　　　你們需要多少時間？

B: We should be able to finish in 2 hours. 　我們應該可以在 2 小時內完成。

A: How long does it take from here to Newark? 從這裡到紐華克要花多少時間？

B: It takes about half an hour. 　　　　　　大約 30 分鐘。

f. 與距離有關

A: How far ^註 is it from Tokyo to Nagano? 　從東京到長野有多遠？

B: It's about 200 kilometers. 　　　　　　　大約 200 公里。

g. 與頻率有關

A: How often do you come here? 　　　　　　你多常來這兒？

B: I come here every day to pick up my mail. 我每天都來拿信。

註 How far 用來問一般的距離，而若與動作有關則可用 as far as ...「一直到……」表達，例如：I ran as far as Hyde Park. 我一直跑到了海德公園。

這樣練習最有效

請運用前面所列以 How 起頭的片語，練習自行造出多個問句並回答。

1. 可針對日常生活中，例如到車站之距離、自己的步行速度、車子速度、最近購買的商品價格、生活費明細、公司企劃案或專案的評價……等等部分，進行問答練習。

2. 看著每天拿到的發票，以 How much was ... ? 的句型來練習與價格、品項有關的英語問答，也是很有效果的。

15. 正確答案：(C) ☆☆

When and where are we having our company picnic this year?

我們今年度的公司野餐活動將在何時、何地舉辦？

(A) We had a nice party last year.   我們去年的派對很不錯。

(B) It's going to be at Hiro Nakayama's place.   會在中山弘的家舉辦。

(C) It's going to be at Jones Beach on July 15th.   **7 月 15 在瓊斯海灘。**

由於是有 when 又有 where 疑問詞的雙重問句，所以同時包含 Jones Beach、July 15th 兩項資訊的 (C) 是正確答案。

💣 小心陷阱

只要漏聽一個疑問詞，就可能落入 (B) 陷阱。當正確答案在最後面時，尤其須小心前面的陷阱選項。

💡 奪分祕笈：包含兩個疑問詞的問題

這種包含了兩個疑問詞的問題不常出現，但是偶爾還是會冒出一題來。例如：

1. A: When and where are you having your exhibit?
   你的展覽將於何時、何地舉行？

   B: I'm having one at the Zen Gallery starting next Sunday.
   我禪美術館的展覽下週日開展。

2. A: What kind and how many donuts would you like to take with you?
   你想外帶哪種甜甜圈、要多少個？

   B: I would like two honey glazed and three chocolate chips, please.
   請給我兩個蜜汁甜甜圈和三個巧克力脆片甜甜圈。

3. A: How and when do you plan to go to San Jose?
   你打算怎麼去、何時去聖荷西？

   B: I'm thinking of driving there next week.
   我正考慮下週開車去。

這樣練習最有效

請練習用 when、where 造出疑問句。

▶ **首先依據自己一天的作息、行動來造句：**

而句子裡必須同時包含 When「何時」、Where「何地」這兩項資訊，然後再轉換成疑問句並好好記住。

I met Ben yesterday at noon in Shinjuku.	我昨天中午在新宿遇到了班。
When and where did you meet Ben?	你在何時、何地遇到了班？

I saw two stray cats in the alley about an hour ago.	大約一小時前我在巷子裡看見了兩隻流浪貓。
When and where did you see the stray cats?	你在何時、何地看見了流浪貓？

▶ **搜尋網路：**

一邊搜尋網路，一邊以 how 和 when 這兩個要素來進行與旅遊計畫有關的造句練習，也可以深入談論自己以往的旅遊經驗。

We plan to take a cruise to Alaska on May 20th.	我們計畫 5 月 20 日搭乘遊輪到阿拉斯加。
How and when do you plan to go to Alaska?	你們打算怎麼去、何時去阿拉斯加？

I flew from Shanghai to Beijing on October 8th.	我 10 月 8 日從上海飛到了北京。
When and how did you get to Beijing from Shanghai?	你是何時、如何從上海到北京的？

16. 正確答案：(C) ☆☆

Jeff didn't lose all the data in the file, did he?

傑夫沒失去檔案中的所有資料，是吧？

(A) Yes, he didn't.	是的，他沒失去所有資料。
(B) No, I'm afraid he did.	不，他恐怕失去了所有資料。
(C) Yes, I'm afraid he did.	**是的，他恐怕失去了所有資料。**

解說

這是在否定句之後加上肯定疑問的附加疑問句型，而問題中的關鍵詞為 did he，所以最合適的答案是 Yes 接著肯定句 I'm afraid he did. 的 (C) 選項。

(B) 的表達邏輯就中文來說是對的，但正如 Part 2 出題要點 ② Yes-No Questions 部分說明過的，英文在 Yes 之後一定要接肯定句，No 則一定接否定句，所以 (B) 非正解。

💡 奪分祕笈：附加疑問句

附加疑問句在 Part 2 中至少會出一題。請記住下列與附加疑問句有關的基本觀念及要點。

a. be 動詞 ▶ 肯定 + 否定

I'm accepted as a member of the team, aren't I? [註1]	我被接納為團隊中的一員了，不是嗎？

b. be 動詞 ▶ 否定 + 肯定

A: You aren't sleepy, are you? [註1]	你不睏，是吧？
B: Yes, I am. / No, I'm not.	是的，我很睏。／不，我不睏。

c. 一般動詞

A: You have a car, don't you?	你有車，不是嗎？
B: Yes, I do. / No, I don't.	是的，我有。／不，我沒有。

d. 完成式的 have

A: You've already eaten, haven't you?	你已經吃過了，不是嗎？
B: Yes, I have. / No, I haven't. [註2]	是的，我吃過了。／不，我還沒吃。

e. there 為主詞

There was a convention last week, wasn't there?	上週有場大會，對吧？

f. these 為主詞

These are for shipping, aren't they? [註3]	這些是要出貨用的，不是嗎？

註1 接在 I am ... 句子之後的附加疑問應為 aren't I?，這點須特別注意。
註2 一般動詞 have 的代動詞為 do，而完成式的 have 則直接留用。
註3 以 these 為主詞的附加疑問句要用 they。

這樣練習最有效

請利用下列的「主詞 + 動詞」來練習附加疑問句,並試著用 Yes, ... / No, ... 回答。

a. I'm ...	b. You have ...	c. You don't have ...
d. You have + -ed ...	e. You haven't + -ed ...	f. She / He is ...　　g. She / He isn't ...
h. There is / are ...	i. These are / aren't ...	

17. 正確答案:(A) ☆☆

Why don't we chip in on a going-away gift for Mr. Ramirez?
我們何不一起出錢為拉米雷斯先生買個送別禮呢?

(A) Good idea. Count me in.　　　　**好主意,算我一份。**
(B) I don't like him. That's why.　　　因為我不喜歡他。
(C) Why is he going away?　　　　　他為什麼要走?

> **解說**
>
> Why don't we ...? 是表達「我們何不……?」的句型,故同意該提議的 (A) 是正解。

 小心陷阱

碰到以 Why dion't ...? 起頭的問句時要特別小心,除非是問「理由」否則不應選 (B) 的答案。這種答案常是 distracter(誘餌選項),請務必小心,千萬別上當。

奪分祕笈:表達提議、建議

日常會話中出現頻率最高的「提議」、「邀請」等說法其實有很多種。英文中常則是透過句子的述說方式來表現禮貌度,必須配合立場改變說法才能順利溝通。

▶ **較輕鬆隨興的說法**

How abou t ... / What about ...? / Why don't we ...

a. How about getting together on Sunday?　　我們週日何不聚聚?
b. What about getting together on Sunday?
c. Why don't we get together on Sunday?

Would you like to ... / Could you ... / I wonder if ... / Might I ...

a. Would you like to meet next Tuesday? 你下週二願不願意見個面？
b. Could you meet me next Tuesday? 您下週二能否與我見個面？
c. I wonder if you could meet me next Tuesday? 不知您下週二能不能和我見個面？
d. Might I be able to meet you next Tuesday? 下週二我是否能夠見到您？

 這樣練習最有效

請在你認識的人當中選定一個朋友和一位長官或長輩，然後以這些人物為藍本，試著造出五、六個問句。透過這種方式，就能實際體會須依據不同立場選用不同說法的感覺。

18. 正確答案：(A) ☆☆ 🔊 08

Shall we put off the final decision until the next board meeting?
讓我們把最終決定延到下一次的董事會議吧？

(A) Yes, let's do that. **好的，就這麼做吧。**
(B) No, let's close the meeting. 不，讓我們散會吧。
(C) We have to decide the time of the meeting. 我們必須決定會議時間。

解說

針對關鍵詞 Shall we ...?，以 let's 表達「讓我們……」之意的 (A) 為正解。

💣 小心陷阱

針對 Shall we ... ? 形式之問句，以 let's 回答的選項事實上有兩個，但是 (B)「不，讓我們散會吧。」根本牛頭不對馬嘴。然而若漏聽了 (A)，便很可能選了作為 distracter 的 (B) 選項。

💡 奪分祕笈：Shall we ... ?（提議、建議句型）

Shall we ... ? 常用於表達提議或邀請之意。針對這類句子，欲表達肯定的回應時可用 Yes, let's. / Yes, sure. / Let's do that. / Why not?註 等說法。否定回應則多半用 No, let's not ... / Well, let's not ... 等說法。另外，注意Shall I ... ? 這樣的提議句型也經常用在一般會話中，請見下方例句：

a. Shall we leave now?	我們是不是該走了？
b. Shall we close for the day?	我們今天是不是就到此為止？
c. Shall we begin the meeting?	我們是不是要開會了？
d. Shall I shut the door?	我是不是該把門關上？
e. Shall I leave now?	我是不是該現在動身？
f. Shall I come to see you?	我是不是該過來看你？

註 Why not? 是 Why not do that? 的簡短版。

這樣練習最有效

請想像職場、學校、社區等環境中會出現的各種行動，並練習以 Shall we ...？或 Shall I ...？等句型來創造相關對話。

A: Shall we leave now?	我們是不是該走了？
B: O.K, but give me 2 minutes.	好，但是再給我 2 分鐘的時間。
A: Shall I drive?	是不是我來開車？
B: Sure. Thanks.	好，謝了。
A: Shall we begin work?	我們是不是該開始工作了？
B: Let's wait until John gets here.	等約翰到了再說吧。
A: Shall I call Jim?	我是不是要打給吉姆呢？
B: No. Let him call us.	不，讓他打過來。

19. 正確答案：(A) ☆☆☆

How disappointed Mr. Benjamin be about your sales figure this month!
班傑明先生對你這個月的銷售數字一定非常失望啊！

(A) I'll have to do better next month.　**我下個月得加油了。**
(B) Yes, it's good news, isn't it?　對，這是好消息，不是嗎？
(C) Your work was disappointing.　你的工作表現令人失望。

解說
這個感嘆句的關鍵詞為 How disappointed ... sales figure，連結到正確答案 (A) 的 have to do better。

(C) 的 disappointing 是特別為題目中的 disappointed「感到失望」所設計的陷阱,企圖讓你以為是同一個字而受騙。請小心別讓它得逞!

💡 奪分祕笈:感嘆、強調、諷刺

感嘆句可算是「直述句的強調版」,句末總是會加上個驚嘆號「!」。在 Part 2 中感嘆句最多不過出個一題,但是在 Part 3 的會話中卻經常會看到。請多練習下列句型,記得別把單字順序弄錯。

▶ 強化了直述句的句子:

a. How nice you are! 你人真好!

b. How nice you are to help me load my suitcases! 你人真好,幫我把行李箱放車上!

c. What a fool that guy is! 那傢伙真蠢!

d. What a fool that guy is to take his kids out sailing on a windy day! 那傢伙真蠢,竟然在刮風的日子帶著他的孩子們出海航行!

▶ 表現強烈情感的句型包括下列這類修辭疑問句:

a. What do you think I am? 你以為我是什麼啊?

b. Who do you think you are? 你以為你是誰啊?

c. Who do you think you're talking to? 你以為你在跟誰講話?
I'm a pro tennis player. 我可是個職業網球選手。

▶ 在修辭疑問句中再加入強調用詞句:

a. How in the world did you get so much work done in one day? 你到底是如何能在一天內完成這麼多工作的?

b. Where on earth did you find that confidential information? 你到底是在哪兒找到那份機密資料的?

✓ 這樣練習最有效

請從周遭事物擷取靈感,並以「怎麼會有這麼……的……!」這種形式造出十句中文句子,然後再改寫成英文,應該就能掌握感嘆句的基本語感了。

Part 2

Strategies

Pre Test

Half Test 1

Half Test 2

Full Test

| a.那隻狗真可愛！ | How cute that dog is! |
| b. 毛毛蟲這種生物真是奇怪！ | What a strange creature the caterpillar is! |

20. 正確答案：(C) ☆☆☆

Could you please give my best regards to your boss, Mr. Nielsen, when you get back to your office?

你回到你的辦公室後，能否請你替我向你的上司尼爾森先生致上最誠摯的問候？

(A) I'll have a meeting with him.　　　　　　　　我將會跟他開會。

(B) He'll say "hello" to you.　　　　　　　　　　他會對你說「你好」。

(C) I'll be sure to convey your regards to him.　　**我一定會將你的問候傳達給他。**

解說

Could you please ... ? 算是表達請求之意時最有禮貌的說法。選項 (C) 的 I'll ... convey your regards to my boss. 明確表示會傳達問候之意。

小心陷阱

(B) 以未來式陳述「上司將說『你好』」，根本沒有在回答問題，請別被 say "hello" 所騙。

奪分祕笈：表達拜託、請求之意

▶ 較輕鬆隨興的請求句型：

Can you ... / Will you ... 和其回答方式：

A: Can you tell me where the bathroom is?　　　可不可以告訴我洗手間在哪兒？

B: Sure. Go to the end of the hall and turn left.　　　當然可以。走到走廊盡頭處左轉。

A: Will you hold this door while I bring in this luggage?　　你可以在我搬進行李時幫我壓住門嗎？

B: Sure. Let me help you with it.　　　當然可以。讓我來幫你。

Could you ... / Would you ... / Would you mind ~ing ...?

A: Could you talk to your staff about the new plan as soon as possible?	能不能請你盡快和你的員工談談這個新計畫？
B: Of course, I'll do that right away.	當然，我馬上就去談。

A: Would you mind signing the contract today?	您是否介意今天就簽約呢？
B: Today might be difficult. I could do that tomorrow for sure.	今天可能有點困難。我明天一定可以簽。

Word List

- ☐ improve [ɪmˋpruv] 動 改善 (No. 6)
- ☐ chair 動 擔任主席、主持會議 (No. 9)
- ☐ branch manager 分公司經理 (No. 10)
- ☐ pick up ... 去接……
- ☐ It's a shame that ... ……是很令人遺憾的 (No. 7)
- ☐ miss 動 想念、錯過
- ☐ committee meeting 委員會
- ☐ be off to ... 朝……前進、出發 (No. 12)
- ☐ going-away gift 送別禮 (No. 17)
- ☐ board meeting 董事會議 (No. 18)

Memo:

Part  Short Conversation 簡短對話題

☆470 分等級 ☆☆600 分等級 ☆☆☆730 分以上

● 21 ～ 23 與機械、汽車故障有關的問題　　🔊 10

Questions 21 through 23 refer to the following conversation.

Woman: Rick, this is Marcy. I've got a van load of tourists and a flat tire. I'm on Highway I-95 about 2 miles past the Powder Road exit.

Man: I'll be right there with another van. Give me 15 minutes.

Woman: Oh, wait, Rick. Here comes a police car. He's stopping. I think he'll be able to change the tire for me.

Man: Good. But I'm still coming to take your van back to the office, so wait for me. It's not good to drive all day on a spare tire, especially with 12 paying passengers.

女： 瑞克，我是瑪西。我用小巴載了一車觀光客但卻爆胎了。我在 I-95 公路上，過了包德路出口約 2 英里處。

男： 我馬上開另一台小巴士過去。給我 15 分鐘的時間。

女： 喔，等等，瑞克。有警車來了。他是要停車了。我想他能幫我換輪胎。

男： 那很好。但是我還是要去把你的小巴士開回辦公室，所以請等我一下。用備胎開一整天的車不太好，尤其是還載了 12 位付了錢的乘客。

Word List

☐ load of ... 大量的……　　☐ flat tire [flæt taɪr] 爆胎

21. 正確答案：(B) ☆☆

What does Marcy do?　　瑪西是做什麼工作的？

(A) She's a police officer.　　她是警察。

(B) She's a tour guide.　　**她是導遊。**

(C) She's a mechanic.　　她是技工。

(D) She's a tourist.　　她是觀光客。

解說

女子在一開始說了 I've got a van load of tourists ...，可知答案為 (B)。

💣 小心陷阱

(D) tourist 和 tour guide 聽來有點像，請小心別混淆。

22. 正確答案：(B) ☆☆

How long will it take Rick to drive to where Marcy is? 瑞克開車到瑪西所在處要多久？

(A) 2 minutes   2 分鐘   **(B) 15 minutes**   **15 分鐘**
(C) 50 minutes   50 分鐘   (D) 95 minutes   95 分鐘

> **解說**
>
> 男子說了 Give me 15 minutes. ，可知正解為 (B) 。另外， (A) 中的數字是瑪西距離公路出口的英里數、(D) 的數字則是從 I-95 公路而來，皆與時間無關。

💣 小心陷阱

(C) 50 分鐘和正確答案的 15 分鐘兩者很容易聽錯，須特別小心以免上當。

23. 正確答案：(D) ☆☆

Who will probably change the flat tire?   誰可能會更換爆胎？

(A) Marcy.   瑪西。   (B) One of the passengers.   其中一名乘客。
(C) Rick.   瑞克。   **(D) A police officer.**   **警察。**

> **解說**
>
> 由女子所說的 Here comes a police car. ... he'll be able to change the tire. 可推論出正解為 (D) 。

💣 小心陷阱

由於會話一開始時瑞克曾說他「15 分鐘會到達現場」，最後又說「用備胎開一整天的車不太好，所以他還是要去現場」，這些都很容易讓人誤以為要換車胎的是瑞克。

💡 奪分祕笈：與汽車故障有關的詞句

TOEIC 中與機械相關的故障、抱怨、維護之類題目的出題範圍包括了汽車、飛機、火車及巴士等公共運輸工具，以及電話、影印機、電腦、冷氣空調、工廠機器等等。初次接受測驗時，很多人可能光聽到機械類問題就開始恐慌，連問題都聽不清楚。但其實 TOEIC 測驗不會出現需要專業知識才能解答的問題，因此只要牢記本書所列的基本詞彙便足以應付。而與汽車相關的詞彙有很多屬於中式英文，在此請務必把正確的基礎英文用詞記起來。例如：

a. 汽車各部分名稱

- accelerator [æk`sɛlə.retə] 名 油門
- directional signal [də`rɛkʃən `sɪgnl] 方向燈
- steering wheel [`stɪrɪŋ hwil] 方向盤
- windshield 名 [`wɪnd.ʃild] 擋風玻璃
- brake [brek] 名 動 煞車
- rearview mirror 後視鏡
- wheels 名 輪胎
- windshield wiper [`wɪnd.ʃild `waɪpə] 雨刷

b. 與汽車有關的麻煩

- had a collision [kə`lɪʒən] 撞車
- The engine stalled. 引擎熄火。
- The battery is dead / ran down. 電池沒電。
- The car skidded / slipped / spun[註] 汽車打滑／滑開／打轉。
- car crash 車禍
- The car is out of gas. 汽車沒油。
- Got a flat tire. 爆胎。

註 spin – spun – spun [spɪn] [spʌn] 動 旋轉；自旋

c. 駕駛規則

- balloon test / breathalyzer test

  [bə`lun tɛst / `brɛθə.laɪzə] 酒測
- parking violation 違規停車
- DUI (driving under the influence)

  在酒精或藥物影響下駕駛
- violation of the traffic regulations

  [.vaɪə`leʃən] [.rɛgjə`leʃən] 違反交通規則
- parking ticket 違規停車罰單
- moving violation 行車違規

● 24 ~ 26 與提案、發表有關的問題 　　　　🎧 11

Questions 24 through 26 refer to the following conversation.

Man: Sarah, your presentation for our new PET VITA HEALTH was fine. But it would have been perfect if you had brought some samples.

Woman: But Mr. Meyers told me not to bring samples because we're still working on the packaging.

Man: Look! Packaging isn't that important. What's important is that the customers have something to take away with them.

男： 莎拉，妳替我們新產品「寵物生命健康」所做的介紹很不錯，不過要是妳有帶些樣品來就太完美了。

女： 但是梅爾斯先生叫我別帶樣品，因為我們的包裝還沒設計完成。

男： 聽好了！包裝不是那麼重要。重點在於要讓顧客能帶些東西走。

24. 正確答案：(C) ☆☆

What was wrong with the presentation?   這場商品介紹有何不妥？

(A) It was too short.   太短了。

(B) It wasn't well-packaged.   沒有妥善包裝好。

(C) There were no product samples.   **沒有商品樣本。**

(D) Some of the samples were defective.   有些樣品有瑕疵。

解說

男子說的第二句 But it would have been perfect if you had brought some samples. 是指向正解 (C) 的關鍵。選項 (B) It was not well-packaged 的 It 指的不是 presentation，而 (D) Some of the samples were defective. 則與實況不符。

小心陷阱

選項 (B) 中提到的 well-packaged 和在對話中出現的 packaging 很容易使人上當，請小心。

25. 正確答案：(B) ☆☆

What did Mr. Meyers tell Sarah?   梅爾斯先生對莎拉說了什麼？

(A) He told her not to make any changes.   他叫她別做任何改變。

(B) He told her not to bring samples to the presentation. 他叫她別帶樣品去產品發表會。

(C) He told her to modify the presentation.   他叫她修改產品介紹方式。

(D) He told her that packaging wasn't the most important thing.   他告訴她包裝設計不是最重要的事。

解說

女子說的 Mr. Meyers told me not to bring samples ... 是指向正確答案的關鍵。而且對話中完全未提及 (C) He told her to modify the presentation.。

小心陷阱

提出選項 (D)「包裝設計不是最重要的事」的是莎拉的會話對象（應該是她上司），不是梅爾斯先生。但是由於會話中僅出現梅爾斯這個名字，因而很容易讓人上當。

26. 正確答案：(C) ☆☆

What is true about the conversation?　　　　關於這段會話，以下敘述何者正確？

(A) The man said the presentation was perfect.　男子說商品介紹很完美。

(B) The man and the woman agreed.　　　　男子與女子的意見一致。

(C) The man and the woman disagreed.　　**男子與女子的意見不一致。**

(D) The woman asked the man to help her.　女子要求男子幫她的忙。

解說

從男子說的 it would have been perfect if you had brought some samples. 和女子說的
But Meyers told me not to bring samples ... 來判斷，可知兩人意見不合，故 (C) 為正解。

小心陷阱

男子的第二句為過去完成假設式，表達的是與過去事實相反的狀況。請別被 (A) 選項裡的
was perfect 這個字所騙。

奪分祕笈：與提案、發表有關的詞句

proposal 用來指針對新的商品企劃、公司系統變更、規定之修正等提出的建議。一般會先
在公司會議中提出建議或企劃案，而提案者會進行 oral presentation（口頭簡報）。為了
介紹企業商品等的 presentation 也稱「商品發表」，和給傳播媒體的 news release「新聞
稿」一樣都屬於商業上的重要策略。因此 TOEIC 在 Part 3、Part 4 部分通常都會出 1 篇
與 presentation 有關的問題。這對尚未進入職場的學生來說或許有些困難，不過只要把
presentation 想成類似學校中論文發表的形式，就較能理解了。

1. 首先利用 Google 或 Yahoo 等搜尋引擎搜尋你有興趣的產品介紹內容。
2. 閱讀搜尋到的各種文章，並把與商品有關的基礎詞彙記起來。

現在，先來記住以下與提案及發表有關的字彙與片語：

▶ **proposal** [prəˋpozḷ] 图 企劃案；提案、提議
　propose [prəˋpoz] 動 提議；建議

☐ make a proposal 提案　　　　　☐ cosponsor [koˋspansə] 共同贊助人

☐ bid for the project 專案競標　　☐ discussion on the proposal 提案討論

☐ proposer / proponent　　　　　☐ vote on a proposal 投票表決提案
　　[prəˋpozə / prəˋponənt] 提案者／提議人

註「for」表示贊成，「against」代表反對，「abstention」則為棄權

> ▶ **presentation** [ˌprɪzən`teʃən] 图 發表；提出；呈現；簡報
> **present** [ˌprɪ`zɛnt] 動 提出；出示；展現

- ☐ do a presentation 發表或介紹新商品、做簡報
- ☐ do research 做調查、研究
- ☐ introduce a new product 介紹新商品
- ☐ news release （新產品等的）新聞稿
- ☐ public speaking 公開演說
- ☐ publicity-friendly 媒體關係良好的
- ☐ publicity campaign [pʌb`lɪsətɪ kæm`pen] 宣傳活動
- ☐ question and answer session （發表會中的）問答時間

● 27 ~ 29 與飛機及旅館的預約有關的問題　　　🔊 12

Questions 27 through 29 refer to the following conversation.

Man: Would it be possible for me to get on an earlier flight?

Woman: There's a 3-o'clock flight leaving in half an hour. Let me check for seat availability. Yes! There's one seat available on it. You can make it if you check in now.

Man: OK, I'll take it. I have no bags to check in—just a backpack for my carry-on.

Woman: Very good. Here's your boarding pass. Gate 27A.

男： 我有沒有可能搭乘較早的班機？

女： 有一班 3 點的飛機將於 30 分鐘後出發。讓我看看還有沒有空位。有！還有一個空位。您現在辦搭機手續還趕得上。

男： 好的，我要搭這班。我沒有行李要託運，只有一個隨身背包。

女： 太好了。這是您的登機證。27A 登機門。

> **Word List**
>
> - ☐ seat availability [sit əˌvelə`bɪlətɪ] 空位
> - ☐ carry-on [`kærɪˌɑn] 图 隨身行李；形 可隨身攜帶的

27. 正確答案：(D) ☆

Who are the two speakers?　　　　　　　說話的兩個人是誰？

(A) A cabin attendant and a passenger　　空服員和乘客
(B) A customs officer and a traveler　　　海關人員與旅客
(C) A gift shop owner and a customer　　　禮品店老闆與顧客
(D) An airline agent and a customer　　**航空公司人員與顧客**

> **解說**
>
> 由對話一開始處的 ... for me to get on an earlier flight 和服務人員所回答的 There's a 3 o'clock flight ... 等關鍵詞句可判斷出正確答案為 (D)。

小心陷阱

(A) 的 cabin attendant 雖然也屬於航空公司的人員之一，但是其工作場所是在機艙內，請別上當。

28. 正確答案：(A) ☆☆

What does the man want?　　　　　　　這名男子想要什麼？

(A) To leave earlier than scheduled　　**提早出發**
(B) To cancel his flight　　　　　　　　取消他的航班
(C) To check in his luggage　　　　　　　託運他的行李
(D) To pay cash for his ticket　　　　　　用現金付機票錢

> **解說**
>
> 男子要的是 get on an earlier flight，這和正確答案 (A) 的 leave earlier 意思相同。而 (B) 和 (D) 都和會話內容無關。

小心陷阱

男子在對話中曾提到 I have no bags to check in ...，所以 (C) 是錯的。千萬不要因為 check in 這個片語在對話裡出現過，就誤選。

29. 正確答案：(A) ☆ ☆

What time is it now, most likely?	現在最有可能是幾點？
(A) 2:30 p.m.	**下午 2 點 30 分**
(B) 2:45 p.m.	下午 2 點 45 分
(C) 3:00 p.m.	下午 3 點
(D) 3:30 p.m.	下午 3 點 30 分

> **解說**
>
> 服務人員說 There's a 3-o'clock flight leaving in half an hour.「有一班 3 點的飛機將於 30 分鐘後出發。」，因此可推斷現在應該是 (A) 下午 2 點 30 分。注意，most likely 表示「最有可能」。

小心陷阱

同屬三點後時間的選項有 (C) 與 (D) 兩個，都很容易讓人誤選。(C) 為實際出發時間、(D) 為出發後的時間，都不對。另外，請記住 "half an hour" = "thirty minutes"。

奪分祕笈：飯店、機場等處報到及預約常用詞句

預約旅遊、飯店、餐廳、劇院等，是 TOEIC 中出題頻率甚高的主題之一。建議讀者可以：

1. 上網搜尋著名飯店及劇院，除了可以看到相關的資訊外，還可以認識關鍵字彙。
2. 在網路上練習填寫相關預約表單。只要不按下預約表單最後的「send」（送出）鈕，要練習幾次都沒問題。

a. 旅遊

- ☐ aisle seat [aɪl] 靠走道的座位
- ☐ window seat 靠窗的座位
- ☐ boarding ticket [`bordɪŋ] 登機證
- ☐ boarding time 登機時間
- ☐ e-ticket (= electronic ticket) [ɪlɛk`trɑnɪk] 電子機票
- ☐ e-ticket kiosk [kɪ`ɑsk] 核發電子機票的機器
- ☐ economy / business / first class 經濟／商務／頭等艙
- ☐ round-trip ticket [`raɪnd.trɪp] 來回票
- ☐ security check [sɪ`kjʊrətɪ] 安全檢查
- ☐ time of arrival / departure [ə`raɪv̩ / dɪ`partʃə] 抵達／出發時間

b. 飯店

☐ B&B (bed and breakfast)
附早餐的住宿

☐ be booked up 預定已滿

☐ book / reserve a hotel / flight
預訂飯店／班機

☐ itinerary [aɪˋtɪnəˏrɛrɪ] 旅遊行程

☐ luxury / economy / budget hotels
[ˋlʌkʃərɪ / ɪˋkɑnəmɪ / ˋbʌdʒɪt hoˋtəl]
豪華／經濟／廉價飯店

☐ off-season discount 淡季折扣

☐ occupancy tax [ˋɑkjəpənsɪ] 住宿稅

☐ package / optional tour
套裝／自選行程

☐ put down someone's name for 2 nights
以某人的名字預約 2 晚住宿

☐ service charge 服務費

☐ single / double occupancy
單／雙人房

☐ suites 套房

☐ visitors information bureau [ˋbjʊro] 遊
客諮詢中心

☐ weekly discount 每週折扣

c. 劇院

☐ matinee / evening performance
[ˏmætənˋe] 日間／夜間公演、秀

☐ preview 預告片、預演

● 30 ～ 32 與請求協助、給予建議等有關的問題　　　🔊 13

Questions 30 through 32 refer to the following conversation.

Man: Hello, this is John Samuels from Accounting, and I'm wondering if you could help me. I've been having trouble with my e-mail. Every time I try to open an attachment, I get an error message. It's driving me crazy.

Woman: OK. It would help if you could tell me what the error message says. Can you read it to me?

Man: Uh ... Wait a minute ... OK. It says,"Error number 134: The file cannot be opened. It may be due to corruption of the file."

Woman: Not to worry. That's a problem that can easily be solved.

男： 喂，我是會計部的約翰・塞繆爾斯，不知道能否請你幫幫我。我用電子郵件時碰到麻煩。每次我要開啟附件的時候，就會出現錯誤訊息。快把我逼瘋了。

女： 好的。如果你能告訴我錯誤訊息的內容那將會很有幫助。你可以唸給我聽嗎？

男： 嗯……。等一下……。好，錯誤訊息寫的是「錯誤編號 134：檔案無法開啟。可能是因為檔案已毀損。」

女： 不用擔心。這問題可以輕易解決。

30. 正確答案：(B) ☆

What was the purpose of the call?	這通電話的目的為何？

(A) To complain　　　　　　　　　　抱怨

(B) To get help　　　　　　　　　　請求協助

(C) To buy something　　　　　　　　買東西

(D) To report an incident　　　　　　通報事件

解說

男子一開始就說 I'm wondering if you could help me.，所以 (B) 為正確答案。另外由於女子並不是必須對此項麻煩負責的人，所以 (A) 的「來抱怨」說法並不成立。

小心陷阱

或許會有人覺得 (D) To report an incident「通報事件」的答案也滿合理的，但是由男子所說的 ... if you could help me. 可知，他打電話是來求助，而非只「通報事件」。別忘了，TOEIC 測驗所需的是選擇「最適當」的答案。

31. 正確答案：(C) ☆

Which department did John probably call?	約翰可能是打電話給哪個部門？

(A) Marketing　　　　　　　　　　行銷部

(B) Accounting　　　　　　　　　　會計部

(C) Technical Support　　　　　　技術支援部門

(D) Quality Control　　　　　　　　品管部門

解說

由男子一開始說的 I'm wondering if you could help me. I've been having trouble with my e-mail.，可推測，他應是打電話到技術支援部求助。而 (D) Quality Control 是管理、統一公司產品品質的「品管部門」，並非正解。

小心陷阱

對話中出現的 Accounting 是男子的所屬部門，顯然 (B) 是此題的 distracter（誘餌選項）。由於對話裡只出現男子的所屬部門，致電目標部門並未出現，很容易讓人上當。

32. 正確答案：(A) ☆☆

How does the caller feel?　　　　　　　　　打電話的人有何感受？

(A) He's frustrated.　　　　　　　　　　　**他很沮喪。**

(B) He's hungry.　　　　　　　　　　　　　他很餓。

(C) He's embarrassed.　　　　　　　　　　他覺得很尷尬。

(D) He's tired.　　　　　　　　　　　　　他很累。

解說

由男子的第 4 句話 It's driving me crazy. 可知，正解為 (A)。而男子屬於會計部，不會修理電腦並沒什麼好尷尬的，所以 (C) He's embarrassed. 不成立。

 小心陷阱

由於 (B) hungry 的發音和 angry 類似，所以漏聽了 (A) 的人便很可能因誤會而上當，請特別小心了。

 奪分祕笈：請求協助、給予建議等的會話

Part 3 的會話題總會出現向人求助、詢問事情及請求指示的時候常用的句型。而實際到英語系國家去時，最需要的也正是這類句型。迷路的時候你會怎樣開口問路呢？先說 Excuse me.，接著該說什麼？這部分若沒能徹底熟記，就很難理解 Part 3 中這類對話的脈絡。以下要注意兩點：

1. 會話裡的問題、麻煩為何？
2. 會話中指示的解決方法為何？

請反覆聆聽對話，並練習找出和這兩個要點相關之關鍵字詞。另外補充，請求或提供協助的表達說法也有較輕鬆或較禮貌之分，請牢記下頁表格內容：

Strategies

Pre Test

Half Test 1

Half Test 2

Full Test

a. 較輕鬆的說法

Help me with this.	幫我做一下這個。
Can you help me with this?	你可以幫我做一下這個嗎？

b. 較有禮貌的說法

Would you happen to know where I could find this information?	你會不會剛好知道我可以在哪裡找到這項資訊？
Might I ask you where I could get the information?	可否請問您我能從何處獲得這項資訊？
Could you (please) sit down first?	您可不可以先坐下來？
Would you mind opening the window for me?	您介不介意幫我打開窗戶？
I wonder if you could help me with this.	不知您是否可以協助我處理一下此事？

▶ 提供協助時的表達方式：

a. 較輕鬆的說法

Need help?	需要幫忙嗎？
Do you want me to help?	你要我幫忙嗎？
Can I help you?	讓我幫忙吧？

b. 較有禮貌的說法

May I help you?	讓我來幫您吧？
Might / Could I be of some help?	你要不要我幫忙？
Would you like me to help you?	我可以幫您嗎？

● 33 ～ 35 與抱怨、投訴有關的問題　　　🔊 14

Questions 33 through 35 refer to the following conversation.

Woman: I canceled my subscription to your magazine three months ago, and you promised to send me a check for a refund, but I haven't gotten it yet.

Man: I apologize for that, ma'am. And how long ago did you receive your last issue?

Woman: Oh, the magazines are still coming. I just got one yesterday. That's why I'm calling.

Man: Well, ma'am, I'm awfully sorry, but we can't pay you back for magazines that you have received. I will cancel your subscription today and refund you for the remaining issues.

女： 我三個月前取消了對你們雜誌的訂閱，而你們答應要寄給我退款支票，但是我到現在都還沒收到。

男： 我向您致歉，女士。請問您最後一次收到雜誌是在多久之前？

女： 噢，雜誌到現在都還一直送來。我昨天剛收到一本。所以我才打電話來問。

男： 嗯，女士，我真的非常抱歉，不過您已經收到的雜誌我們無法退款。我今天會替您取消訂閱，並退還您剩下幾期的金額。

Word List

☐ subscription [səb`skrɪpʃən] 名 訂閱　　☐ refund [rɪ`fʌnd] 動 退款

33. 正確答案：(A) ☆☆

What is the woman complaining about?　　這名女子在抱怨什麼？

(A) She hasn't received her refund yet.　　**她還沒收到退款。**

(B) She hasn't canceled her subscription.　　她還沒取消雜誌的訂閱。

(C) She is disappointed with the contents of the magazine.　　她對雜誌內容很失望。

(D) She thinks the magazine subscription is too expensive.　　她覺得雜誌的訂閱費太貴了。

解說

由女子在第一句裡說的 ... you promised to send me a check for a refund, but I haven't gotten it yet. 可知，正解為 (A)。而由於她還說 I canceled my subscription three months ago ...，所以 (B) 是錯的。另外，對話中完全沒談到和 (C) 與 (D) 有關的內容。

34. 正確答案：(B) ☆☆

When did the woman get her last issue?　　這位女性在何時收到她最近一期的雜誌？

(A) Three months ago　　三個月前

(B) Yesterday　　**昨天**

(C) Today　　今天

(D) Last year　　去年

解說

女子在第二次發言時說 I just got one yesterday.，可知 (B) 是正解。

選項 (A) 「三個月前」是她取消雜誌訂閱的時間點,可知此非正解。原本從該時間點起,女子不應再收到雜誌,但因雜誌社出錯,所以直到昨天為止,女子都持續收到雜誌。

35. 正確答案:(D) ☆

What will probably happen after this?	在這之後可能會發生什麼?
(A) The company will go bankrupt.	該公司會破產。
(B) The woman will continue to subscribe to the magazine.	這位女士會繼續訂閱雜誌。
(C) The magazines will continue to come for 3 months.	該雜誌會持續寄來三個月。
(D) The woman will receive her refund.	**這位女士會收到退款。**

解說

男子最後說了 I will cancel your subscription today and refund you for the remaining issues.,可知,正確答案是 (D)。

小心陷阱

選項 (C) The magazines will continue to come for 3 months. 是依據對話裡的 I canceled my subscription to your magazine three months ago. 這項資訊所設計的陷阱。

💡 奪分祕笈:用於抱怨、投訴時的表達方式

與抱怨、投訴有關的問題可說是 TOEIC 的必出題型。常見主題除了上列外,還有「訂購的商品沒送到」、「收到不對的商品」、「商品壞了」、「扣款金額不正確」……等等相關的問題也常出現。面對此類題型,以下提供筆者增進實力的小技巧,請讀者一起實行,並記住下方詞彙:

1. 錄下 ICRT 之廣告、產品介紹等內容,然後進行 shadowing(跟讀)及 dictation(聽寫)練習。
2. 上網搜尋各類商品宣傳及說明之文章。
3. 閱讀各種英語雜誌的宣傳文案,試著掌握各雜誌的特色。

Word List

☐ cancel the subscription / order
[səb`skrɪpʃən] 取消訂閱／訂購

☐ compensate for the damage / loss
[`kɑmpən.set] [`dæmɪdʒ] 賠償損害／損失

☐ claim check（行李等的）提取單[註]

☐ damaged merchandise [`mɜtʃən.daɪz]
破損商品

☐ defective product [dɪ`fɛktɪv] 瑕疵品

☐ not live up to the standard
未達標準

☐ get a refund / reimbursement
[rɪ`fʌnd / .riɪm`bɜsmənt] 獲得退款／退費

☐ impolite attitude [.ɪmpə`laɪt `ætət.jud]
不禮貌的態度

☐ inferior quality of work [ɪn`fɪrɪr]
低劣的工作品質

☐ liable / responsible for the damage
[`laɪəbl̩ / rɪ`spɑnsəbl̩] 負有損害賠償責任

☐ make / place a complaint 提出申訴

☐ money back guaranteed [gæərən`tid]
退款保證

☐ warranty / guarantee period [`wɔrəntɪ]
[`pɪrɪəd] 保固期

註 claim 在此指「領取、提取」，check 指「單據」。

Memo:

● 36 ~ 38 錄音訊息 🎧 16

Questions 36 through 38 refer to the following recorded message.

Thank you for calling New Canaan Public Library. The main branch of the public library is located at 66 East Main Street. Library hours are as follows: Tuesday through Friday from 9 a.m. to 9 p.m., Saturday from 10 a.m. to 9 p.m., and Sunday from 12 noon to 8 p.m. We are closed on Mondays and on all state and federal holidays. Also, the library will be closed the entire month of July due to extensive renovations. To hear this message again, press 1. To go back to the main menu, press 2.

感謝您來電新迦南公共圖書館。公共圖書館本館位於東大街 66 號。開館時間如下：週二至週五上午 9 點到晚上 9 點，週六為上午 10 點到晚上 9 點，週日則從正午 12 點到晚上 8 點。週一及所有州定假日、聯邦假日均休館。此外，由於大規模改裝工程，7 月全月圖書館都將休館。若要重聽此語音訊息，請按 1。要回到主選單，請按 2。

Word List

- □ federal holiday [ˈfɛdərəl ˈhaləde]　（美國）聯邦假日
- □ renovation [ˌrɛnəˈveʃən] 图 改裝、翻新
- □ due to ... 由於…
- □ extensive [ɪkˈstɛnsɪv] 圈 大規模的

---

36. 正確答案：(D) ☆

Where is the library located?　　　　該圖書館位於何處？

(A) The main branch　　　　　　　　本館
(B) The state and federal building　　州政府與聯邦政府大樓
(C) Next to the book store　　　　　　在書店旁
(D) On East Main Street　　　　　**在東大街上**

> 解說
>
> 第二句提到 ... library is located at 66 East Main Street.，因此可知正解為 (D)。

 小心陷阱

選項 (A) 的 main branch 是因語音內容中提及的 Main Street. 而設的陷阱，而 (B) 的 state and federal building 則是為 state and federal holidays 所設的陷阱，請小心。

37. 正確答案:(B) ☆☆

What hours is the library open on Fridays?   圖書館週五何時開放?

(A) From10 in the morning until 9 in the evening   從早上 10 點到晚上 9 點

(B) From 9 in the morning until 9 in the evening   **從早上 9 點到晚上 9 點**

(C) From 10 in the morning until 8 in the evening   從早上 10 點到晚上 8 點

(D) From 12 noon until 8 in the evening   從中午 12 點到晚上 8 點

> **解說**
>
> 訊息中提到 Tuesday through Friday from 9 a.m. to 9 p.m., ...,可知正解是 (B)。

小心陷阱

只要是與數字有關的問題,所有選項幾乎都可說是陷阱。由於要記住說明文中所有的開放時間實在太難,所以請事先瀏覽過問題、並記住 What hours ... on Fridays? 等關鍵詞後再聽文章內容,否則會無法作答。

38. 正確答案:(A) ☆☆

What will happen in July?   7 月會發生什麼事?

(A) The library will be renewed.   **圖書館將改建。**

(B) All the library personnel will go on vacation.   圖書館館員都將去度假。

(C) The library will be relocated.   圖書館將會搬遷。

(D) The library will be open every day.   圖書館每天都會開放。

> **解說**
>
> 若掌握了訊息中的關鍵詞 closed ... July ... renovations.,便可知正解為 (A)。注意,語音裡的 renovation 在 (A) 選項裡被替換成了同義的 renewed。

小心陷阱

第二句 The main branch of the public library is located ... 被設計成 (C) 選項裡的 library will be relocated 陷阱。locate「位在」和 relocate「搬遷」兩者意義完全不同,請特別注意。

奪分祕笈：聽取錄音訊息

錄音訊息是 TOEIC Part 4 中的必出考題之一。內容包括公共機關及活動的介紹，航空公司、火車、巴士的訂位，要求再次遞送郵件或行李、劇院訂票等。問題種類有（1）與主題有關的大範圍問題，及（2）打電話的人該怎麼做，和（3）哪個數字鍵對應到哪個功能等小範圍問題。有關數字的問題，若沒能確實記住數字，光靠隱約的記憶通常都無法答對。因此在聆聽文章內容前，一定要先掌握問題裡的關鍵詞才行。就公司機構等的錄音訊息來說，一開始都會先以類似 Thank you for calling Victoria Airlines. 這樣的句子來介紹公司名或部門名稱，請千萬別漏聽。

▶ 常見於電話語音的表達方式：

a. To make a reservation, press 1. 　　　　　　　　　預約請按 1。

b. To place an order, press 2. 　　　　　　　　　　　訂購請按 2。

c. To reach the customer service, press 3. 　　　　需要顧客服務請按 3。

d. To have your package delivered again, press 2. 需要再次配送包裹請按 2。

e. To talk to one of our agents, please hold the line. 若要與服務人員對話，請稍候別掛斷。

f. Hold the line. 　　　　　　　　　　　　　　　　　　　請稍候別掛斷。

g. The first available agent will be with 　　　　　第一位空出來的服務人員很快就會
   you shortly. 　　　　　　　　　　　　　　　　　　　　與您對話。

▶ 辦公室等地方下班後的語音訊息：

a. Our office is closed for the day. 　　　　　　　　我們辦公室今日已關閉。

b. Please call again tomorrow or dial direct. 　　　請明日再來電，或撥打專線。

c. Please call back tomorrow 　　　　　　　　　　　請於明日 8 點 30 分到 5 點之間
   between 8:30 and 5:00. 　　　　　　　　　　　　　再次來電。

▶ 常見於電話留言的表達方式：

a. This is Tim. 　　　　　　　　　　　　　　　　　　　我是提姆。

b. Hi, thank you for calling Tim. 　　　　　　　　　嗨，謝謝你打給提姆。

c. You've reached the Swenson residence. 　　　　這是史文生家。

d. I'm out right now. 　　　　　　　　　　　　　　　　我現在不在家。

e. I'm not available now. 　　　　　　　　　　　　　我現在不方便接電話。

f. I can't come to the phone right now. 　　　　　　我現在無法接電話。

g. Please leave your number so I can call back later. 請留下你的電話號碼，以便我稍後回電。

h. Start your message after the tone / beep. 　　　請在嗶聲後開始留言。

● 39 ~ 41 天氣預報

🔊 17

Questions 39 through 41 refer to the following weather forecast.

And now for the weather forecast. Tonight promises to bring us more rain–lots and lots more rain. We're still feeling the effects of that hurricane that passed through on Tuesday. The rain is expected to continue through tomorrow morning, clearing up in the early afternoon. So drive carefully tomorrow morning, and bring an umbrella.

那麼現在開始提供天氣預報。預計今晚會下更多雨，雨量會非常、非常多。我們仍受到週二通過的颶風影響。降雨預計會持續至明天整個早上，午後會放晴。所以明天早上開車時請特別小心，並記得帶傘。

39. 正確答案：(C) ☆

What kind of weather is predicted for tonight?　今晚的天氣預測會是如何？

(A) Clear skies　　　　　　　　　　　　晴朗無雲
(B) Storm　　　　　　　　　　　　　　暴風雨
(C) Rain　　　　　　　　　　　　　　**下雨**
(D) Clouds　　　　　　　　　　　　　　陰天

> 【解說】
> 依據預報第二句 Tonight promises to bring us more rain. 可知正解為 (C)。

> 🅑 小心陷阱
>
> 小心不要因第三句提到了 effects of that hurricane 而誤選 (B) storm。

40. 正確答案：(B) ☆☆

What happened on Tuesday?　　　　　　週二發生了什麼事？

(A) The rain finally stopped.　　　　　　雨終於停了。
(B) There was a storm.　　　　　　　**有暴風雨。**
(C) It snowed a lot.　　　　　　　　　　下了很多雪。
(D) It was a very hot day.　　　　　　　天氣非常熱。

> 【解說】
> 由預報第三句中的 ... hurricane that passed through on Tuesday. 可知正解為 (B)。

41. 正確答案：(D) ☆☆

When will it be sunny again?　　　　　　　　何時會再放晴？

(A) This morning　　　　　　　　　　　　今天早晨
(B) Tuesday afternoon　　　　　　　　　　週二下午
(C) Tomorrow morning　　　　　　　　　　明天早晨
(D) Tomorrow afternoon　　　　　　　　**明天下午**

> 解說
>
> 根據預報第四句裡提到的 ... rain ..., clearing up in the early afternoon. 等關鍵詞可知正解為 (D)。

小心陷阱

由於第四句中同時包含了 tomorrow morning 和 early afternoon 這兩個表示時間的副詞片語，因此需小心別誤選了 (C) tomorrow morning。

這樣練習最有效

即使住在台灣，你仍能透過 ICRT 及部分的 FM 廣播聽到英語天氣預報。若想眼耳並用，還有有線電視的 CNN、BBC 等頻道可利用。天氣預報的相關詞彙有限，除了特殊狀況外，只要多練習個幾次就不覺得那麼困難了。而練習時若能同時將天氣預報 visualize（想像該情景），便會更有效果。另外，也可以練習一邊看英文報紙的天氣預報與天氣圖，一邊自行嘗試以英語播報出來。總之，重點就在於「開口練習」。

奪分祕笈：與天氣預報有關的詞句

請熟記下列常出現在天氣預報中的相關詞句。

Word List

☐ fair / clear / sunny / fine 形 晴朗的
☐ rain 名 動 下雨
☐ light shower 小雨
☐ heavy shower 大雨
☐ drizzle [drɪzl] 動 名（下）毛毛雨
☐ downpour [`daʊn͵por] 名 豪雨
☐ flood [flʌd] 名 洪水 動 淹沒
☐ storm 名 暴風雨

☐ thunderstorm [`θʌndɚ͵stɔrm] 名 雷雨
☐ tornado [tɔr`nedo] 名 龍捲風
☐ tornado funnel [`fʌnl] 龍捲風的漏斗狀部分
☐ typhoon 名 颱風、（亞洲的）熱帶性低氣壓
☐ cyclone [`saɪklon] 名 氣旋、（印度洋的）熱帶性低氣壓

- □ hurricane [`hɜɪˌken] 图 颶風、（大西洋的）熱帶性低氣壓
- □ snow 图 雪
- □ hailstone [`helˌston] 图 冰雹
- □ avalanche [`ævlˌæntʃ] 图 雪崩 動 崩塌
- □ snow coverage [`kʌvərɪdʒ] 積雪量
- □ warning [`wɔrnɪŋ] 图 警報 形 警告的
- □ alert [ə`lɜt] 形 警戒的 图 警戒 動 向……報警
- □ temperature [`tɛmprətʃɚ] 图 溫度

- □ high 30s and low 10s （一天的）最高氣溫 30 幾度與最低氣溫 10 幾度
- □ 5 (5 degrees Celsius / Centigrade) [`sɛlsɪəs / `sɛntəˌgred] 攝氏 5 度
- □ -5° F (minus 5 degrees Fahrenheit) [`færənˌhaɪt] 華氏 -5 度
- □ devastating damage [`dɛvəsˌtetɪŋ] 毀滅性的破壞
- □ serious damage 嚴重損害

● 42 ~ 44 新聞

🔊 18

Questions 42 through 44 refer to the following news.

... And in local news, about 40 park rangers and local police are still searching for a missing hiker. Frank Dobbs, a 52-year old man, was last seen driving into Great Mountain National Park around 8:00 on Sunday morning. When he didn't come home Sunday evening, his wife called the police. Helicopters flew into the park Monday and again today, to look for the hiker. Although his car was found in the parking lot at the beginning of the 20-mile hiking trail, no sign of Dobbs has been found. Dobbs' wife, Mary, told reporters that her husband was an experienced hiker and had already hiked in the park more than 80 times. But, she also added that he had forgotten to take his cell phone with him even though he had taken plenty of drinking water and snacks with him.

……接著是地方新聞。大約 40 名的公園巡查員與地方警察仍在持續搜尋一名失蹤的登山客。這位名為法蘭克‧多布斯的 52 歲男子被人目擊在週日上午 8 時許開車進入大山國家公園，之後便失去了蹤跡。週日晚上他沒回家，於是其妻子打電話報警。週一和今天，直升機二度至國家公園尋找該名登山客。雖然他的車在 20 英里登山步道的入口處停車場被發現，但是並未見到多布斯先生的身影。多布斯的太太瑪莉告訴記者，她先生是個經驗豐富的登山客，到該公園登山健行已經超過 80 次。不過，她也補充說到，她先生雖然帶了足夠的飲水與乾糧，卻忘了帶手機。

Word List

- □ hiking trail [haɪkɪŋ trel] 登山步道

42. 正確答案：(A) ☆☆

What is this news about? 　　　　　　　　　　　這則新聞報導的是什麼？

(A) A man went hiking and hasn't come home yet. 一名男子去登山還沒有回家。

(B) A helicopter crashed in the mountains, 一台直升機在山區墜毀，飛行員失蹤。
　　and the pilot is missing.

(C) Police are looking for a man who killed his wife. 警方正在搜索一名殺妻男子。

(D) A dangerous criminal has escaped from jail. 有一名危險犯人逃出了監獄。

> **解說**
>
> 由報導第一句中的 searching for a missing hiker 和第二句的 man ... was last seen 等關鍵字詞可知正確答案為 (A)「一名男子去登山但是還沒有回家。」。

 小心陷阱

若是沒聽出 missing hiker 的話，便可能因報導中的 helicopter 一詞而誤選 (B)，或因 police 一詞而誤選 (C)。請特別留意。

43. 正確答案：(C) ☆

How old is Frank Dobbs? 　　　　　　　　　　　法蘭克‧多布斯多大年紀？

(A) 20 　　　　　　20 歲 　　　　　　(B) 40 　　　　　　40 歲

(C) 52 　　　　　**52 歲** 　　　　　(D) 80 　　　　　　80 歲

> **解說**
>
> 第二句提到 Frank Dobbs, a 52-year old man, 故 (C) 為正解。

 小心陷阱

選項 (A) 中的數目 20 是登山步道的長度，(B) 中的 40 為搜救隊人數，(D) 中的 80 是多布斯先生去登山的次數，這些都是為沒聽到 52 歲這項資訊的人所設計之陷阱。

44. 正確答案：(D) ☆☆

What did Frank Dobbs take with him? 　　　　　法蘭克‧多布斯帶了什麼出門？

(A) A gun and a cell phone 槍與手機

(B) A cell phone and a map 手機和地圖

(C) A map and drinking water 地圖和飲用水

(D) Drinking water and food **飲用水和食物**

解說

由最後一句,多布斯太太瑪莉對記者所說話裡的 plenty of drinking water and snacks 可知正解為 (D)。

小心陷阱

選項 (B) 的手機是多布斯先生「忘了帶」的東西。請注意,最後一句 ... forgotten to take his cell phone ... even though ... drinking water and snacks ... 中的 even though 為逆接連接詞。

奪分祕笈:與休閒活動有關的表達方式

與各種活動(activities)及休閒娛樂(leisure)相關的文章至少會出現 1 篇。題目中不會出現專業術語,但請務必牢記正確的英語表達方式。

▶ 以「go V -ing」形式表達的活動:

☐ go bicycling / cycling 去騎腳踏車 ☐ go camping 去露營
☐ go fishing 去釣魚 ☐ go hiking 去登山健行
☐ go mountain-climbing 去爬山 ☐ go swimming 去游泳
☐ go scuba-diving [`skubə͵daɪvɪŋ] 去潛水 ☐ go skiing 去滑雪
☐ go shopping 去購物

▶ 以「play + 名詞」形式表達的活動

a. 與球技有關的活動
play baseball 打棒球 play basketball 打籃球
play soccer 踢足球 play tennis 打網球
b. 與競賽有關的活動
play chess [tʃɛs] 下棋 play go 下圍棋
play cards 打撲克牌 play scrabble [`skræbl] 玩拼字遊戲

▶ 以「do / practice + 名詞」形式表達的活動(通常用於武術類)

☐ do / practice judo [`dʒudo] 練習柔道 ☐ do / practice karate [kə`ratɪ] 空手道
☐ do / practice fencing [`fɛnsɪŋ] 擊劍 ☐ do / practice boxing [`baksɪŋ] 拳擊

▶ 以「go to + 名詞」形式表達的活動

☐ go to the beach 去海邊 ☐ go to church[註] 做禮拜
☐ go to the movies 去看電影 ☐ go to school[註] 去上學
☐ go to the theater 去看戲劇表演

註 由於 go to church、go to school 指的是「活動」,所以不加 the。

● 45 ~ 47 廣告

🎧 19

Questions 45 through 47 refer to the following advertisement.

This program has been brought to you by Charlie's Used Cars, the most honest car dealer in town. We are conveniently located at 1500 Waterloo Street, right next to the Hynes Shopping Mall. Look for our red, white, and blue banners and come right in. Come right over and see us today and tell Richard you heard this message on the Morning Show. You'll get an instant 10% discount on any car you choose today. Today only! That's right, 10% off on any car just for telling Richard that you heard our ad on the radio. This offer expires at our six-o'clock closing time today, so hurry up and come on down!

本節目由本地最誠實的汽車經銷商：查理中古車提供。我們位於交通便利的滑鐵盧街 1500 號，就在海因斯購物中心旁。找到我們紅、白、藍三色的旗幟之後請直接入內。請您今天就馬上過來，並告訴查理您在晨間節目中聽到了這段廣告訊息。當日您所選的任何車款，都能立即享有九折優惠。只有今天！沒錯，只要告訴查理您在廣播上聽到我們的廣告，任何車種都可獲得 10% 的折扣。這項優惠只到今天 6 點本店打烊為止，請儘快過來！

45. 正確答案：(A) ☆

What kind of business is being advertised? 這是哪個行業的廣告？

(A) A car dealer **汽車經銷商**
(B) A discount store 折扣商店
(C) An electronics store 電器行
(D) A supermarket 超市

> **解說**
> 由廣告第一句中的 Charlie's Used Cars 和緊接著的 car dealer 等關鍵詞，可知正解為 (A)。

💣 小心陷阱

請小心，漏聽了第一句的人很可能會因為第二句的 Hynes Shopping Mall 而誤選 (D)，也可能因為第五句的 10% discount 而誤選 (B)，或因為第七句的 radio 而誤選 (C)。

46. 正確答案：(D) ☆☆

How can you qualify for a discount?

(A) By going to the shopping mall and picking up a coupon

(B) By going to Richard's any time

(C) By attending the demonstration this afternoon

(D) By telling Richard you heard the ad on the Morning Show

如何才能獲得折扣？

去購物中心拿優惠券

任何時候去查理的店都可以

參加今天下午的展示／示威活動

告訴查理你在晨間節目上聽到這段廣告

解說

關鍵就在第七句的 10% off ... for telling Richard that you heard our ad on the radio，可知正解為 (D)。

小心陷阱

注意，(B) 指「任何時候去都能獲得折扣」，並不正確，勿誤選。

47. 正確答案：(B) ☆☆

How long is this special offer good for?

(A) Until all the goods have been sold

(B) Until closing time today

(C) Tomorrow at 6 p.m.

(D) For one week starting today

這項優惠將延續多久？

直到所有商品賣完

直到今天打烊為止

到明天下午 6 點

從今天起持續 1 週

解說

由最後一句 This offer expires at our six o'clock closing time today ... 可知正解為 (B)。

小心陷阱

要是漏聽了最後一句中的 today，可能誤選 (C)，因此一定得仔細聆聽。

奪分祕笈：廣告特有的表達方式

Part 4 不只會出現商品廣告，也會出現與商店、辦公室及各種機構設施開幕有關的問題。在這類充滿艱澀用詞的商務相關說明文中，往往也包含許多廣告特有的表達方式，一旦習慣，便能輕鬆得分。別只是依據網路上的大分類來找，最能輕鬆記住相關表達的做法，就是依據本身興趣，以 Google 等搜尋引擎來搜尋各種領域的廣告並閱讀其內容。例如，下列這些廣告中常見的說法，很值得好好熟記。例如：

a. 10% discount on all items　　　　　所有商品皆打九折
b. on a first-come-first-served basis　　以先後順序決定；先到先贏
c. annual / semi-annual / quarterly sale　年度的／半年一次的／一季一次的特賣

● **48 ~ 50 公告**　　　　　　　　　　　　　　　　　　　　　　　🔊 20

Questions 48 through 50 refer to the following public announcement.

Attention Employees!

The refrigerator in the employee lunch room will be shut off for repairs over the holidays. Therefore, if you have any food items in the refrigerator, please take them home by Friday, December 20. Any remaining items will be discarded. And don't forget to check the freezer, too! Last year someone left a whole box of ice cream, and we had to throw it away! Happy Holidays from the Maintenance and Janitorial Services!

各位員工請注意！

員工午餐室裡的冰箱將於假期期間關閉電源維修。所以，如果你有任何置放於冰箱的食物，請於 12 月 20 日週五前帶回家。任何留下的東西都會被丟棄。同時也別忘了檢查一下冷凍庫！去年就有某人留下了一整盒冰淇淋，而我們不得不把它扔掉！維護及清潔服務部門祝您佳節愉快！

Word List

☐ be discarded [dɪsˋkɑrdɪd] 被丟掉

48. 正確答案：(B) ☆

What will happen to the refrigerator during the holidays?

假期期間冰箱會發生什麼事？

(A) It will be replaced with a new one.
會被換成新的。

(B) It will be repaired.
會進行維修。

(C) It will be moved to another floor.
會被搬到其他樓層。

(D) It will be donated to charity.
會捐給慈善機構。

解說

由第一句 The refrigerator ... will be shut off for repairs ... 可知正解為 (B)。

小心陷阱

若漏聽了第一句的 for repairs，可能會誤選 (A)「換成新冰箱」，須多加注意。

49. 正確答案：(C) ☆☆

What are employees asked to do?
員工們被要求做什麼？

(A) Eat lunch at home on Fridays.
週五在家吃午飯。

(B) Throw away any food left in the lunch room.
把任何留在午餐室裡的食物扔掉。

(C) Remove their food from the refrigerator.
將冰箱裡屬於他們的食物拿走。

(D) Clean up their own mess at the end of each day.
在每天結束時清理自己弄亂的東西。

解說

第二句裡曾提到 ... If you have any food items ... take them home ... 故 (C) 為正解。不過請注意，原句中的 take them home 被替換成了同義的 remove their food。

小心陷阱

(A) 選項中的 lunch、Friday 和 (B) 選項中的 throw away、lunch room 等皆為公告裡提到的詞彙，小心不要掉入陷阱。

50. 正確答案：(C) ☆☆

What happened last year?

(A) The freezer broke down and had to be fixed.

(B) A box of food was left in the lunch room.

(C) Someone forgot to take their ice cream home before the holidays.

(D) There was a Christmas party, and nobody cleaned up.

去年發生了什麼事？

冷凍庫壞了，必須修理。

有一盒食品被遺留在午餐室裡。

某人忘了在放假前把冰淇淋帶回家。

舉辦了聖誕派對，但是卻沒人清理。

解說

依據倒數第二句 Last year someone left a whole box of ice cream, and we had to throw it away! 可知，正確答案為 (C)。注意，(C) 選項用了同義的方式表達：Someone forgot to take their ice cream home before the holidays.。

小心陷阱

(A) 選項中的 freezer 和 (B) 選項中的 a box of、lunch room 都是曾出現在公告中的詞彙，而 (D) 選項中的 Christmas 則可能讓人聯想到公告中的 the holidays。這些都很容易使人上當以致誤選，請務必小心。

這樣練習最有效

公告（public announcement）的特徵就在於一定包含「由誰」、「給誰」等資訊。有時即使沒有明確提到這些資訊，文中也必定存在可推測出該資訊的關鍵詞。而其題目大致可彙總為「主旨為何？」、「由誰提出？」、「是給誰的訊息？」、「該做什麼？」、「應注意什麼事？」、「去哪裡就能取得所需物品？」等幾種。public announcement 幾乎每次都一定會出現在 TOEIC 的 Part 4 中，且其種類繁多。為了能多接觸一些 announcement，請別只靠本書，也要多多收聽 ICRT 等的廣播節目。建議讀者錄下來幾個節目，然後進行 dictation 練習。

奪分祕笈：常用於公告的詞句

a. 給公司員工的公告

☐ promotions / transfers of personnel 升遷／人事異動

☐ changes in regulations / rules 與條例／規則有關的變動

☐ complaints / compliments / apologies to employees 向員工表達的抱怨／讚美／致歉

☐ restructuring of organization 組織結構調整

☐ notices from maintenance 管理部發布的通知

b. 與公共交通有關的公告

☐ delays in arrival / departure time 抵達／出發時刻的延遲

☐ reports on accidents 事故相關報告

☐ temporary changes of routes due to construction work / parades / accidents
因施工／遊行／事故而臨時更改路線

c. 與公共設施有關的公告

☐ opening of new facilities 新設施的啟用

☐ business hours of library / city hall 圖書館／市政府的服務時間

☐ notices from the Water Bureau / the Internal Revenue Service / election board
由水資局／國稅局／選舉委員會發布的通知

d. 住宅社區內的公告

☐ notices from the superintendent / management office / maintenance
由管理人／管理室／保養維修部門發出的通知

☐ warning against some criminal actions 防範某些犯罪行為的警語

☐ announcements from the residents' association 由居民自治會所發布的公告

e. 大型商店內的公告

☐ advertisements for sales / discounts / gift coupons 特賣／折扣／禮券廣告

☐ announcements about lost and found information / a lost child looking for his or
her parents 失物招領／孩童走失公告

☐ announcement of a fire drill 消防演習公告

f. 醫院內的公告

☐ paging patients / doctors / visitors 呼叫病患／醫師／訪客

☐ announcements about changes of hours / doctors-in-charge
門診時間／看診醫師異動之公告

☐ directions to outpatients 給門診病人的指示

51. 正確答案：(A) ☆☆

The new desktop model is the most _____ computer I have ever used. I can't do without it.

這台新的桌上型機種是我所用過最可靠的電腦。我不能沒有它。

(A) reliable 可靠的　　　　　　　　　(B) reliability 可信賴度

(C) relying 倚賴著的　　　　　　　　　(D) relied 倚賴的

解說

computer 為名詞，接在它前面的應是形容詞以修飾名詞。其中 (B) 選項為名詞，不予考慮，而餘三個選項中，唯一符合題意的只有 (A)。

💣 小心陷阱

由於形容詞選項共有 (A)、(C)、(D) 三個，因此意義雖各自不同卻很容易造成誤導。不過只要知道 (A) reliable 的意思是「可靠的」，就能答對。

💡 奪分祕笈：詞性（Word Form）類問題

觀察空格前後的字詞，然後選擇出詞性正確、意思恰當的選項。記住相關衍生詞與其意義，答題就可以快速又準確。例如：

Word List

☐ attend [ə`tɛnd] 動 參加、出席　　　☐ attendance [ə`tɛndəns] 名 出席
☐ attendant / attendee [ə`tɛndənt / ə`tɛndi] 名 參加者

☐ child [tʃaɪld] 名 小孩　　　☐ childlike [`tʃaɪldˌlaɪk] 形 天真的、孩子般的
☐ childish [`tʃaɪldɪʃ] 形 幼稚的、孩子氣的

☐ employ [ɪm`plɔɪ] 動 雇用　　　☐ employment [ɪm`plɔɪmənt] 名 雇用
☐ employer [ɪm`plɔɪɚ] 名 雇主　　　☐ employee [ˌɛmplɔɪ`i] 名 受雇者

☐ differ [`dɪfɚ] 動 不同、相異　　　☐ different [`dɪfərənt] 形 不同的
☐ difference [`dɪfərəns] 名 差異　　　☐ differentiate [ˌdɪfə`rɛnʃɪˌet] 動 區別

☐ depend [dɪ`pɛnd] 動 倚賴、依靠　　　☐ dependable [dɪ`pɛndəbl] 形 可倚賴的
☐ dependence [dɪ`pɛndəns] 名 依賴（性）
☐ dependent [dɪ`pɛndənt] 形 倚賴的、名 受撫養的家屬

☐ instruct [ɪn`strʌkt] 動 指導　　　☐ instruction [ɪn`strʌkʃən] 名 指示、教學、說明書
☐ instructive [ɪn`strʌktɪv] 形 有教育性的、有益的

52. 正確答案：(C) ☆☆

Frank is a mail clerk, so his _____ is to sort out and deliver the mail to each department every morning.

法蘭克是（公司裡的）郵件管理員，所以他的責任就是每天早上整理郵件並送到各部門去。

(A) behavior 態度、行為   (B) action 行動、行為

(C) responsibility 責任、任務   (D) hobby 興趣、嗜好

解說

只要了解 mail clerk 的意義，就應知道 sort out、deliver the mail 等都是法蘭克須負責的工作，(C) 為正確答案。只要能夠確實掌握整句的意義，就能答對。

小心陷阱

雖然 (A)、(B)、(D) 三個選項都與人的工作有關，但是皆非「工作責任」之意。

奪分祕笈：詞彙類問題（區別意義相近的單字）

為了能選出最符合文意的單字，請多熟記各種意思相近但其實又不太一樣的詞彙。例如：

Word List

☐ award [əˋwɔrd] 图 獎 動 授予
☐ grant [grænt] 图 補助金、獎學金 動 授予獎學金

☐ co-worker 图 同事   ☐ partner 图 合夥人
☐ collaborator [kəˋlæbəˌretə] 图 合作夥伴

☐ crisis [ˋkraɪsɪs] 图 重大危機   ☐ emergency [ɪˋmɝdʒənsɪ] 图 緊急情況
☐ urgency [ˋɝdʒənsɪ] 图 緊急、迫切

☐ drive 動 驅使   ☐ force [fors] 動 強迫 图 力量

☐ income [ˋɪnˌkʌm] 图 收入   ☐ proceeds [ˋprosidz] 图 收益

☐ policy [ˋpaləsɪ] 图 保險單   ☐ premium [ˋprimɪəm] 图 保險費
☐ surcharge [ˋsɝˌtʃardʒ] 图 附加費用、額外費用

☐ profitable [ˋprafɪtəbl] 形 有利的、能賺錢的
☐ beneficial [ˌbɛnəˋfɪʃəl] 形 有益的、有用的

53. 正確答案：(B) ☆☆☆

In order to promote our sales in agricultural produce, we will _____ Bill Rush and his staff attend the Farmers' Convention in Atlanta this year.

為了提高我們農產品的銷量，本公司將派比爾・拉許及其屬下去參加今年在亞特蘭大舉辦的農民大會。

(A) let 讓　　　　　　**(B) have 派**　　　　　(C) make 強迫　　　　　(D) tell 告訴

> **解說**
> 依前後文意思，由公司「派」比爾・拉許及其屬下出席農民大會最合理，(B) 為正確答案。有關使役動詞的說明，請見後續「奪分秘笈」部分。

Word List

☐ agricultural produce [ˌægrɪˈkʌltʃərəl prəˈdjus] 農產品

小心陷阱

欲表達「派某人去做某事」之意時，應使用「have + someone + 動詞原形」的形式。選項 (A) let 指「讓」、選項 (C) make 指「強迫」，雖然用法與 have 相同（見下方說明），但意思不正確。

奪分祕笈：使役動詞（causative verbs）

使役動詞可分為 （1）不加 to 的不定詞和 （2）要加 to 的共兩種。而使役動詞在 TOEIC 測驗裡的出現頻率非常高，是固定必出的重點題型。例如：

▶ **不加 to 的使役動詞：**

a. have + someone + 動詞原形：派……做……
   I'll have one of our staff come to see you. 我會派我們一位工作人員來見你。

b. let + someone + 動詞原形：讓……做……
   Let me pay you for the extra hours you've put in.
   讓我針對你已額外投入的工時支付你費用。

c. make + someone + 動詞原形：強迫、……做……
   My father made me walk 20 miles to school as punishment.
   我爸強迫我走 20 英里路上學以做為懲罰。

▶ 要加 **to** 的使役動詞：

a. allow + someone + to + 動詞原形：允許……做……

His father allowed him to stay at home.

他爸爸允許他待在家裡。

b. force + someone + to + 動詞原形：迫使……做……

They force him to resign.

他們迫使他辭職。

54. 正確答案：(D) ☆

Our financial advisor was so reliable that she _____ exactly when the stock market would begin to pick up and when it would fall.

我們的財務顧問非常可靠，她總是知道股市何時會開始上揚，何時又會下跌。

(A) will know　　　　(B) has known　　　　(C) knows　　　　**(D) knew**

解說

由於此句前半的 Our financial advisor was so reliable ... 為過去式，其後 that 子句的動詞也必須用過去式，正解為 (D)。

Word List

☐ pick up （經濟狀況）回升、復甦

☐ fall 下跌

💣 小心陷阱

若漏看了過去式 was，便很可能誤選現在式的 (C)，請多注意。

💡 奪分祕笈：時態的一致與完成式

所謂時態的一致，並不是讓句子裡所有的時態都一樣，而是要配合句子中的各時間點來運用正確的時態。例如：

▶ 現在

She says she will be going to the dentist today.　　她說她今天會去看牙醫。

▶ 過去

She said she would be going to the dentist that day.　　她說過那天她會去看牙醫。

（will 變成過去式 would）。

Strategies　Pre Test　Half Test 1　Half Test 2　Full Test

過去完成式用於必須明確表達兩個行動的前後關係時：

> ▶ **過去完成**
> Kim had already left when Joe came back to the office.
> 在喬回辦公室之前，金已經離開了。

過去完成式也可用於敘述到過去一個時間點為止所發生的狀態：

> Before I started working for this company, I had been out of work for six months.
> 在我開始為本公司工作前，我待業了六個月。

未來式是用來說明往後將發生的事，而未來完成式則用於必須敘述在未來某個時間點「什麼事將結束」時：

> ▶ **未來式**
> They will arrive in Cairo at 5 p.m.   他們會在下午 5 點到達開羅。
> ▶ **未來完成式**
> I'll have arrived in Cairo by 5 p.m.   下午 5 前後我應該已經抵達開羅了。

55. 正確答案：(B) ☆☆

After snatching a bag from an elderly woman, the criminal ran into a police officer and _____ right away.

從一位老婦人那兒搶到手提包後，該罪犯撞見一位警察，立刻被逮捕。

(A) caught   **(B) got caught**   (C) will catch   (D) catchy

> **解說**
> 因為 criminal 是「被」逮捕的，所以應選 (B) got caught。注意，本題的被動式是以「get + 過去分詞」的形式表達。（見下方「奪分秘笈」被動式說明。）

> **Word List**
> ☐ snatch [snætʃ] 動 名 奪取、搶奪　　☐ criminal [`krɪmən!] 名 罪犯

🔸 小心陷阱

由於空格前面接有 police officer，所以請小心別受引誘而選了主動式的 (A) caught。

奪分祕笈：被動式

請看看以下這些常出現於 TOEIC 測驗的各種被動式時態及用法：

▶ 一般被動式：be + 過去分詞

a. 現在進行式

A house is being built.　　　　　房子正在建造中。

b. 現在完成式

A house has been built.　　　　　房子已建造完成。

c. 過去完成式

The house had been built before we moved here.

在我們搬來之前那間房子就已經蓋好了。

▶ 特殊被動式：get + 過去分詞（用來強調「受害」、「受災」之意）

a. get 加被動式句型

The log house got burnt down by the forest fire.

那間小木屋被森林大火給燒個精光。

56. 正確答案：(B) ☆

For the barbecue next Saturday, I'll bring beef and chicken, so you _____ buy them.

我會帶牛肉和雞肉去下週六的烤肉大會，所以你不用買了。

(A) have to 必須　　　　　　　　**(B) don't have to 不必**

(C) must 一定要　　　　　　　　(D) mustn't 絕不可

解說

根據前後文意 (B) don't ha ve to 為正確答案。

 小心陷阱

這題考的是你能否區別 don't have to「不必」與帶有禁止意義之 (D) mustn't「絕不可」之間的差異。這算是 TOEIC 相當偏好的出題方式之一。

奪分祕笈：助動詞 may / might / have to / don't have to / must / mustn't

這是相當典型的 TOEIC 考題，所以請好好記住以下各語句的意思。例如：

▶ may

a. 許可

You may leave when you finish the test.　　　你考完就可以離開。

b. 可能性

I may join you later.　　　我稍後也許會去找你。

▶ might

a. 可能性

Melanie might be interested in joining the team.　　米蘭妮或許會想加入該團隊。

b. 建議

You might want to take extra water with you.　　今天會變得很熱。
It's going to be hot today.　　你或許想多帶點水。

▶ have to

a. 義務

I have an appointment. I have to go now.　　我有個約，現在必須走了。

▶ don't have to

b. 否定義務

You don't have to hurry. We still have time.　　你不必急，我們還有時間。

▶ must

a. 義務註

You must fasten your seatbelt while driving.　　你開車時一定要繫安全帶。

b. 強烈建議

You must buy this hybrid car.　　你一定要買這台油電混合車。
It really saves gas.　　它真的很省油。

▶ mustn't

禁止

You mustn't use a cell phone in the priority seating zone.
在博愛座附近絕不可使用手機。

註 must 的語氣比 have to 強烈。

57. 正確答案：(A) ☆☆

The building was burning so fiercely that there was _____ the firefighters could do to save it.

大樓火災的火勢猛烈，消防隊員們幾乎是束手無策。

(A) little 幾乎沒有　　　(B) a little 有一點點　　　(C) few 幾乎沒有（可數）　　　(D) a few 有幾個

> **解說**
>
> 因為火勢猛烈，所以消防隊員「幾乎沒能做什麼事」，因空格前為單數動詞，故(C)、(D) 選項不必考慮；而依句意，應選表否定的 (A) little。TOEIC 很常出現「可數名詞、不可數名詞」及數量形容詞相關考題。這裡的 (A)、(B) 選項都用於不可數名詞，(C)、(D) 則用於可數名詞。另，不加 a 時表示「幾乎沒有」，為否定之意。

Word List

☐ fiercely [ˋfɪrslɪ] 副 猛烈地、強烈地

小心陷阱

請特別注意，(A) little 和 (B) a little 分別表示「幾乎沒有」和「有一點點」的否定與肯定兩種相反語氣。

奪分祕笈：數量形容詞 few / little 與可數名詞、不可數名詞

a. a few / few

I have a few friends.	我有幾個朋友。
I have few friends.	我幾乎沒有朋友。

b. only a few + 可數名詞

I've only got a few dollars left.	我只剩下幾美元。

c. only a little + 不可數名詞

I've got only a little money left.	我只剩一點錢。

d. not much + 不可數名詞

There wasn't much hope for the survival.	生存機會渺茫。

e. any + 可數名詞（複數形）

Do you carry any birthday cards?	你們沒有賣生日賀卡？

f. any + 不可數名詞

Do you have any milk?	你們有牛奶嗎？

58. 正確答案：(D)

As _____ as I know, the order was shipped out the day before yesterday, and was scheduled to arrive at the client company this morning.

就我所知，訂購的商品已於前天出貨，預計將於今早送達客戶的公司。

(A) well　　　　(B) little　　　　(C) many　　　　**(D) far**

解說 ▶ as far as

as far as 為固定片語，表「就……而言」，所以正確解為 (D)。而 as far as 其實有兩種主要意思，詳情請見以下「奪分秘笈」的說明。

Word List

☐ client company 客戶的公司

 小心陷阱

請小心，別誤以為「據我所知」是用 (A) as well as I know 來表達。

奪分秘笈：擁有多種含意的 as ... as

▶ **as far as**

a. as far as「到……為止」

　 I walked as far as the hill.　　　　　　　我一直走到山丘那邊。

b. as far as I'm concerned「就……而言」

　 As far as we are concerned, that　　　　對我們來說，那家公司和我們
　 company has no future with us.　　　　　並無未來可言。

▶ **as much as「到……的程度」**

　 We'll provide as much fuel as you need.　我們將提供你所需要的一切燃料量。

▶ **as well as**

a. 「和……一樣」、「不亞於……」

　 My son can play the violin as well as I do.　我兒子的小提琴拉得不比我差。

b. 「不僅……還……」

　 These new batteries last longer than the　這些新電池不僅比舊型的更持久，
　 old ones as well as being lighter.　　　　也更輕巧。

59. 正確答案：(A) ☆☆

Our business this year has dropped so drastically that we will have to let _____ Fred or Nelly go.

由於我們今年的業績大幅滑落，以至於我們必須解雇弗雷德或娜麗。

(A) either　　　　　(B) neither　　　　(C) both　　　　(D) that

> **解說**
>
> let ... go 有「解雇……」之意。由於問題裡兩個人的名字之間夾著 or，故剛好符合 either A or B「或 A 或 B」的句型。另外，neither 則要搭配 nor，意思是「既非 A 也非 B」。

> **Word List**
>
> ☐ drastically [`dræstɪk｜ɪ] 副 大幅地、激烈地

小心陷阱

以此題來說，由於有兩個人名，所以或許有人會想選 both，但別忘了人名之間還夾著個 or。若要使用 both，應為 both Fred and Nelly。

奪分祕笈：both / either / neither

連接詞不只有 and、but、or，更有可將前後兩個元素統整起來的 both A and B、either A or B、neither A nor B 等，這是考生們最討厭的文法類型之一，卻也是 TOEIC 的常見考題。因此請將以下例句好好熟記起來。

a. both A and B

I like both purple and red, so I'm taking both sweaters.

我喜歡紫色也喜歡紅色，所以我兩件毛衣都要了。

b. either A or B

You can't have both of us as assistants. You have to choose either Nelly or me.

你不能同時雇用我們倆做助理。你要嘛選娜麗，要嘛選我。

c. neither A nor B

The office wants to cancel the whole deal. So neither Danny nor I have^註 to go to the meeting tomorrow.

該辦公室打算取消整個交易。所以丹尼和我都不必去參加明天的會議。

註 這種語法的動詞應配合接在其 or 或 nor 後方的名詞。以此例來說，前面接的是名詞 I，所以用 have。

60. 正確答案：(C) ☆☆

I'm all for Norman to be elected class monitor. _____ busy he was, Norman always treated us warmly and gave us lots of constructive advice.

我完全贊成諾曼被選為班長。不論他多忙，諾曼總是能親切待人並提供我們許多有建設性的意見。

 (A) How　　　　　　(B) How much　　　**(C) No matter how**　　(D) Whenever

> **解說**
>
> 只要能掌握 no matter how「不論多麼……」這個常用片語的意思，就會知道它是最合適的選擇。其他選項的意思都說不通。

Word List

　☐ I'm all for ... 我完全贊成……　　　　　☐ constructive [kən`strʌktɪv] 形 有建設性的

💣 小心陷阱

若沒能確實理解 no matter how 的意思，很可能被 (A) How 所騙，請小心。

💡 奪分祕笈：no matter how / what / when

no matter how「不論多麼」、no matter what「無論什麼」、no matter when「不論何時」、no matter where「無論何處」等以「強調句子」為目的之常用片語可分別應用在各式各樣的情況下。而這些常用片語還可各自替換為 however、whatever、whenever、wherever。例如：

> a. My mom always took time to teach us English no matter
>   how / however busy she was at work.
>   不論工作有多忙，我媽總是會撥出時間教我們英文。
> b. No matter what / Whatever happens, I'll always support you.
>   不論發生什麼事，我都會支持你。
> c. No matter when / Whenever you go, I'm willing to go with you.
>   不論你何時要走，我都願意跟隨。
> d. We can communicate by e-mail no matter where / wherever you are in the world.
>   不論你在這世上的哪個角落，我們都可透過電子郵件聯絡。

61. 正確答案：(D) ☆☆

Samantha will be going to Beijing next week and plans to visit the Great Wall _____ she stays there.

莎曼莎下週要去北京，她打算在停留期間去參觀萬里長城。

(A) where 在該處

(B) during ……的時候

(C) as 做為……

(D) while 在……期間

解說

最後的 she stays there 為子句，所以連接詞 (D) while 為正確答案。(B) during 為介系詞，後面必須接名詞（片語）（例如：her stay），而 (A)、(C) 則文意不通。

小心陷阱

要注意別搞混了 while 和 during 而選錯答案。

奪分祕笈：during、after、before、while、within 等介系詞與連接詞

- a. during / within 之後接名詞（片語）

  We'll be busy during the harvest season.　在收穫季節時我們會非常忙碌。

- b. after / before 可接名詞（片語）或子句

  Tell me after the game. / Tell me after you finish the game.　遊戲結束後請告訴我。

- c. while 之後必須接子句

  Stop by while you are in Tokyo.　當你在東京時請順道過來。

62. 正確答案：(B) ☆☆☆

_____ everyone's surprise, Tim, who was considered the shyest person in class, won first prize in the speech contest.

出乎大家的意料，被認為是班上最害羞的人提姆，竟在演講比賽中贏得第一。

(A) By

(B) To

(C) On

(D) For

解說

表示「出乎意料」之意的常用片語就說成 to someone's surprise，正確答案為 (B)。

小心陷阱

選項 (B) 的 by 只能用於 catch someone by surprise「出其不意、讓某人措手不及」這類的片語中，並不適用於此句。

常見的介系詞包括 at、by、for、on、to 等，但較常出現於 TOEIC 的是與名詞、形容詞、副詞等合併使用的介系詞片語。請牢記以下幾種相關用法。

a. **at ease 輕鬆自在地**

   Vic looked like he was at ease. 維克看來輕鬆自在。

b. **at one's expense 因……的犧牲、因……付出的代價**

   Don't forget that you've learned a lesson at our expense!
   別忘了你因為我們所付出的代價而學到了一課！

c. **at all costs 無論如何、不惜一切代價**

   I want to buy back the Chagall at all costs.
   不論付出多少代價我都要買回那件夏卡爾的作品。

d. **for free 免費地**

   The store is giving away the new detergent samples for free.
   該商店正在免費贈送新的清潔劑樣品。

e. **for good 永遠地**

   Ken fell in love with the house in the country and decided to live there for good.
   肯恩愛上了那棟鄉間的房子，且決定永遠住在那兒。

f. **for sure 肯定地、一定**

   I'll bring back this file by tomorrow for sure. 我明天一定會把這份檔案帶回來。

g. **to no avail 無濟於事**

   We've tried to save the company to no avail.
   我們已試過挽救公司，但是無濟於事。

h. **to one's disappointment 令人失望地**

   To our disappointment, the musical turned out to be a flop.
   令我們失望的是，該齣音樂劇結果是個失敗作。

i. **on and off 斷斷續續地、時有時無地**

   It's been raining on and off since yesterday.
   從昨天起雨就一直斷斷續續地下著。

j. **on arriving 一到達……就**

   On arriving at the office, Frances had to answer three calls in succession.
   一到辦公室，法蘭西斯就不得不連續接了三通電話。

k. **on the hour every hour 每個整點**

   WXNY news broadcasts on the hour every hour.
   WXNY 新聞在每個整點播放。

63. 正確答案：(B) ☆☆

Although Joe has been working in the factory for only two weeks, he is already getting used to _____ heavy machinery.

雖然喬在該工廠只做了兩個禮拜，但是他已習慣操作重型機具。

(A) handle   **(B) handling**   (C) have handled   (D) handled

 解說

> 這是「be / get used to + 動名詞或名詞」形式的慣用句型。

Word List

☐ heavy machinery 重型機具

 小心陷阱

很多人都會誤以為 be / get used to 和 used to 一樣後面接原形動詞，這是個錯誤，請留意。

💡 **奪分祕笈：be used to + V-ing、look forward to + V-ing**

請牢記經常出現在 Part 5 且相當容易答錯的三種表達方式。而 to 在此當介系詞。

> a. be / get used to + 名詞（片語）
> I'm already getting used to living in this busy sleepless city.
> 我已漸漸習慣生活在這個忙碌的不夜城。
>
> b. be / get accustomed to + 名詞（片語）
> You will have to get accustomed to sleeping in broad daylight if you live in Stockholm.
> 如果你住在斯德哥爾摩，就必須習慣在白日的亮光中入睡。
>
> c. look forward to + 名詞（片語）
> We are very much looking forward to attending your lecture.
> 我們非常期待上您的課。

64. 正確答案：(C) ☆☆

Mary-Ann has been working night shifts at a convenience store, so her husband _____ sees her. 瑪麗安一直在便利商店上夜班，所以他先生幾乎見不到她。

(A) not always 不總是   (B) not often 不常

(C) hardly ever 幾乎從不   (D) almost 幾乎都

 解說

> 依前後文意表示「極少……、幾乎從不……」之意的 (C) hardly ever 為正確答案。

□ night shift 夜班

小心陷阱

若是不夠小心，也很可能會誤選 (B) not often，但是 not often 的正確說法應為 does not often see her。

奪分祕笈：表示頻率的否定型副詞

在準備 TOEIC 測驗時一定要記住結合否定意義的頻率副詞。

a. not always 不總是……
   I don't always eat lunch at the company cafeteria.　　我並不總是在公司的餐廳吃午飯。

b. not usually 通常不
   We don't usually eat out on weekdays.　　平常日我們通常不在外面吃飯。

c. not often 不常……
   Harry doesn't often make mistakes.　　哈利不常犯錯。
   It's not like him.　　這實在不像他。

d. almost didn't ... 差一點就不……、幾乎就要無法……
   I almost didn't make it to the meeting.　　我差點就要趕不上會議了。

e. never 從不……、從未……
   I've never eaten jellyfish salad before.　　我從未吃過海蜇皮沙拉。

f. rarely / seldom / hardly ever 極少……、幾乎不……
   I rarely / seldom / hardly ever drive to work.　　我幾乎不開車上班。

65. 正確答案：(A) ☆☆☆

I suggest we hire Omega Works Studio for our next TV commercial because they will probably come up with _____ innovative design than any other company.

我建議聘請歐米茄工作室來製作我們的下一個電視廣告，因為他們應該能提出比任何其他公司都更創新的設計。

(A) more 更……
(B) some 一些
(C) the most 最……的
(D) the only 唯一的

解說
本句的關鍵字為 than，前面應用 more，構成比較結構。

小心陷阱

more ... than any other 這種語法相當刁鑽，表面使用比較級，表達的卻是最高級之意，請務必小心。

 奪分祕笈：less / fewer / more ... than any other + 單數形名詞

less 用於不可數名詞、fewer 用於可數名詞、more 則兩者皆可用。另外需注意的是 any other 之後要接單數形名詞。

> a. less
>
> Fried chicken at Jimmy's costs less than at any other store in town.
> 吉米炸雞店賣的炸雞比鎮上任何其他店的都便宜。
>
> b. fewer
>
> I've made fewer mistakes than anybody who works in the Accounting Section.
> 我犯的錯比會計部裡的任何人都少。

66. 正確答案：(B) ☆☆☆

The company manufactures hybrid cars _____ gas consumption is 30% lower than gas-powered cars.
該公司製造油耗比汽油動力車低 30% 的油電混合車。

(A) that (B) **whose** (C) what (D) why

> **解說**
>
> 空格後的 gas consumption 為其後 is 30% ... 之主詞，其前缺乏的應是具形容詞功能的所有格關係代名詞 whose。故正確答案為 (B)。

> **Word List**
>
> □ manufacture [ˌmænjəˈfæktʃə] 動 製造　□ consumption [kənˈsʌmpʃən] 名 消耗、消耗量

 小心陷阱

若沒能清楚理解此句結構，便可能會誤選關係代名詞 that。但若將 that 置於 gas consumption 之前，會形成「雙主詞」，不可不慎。

 奪分祕笈：關係詞

與關係詞有關的考題每次在 Part 5 中都免不了要出現好幾個。因此請將下列的基本關係代名詞、關係副詞例句一一熟記起來。

右側標籤：Strategies　Pre Test　Half Test 1　Half Test 2　Full Test

a. which / that（主詞）

Iwojima is an island which / that lies south east of the Japanese Archipelago.

硫磺島是位於日本列島東南方的一個島嶼。

b. which / that（受詞）

This is the T-shirt (which / that) [註1] you gave me last year.

這就是你去年給我的那件 T 恤。

c. that（主詞・受詞）

The only thing that [註2] matters to Sam is his son's happiness.

對山姆來說唯一重要的事就是他兒子的幸福。

d. whose（所有格）

I ran into one of the neighbors whose house is [註3] right across the street from mine.

我偶然遇見了住在我家對街的一位鄰居。

e. when（關係副詞）

Jim is looking forward to the time when he can meet Nelly again.

吉姆很期待能再次見到娜麗的那一刻。

f. why（關係副詞）

I don't know the reason why Ned quit his job.

我不知道奈德辭職的理由。

註1 作受詞的關係代名詞在會話中經常被省略

註2 若先行詞前用了 all、the only、the first 等現定或強調時，關係代名詞要用 that。

註3 接著的動詞應配合 one of 而使用單數形的 is。這是 TOEIC 常考的題目之一。

67. 正確答案：(C) ☆☆

_____ do you think I could have your answer to my application for the housing loan?

你認為我申請的房屋貸款何時會給我回覆？

(A) Who   (B) Which   **(C) When**   (D) What

解說

本句其實是 When could I have your answer ... ? 的變形。因為插進了 do you think，因此 I 和 could 不須倒裝，正確答案為 (C)。

Word List

□ application [ˌæpləˈkeʃən] 图 申請

Part 5

Strategies

Pre Test

Half Test 1

Half Test 2

Full Test

 奪分祕笈：間接疑問句（embedded questions）

這題是將疑問句 When could I have your answer 和 do you think 合併成 When do you think I could have your answer to my application for the housing loan?。困難的部分就在於插入的 do you think 為疑問形式，而原本的疑問形式的 could I have ... 須還原成 I could have ... 這樣的直述形式。這類間接疑問句用於須向對方表達更多敬意的情況，在商務英語中屬常態句型，因此必須好好練習並熟記。今後一旦遇上較長的句子，別猶豫，只要確實掌握句首疑問詞及內容關鍵詞即可。

68. 正確答案：(A) ☆☆☆

If _____ you, I wouldn't buy that condominium right now. The real estate market is booming and the prices are the highest they have ever been.

如果我是你，就不會現在買那間公寓。不動產市場現正蓬勃發展，價格已達歷史新高了。

(A) I were　　　　(B) I am　　　　(C) I could be　　　　(D) I might be

> 解說
> 此題考的是與「現在事實相反的過去假設式」，正確答案為 (A)。

> **Word List**
> □ real estate [ɪs`tet] 不動產、房地產　　□ boom [bum] 名動 繁榮、興旺

小心陷阱

(C) I could be you 和 (D) I might be 皆符合假設語氣的用法，但是在此的意思說不通。不過因為容易引人誤選，因此須多加注意。

 奪分祕笈：過去假設式、過去完成假設式

請仔細檢視以下所列各假設式的時態。

> ▶ 過去假設式
> 「If + 過去式」，「助動詞過去式 + 原形動詞」用於描述與現在事實相反的情況。
> If I had 100 dollars, I would lend it to you.
> 要是我有 100 美元，就能借給你了。（但是我沒錢，所以不能借你。）。

> ▶ 過去完成假設式
> a. 「if + 過去完成式, 助動詞過去式 + 現在完成式」（過去 → 過去）用來描述與過去事實相反的情況。

If I had had money, I would have lent it to you. Too bad.

要是我當時有錢，我早就借你了。（但是我當時沒錢，所以也沒借你。）

b. 「if + 過去完成式, 助動詞過去式 + 原形動詞」（過去 → 現在）用於表達與過相反的情況影響到現在。

If I had lent him money at that time, we would still be good friends now.

要是當時我有借錢給他，我們現在還會是好朋友。

（但是我當時沒借他錢，所以我們現在不再是好朋友。）

69. 正確答案：(D) ☆☆☆

We'll have to _____ do with oil and vinegar for the potato salad since we are all out of mayonnaise.

由於我們的美乃滋都用光了，所以不得不湊合著用油醋來拌馬鈴薯沙拉。

(A) work (B) have (C) take **(D) make**

> **解說**
>
> 本題考的是 make do with「湊合著、將就著」這個慣用片語。正確答案為 (D) make。

奪分祕笈：使用 do、make 的常用片語

慣用片語也是 TOEIC 的常考項目之一。很多用了 do / make 的慣用片語都很難翻成中文，因此牢記例句是很重要的。

a. do damage to ... 對……造成損害

You bumped into my car and did a lot of damage to it.

你撞上我的車，造成了很大的損壞。

b. do a good job / work 做好工作

Nelly always does a good job / good work.[註]

娜麗總是把工作做得很好。

c. do away with ... 丟棄……、廢除……

We'd better do away with this old printer and get a new model.

我們最好把這個舊印表機扔掉，換一台新型的。

d. do without ... 沒有……也可以

I love this new wide-screen lightweight laptop. I can't do without it.

我很喜歡這個新的寬螢幕輕薄筆記型電腦。我不能沒有它。

e. make room for ... 騰出空間給……

Make room for the baby. 請騰出空間給寶寶。

Strategies

Pre Test

Half Test 1

Half Test 2

Full Test

f. make do with ... 湊合著⋯⋯、將就著⋯⋯

We'll have to make do with the present budget.

我們必須將就著使用現有的預算。

g. make it 趕上、做到

I don't think I can make it tonight.

我想我今晚是趕不上了。

註 請注意 job 為可數名詞，work 為不可數名詞。

70. 正確答案：(A) ☆☆☆

As a door-to-door sales representative, Stella _____ on over 200 homes every day selling Devon cosmetics.

身為一位挨家挨戶推銷的推銷員，史黛拉每天拜訪超過 200 戶銷售黛文化妝品。

(A) calls   (B) gives   (C) picks   (D) visits

> **解說**
>
> 本題考的是 call on「拜訪」這個動詞片語。正確答案為 (A)。

Word List

☐ sales representative [selz rɛprɪ`zɛntətɪv] 推銷員

小心陷阱

請注意，(C) pick on 是「找碴、指責」之意，不可誤選。

奪分祕笈：動詞片語

以下列出 TOEIC 常考的動詞片語，請牢記。

Word List

☐ come across 偶遇   ☐ find out 發現

☐ get over 熬過（痛苦的事或辛苦的時期）   ☐ go over 重溫、複習

☐ pick up 接（人）、撿起（事物）   ☐ take away 帶走

☐ take place 發生   ☐ take up 著手進行

☐ throw away 扔掉   ☐ try out 試用

☐ try on 試穿   ☐ turn off 關掉（機器、開關等）

☐ rely on 依賴、依靠

● **71 ~ 73 廣告**

第 71 ~ 73 題與以下廣告有關。

慈善音樂會

各位熱愛古典樂的朋友們，我們（71）很高興宣布一場由世界知名聖羅莎交響樂團擔綱演出的特別追加音樂會已確定排進哈特菲爾德音樂廳的公演時間表中。

該場音樂會將於 5 月 14 日週二晚上 7 點 30 分舉行。這是場慈善音樂會，因此所有收益都將（72）捐贈給國家兒童癌症基金會。

這場追加公演將以該交響樂團的創辦人兼前指揮佛雷德列克‧查爾斯為號召。雖然查爾斯先生已在去年退休，（73）不過他將特別為此次演出重新站上指揮台。他已選了他最愛的幾首莫札特、貝多芬及德布西作品做為本次曲目。而門票分成 50、80、100 美元共三種，您可直接在哈特菲爾德音樂廳購票。若欲訂票請撥打 1-800-888-8811，或上我們的網站 www.hatfieldhall.org 進行線上訂票。

Word List

□ proceeds [ˋprosidz] 图 收益、銷售獲得的款項
□ feature [fitʃə] 動 以……為特色、由……主演、以……為號召

71. 正確答案：(B) ☆

選項翻譯： (A) 取悅 **(B) 高興的** (C) 討人喜歡的 (D) 令人愉悅的

解說

we are pleased to announce that ...「我們很高興宣布……」是一種固定說法。正確答案為 (B)。

💡 **奪分祕笈**

請牢記下列幾個相關固定說法。

a. It is our pleasure to announce ...	我們很榮幸地宣布……。
b. It is my great honor to introduce ...	我非常榮幸能介紹……。
c. I am honored to introduce our new director.	我很榮幸能介紹我們的新總監。
d. There's no other pleasure than to introduce you to our new director.	能夠為您介紹我們的新總監真是我無上的榮幸。

72. 正確答案：(C) ☆☆

選項翻譯： (A)（被）收費 (B)（被）支付 **(C)（被）捐贈** (D)（被）分配

解說

依上下文來看，proceeds will be donated to charity 最為合理，正確答案為 (C)。注意，和 donate 意義近似的 contribute 多用來指「貢獻勞力或技術」之意，故有關金錢上的捐贈一般用 donate。

小心陷阱

(B) paid 只能用來表示支付費用，不能用在與捐贈有關的描述上。另外， (D) 的 distribute 是指「分配、經銷（商品等）」，亦非正確答案。

73. 正確答案：(C) ☆☆

選項翻譯： (A) 雖然 (B) 相反地 **(C) 然而** (D) 結果

解說

前半句提到了 Mr. Charles retired ...，而後半句卻說 he will return to conduct ...，兩者為相反情況，所以須使用逆接型連接詞 however。正解為 (C)。

小心陷阱

請注意用來引導子句的連接詞 although 和副詞 however 的不同之處。

▶ The company is prospering；however, employees are underpaid.
該公司蓬勃發展，不過是員工的薪資卻偏低。

▶ She didn't eat anything although she was hungry.
雖然她餓了，但是什麼都沒吃。

奪分祕笈

看到廣告文章時，請先由上而下掃描一次，大略掌握該廣告主題及重要關鍵詞後，再看題目。另外，在此也讓我們好好了解一下帶有「然而、與……不同」含意的逆接詞。

a. although 雖然……（連接詞）

Although the business seemed to be prospering, it turned out to be in the red at the end of the fiscal year.
雖然業務看似蓬勃發展，但是在本會計年度結束時竟然是赤字。

b. however 然而、不過（副詞）

We all know you have been trying hard to raise the funds. However, we do not finance nonprofit organizations.

我們都知道你一直很努力地募集資金。然而，我們並不資助非營利組織。

c. in contrast to 相對於……、和……不同

In contrast to his predecessor, the new manager is very serious.

不同於前任經理，新的經理非常嚴肅。

d. on the contrary 相反地、反之

He didn't become thinner–on the contrary, he grew even fatter.

他沒變瘦，相反地還變得更胖。

e. on the other hand 另一方面

The wheat harvest was good this year. On the other hand, rice didn't do well.

今年小麥的收穫很不錯。另一方面，稻米收成則不理想。

● 74 ~ 76 商務信函

第 74 ~ 76 題與以下信函有關。

GHG 貿易公司
康尼庫斯藍 35，鹿特丹，荷蘭
電話（31）437-8760；傳真（31）437-8761
電子郵件信箱 info@ghg.co.ne

凱文・佛伊爾 先生
執行長
布拉班特工業
468 索倫特大道
得梅因市，愛荷華州 50301
美國
2008 年 3 月 22 日

親愛的佛伊爾先生，

感謝您同意授權 GHG 貿易為貴公司在荷蘭與比利時的銷售代理商。我們對貴公司產品印象深刻。正如您所建議的，我們也和貴公司的其他代理商談過，他們都（74）極度推薦貴公司作為商業夥伴。

首先，我們想在今年 10 月 23 至 26 日於鹿特丹（75）舉辦的貿易展上把貴公司的一些最新產品介紹給潛在買主。這次的貿易展讓我們有機會將貴公司的產品展示給來自許多不同國家的人。（76）接下來我們也打算在西歐各地的貿易展中介紹貴公司產品。

我已隨信附上包含了該展覽詳細資訊的宣傳手冊供您參考。

很期待盡快收到您的回應。

皮耶‧方‧多倫

業務經理

謹啟

Word List

☐ be impressed by ... 對……印象深刻 ☐ potential buyer [pə`tɛnʃəl `baɪə] 潛在買主

74. 正確答案：(A) ☆☆

選項翻譯：　**(A) 推薦**　　　　(B) 抱怨　　　　(C) 批評　　　　(D) 說

解說

第三句的 they 指的是 some of your other sales agents，而由於前一句說了「貴公司產品相當優秀」，所以可判斷這些代理商 recommend you very highly 這樣的說法較為合理，因此本題選 (A)。

小心陷阱

英文中也有 speak highly of someone「對某人評價很高」的說法，但由於原句中並未出現介系詞 of，故不可選（D）。

75. 正確答案：(D) ☆

解說

taking place 是「舉辦」之意，為慣用動詞片語，而本句中使用的是「未來進行式」。(A) 為正解。

小心陷阱

(A) hold 很容易讓人想到和 take place 同義的 will be held 而造成誤選，請特別小心。

Strategies　Pre Test　Half Test 1　Half Test 2　Full Test

76. 正確答案：(B) ☆☆

選項翻譯： (A) 結果 **(B) 接下來** (C) 另一方面 (D) 相反地

解說

由於前一句說了 demonstrate your products to people from many different countries，所以應銜接 subsequently introduce your products all over Western Europe「接下來在西歐各地介紹貴公司產品」。正確答案為 (B)。

小心陷阱

(A) consequently 是指因某事而產生的某些「結果，或理所當然的結局」之意，並不適用於此句。

奪分祕笈：順接型的連接詞

在面對商業信函類問題時，最好先由上而下掃描信件內容，確實掌握寄信人、收信人及信件主旨後，再閱讀空格前後的內容來作答。在這類題目裡，具連接功能的詞語相當常考，所以在此讓我們一起來學習和 and、so 等連接詞意義相近的順接詞。

a. therefore 因此、所以 （副詞）

The chairperson has resigned. Therefore, we will have to select a new chair as soon as possible.

主席辭職了。因此，我們必須儘快選出新的主席。

b. accordingly 相應地、於是 （副詞）

A huge hurricane was forecast. Accordingly, the city government organized rescue teams to deal with possible natural disasters.

預報會有大型颶風來襲。於是市府組織了救援隊，以應付可能發生的自然災害。

c. subsequently 接下來、隨後 （副詞）

There was an accident at the construction site. Subsequently, the company postponed the date of completion of the building by 1 month.

建築工地發生了意外事故。隨後，該公司便將建築完工日延後了一個月。

d. consequently 結果、因此（副詞）

The country encouraged people to learn at least two foreign languages. Consequently, most of the people nowadays are bilingual or trilingual.

該國鼓勵人們學習至少兩種外語。結果，現在大部分的人都會兩到三種語言。

e. as a result 結果

Marge invested her money in the stock wisely. As a result, she became a member of the new riches.

瑪姬明智地把她的錢投資於股市。結果，她成了新富一族。

Part  **Reading Comprehension 文章理解題**

☆470 分等級 ☆☆600 分等級 ☆☆☆730 分以上

● 77 ~ 78 廣告（advertisement）

第 77 ~ 78 題與以下廣告有關。

超廉超市
7 月 18 日星期六全新開幕！

超廉很高興宣布旗下最新、最現代化的一間超市將於 2008 年 7 月 18 日星期六，在沃森維爾開幕。剪彩儀式預計於上午 8 點 15 分在停車場舉辦，而新店會在上午 9 點開始營業。自週日起，新超市每天將從上午 6 點營業至晚上 11 點。

為了慶祝全新開幕，超廉將捐款贊助沃森維爾圖書館分館的兒童閱讀計畫，以及沃森維爾高中的鼓號樂隊，而該樂隊也將在剪綵儀式中提供表演。

在廣達 4,000 平方公尺的全新超廉超市中，將有提供精選多樣美國牛肉的肉品區，以及新鮮海產區。超廉最著名的熟食店更會提供選項豐富的新鮮沙拉與種類繁多的國產和進口起司。另外，也別忘了順道到有賣超廉知名南方炸雞的餐點外帶區逛逛。

要是逛累了，還可在熟食店的點心吧找個位子坐下，享受點熱湯、新鮮沙拉、美味三明治、汽水或現煮咖啡。

何不帶著全家大小一同參加我們的開幕活動，當天還有許多好康優惠等著你喔！

Word List

☐ ribbon-cutting ceremony [ˋrɪbənˋkʌtɪŋ ˋsɛrəˏmonɪ]（開幕的）剪綵儀式
☐ make a donation [doˋneʃən] 捐助（給慈善團體等）
☐ deli [ˋdɛlɪ] 图 熟食、熟食店
☐ fresh-brewed [frɛʃbru] 圈 現煮的

77. 正確答案：(C) ☆☆

What will people be able to enjoy on the opening day of the new supermarket?
在新超市開幕那天，大家可以享受到些什麼？

(A) Extended opening hours　　　　　　營業時間延長
(B) Free food and drink　　　　　　　　免費的食物和飲料
(C) A musical performance　　　　　　**音樂演奏**
(D) People dancing with ribbons　　　　有人會跳彩帶舞

由第二段提到的 ... the Watsonville High School Marching Band ... perform at the ribbon-cutting ceremony. 可知，正確答案為 (C)。開幕日為週六，而營業時間是從週日起才延長，因此 (A) 是錯的。另外文中並無與 (B)、(D) 有關的敘述。

小心陷阱

(D) People dancing with ribbons 是專為本文中 A ribbon-cutting ceremony 設計的陷阱選項，請小心。

78. 正確答案：(B) ☆☆

What can people NOT find at the Deli section?

在熟食店找不到什麼東西？

(A) Meals to take out	外帶餐食
(B) Fresh beef	**新鮮牛肉**
(C) A place to sit and eat	坐著吃東西的地方
(D) Food from overseas	外國食品

解說

此題要選在熟食區找「不」到的東西，所以只要聚焦於第三、四段提到食物的部分即可。在第三段最後關於熟食店的敘述中曾提到 meals-to-go ...，因此 (A) 找得到；第四段第一句提到 ... find a table in the Deli snack bar ...，所以 (C) 也找得到；而第三段第二句最後的 imported cheeses 則指向 (D)。而與 (B) fresh beef 相關的敘述則出現在第三段的第一句中：... Meat Department offering a selection of the finest US Choice beef ...。 由此可知，牛肉並非熟食區的產品。

小心陷阱：請試著想像賣場情境

第三段的第一和第二句連續介紹了許多食品，由於各式各樣的品名一一出現，所以在此須小心別把各項食品弄混了。只要試著 visualize「想像」賣場情境，就會比較容易理解。此題 What can people NOT find at the Deli section? 雖以大寫 NOT 做了強調，但考試時依舊很容易漏看，要特別注意。另外，畢竟解答此題時必須一一確認文章內資訊，所以花的時間難免比其他題目更多。一找到正確答案，就請馬上畫進答案卡並繼續下一題。

● 79 ~ 80 信件（letter）

第 79 ~ 80 題與以下信件有關。

康普菲克斯公司

34 室，瓦萊里奧大廈，483 布萊蕭大道，沙加緬度，加利福尼亞州 94230

電話 916-8754-5473

西里爾·愛德華 先生
GFS 家具公司
3785 羅伯森街
弗雷斯諾，加利福尼亞州 93650

2008 年 8 月 6 日

親愛的愛德華先生，

我寫此信的目的是為了告知您有關一筆我們向貴公司訂購之辦公家具（訂購編號 #4699570）的問題。7 月 10 日時，我們曾向貴公司訂購 6 張型號為 OC5475 的辦公椅，該辦公椅在貴公司的網站廣告上標價為每張 95.99 美元。一如承諾，訂購後一週內商品就送到了。然而當我們打開箱子時，卻發現你們只送來了 5 張椅子。不僅如此，這些椅子也都不是我們訂的那一款。貴公司送來的椅子型號為 OC4755，和 OC5475 的很像，不過比較便宜、坐起來也比較不舒適。然而，當我們檢查貴公司給的發票時，卻發現你們是按原訂單，向我們收取的六張較高價椅子費用。

當然，我們立刻打電話給貴公司的客服中心回報這項錯誤。貴公司隔天便派了一台卡車把錯誤的椅子載走，並送來正確的椅子。但是，這已是貴公司今年以來第二次弄錯我們的訂單。日後若再發生此事，則即使我們兩家公司有著長久合作關係，我們仍不得不考慮找個新的供應商。

瑪莎·哈洛倫
執行長

Word List

- [ ] invoice [ˋɪnvɔɪs] 名 發票、單據
- [ ] supplier [səˋplaɪɚ] 名 供應商
- [ ] i.e. 亦即（拉丁文 id est 之縮寫）

Strategies | Pre Test | Half Test 1 | Half Test 2 | Full Test

79. 正確答案：(B) ☆

What is the purpose of this letter? 這封信的目的為何？

(A) To order some office chairs 訂購辦公椅

(B) To complain about poor service **抱怨服務差**

(C) To ask for a discount on merchandise 要求商品的折扣優惠

(D) To let GFS know the merchandise hasn't arrived 讓 GFS 公司知道貨還沒送到

 解說

信中第一句就提到 ... about a problem with an order ...，所以正確答案是 (B)。

80. 正確答案：(D) ☆☆

What mistake was made with the client's order? 顧客的訂單出了什麼錯？

(A) Delivery was late. 商品太晚送到。

(B) A more expensive model was delivered. 送來的是較貴的商品。

(C) The wrong chairs were delivered twice. 椅子送錯兩次。

(D) Both the quantity and model were wrong. **數量和商品型號都錯了。**

解說

由第一段第四句提到的 ... supplied us with only five chairs. 和第五句 Not only that, they were not the chairs we ordered. 可知，正確答案為 (D)。

🔴 **小心陷阱：務必確實掌握整體情況**

注意，該公司確實是第二次弄錯訂單，但是信中沒提到弄錯的是否都是「椅子」，因此不可選 (C)。

💡 **奪分祕笈：商務信函**

商務信函類題目每次都會出 2 ~ 3 題左右。

1. 首先掃描各段的第一句。英文文章原則上提到新主題、新狀況時，都會換新段落。因此各段落的第一句通常都會包含重要資訊，務必看過一遍。

2. 商務信函和電子郵件的差異點在於「文章較長」、「內容較複雜」、「使用的社交辭令較多」等。以此信為例，第一段寫的是寄信人撰寫此信的目的及事情發生的詳細經過，到了第二段才開始抱怨。讀者最好能事先了解各類文章的大致架構及脈絡。尤其是像本篇以及雙篇文章 91 ~ 95 題的「客訴相關」電子郵件等文章，最是需要好好掌握整體情況。至於與抱怨、客訴有關的解題策略，請參考 91 ~ 95 題的「小心陷阱」說明。

● 81 ~ 84 申請表（application form）

第 81 ~ 84 題與以下申請表有關。

「為生命而跑」
贊助申請表
溫徹斯特國際馬拉松賽

非常感謝您選擇為慈善而跑！請填寫此表並記得將複本寄給溫徹斯特國際馬拉松賽辦事處。我們希望能記錄下您的努力，並於稍後發表在我們的「為生命而跑」雜誌上。而於賽後，您將收到我們所頒發的證書。祝您好運！

申請人兼跑者：丹妮拉・金
電話號碼：020-8563-9980　電子郵件：dking250@telbank.co.uk
地址：57 號，特拉法加・派瑞德，倫敦，N16 5GT

跑者的話
我參加此次比賽的目的是為了替我最喜歡的慈善團體「無國界醫生募款」。希望您能贊助我參賽，以協助我募款。這是我第一次跑馬拉松，所以如果我沒能跑完全程，那就贊助我跑完的部分即可！謝謝您！

丹妮拉・金的贊助者名單

贊助者姓名	贊助金額	賽後支付的金額
1. 布魯斯・哈德	50 英鎊	50 英鎊
2. 瓦爾・葛拉罕	40 英鎊	40 英鎊
3. 古瑪爾・崔罕	100 英鎊	100 英鎊
4. 派特・歐瑪莉	50 英鎊	50 英鎊
5. 克勞斯・施密特	80 英鎊	
6. 瑪麗亞・舒瑞茲	30 英鎊	30 英鎊
7. 基斯・伊凡斯	120 英鎊	150 英鎊
8. 菲歐娜・摩爾	40 英鎊	

Word List

☐ run for life 原有「拼命地跑」的意思，在此可譯為「為了生命而跑」
☐ raise funds 募款

81. 正確答案：(A) ☆☆

How much of the race did Daniella King probably complete?

丹妮拉・金在比賽中大概跑完了多少距離？

(A) All of it　　　　**全程**　　　　(B) Some of it　　　　一部分

(C) Half of it　　　　一半　　　　(D) One quarter of it　四分之一

> **解說**
>
> 「跑者的話」倒數第二句提到 ... if I don't finish the race, just pay me for the part I completed.，而下方表格顯示，贊助者提供的贊助金額與實際支付金額一致。由此可判斷她應該已跑完全程，故本題選 (A)。

🔘 **小心陷阱：要注意該數字到底代表的是什麼**

注意，(D) One quarter of it「四分之一」為清單中未付款人數的比例，不可誤選。

82. 正確答案：(D) ☆☆

Why is Daniella King taking part in this race?　　丹妮拉・金為何要參加這場比賽？

(A) Because she needs the money　　　　因為她需要錢

(B) Because she loves to run marathons　　因為她愛跑馬拉松

(C) Because her friends asked her to　　　因為她朋友拜託她

(D) Because she wants to help people　　**因為她想幫助別人**

> **解說**
>
> 首先注意，文章中用的 participating 在問題裡改述成了 take part in。由「跑者的話」於第一句提到的 I'm participating 提到 ... to raise money for ... charity 可知，正確答案是 (D)。 另外，「跑者的話」裡的第三句提到 This is my first ever marathon ...，由此可推測跑馬拉松並非她的興趣，所以 (B) 是錯的。

🔘 **小心陷阱**

「需要錢」與「為了幫助人兒募款」是兩件事。二者的意思或許有重疊，但是在意義上有相當大的落差。因此，不可誤選 (A)。

83. 正確答案：(D) ☆☆

What is true about Daniella King's sponsors?
有關丹妮拉・金的贊助者之敘述，何者為真？

(A) Everyone has paid her except one person.　　只有一個人沒付款。
(B) The three biggest sponsors have all paid her.　3 位贊助金額最高的人都付款了。
(C) Everyone promised to pay more than £50.　每個人都承諾要捐超過 50 英鎊。
(D) One person paid more than he or she promised. **有個人付了比她或他原本承諾的金額還多的錢。**

解說

從表格可看出 (A) 是錯的，因為共有 2 人還沒付款；(B) 也錯，因為贊助金額第三高的克勞斯・施密特還沒付錢；而 (C) 也不對，因為捐款低於 50 英鎊的就有兩人。而由於基斯・伊凡斯捐出了 150 英鎊，比原本答應的 120 英鎊還多，所以 (D) 為正確答案。

奪分祕笈

與前面提到的「包含 NOT 的問題」相同，在回答這種 What is true ... ? 型的題目時，若發現 (A) 為正確答案，那麼請務必立刻畫上答案卡然後移至下一題。

84. 正確答案：(B) ☆☆

The phrase "keep track of" in line 2, is closest in meaning to第二行中 keep track of 意思最接近？

(A) praise　　　　　稱讚
(B) follow　　　　**追蹤（記錄等）**
(C) record on video　錄在影帶上
(D) write about　　　撰寫關於……

解說

Part 7 中必定會出現 1 ~ 2 題與詞彙意義有關的問題。就算不知道 keep track of 的意思，依據 fill in this form and return a copy 也可推測出目的是要「留下記錄」。此外，在「做了記錄」後，下一句的 After the race you will receive a certificate ... 也才可能成立。選項 (B) follow 有追蹤（記錄）的意思，故為正解。

小心陷阱：別只看包含特定單字的句子，而要看前後文

若只看包含 keep track of 的那句話，有可能會誤選 (D) write about，但這樣與前後文的意思銜接不起來。

▶ 圖表可能做為單篇文章的一部分，也可能搭配商業信函等文章以雙篇文章形式出題。這類題目多半問得直截了當，甚至只需抓對數字就能答對，所以除非看錯，不然應該可輕鬆得分。

▶ 圖表題的內容通常包括「時刻表、行事曆」、「商品與價格表」、「發票、帳單」、「天氣預報」等幾種。

▶ 圖表種類 ：(1) column / chart 在縱向、橫向欄位中標記資料的表格，及 (2) graphs，而graphs包括：

a. line graph 折線圖：
以線條連接各點資料而形成的圖表。經常用來表示價格或股價的漲跌狀況。

b. histogram 柱狀圖：
沿 Y 軸垂直繪製多條長方形的圖表，常用於表示偏差分布狀態或人數差異等資料。

c. pie-graph 圓餅圖：
依據各資料元素來分割圓形，以表示出各元素的百分比關係。經常用於民意調查（opinion poll）等的資料說明。

● 85 ~ 87 指示說明（instructions、directions）

第 85 ~ 87 題與以下的指示說明有關。

如何戒菸

1. 在行事曆上標出你要戒菸的日期。記得告訴所有家人和朋友你的計劃，好讓他們支援你。

2. 做些明智的準備工作。丟掉所有的香菸和菸灰缸。你可能會懷念嘴裡叼著香菸的感覺，所以可準備一些香菸的替代品，例如無糖口香糖、紅蘿蔔條，或糖等。

3. 去參加戒菸課程。練習說「不，謝謝。我不抽菸。」如果你以前曾試過戒菸，那麼請想想以前有哪些事對你戒菸有幫助、哪些事沒有幫助。

4. 找出能支持你努力戒菸的人。這些人可以是已成功戒菸的朋友或家人。如果你有朋友及家人仍在抽菸，可以禮貌地請求他們別在你周圍抽菸。

5. 參與全國禁菸協會舉辦的有趣活動。以往有過的一些活動，包括鼓勵抽菸者交出未抽完的菸盒以換取免費禮物等。

6. 別太心急。先戒菸 24 小時試試。以此為起點來幫助你終生戒菸。去認識一些不抽菸的新朋友，或找其他也正在嘗試戒菸的人，這樣你們就能幫助彼此永久戒菸。

Word List

- □ attempt [ə`tɛmpt] 動 試圖
- □ campaign [kæm`pen] 名 活動
- □ sensible [`sɛnsəbl] 形 合理的、明智的（勿與 sensitive「敏感的」混淆）
- □ substitute [`sʌbstətjut] 名 替代品

85. 正確答案：(C) ☆☆

What advice is given to people who want to quit smoking?
此文章給了想戒菸的人什麼建議？

(A) Do not go to places where people smoke.	別去有人抽菸的地方。
(B) Try not to smoke for at least one week.	試著不抽菸至少一個禮拜。
(C) Get help from friends and relatives.	請朋友和親屬幫忙。
(D) Become a member of the National Anti-Smoking Society.	**成為全國禁菸協會的一員。**

解說

由第一點第二句提到的 ... tell all of your family and friends ... so they can support you.，可知，正確答案為 (C)。不過注意，原文的 family and friends 換成了 friends and relatives。而第四點的第三句 If you have friends and family who still smoke, ask them politely not to smoke around you. 並不等於 (A) 別去有人抽菸的地方。另外，第六點建議 Quit smoking for 24 hours.，但沒有提到 (B) 選項所說的一週，所以 (B) 也不是正確答案。

小心陷阱：不要自行擴大解釋內容

請注意，第五點第一句 Participate in the fun events organized by the National Anti-Smoking Society.，是建議「參加活動」，並非建議「成為會員」，因此不可誤選。

86. 正確答案：(A) ☆☆

In this passage, what is NOT mentioned as a way to give up smoking?
在這段文章中，並未提到哪種戒菸方法？

(A) Consult a doctor.	**諮詢醫師。**
(B) Throw away your cigarettes.	丟掉你的香菸。
(C) Join a group of people trying to quit.	加入嘗試戒菸者的群體。
(D) Try to do it slowly.	慢慢地努力戒菸。

87. 正確答案：(C) ☆☆

What is one thing people should do to help themselves quit smoking?

人們應該做哪件事來幫助自己戒菸？

(A) Mark their calendar on days they didn't smoke.		在行事曆上標出沒有抽菸的日子。
(B) Give up gum and candy also.		把口香糖和糖果也一併戒掉。
(C) Practice refusing cigarettes.		**練習拒絕香菸。**
(D) Read books about celebrities who have also quit.		閱讀與已戒菸名人有關的書。

解說

由第三點第二句中提到的 "No, thank you. I don't smoke." 這個關鍵句可知，正解為 (C)。另，文中完全沒有和 (D) 有關的資訊。

小心陷阱：請正確掌握文中建議要標記的東西

第一點說的是 Mark a day on your calendar for when you are going to quit smoking.「在行事曆上標出你要戒菸的日期」，而不是 (A) 的「在行事曆上標記出你沒有抽菸的日子」。而第二點提到的是 ... prepare some substitutes for cigarettes, such as sugarless gum, carrot sticks, or hard candies. 而不是 Give up gum and candy，所以 (B) 也不對。請小心別掉進這兩個陷阱。

奪分祕笈：指示說明

請先確認團體名稱、對象名稱及主旨等資訊。若是編號條列式文章，則題目也會依編號順序出題，所以能快速作答。另外像「公共工程及交通機關之變更通知」等文章，通常都會明確記載期限，且這期限也往往會成為考題。一般來說，與日期時間或期限有關的題目都很直截了當，只要不看錯選項就能輕鬆得分。但若是像「公車路線變更」或「因工程、事故而封鎖道路」等關於突發事件的公告，就常會出現改述詞彙及誘餌選項，這時就要多加小心。

● 88 ~ 90 電子郵件

第 88 ~ 90 題與以下的電子郵件有關。

Strategies
Pre Test

日期：2009 年 1 月 4 日
收件人：伊馮・迪馬可，業務部副總
寄件人：布蘭特・歐茲沃特，地區業務經理
主旨：追加行程

親愛的伊馮，

我想問問是否可延長我即將進行的歐洲之旅。誠如妳所知，我將去瑞士和我們在那兒的合作夥伴討論明年度的生產計劃。目前我計劃在 2 月 25 日出發，3 月 2 日回來。不過我剛聽說我們的德國合作夥伴發生了財務問題。我不確定問題有多嚴重，但是我想可以趁這個機會去法蘭克福與該公司面對面談一下這件事。我無法提早出發，因為 2 月 23 日有一場銷售會議。因此我想延長待在歐洲的時間，在去過瑞士之後繼續前往德國。我可以在 3 月 1 日離開日內瓦，飛往法蘭克福。我可能得在那兒待兩天，然後在 3 月 4 日回芝加哥。能否請妳告訴我這樣是否可行？而在此同時，我會儘量收集有關那家德國公司所發生的問題的相關資訊，並寄一份報告給妳。

謝謝
布蘭特

Half Test 1
Half Test 2
Full Test

Word List

□ meanwhile 副 在此同時

---

88. 正確答案：(B) ☆☆

Why did Brent Oswald send this message? | 布蘭特・歐茲沃特為何要寄這封電子郵件？

(A) To inform his boss of his plan to make a business trip | 為了通知上司他的出差計畫

(B) To inform his boss about a possible change of plans | 為了通知上司可能的計畫變更

(C) To give his boss a report about a German company 　為了給上司一份有關一家德國公司的報告

(D) To ask his boss to go to Europe with him 　為了請上司與他一同去歐洲

> **解說**
>
> 電子郵件文章不像傳統信件那樣會明確分段，而其主旨多半就寫在開頭，因此最好一開始就把它記起來。這封電子郵件的第一句 I wanted to ask you if I could extend my upcoming trip to Europe. 就是指向正確答案 (B) 的關鍵。

小心陷阱：請正確掌握文中建議要標記的東西

由第二句開頭的 As you know ...，可知，出差一事並非現在才通知，故 (A) 是錯的。另外，由第四句的起頭 However, I just heard ... 可知，德國公司的問題並非此信的主要目的，所以 (C) 也不對。(D) 選項的內容在文中完全無任何相關描述。如果沒掌握住一開始就提到的主旨就可能錯選 (A) 或 (C)。

89. 正確答案：(A) ☆☆

What does Brent Oswald want to do? 　布蘭特・歐茲沃特想做什麼？

(A) Attend a sales conference, go to Switzerland, then go to Germany.
出席一場銷售會議，去瑞士，然後再去德國。

(B) Go to Chicago, attend a sales conference, then fly to Frankfurt.
去芝加哥出席一場銷售會議，然後飛去法蘭克福。

(C) Go to Germany, then to Switzerland and return to Chicago.
去德國，然後去瑞士，再回芝加哥。

(D) Go to Switzerland, go to Germany, then attend a sales conference.
去瑞士，再去德國，然後出席一場銷售會議。

> **解說**
>
> 由第六句的 sales conference on February 23 和第七句的 go to Germany after I visit Switzerland 可知正確答案為 (A)。而在此須注意的是 Germany after Switzerland 所表達的順序，和國名單字的排列順序是相反的。

小心陷阱：務必清楚理解行程細節

(B)、(C)、(D) 都是誘餌選項，而且各個都很誘人。和旅行團那種固定模式的行程不同，商務旅行（出差）的行程通常是由「要去幾個地點」、「和誰見面」、「在哪裡開會」及「要談那些事」等元素組合而成。閱讀時，請同時在腦海中好好 visualize 情境。

90. 正確答案：(B) ☆

What does Brent find out about their partner company in Germany?

布蘭特發現了關於他們德國合作夥伴的什麼事？

(A) They feel satisfied with the German company.

　　他們對該德國公司很滿意。

(B) They think the German company is not doing well.

　　他們覺得該德國公司狀況不太好。

(C) They want to continue doing business with the German company.

　　他們想繼續和該德國公司做生意。

(D) They want to stop doing business with the German company.

　　他們想停止和該德國公司做生意。

解說

由第四句中提到的 ... our partner in Germany is having financial problems. 可知，正確答案應為 (B)。另，文中並無與 (A) 或 (C) 有關的資訊。

💣 小心陷阱：考試時最忌諱擅自臆測

一看到第四句的 our partner in Germany is having financial problems，有些人或許就會擅自猜測「那他們應該會想和該公司斷絕往來了吧」。但要注意的是，「猜測」不能視為正確答案，請千萬別掉入這陷阱。

● 91 ~ 95 廣告與電子郵件（advertisement、e-mail）

第 91 ~ 95 題與以下的廣告和電子郵件有關。

廣告

伊世美德旅行社

伊世美德旅行社是一家獨立的旅遊公司，專營各式各樣的度假行程，包括在希臘、賽普勒斯、土耳其與埃及等地的潛水之旅及婚禮套裝行程。我們承諾會熱烈歡迎前往各目的地的所有顧客。伊世美德保證只要客人一到達目的地，就會有我們的一位旅遊代表，隨時準備回答有關該度假勝地或當地設施及短程旅遊相關的任何問題。

以顧客可負擔的價格提供高品質服務，是我們最主要的優先任務。自 1981 年創業以來，我們已在所經營的市場中站穩腳步，並在我們的專營地區累積了豐富的經驗。我們所有員工都充分了解顧客的重要性。我們非常謹慎，只聘僱具備積極、樂於助人的態度與良好溝通能力的員工。

所以事不宜遲，現在就上我們的網站 www.eastmedtravel.com，或撥電話給我們紐約辦公室 1-222-355-0331 的凱文，了解該如何預約讓您終身難忘的美好假期！

電子郵件

日期：2008 年 8 月 6 日
收件人：kevin_grayson@eastmed.co.uk
寄件人：cnoonan@bright.net
主旨：貴公司的當地代表

親愛的凱文，

我向貴公司預訂了一套旅遊行程，而我現在正和兩個朋友待在賽普勒斯島拉納卡的德爾洪酒店。依據你們的廣告，你們的當地旅遊代表都很積極、樂於助人而且有良好溝通能力。很遺憾地我必須告訴你，以你們此地的旅遊代表來說，這件事完全不是事實。我們原本期待他會到機場與我們會面，並帶我們到飯店。但是到處都找不到他人，結果我們只好坐計程車。等我們終於見到他本人的時候，他卻說他以為我們隔天才到。我們昨天安排了潛水之旅，但是他不僅遲到，還只帶了兩人份而不是三人份的裝備。接著他花了一小時才找到另一套裝備來。最後，我們的潛水之旅從全天被縮短成半天。儘管貴公司的廣告提出了多項保證，但是我的朋友和我對貴公司的服務都極為失望。

克萊兒・努南

91. 正確答案：(C) ☆☆☆

What kind of vacations does EastMed Travel specialize in?

伊世美德旅行社專營哪種假期行程？

(A) Trips to all parts of the world　　　　　前往世界各地的旅遊

(B) Outdoor vacations only　　　　　　　　只有戶外活動型的假期

(C) Trips to one particular region　　　**前往特定區域的旅遊**

(D) Vacations for senior citizens　　　　　適合高齡者的假期

> 解說
>
> 依據廣告中第一段的第一句提到的 EastMed Travel ... tour operator ... in Greece, Cyprus, Turkey and Egypt. 可知這是一間專營近東和中東區域的旅行社，所以正確答案為 (C)。而文中並無任何與 (A)、(D) 選項有關的資訊。

小心陷阱：不能只靠單一資訊來判斷

廣告第一句裡提到的 diving excursions 可能會讓人想選 (B)，但接下來還提到 wedding packages，所以 (B) 並非正確答案。

92. 正確答案：(D) ☆☆

What special features does EastMed Travel mention in its publicity?

伊世美德旅行社在其宣傳文裡提出了哪些特色？

(A) Low prices and comfortable hotels　　　　低廉的價格和舒適的飯店

(B) Excellent service and good food　　　　　優秀的服務與美味的食物

(C) Good food and a variety of activities　　　美味的食物和各種活動

(D) Reasonable prices and high-quality service　**合理的價格與高品質的服務**

> 解說
>
> 廣告第二段的第一句 Our main priority ... quality service ... with a price they can afford. 就是指向正確答案 (D) 的關鍵。

小心陷阱

廣告第一段的最後一句提到他們的代表可以回答有關 resort 和 local facilities 的問題，但這與 (A) 中的 comfortable hotels 無關，不可誤選。

93. 正確答案：(B) ☆

What was Claire Noonan's first problem?

(A) She was taken to the wrong hotel.

(B) No one met her at the airport.

(C) Her flight arrived late.

(D) The hotel was not expecting her.

克萊兒‧努南首先碰到什麼問題？

她被帶到錯的飯店去了。

沒人在機場與她碰頭。

她的飛機晚到了。

飯店不知道她要來。

解說

由電子郵件的第四句 We were expecting him to meet us at the airport ... 和第五句 He was nowhere to be found ... 可知，正確答案為 (B)。

🗯 小心陷阱：務必看清主詞

電子郵件第七句中的 ... but he arrived late ... 有可能讓人看錯並誤以為答案是 (C) Her flight arrived late。

94. 正確答案：(A) ☆

What was the problem with the scuba diving excursion? 潛水之旅出了什麼問題？

(A) It was delayed by the mistakes of the representative.
   因旅行社的旅遊代表犯錯而延誤了。

(B) The representative brought the wrong kind of equipment.
   旅行社的旅遊代表帶錯裝備。

(C) They couldn't get back to the hotel during the day.
   他們無法白天時回到飯店。

(D) The representative did not meet them.
   旅行社的旅遊代表並未現身。

解說

由電子郵件第七句的後半 ... he arrived late and only brought enough equipment for two people, not three. 和第八句 He then spent the next hour finding one more set. 可知，正確答案為 (A)。

🗯 小心陷阱：要注意日期與時間

旅行社代理是「少帶」裝備而不是「帶錯」裝備，因此 (B) 為錯誤選項。另，沒見到面的狀況是發生在前一天抵達機場時，所以 (D) The representative did not meet them. 的敘述也不對。小心不要誤選這兩個答案。

95. 正確答案：(D) ☆☆

In the advertisement, the phrase "main priority" in paragraph 2, line 1, is closest in meaning to
廣告第二段第一行裡的片語「main priority」意思最接近

(A) favorite activity   最喜歡的活動
(B) longest experience   最長的經驗
(C) most profitable business   最賺錢的行業
(D) most important aim   **最重要的目標**

解說

由整句 Our main priority is to offer our customers quality service combined with a price they can afford. 可推斷 main priority 的意思就是 most important aim「最重要的目標」，所以正確答案為 (D)。

小心陷阱：依據前後文來掌握實際含意

若不仔細看前後文，(C) 選項 most profitable business 可能是相當誘人的答案，小心不要上當。

奪分祕笈：客訴類的電子郵件與信件

1. 客訴類的電子郵件或信函每次測驗大概都會出個一篇。面對這類文章時，若只是從頭到尾乖乖讀完，則不但不易理解，也會因此花費過多時間。建議讀者：
   a. 一定要先快速讀過問題，如此才能掌握文章的整體概念。
   b. 為了在文章中快速找出問題的答案，請圈選出關鍵詞。由於問題通常都會問得很直接，所以可先從問題找出線索，然後再著手閱讀文章。

2. 客訴類文章的分類：
   a. 如第 91 ~ 95 題，廣告和實物不符的狀況
   b. 如第 79 ~ 80 題，與單據有誤、送錯商品有關的狀況
   c. 與商品品質有關的內容
   d. 與店家服務品質惡劣有關的內容
   e. 與公共交通工具上的禮儀與待客有關的內容
   f. 與交通運輸延遲等有關的內容

3. 題目種類：
   a. 較大範圍的問題：主要抱怨什麼？

   What is the nature of the problem?   問題屬於哪種性質？
   What is the customer complaining about?   顧客在抱怨什麼？
   What's wrong with the merchandise?   商品有何問題？
   Why is the customer upset?   顧客為何生氣？

b. 較小範圍的問題：投訴的細節

When did it happen?	問題何時發生？
How did it happen?	問題如何發生？
Who is responsible for the problem?	誰該為此問題負責？

c. 較小範圍的問題：如何解決？

What will be done in the end?	最後會採取什麼行動？
How will they cope with the problem?	他們將如何處理這問題？
Who will take care of the situation?	誰將處理這情況？

● 96～100 商務信函（business letters）

第 96～100 題與以下的商務信函有關。

信函

G&L 工業

3317 亨廷頓路，斯普林菲爾德，伊利諾州 62704，美國

電話：217-9873-0081；傳真：217-9873-0085

莫辛德・辛格 先生
PTC 有限公司
38 室，歌帝梵商務園區
希斯金路
考文垂 CV1 5TY
英國

2008 年 4 月 24 日

親愛的辛格先生，

感謝您提供的最新銷售報告。很高興知道本公司的產品賣得不錯，我們之間的業務關係也因此有了如此好的開始。

我寫這封信的目的是為了讓您知道我計畫於 6 月拜訪英國。我已經有將近 2 年的時間沒去那兒了。我想花點時間到倫敦看看一些大型購物中心，以便感受一下零售市場的變化情形。之後，我想去考文垂，到貴公司拜訪您。我想看一下貴公司的運作情況並見見一些員工，對我真的會很有幫助。我將與我們國際業務部的主任黛娜・梅斯葛女士一同前往，我們希望能與貴公司的業務部人員見個面，並針對英國市場討論一些可能的新策略。

您若能告知我您 6 月中旬的行程安排,我將會非常感激,如此我就能將這次的拜訪安排在我們雙方都方便的時間。

很期待您的回覆。
里昂・羅許
執行長
敬上

信函

PTC 有限公司
38 室,歌帝梵商務園區
希斯金路,考文垂 CV1 5TY
電話:24-7525-9523;傳真:24-7534-6646

G&L 工業
3317 亨廷頓路
斯普林菲爾德,伊利諾州 62704
美國

2008 年 4 月 29 日

親愛的羅許先生,

非常感謝您的來信。對於銷售順利一事我也十分欣喜。我們所收到從貴公司運送來的第一批貨,現在已幾乎全數賣完,因此我們計畫在下個月中旬左右再訂一批。

很高興聽到您要來拜訪我們。有很多事我們都需要談一談,而見面談總是比較好的。關於如何在英國市場上更有效率地行銷貴公司產品這方面,我們也有一些新的點子,因此我們十分樂意與您和黛娜・梅斯葛女士一起坐下討論。至於較方便的拜訪時機,由於我 6 月 12 日到 20 日必須去印度見一些客戶,因此是否有可能將您的來訪日期安排在 6 月 21 日或之後呢?

很期待您的回信。

莫辛德・辛格
總經理
謹啟

96. 正確答案：(D) ☆☆☆

What is the relationship between the two companies?　這兩家公司間的關係為何？

(A) One is the parent company of the other.　其中一家是另一家的母公司。

(B) One wants to take over the other.　其中一家想併購另一家。

(C) They have a long-established business relationship.　他們有建立已久的業務合作關係。

(D) They have just recently started doing business together.　**他們最近才剛開始業務合作。**

> **解說**
>
> 由第一封信函中第一段第二句後半提到的 ... our business relationship has gotten off to such a good start. 可知，正解為 (D)。

 小心陷阱

如果沒看懂或沒留意第一段第二句後半提到的資訊，可能會誤選 (C)，請特別注意。

97. 正確答案：(C) ☆☆

When is the best time for Mr. Rausch to visit Mr. Singh's company?
對羅許先生來說，何時是拜訪辛格先生的公司的最佳時機？

(A) June 21　6 月 21 日　　　　(B) Early June　6 月初

(C) Mid-June　6 月中旬　　　(D) Late June　6 月下旬

> **解說**
>
> 由第一封信函第三段的 ... let me know what your schedule is in mid-June so that I can arrange my visit ... 可知，正解為 (C)。

 小心陷阱：務必看清楚寄件人是誰

可能有人會因為第二封信函第二段的最後一句 Would it be possible for you to arrange your visit on or after June 21? 而認為答案應是 (A)。但這題問的是「對羅許先生來說，何時是最佳時機？」，所以請小心別上當。

98. 正確答案：(B) ☆☆

What does Mr. Rausch want to do in London? 　羅許先生想在倫敦做什麼？

(A) Visit Mr. Singh's company. 　　　　　拜訪辛格先生的公司。

(B) Look around some shops. 　　　　　**到處看看一些商店。**

(C) Have a sales meeting. 　　　　　　　召開銷售會議。

(D) Sell his company's products. 　　　　販賣他公司的產品。

解說

由第一封信函第二段的第三句 I want to spend some time in London looking around some of the major shopping centers ... 可知，正確答案為 (B)。

⬤💥 小心陷阱：確定地點

由第二段第四句裡提到的 ... I'd like to go to Coventry and visit you at your company.，可知，辛格先生的公司不在倫敦，而是在考文垂，所以選項 (A) 並不正確，千萬別誤選。

99. 正確答案：(A) ☆

What will Mr. Singh be doing in the middle of June? 辛格先生 6 月中旬時會是在做什麼？

(A) Visiting overseas clients 　　　　　**拜訪海外客戶**

(B) Welcoming some clients from India 　　招待一些來自印度的客戶

(C) Preparing for a conference 　　　　　準備一場會議

(D) Making a new order 　　　　　　　　下新的訂單

解說

在第二封信函第二段的第四句提到 ... I have to go to India to meet some clients from June 12 to 20.，因此正確答案為 (A)。

⬤💥 小心陷阱：別被具體的地名所騙

是辛格先生要去印度見客戶，而不是要接待印度來的客戶，所以 (B) 為非，不可誤選。

100. 正確答案：(C) ☆☆

In the first letter, the word "strategies" in paragraph 2, line 8 is closest in meaning to

第一封信函第二段第八行裡的 strategies 的意思最接近

(A) figures	數據	(B) staff	員工
(C) plans	**計畫**	(D) offices	辦公室

解說

兩個公司的業務人員見面針對市場所討論的當然是「策略」、「計畫」等，故最合理的答案為 (C)。

小心陷阱：選擇意義相近的單字

選項 (A) figures 似乎頗具吸引力，但是至於該句中會與全文之語意不符，因此不可選。

Memo:

解答與解說
Half Test 1（100 題）

解答一覽表

Listening Section

Part	No.	正解	你的答案
Part 1	1	A	
	2	A	
	3	C	
	4	C	
	5	B	
Part 2	6	B	
	7	C	
	8	A	
	9	B	
	10	C	
	11	B	
	12	B	
	13	C	
	14	A	
	15	A	
	16	C	
	17	B	
	18	A	
	19	A	
	20	B	
Part 3	21	D	
	22	A	
	23	C	
	24	B	
	25	C	
	26	A	
	27	C	
	28	A	
	29	C	
	30	D	
	31	A	
	32	D	
	33	D	
	34	A	
	35	B	
Part 4	36	B	
	37	B	
	38	D	
	39	D	
	40	C	
	41	A	
	42	D	
	43	B	
	44	B	
	45	D	
	46	A	
	47	C	
	48	B	
	49	A	
	50	D	

Reading Section

Part	No.	正解	你的答案
Part 5	51	C	
	52	A	
	53	A	
	54	D	
	55	C	
	56	A	
	57	B	
	58	A	
	59	D	
	60	B	
	61	D	
	62	A	
	63	C	
	64	B	
	65	C	
	66	C	
	67	C	
	68	A	
	69	B	
	70	C	
Part 6	71	B	
	72	D	
	73	C	
	74	D	
	75	C	
	76	A	
Part 7	77	C	
	78	B	
	79	B	
	80	B	
	81	A	
	82	C	
	83	C	
	84	D	
	85	B	
	86	A	
	87	B	
	88	A	
	89	D	
	90	B	
	91	B	
	92	C	
	93	A	
	94	D	
	95	B	
	96	B	
	97	A	
	98	A	
	99	C	
	100	D	

請記下 Half Test 1 的成績。

	答對題數	答對率	目標答對率
Part 1	/ 5	%	90%
Part 2	/ 15	%	80%
Part 3	/ 15	%	70%
Part 4	/ 15	%	70%
合計	/ 50	%	75%

	答對題數	答對率	目標答對率
Part 5	/ 20	%	70%
Part 6	/ 6	%	70%
Part 7	/ 24	%	70%
合計	/ 50	%	70%

Part 1 Photographs 圖片題

☆470 分等級 ☆☆600 分等級 ☆☆☆730 分以上

1. 正確答案：(A) ☆☆　　　　　　　　　　　　　　　　　　　🔊 22

(A) A craftsman is at work.　　　　　　**一名工匠正在工作。**

(B) A weaver is making a rug.　　　　　　一名紡織工人正在織地毯。

(C) The man's works are being shown at the exhibit.　這名男子的作品正在展覽館展示。

(D) The man is taking a break.　　　　　　這名男子正在稍作休息。

> **解說** 人的狀態 ➲ Pre 1
>
> 該名男子正在使用黏土工作，所以 (A)「一名工匠正在工作」是正確答案。此題的答題關鍵在於是否能聽出 craftsman「工匠」和 at work「在工作」。注意，選項 (C) 使用的複數形works，意思為「作品」、「工廠」、「工程」。

2. 正確答案：(A) ☆☆

(A) The truck is parked along the curb.　　　**這輛卡車停在路邊。**

(B) The cars are bumper-to-bumper on the street.　街道上車多壅塞。

(C) The truck is carrying packages.　　　　這輛卡車載著行李。

(D) The truck is now in operation.　　　　這輛卡車正在作業中。

> **解說** 以物為主題 ➲ Pre 2
>
> 此照片中的車為形狀特殊的道路清潔車，請小心別因它怪異的外表而分神答錯。本題的關鍵不在於卡車的功能，而在於 (A) along the curb「沿著路邊」。

3. 正確答案：(C) ☆☆

(A) The woman and the dog are about to cross the street.　這名女子和狗正要過馬路。

(B) The woman is patting her pet.　　　　這名女子正在輕拍她的寵物。

(C) The woman has a working dog.　　　**這名女子擁有一隻工作犬。**

(D) The woman is walking her dog.　　　　這名女子正在遛狗。

> **解說** 人的動作、狀態 ➲ Pre 1
>
> 由照片裡的狗套著代表工作中的挽具可知，這一隻是工作犬，因此 (C) 為正確答案。由於女子並未做任何動作，所以 (A)、(B)、(D) 都不對。

4. 正確答案：(C) ☆☆☆

(A) The sign prohibits anyone from standing there.　此告示牌禁止任何人站在那兒。

(B) "Off Hours" on the sign means only holidays.　此告示牌所指的「離峰時間」只有假日。

(C) Passengers should wait here between　**在晚上 9 點到早上 6 點之間，**
9:00 p.m. and 6:00 a.m.　**乘客應該在此等待。**

(D) Passengers should not wait here from　從晚上 9 點到早上 6 點，
9:00 p.m. to 6:00 a.m.　乘客不該在此等待。

> **解說** 物與人的狀態 ⊃ Pre 2
>
> 此告示牌指示於離峰時間該在何處下車。告示牌上提到的離峰時間包括星期一至星期五的晚上 9 點到早上 6 點，以及星期六、日和假日全天。只有 (A) 為正確敘述，其他選項皆為誤。

5. 正確答案：(B) ☆☆

(A) A cook is sitting on the right.　一名廚師正坐在右側。

(B) A rice cooker is sitting on the table.　**桌上有一個電鍋。**

(C) The dinner has already been finished.　晚餐已經吃完了。

(D) Dessert is being served.　正在提供甜點。

> **解說** 物的狀態 ⊃ Pre 2
>
> 圖中明顯看到桌上有個電鍋，故正解為 (B)。由於桌上還有主菜與沙拉等，可見晚餐還沒結束，所以 (C)、(D) 都不對。另，注意 (A) 中的 cook 指「廚師」，與 (B) 中的 cooker「電鍋、電子鍋」容易混淆，所以請特別注意。

Word List

- [ ] craftsman [`kræftsmən] 名 工匠
- [ ] take a break 稍作休息
- [ ] bumper-to-bumper 形 （車輛）一輛接一輛的（bumper指「保險桿」）
- [ ] working dog 工作犬（導盲犬稱為 seeing-eye dog 或 guide dog）
- [ ] prohibit [prə`hɪbɪt] 動 禁止
- [ ] cook 名 廚師
- [ ] cooker 名 電鍋

Part ② Question–Response 應答題

☆470 分等級 ☆☆600 分等級 ☆☆☆730 分以上

6. 正確答案：(B) ☆☆ 🔊 24

Great news! I was elected chairperson of the debate club!

好消息！我獲選為辯論社的主席了！

(A) You're a good person. 你是個好人。

(B) You're the right person for it. 你是合適人選。

(C) You can do better. 你可以做得更好。

> **解說** 陳述與反應 ⊃ Pre 6
>
> 此題要考驗的是對對方所做之 statement 的反應能力。針對說話者被選上 chairperson of the debate club，(B) 的 the right person「適任者」為最合理的反應。

7. 正確答案：(C) ☆

The company will pay us back for our plane tickets, won't they?

公司會退還給我們機票錢，不會嗎？

(A) The tickets will be reserved. 票會先訂好。

(B) They always travel by plane. 他們總是坐飛機旅行。

(C) I'm sure they will. 我很肯定他們會退的。

> **解說** 附加疑問句 ⊃ Pre 16
>
> 此附加疑問句的完整意思為 Won't they pay us back?「他們不會把錢退還給我們嗎？」，所以應請選擇回答「會或不會」的選項。(C) 為正解。

8. 正確答案：(A) ☆☆

Does the ink cartridge have to be changed often? 這墨水匣必須常換嗎？

(A) Yes, if you use it a lot. 是的，如果你很常用的話。

(B) Yes, the printer has black and color cartridges. 是的，該印表機有黑色與彩色的墨水匣。

(C) Yes, the printer ink is running low. 是的，該印表機的墨水所剩不多。

> **解說** Yes-No 疑問句 ⊃ Pre 7
>
> 此題的關鍵詞為 be changed often，所以只有 (A) if you use it a lot 回答了問題。注意，選項 (A) 中的 a lot 呼應了原句中的 often。

Strategies

Pre Test

Half Test 1

Half Test 2

Full Test

9. 正確答案：(B) ☆☆☆

Don't you suddenly go on a trip without telling me! 你可不要沒通知我就突然出去旅遊！

(A) No, you don't.   不，你不要。

(B) I'll try not to.   **我會盡量不這麼做。**

(C) Tell me first.   先告訴我。

> **解說 禁止與回應**
>
> Don't you ...! 這種句型是用來向對方強調「別做……」。本句雖然看起來是疑問句形式，實際是個否定的命令，因此 (B) I'll try not to.「盡量不」為合理回應。

10. 正確答案：(C) ☆☆   🔋 25

Would you let us know the results of the experiment when you get them?
可否請您在實驗結果出來後通知我們？

(A) You're very efficient.   你很有效率。

(B) Nobody knows the results yet.   還沒人知道結果。

(C) We certainly will.   **我們一定會的。**

> **解說 表達拜託、請求之意 ⊃ Pre 20**
>
> 請注意 Would you ...? 這樣的問句不見得都以 I 回答，也可能以 We 回答。(C) 為正確選項。有些人可能誤以為 (C) 選項的主詞 We（複數形）與 you 不對應，而因此錯過正確答案。另外，雖然 (B) 選項提到了 the results，但並未針對關鍵的 Would you let us know 做回應，故為誤。

11. 正確答案：(B) ☆☆

How long does it take to get from Charing Cross to London Bridge by train?
從查令十字到倫敦大橋坐火車要花多久時間？

(A) London Bridge is down today.   倫敦大橋今天是放下的。

(B) To London Bridge is about 12 minutes.   **到倫敦大橋約 12 分鐘。**

(C) It's about 10 miles from Charing Cross.   距離查令十字大約 10 英哩。

> **解說 使用 How 的疑問句 ⊃ Pre 14**
>
> 即使是不熟悉倫敦市內地理狀況的人，只要有聽到 How long ...「多久？」與 from ... to「從某處到某處」，一定就能答對。由於問的是所需的時間，因此 (B) 的 12 minutes 即是答案關鍵。另外，(C) 的 10 miles 是針對 How far ...「距離多遠？」的回答，所以是陷阱而非正解。

12. 正確答案：(B) ☆☆

I just can't get over the beautiful sunset I saw on the beach.

我就是忘不了在沙灘上看見的美麗夕陽。

(A) It certainly was a nice beach, wasn't it?　　那沙灘真是不錯，不是嗎？

(B) I can't either. Let's go again.　　　　**我也忘不了。我們再去一次吧。**

(C) You should try to get over it, though.　　不過你該把它給忘了。

> **解説** 陳述與反應 ➲ Pre 6
>
> 針對 I can't get over ...「無法忘懷（經驗或所見所聞的事物）」這樣的陳述，(B) 以 I can't either.「我也無法。」表達認同之意，故為正確答案。選項 (C) 中的 get over 有「把不好的事忘掉」的意思，與原句的 get over 所指的對象顯然不同，故為誤。

13. 正確答案：(C) ☆☆

Where can I get this traveler's check cashed?

我到哪裡可以兌現這張旅行支票？

(A) We don't sell traveler's checks.　　　　我們不賣旅行支票。

(B) You can buy them at the cashier's.　　　你可以在出納員那邊購買（旅行支票）。

(C) Go to the service counter on the first floor. 請至 1 樓服務台辦理。

> **解説** 使用 Where 的疑問句 ➲ Pre 12
>
> 問題中的關鍵詞 get traveler's check cashed 連結到「可在 service counter（服務台）兌換」之提示，所以 (C) 為正確答案。(A) 並未回答問題；(B) 則用字原與 cash 相同的 cashier 來混淆視聽。

14. 正確答案：(A) ☆☆　　　　　　　　　　　　　　　🎧 26

Which do you prefer to live in, a condominium or a private home?

你比較喜歡住在公寓還是獨棟私人住宅？

(A) I wouldn't mind living in a condominium.　　**我不介意住公寓。**

(B) My private cottage is located in the mountains.　我的私人小屋位在山裡。

(C) You live in a private home, don't you?　　　你住在獨棟私人住宅裡，不是嗎？

> **解説** 使用 Which 的疑問句 ➲ Pre 11
>
> 這是 A 和 B 二選一型的問題，因此有針對問題做回應的 (A) I wouldn't mind living in a condominium. 為正確答案。

15. 正確答案：(A) ☆☆

What is our branch's sales target for next year?　　　我們分店下一年度的銷售目標為何？

(A) We have to increase sales by 10 million dollars. **銷售額必須增加 1,000 萬美元。**

(B) We have to meet the target.　　　　　　　　　　我們必須達成目標。

> **解說** 使用 What 的疑問句 ⊃ Pre 8 ──
> 由於此問題的關鍵詞為 sales target，(A) 選項提到 increase by sales 10 million dollars，
> 因此為正解。而 (B) 選項包含了 target，(C) 選項包含了 sales，二者皆為問題裡提到的單
> 字，因此一旦漏聽或沒聽懂 (A) 便很容易受騙上當，請務必小心。

💡 奪分祕笈

將英文的數字轉換成中文時總是很容易搞錯。數字的位數在英文裡叫 digit，而阿拉伯數字每
3 digit 會加上逗號分隔。請牢記如下的三位數單位。

a. 第一個逗號	1,000	one thousand	千
b. 第二個逗號	1,000,000	one million	百萬
c. 第三個逗號	1,000,000,000	one billion	十億

✓ 這樣練習最有效

參加 TOEIC 測驗時，數字是無法避免的重要考題。請在平日進行看車廂廣告或英文報紙之財
經版並讀出數值的練習。

寫法	讀法
a. 金額	
1,110,000	one million one hundred and ten thousand
b. 電話號碼	
123-456-7890	one-two-three (pause)^註 four-five-six (pause) seven-eight-night-0

註 在有橫線的位置停頓一下

16. 正確答案：(C) ☆☆

Who's in charge of filling the orders for Jill Metz's book?　是誰負責吉爾‧梅斯的書出貨？

(A) The order has already been filled.　　　　　該筆訂單已出貨了。

(B) The book is selling like hotcakes.　　　　　那本書非常暢銷。

(C) Lenny is.　　　　　　　　　　　　　　　**是萊尼。**

解說 使用 Who 的疑問句 ⊃ Pre 9

只有 (C) 中的 Lenny 針對問題 Who 做出了回應。(A) 答非所問,而 (B) 的sell like hotcakes 是指有「如鬆餅不斷現煎現賣般的熱銷狀況」,亦是牛頭不對馬嘴。

17. 正確答案:(B) ☆☆☆

Has the committee decided which proposal to adopt yet?
委員會已決定要採用哪一份提案了嗎?

(A) No, their proposal won't be accepted. 不,他們的提案不會被採納。

(B) Yes, they like Craig's idea. **是的,他們喜歡克雷格的構想。**

(C) The committee made a proposal. 該委員會提出了一個方案。

解說 Yes-No 疑問句 ⊃ Pre 7

本題為 Yes-No 問句,除了答Yes外,(B) 的 Craig's idea 也回應了 which proposal,故為正確選項。而 (A) 的回答「不,他們的提案不會被採納。」雖然不是完全不可能,但就如 Part 2 一開始的說明提到的,永遠要選擇 best answer。 另外,(C) 的描述完全與題目情況不符,不過由於包含了題目裡也有的單字 committee、proposal 等,所以很容易引人上當,請務必小心。

18. 正確答案:(A) ☆☆ 🎧 27

Shall we schedule the brainstorming session for next Thursday afternoon?
我們把腦力激盪會議安排在下週四下午吧?

(A) Let's hold it in the morning instead. **讓我們改在上午舉行吧。**

(B) Let's take a break. 讓我們休息一下吧。

(C) Let's wait until the storm is over. 讓我們等暴風雨結束吧。

解說 Shall we ... ? / Let's ... ⊃ Pre 18

選項 (A) 的 morning instead 針對原問句的 (Thursday) afternoon 做出回應,故為正確答案。另外要小心的是,問題中的 brainstorming 在 (C) 選項被刻意改成 storm「暴風雨」來混淆視聽,請別上當。

19. 正確答案:(A) ☆☆

I wonder who the black dog in the dog run belongs to.
不知道在狗兒專用活動區裡的那隻黑狗是誰的?

(A) My friend. **我朋友的。**

(B) The park. 公園的。

(C) The dog. 那隻狗的。

20. 正確答案：(B) ☆☆

Jessy fell off the bike and got 10 stitches at the emergency room.

潔西從腳踏車上摔下來，在急診室裡縫了 10 針。

(A) Shall I ask her about the stitches?	我是不是該問問她有關縫線的問題？
(B) How terrible! I hope she gets well soon.	**太可怕了！希望她早日康復。**
(C) I don't like sewing stitches by hand.	我不喜歡用手縫製東西。

解說 陳述與反應 ⊃ Pre 6

stitches 可指「外科上的縫合」或「裁縫上的縫製」。由題目中的 fell off the bike 和 emergency room 等描述來判斷，此處的 stitches 應為第一個意思。只有 (B) How terrible! I hope she get well soon. 適當回應了原句提到的狀況。

Word List

- [ ] run low 所剩不多 (No. 8)
- [ ] experiment [ɪkˋspɛrəmənt] 图 實驗 (No. 10)
- [ ] condominium [ˋkɑndəˏmɪnɪəm] 图 擁有獨立產權的公寓 (No. 14)
- [ ] private home 獨棟私人住宅
- [ ] fill the order 供貨、出貨 (No. 16)
- [ ] brainstorming [ˋbrenˏstɔrmɪŋ] 图 腦力激盪 (No. 18)
- [ ] fall off 從……跌落 (No. 20)
- [ ] emergency room 急診室

- [ ] go on a trip 外出旅遊 (No. 9)
- [ ] cashier [kæˋʃɪr] 图 出納員、收銀員 (No. 13)
- [ ] mansion [ˋmænʃən] （較高級的）大廈
- [ ] cottage [ˋkɑtɪdʒ] 图 鄉間小屋
- [ ] adopt [əˋdɑpt] 動 採用、採納 (No. 17)
- [ ] belong to 屬於……
- [ ] dog run 狗專用的活動區 (No. 19)
- [ ] stitch [stɪtʃ] 图 針腳、（外科的）縫線

Part  Short Conversation 簡短對話題

☆470 分等級 ☆☆600 分等級 ☆☆☆730 分以上

● 21～23 購物 29

Woman: I bought this pretty piece of gemstone, and I'm looking for a chain for it. See, there's a hole here for the chain to go through.

Man: We have chains right over here of various sizes and lengths, 50 dollars and up. Gold or silver?

Woman: Gold. I like the one that says 310 dollars, but it looks like it might be too thick to go through the hole. May I try it on, please?

Man: Certainly. Here you are. And it's just the right size for the hole.

女： 我買了這顆漂亮的寶石,正在找一條合適的鍊子。你看,這兒有個洞可穿鍊子。

男： 我們有各種粗細和長度的鍊子,就在這邊,50 美元起。您喜歡金的還是銀的?

女： 金的。我喜歡那條標價 310 美元的,但是看來似乎有點太粗,可能穿不過這個洞。 我可以試一下嗎?

男： 當然,請試。粗細剛好符合這個洞。

> **Word List**
>
> □ gemstone [ˈdʒɛmˌston] 名 寶石

21. 正確答案:(D) ☆

What kind of store is this?	這是什麼商店?
(A) An electronics store	電器行
(B) A boutique	精品店
(C) A furniture store	家具行
(D) A jewelry store	**珠寶店**

> **解說**
>
> 女子一開始提到的 gemstone 以及後來店員提到的 gold、silver 可知,正確答案為 (D)。

小心陷阱

若不知會話中 gemstone 的意思,便可能被 (B) 給誘惑了,務必多加注意才行。

22. 正確答案：(A) ☆

What does the customer want to do?   客人想做什麼？

(A) To buy a gold chain   **想買金項鍊**

(B) To exchange a sweater that has a hole in it   想更換破了一個洞的毛衣

(C) To return a silver pin   想退還銀製別針

(D) To look at chairs and sofas   想看椅子和沙發

解說

女子在第一句中就提到 ... I'm looking for a chain，因此正解為 (A)。附帶一提，真正以黃金製作的東西用 gold 修飾，如 (A) 中的 gold chain；而不是真金、只是呈金色的事物則用 golden，如 golden hair。

小心陷阱

由女子說了 See, there's a hole here.，因此答題時很有可能會被 (B) 的 a sweater that has a hole in it「破洞的毛衣」給騙了。

23. 正確答案：(C) ☆☆

What is the customer concerned about?   客人擔心的是什麼？

(A) Price   價格

(B) Quality   品質

(C) Size   **粗細**

(D) Brand   品牌

解說

由女子第二次發言時說的 ... it might be too thick to go through the hole. 可知，她擔心的是鍊子的粗細。 (C) 為正解。

小心陷阱

由於會話中男子提到了 50 dollars and up，和女子提到了 310 dollars，因此可能會讓人物以為女子擔心的是價格，所以請小心別誤選 (A)。

● 24 ～ 26 與討論提案有關的對話 ⊃ Pre 24 ～ 26

Man: Linda, we have to present three of our five proposals to Mr. Baines at 4:00 today. Which three do you think he would like the most?

Woman: Well, based on his comments at the meeting last week, I think the only one he wouldn't like is proposal B. He thought the idea was not original enough. And personally, I'm not very happy with proposal D, although I like the other four. D is just too costly. What do you think?

Man: Yeah, I don't think D is very realistic. So we'll take proposals A, C and E to him and see what he says.

男： 琳達，我們今天四點必須向拜恩斯先生提出我們五個提案當中的三個。妳覺得他可能最喜歡哪三個？

女： 嗯，依據他上週在會議裡的評論，我想他會不喜歡的只有提案 B。他覺得那個構想不夠有原創性。而我個人雖然喜歡其他的四個提案，但是對提案 D 不太滿意。D 的成本太高了。你覺得呢？

男： 是啊，我覺得 D 不太實際。那麼我們就給他提案 A、C、E，然後看他怎麼說吧。

24. 正確答案：(B) ☆☆

How many proposals do they have to present to Mr. Baines?

他們必須提出幾個提案給拜恩斯先生？

(A) One 1　　　　　　(B) Three 3　　　　　　(C) Four 4　　　　　　(D) Five 5

> 解說
>
> 根據對話一開始男子所說的 ... we have to present three of our five proposals ...「我們必須提出我們五個提案中的三個……」，可知正確答案為 (B)。(A) 選項是以拜恩斯先生不喜歡 B、女子不喜歡 D 所設計的陷阱。(C)「Four」為女子喜歡的提案之數目。(D)「Five」則為原有提案的數目。

25. 正確答案：(C) ☆☆☆

Which of the proposals are they going to submit?　　他們將送出哪幾個提案？

(A) All of them　　　　　　　　　　　　　　全部

(B) Everyone except proposal D　　　　　　除了提案 D 以外的每一個

(C) Everyone except proposals B and D　　**除了提案 B、D 以外的每一個**

(D) None of them　　　　　　　　　　　　都不送

26. 正確答案：(A) ☆☆

Why don't they like proposal D?	他們為何不喜歡提案 D？
(A) It's too expensive.	**它太貴了。**
(B) It's not original.	它缺乏原創性。
(C) It's not innovative.	它並不創新。
(D) It's too abstractive.	它太抽象。

● 27 ~ 29 時程變更   🎧 30

Man 1: There have been some changes in your schedule, Mr. White. The meeting that was supposed to be held this morning will take place in the conference room at 9:00 tomorrow morning, and the board meeting has been pushed back from tomorrow afternoon until Friday at 10 o'clock.

Man 2: Friday at 10:00? Oh, that's no good. I already have an appointment. I'm supposed to spend the entire day at our new plant. Contact the board room and see if the date can be changed, would you?

Man 1: Of course. Oh, I almost forgot. Since your meeting today has been postponed, I told Mr. Jenkins you could see him now. He's waiting in the lobby.

男 1： 懷特先生，您的行程安排有些更動。原本應於今天早上開的會將改在明天早上 9 點於會議室舉行，而董事會議也從明天下午延後到週五的 10 點。

男 2： 週五 10 點？噢，那不行。我已經有約了。那天我一整天都得待在我們的新工廠才對。麻煩你和董事會室聯繫，看看是否能改期，好嗎？

男 1： 當然沒問題。噢，我差點忘了。因為你今天的會議已經延後，所以我告訴詹金斯先生你現在可以見他。他正在大廳等。

Word List

- [ ] take place 舉行
- [ ] push back 延期
- [ ] board meeting 董事會議
- [ ] be postponed [post`pond] 被延後

27. 正確答案：(C) ☆☆

Where will the meeting that was originally scheduled for today take place?

本來安排在今天的會議將在哪裡舉行？

(A) At 9:00 tomorrow   明天 9 點

(B) At 10:00 tomorrow   明天 10 點

(C) In the conference room   **在會議室**

(D) In Mr. Jenkins' office   在詹金斯先生的辦公室

> **解說**
>
> 第一位說話者（助理）提到的 The meeting ... will take place in the conference room ...「……的會將……於會議室舉行」，可知，正確答案是 (C)。注意，本題問的是 Where，所以與 When 有關的 (A) 和 (B) 皆為誤導的選項，請特別小心。

28. 正確答案：(A) ☆☆

What does Mr. White ask his assistant to do?   懷特先生要他的助理做什麼？

(A) Call the board meeting organizer.   **打電話給董事會議承辦人。**

(B) Call the conference room.   打電話到會議室。

(C) Spend Friday at the conference.   週五去參加會議。

(D) Tell Mr. Jenkins he cannot see him.   告訴詹金斯先生他不能見他。

> **解說**
>
> 由懷特先生對助理說的 contact the board room ...「和董事會室……聯繫」可知，正確答案為 (A)。懷特先生並未要求助理參加星期五的會議，故 (C) 為誤。另外，(D) 是依助理所說的 I told Mr. Jenkins you could see him now.「我告訴詹金斯先生你現在可以見他。」而設計的陷阱，不可誤選。

29. 正確答案：(C) ☆

What is Mr. White expected to do next?   懷特先生接下來應該要做什麼？

(A) Attend a conference.   出席會議。

(B) Go to the new plant.   前往新工廠。

(C) Meet Mr. Jenkins.   **和詹金斯先生見面。**

(D) Tell the board he is on his way.   告訴董事會他現在正要過去。

助理說的 I told Mr. Jenkins you could see him now. 可知，正解為 (C)。因為會議已延期，所以 (A) 是錯的。另，是週五才要去新工廠，所以 (B) 也不對。最後，董事會改在週五，且他無法出席，因此 (D) 亦不正確。

● 30 ~ 32 尋求協助或建議 ⊃ Pre 30 ~ 32

Man: Remember I told you I bought a new condominium about two months ago? It's been completed and the residents can move in starting this weekend. If you don't have any plans, is there any chance you could help me this Saturday?

Woman: Saturday? I'm not sure. I'm waiting to hear from a friend about his schedule. We plan to go scuba diving on Saturday.

Man: Oh, okay. When you find out, could you call me on my cell phone? I've already asked Jim and Akiko, and neither of them can make it.

Woman: Have you asked Takeshi? If he knew you needed help, I'm sure he'd be glad to lend you a hand. There's also the fact that he's much stronger than I am.

男： 還記得我告訴過妳大約兩個月前我買了間新公寓嗎？那棟公寓已經完工，這個週末起住戶就可以搬進去了。如果妳沒其他計畫，本週六有可能幫我忙嗎？

女： 週六？我不確定耶。我正在等一個朋友告所我他的行程。我們計畫週六去潛水。

男： 噢，好吧。等你確定了，可以打我的手機通知我嗎？我已經問了吉姆和明子，他們都不能來。

女： 你問過健志了嗎？我很確定如果他知道你需要幫忙，一定會很樂意伸出援手的。而且事實上他也比我強壯很多。

Word List

□ resident [`rɛzədənt] 图 居民、居住者

---

30. 正確答案：(D) ☆

Why does the man need help?　　　　　　　　這名男子為何需要幫忙？

(A) He wants to learn scuba diving.　　　　　他想學潛水。

(B) He has to drive to the beach.　　　　　　他必須開車到海灘去。

(C) He wants to buy an apartment.　　　　　他想買一間公寓。

(D) He is going to move.　　　　　　　　**他即將要搬家。**

解説

由男子說的 ... the residents can move in starting this weekend. ... help me this Saturday? 「這個週末起住戶就可以搬進去了。……本週六有可能幫我忙嗎？」可知，他是因為要搬家，所以需要人幫忙。正確答案為 (D)。而要去潛水的是女生，所以 (A) 不對；對話中完全沒提到要開車去沙灘的事，所以 (B) 也不對；最後，公寓兩個月前就買了，所以 (C) 當然是錯的。

31. 正確答案：(A) ☆☆

Why can't the woman give an answer immediately? 　　女子為何無法立即給一個答案？

(A) She is not sure about her plans. 　　　　　　**她還不確定她的計畫為何。**

(B) She does not want to cancel her appointment. 　　她不想取消她的約會。

(C) She does not want to help the man. 　　　　　　她不想幫這名男子。

(D) She is still wondering what to do. 　　　　　　她還在想該怎麼做。

解説

由女子說的 I'm waiting to hear from a friend about his schedule.「我在等一個朋友告訴我他的行程」可知，正確答案為 (A)。另外，由於還沒約好當然就沒得取消，所以 (B) 是錯的；她只是還沒確定行程，並沒有說不想幫忙，所以 (C) 也不正確；最後，她並沒有猶豫不決，而是她朋友還沒確認行程，因此 (D) 也不能選。

32. 正確答案：(D) ☆

What does the woman recommend that the man do? 　　這名女子建議這名男子做什麼？

(A) Build up his strength. 　　　　　　　　　　　　鍛鍊體力。

(B) Postpone the moving date. 　　　　　　　　　　延後搬家日期。

(C) Cancel the moving van the man reserved. 　　　取消搬家用貨車的預約。

(D) Talk to Takeshi about having him help. 　　　**和健志商量請他幫忙。**

解説

女子第二次發言時說 Have you asked Takeshi? ... I'm sure he'd be glad to lend you a hand.，所以正確答案為 (D)。而選項 (A)、(B)、(C)，的內容皆未提及。另外，請注意本題問句中 recommend 後的 that 子句裡必須用原形動詞。

● 33 ～ 35 回應抱怨 ⊃ Pre 30 ～ 32，33 ～ 35　　　　　　　　　🔊 31

Woman: Wow, our seats are really far away from the stage. Couldn't you get seats closer to the front?

Man: No. The ticket agent said that we were lucky to get tickets at all. This performance sold out in less than six hours.

Woman: Really? Well, I guess I shouldn't complain. Let's just enjoy the show!

女： 哇，我們的座位離舞台真的好遠。你買不到比較靠近前面的位子嗎？

男： 買不到。票務代理員說我們能買到票已經算幸運的了。這場表演的票不到六小時就賣光了。

女： 真的嗎？嗯，那我想我就不應該抱怨了。讓我們好好欣賞表演吧！

33. 正確答案：(D) ☆

Where does this conversation take place?　　　這段對話發生在何處？

(A) At a basketball game　　　在一場籃球比賽中
(B) On an airplane　　　在飛機上
(C) At a ticket window　　　在售票窗口
(D) In a theater　　　**在劇院裡**

> 解說
>
> 根據女子一開始所說的 ... our seats are really far away from the stage.「我們的座位離舞台真的好遠。」以及最後說的 Let's just enjoy the show!「讓我們好好欣賞表演吧！」可知，正確答案應為 (D)。

34. 正確答案：(A) ☆☆

Why could they not get better seats?　　　他們為何無法取得更好的位子？

(A) The tickets sold out quickly.　　　**票很快就賣完了。**
(B) The performance took six hours.　　　整場表演花了六個小時。
(C) They arrived too late.　　　他們太晚到了。
(D) The ticket agent was too busy.　　　票務代理員太忙了。

> 解說
>
> 由男子生所說的 This performance sold out in less than six hours.「這場表演的票不到 6 小時就賣光了。」可知，正確答案為 (A)。請注意不要誤選包含了 six hours 的 (B)，因為對話中根本沒提到表演多久的問題。

35. 正確答案：(B) ☆

What is the woman going to do?　　　　　　　　這名女子打算怎麼做？

(A) Complain about the seats.　　　　　　　　抱怨座位問題。

(B) Enjoy the performance.　　　　　　　　**盡情欣賞表演。**

(C) Guess why the seats are far from the stage.　猜測座位為何離舞台很遠。

(D) Complain about the performance.　　　　　抱怨該場表演。

解說

這名女子雖然一開始在抱怨，但是經男子解釋後，她最後說了 Let's just enjoy the show!，所以正確答案為 (B)。

Memo:

● **36 ~ 38 宣布**　　　　　　　　　　　　　　　　　　　　　　🎧 33

Questions 36 through 38 refer to the following announcement.

Im glad you could be here today. I know you're all busy, so I'll get right to the point. We've suddenly found ourselves with far more work than we are accustomed to handling, so some rearrangement of the schedule and project teams is necessary. The bridge design project is our number-one priority, and it is the only job with no flexibility regarding the schedule. We must have preliminary designs submitted no later than three weeks from today. So, for now, five members of the highway rest-stop renovation project must be moved over to the bridge design project. I'll keep all department heads informed of any other changes. Thank you for your time.

第 36 ~ 38 題與以下宣布有關。
我很高興各位今天能來到這兒。我知道你們都很忙，因此我將直接切入重點。我們突然發現我們的工作量已大幅超出我們所習慣應付的分量，因此有必要重新調整一下時程安排與專案團隊的編制。橋梁設計專案是我們第一優先的案子，也是在時程安排上唯一沒有彈性的工作項目。我們必須在從今天起的三週內提交初步設計。所以現在五位原屬高速公路休息站更新專案的成員們必須轉調至橋梁設計專案。如果有任何其他變更，我將隨時通知各部門主管。感謝各位撥冗參與。

Word List

☐ be accustomed to ... 習慣於......　　☐ flexibility [ˌflɛksə`bɪlətɪ] 图 彈性、靈活性
☐ preliminary [prɪ`lɪməˌnɛrɪ] 彨 初步的　☐ submit [səb`mɪt] 働 提交

---

36. 正確答案：(B) ☆☆

What problem is the speaker addressing?　　說話者提出的是什麼問題？

(A) One of the projects was canceled.　　　專案之一被取消了。

(B) There is more work than they can handle.　**工作量超出了他們所能應付的分量。**

(C) Some members of the team are quitting.　有些團隊成員要辭職。

(D) The highway rest-stop project has to be delayed.　高速公路休息站的案子必須延後。

解說

由宣布第三句提到的 ... far more work than we are accustomed to handling ... 可知，正確答案為 (B)。

37. 正確答案：(B) ☆☆☆

What is the company's most important project?　　該公司最重要的專案是哪個？

(A) The highway rest-stop　　　　　　　　　　高速公路休息站
(B) The bridge design　　　　　　　　　　　**橋梁設計**
(C) Rearrangement of personnel　　　　　　　人力的重新配置
(D) Rearrangement of the work schedule　　　工作時程的重新安排

> 解說
>
> 由第四句提到的 The bridge design project is our number one priority ... 可知正解為 (B)。

38. 正確答案：(D) ☆

How many members of the highway rest stop　　高速公路休息站專案有幾位成員將轉調？
project will be transferred?

(A) None 0 位　　　　(B) One 1 位　　　　(C) Three 3 位　　　　**(D) Five 5 位**

> 解說
>
> 由第六句提到的 ... five members of the highway rest-stop renovation project must be moved over to the ... 這句可知，正解為 (D)。

● 39 ~ 41 指示說明

Questions 39 through 41 refer to the following instructions.

Today's final examination will determine whether you pass or fail the course. Part one is on recognizing road signs, and you'll have twenty minutes to complete it. Part two is about potentially dangerous situations you have experienced. You will have forty minutes to finish this short-essay exercise. The last portion of the exam covers minor auto maintenance, basic first aid, automatic and manual transmissions, and essential rules of the road. You will have one hour and fifteen minutes to finish. Do not begin a new section until instructed to do so by your proctor. When you've finished the exam, put your answer sheets and test booklets in the envelope provided and hand them to the proctor as you leave the room. Now you may begin.

第 39 ~ 41 題與以下的指示說明有關。
今天的期末測驗將決定各位是否通過本課程。第一部分考的是辨識道路標誌，你們有 20 分鐘可作答。第二部分與各位曾經歷過的潛在危險狀況有關。你們將有 40 分鐘時間來完成這

段短文作答。本測驗的最後一部分則包括簡易車輛維修、基本的急救處理、自動及手動換檔，以及基本道路規則等。各位將有 1 小時又 15 分鐘來完成這部分。在監考人員下指示前，請勿擅自開始下一部分的測驗。在完成整個測驗後，請將答案卷和考題本放進我們提供的信封袋，並於離場時交給監考人員。現在請開始作答。

Word List

☐ proctor [`prɑktə] 名 監考人員

39. 正確答案：(D) ☆☆

Where is this talk being given?	這段話的地點是何處？
(A) At a high school	一所高中
(B) At a medical clinic	一家診所
(C) At a police academy	警察學校
(D) At a driving school	**駕訓班**

解說

談話中提到的 recognizing road signs、auto maintenance、automatic and manual transmissions 等都指向正確答案 (D)。不過由於提到了 pass or fail the course 很容易讓人誤以為答案是 (A)，請特別留意。

💡 奪分祕笈：與指示說明有關的表達方式

指示說明類文章句型較特別，多半採命令句或類似 You will do ... 等句型。

a. 測驗指示
   You will have 20 minutes to complete the test.
   你們有 20 分鐘可完成此測驗。

b. 機器的使用方法
   Wait until all the papers are spitted out of the printer.
   等所有紙張都從印表機吐出為止。

c. 藥品的服用方式
   Take 1 tablet after every meal. 每餐飯後吃一錠。

d. 料理方法
   Bake the meat in the oven for 40 minutes.
   將肉以烤箱烤 40 分鐘。

e. 路線說明
   Go straight for seven blocks, and you'll see the Bic Car Dealer on your left.
   往前直行七個街區，你就會在左手邊看見比克汽車經銷店。

40. 正確答案：(C) ☆☆

How much time do they have to complete the essay?　　　他們有多少時間來完成短文？

(A) Two hours and fifteen minutes　　　　　2 小時又 15 分鐘

(B) One hour and fifteen minutes　　　　　1 小時又 15 分鐘

(C) Forty minutes　　　　　　　　　　**40 分鐘**

(D) Twenty minutes　　　　　　　　　　20 分鐘

> **解說**
>
> 指示的第四句明確提到 You will have forty minutes to finish this short-essay exercise，所以正確答案為 (C)。而 (A) 是指整個測驗的時間，(B) 做為最後一部分的時間，(D) 則是做第一部分的時間。

41. 正確答案：(A) ☆☆☆

Which of these areas is covered in part three of the test?

此測驗的第 3 部分包含以下哪個領域？

(A) Automobile maintenance　　　　　**車輛維修**

(B) Automobile designs　　　　　　　　車輛設計

(C) Buying a used car　　　　　　　　中古車的購買

(D) Types of cars　　　　　　　　　　各類車種

> **解說**
>
> 由第五句 The last portion ... covers minor auto maintenance、basic first aid、automatic and manual transmissions, and essential rules of the road. 可知，正確答案為 (A)。而 (B)、(C)、(D) 的內容皆未包括在內。

● 42 ~ 44 廣告宣傳　　　　　　　　　🔊 34

Questions 42 through 44 refer to the following advertisement.

Don't you just love to sit down with a cup of coffee and check your e-mail during the lunch break or after work? At CoffeeNet Café, you can log on for up to 1 hour on our brand-new laptops just by buying a cup of coffee! And if you want to bring your own laptop from home, you can stay on the Internet for as long as you want—all for $2.25—the price of just a cup of coffee! CoffeeNet Café. We're located on University Avenue between First National Bank and Clifford's Bicycle Shop. See you soon at CoffeeNet Café!

第 42 ~ 44 題與以下廣告有關。

難道您不喜歡在午休時間或下班後，坐下來喝杯咖啡並檢查一下您的電子郵件嗎？在咖啡網咖啡廳，只要買 1 杯咖啡，您就可用我們的全新筆記型電腦上網達 1 小時之久！而如果你想從家裡帶自己的筆記型電腦來，那麼您想上網多久就上多久──只需 2.25 美元──不過是 1 杯咖啡的價格！咖啡網咖啡廳。我們位在大學路上，第一國家銀行與克利福自行車店之間。咖啡網咖啡廳期待您的光臨！

Word List

☐ log in / on the Internet 登入／連上網路

---

42. 正確答案：(D) ☆☆

Which of the following can you do at CoffeeNet Café?
你可以在咖啡網咖啡廳做以下哪件事？

(A) Have as much coffee as you want.	要喝多少咖啡就喝多少。
(B) Get a free cup of coffee if you bring your own laptop.	如果你帶自己的筆記型電腦來，就能免費獲得 1 杯咖啡。
(C) Log on to the Internet while your laptop is being repaired.	在你的筆記型電腦送修的同時登入網路。
(D) Buy a cup of coffee and check your e-mail.	**買杯咖啡並檢查你的電子郵件。**

解說

第一句裡提到的 sit down with a cup of coffee and check your e-mail 就指向正確答案 (D)。其他的 (A)、(B)、(C) 皆為錯誤，廣告中並未提及這些資訊。

小心陷阱

請注意，廣告的第二句和第三句都提到 a cup of coffee，但全文皆未提及 (A) 的 as much coffee 或 (B) 的 free cup of coffee。

43. 正確答案：(B) ☆

How much is a cup of coffee at CoffeeNet Café?	在咖啡網咖啡廳一杯咖啡賣多少錢？

(A) $2.00	2 美元	**(B) $2.25**	**2 美元 25 分**
(C) $3.00	3 美元	(D) $3.25	3 美元 25 分

解說

由第三句裡提到的 ... all for $2.25 ── the price of just a cup of coffee! 可知，(B) 2 美元 25 分為正確答案。

小心陷阱

由於有多個類似數字並列，很容易令人困惑，因此一定要先瀏覽過題目再聽本文。若採相反順序進行，就不易答對。

44. 正確答案：(B) ☆☆

Where is CoffeeNet Café located?　　　　咖啡網咖啡廳位於何處？

(A) Between the university and the bank　　大學和銀行之間

(B) Next to a bicycle shop　　　　**自行車店旁**

(C) Across from a bank　　　　銀行對面

(D) On the university campus　　　　在大學校園內

解說

由第五句 We're ... between First National Bank and Clifford's Bicycle Shop. 可知，(B) 為最正確的敘述。

小心陷阱

(A) 與 (D) 選項裡都出現了 university 這個字，但在這則廣告中是路名，請小心別上當。另外，(A) 與 (C) 都提到 bank，但都為錯誤敘述，不可誤選。

● 45 ～ 47 新聞

Questions 45 through 47 refer to the following news item.

Leading off the news tonight is the crash of a 747 bound for Washington's Dulles Airport. The aircraft reportedly went down in the sea approximately 200 miles off the coast. Rescue operations have commenced, but high winds and rough seas are hindering the rescue efforts. The exact cause of the crash is unknown. There are unconfirmed reports, however, of a witness in Maryland who happened to see an object traveling at high speed on a downward angle through his telescope. According to the witness, the object appeared to be on fire. The rescue team, while attempting to find and help anyone who may have survived the impact, is also trying to locate the flight recorder in the hope that it will give some information on what actually happened.

第 45 ~ 47 題與以下的新聞報導有關。

今晚的頭條新聞是一架飛往華盛頓杜勒斯國際機場的波音 747 墜毀事件。據報導，這架飛機墜落在距離海岸約 200 英里的海上。救援行動已經展開，但是強風與大浪阻礙了救援行動。確切的墜機原因仍不明。然而有未經證實的報告指出，馬里蘭州有位目擊者恰巧透過他的望遠鏡看見有個高速下墜的物體。據目擊者指出，該物體看起來是著火了。救難小組一方面在努力尋找並救出此次墜機中任何可能的生還者，一方面也試圖找到飛航記錄器，希望該記錄器能提供一些資訊以了解實際上到底發生了什麼事。

Word List

- crash [kræʃ] 名 墜毀
- witness [ˋwɪtnɪs] 名 目擊者
- hinder [ˋhɪndə] 動 妨礙

45. 正確答案：(D) ☆☆

Where did the plane go down? 這架飛機墜落於何處？

(A) At Dulles Airport in Washington 華盛頓的杜勒斯國際機場
(B) In Maryland 在馬里蘭州
(C) In the air 在空中
(D) In the sea **在海上**

> **解說**
>
> 報導第二句提到 The aircraft reportedly went down in the sea ...，所以正確答案為 (D)。而 (A) 為該飛機之目的地，(B) 則是目擊者所在位置，不可誤選。

46. 正確答案：(A) ☆☆

Why are the rescue workers having difficulty? 救難人員在救援時為何會有困難？

(A) The sea is rough and stormy. **海上風浪很大。**
(B) The cause of the crash is not known. 墜機原因不明。
(C) The reports of a witness are unconfirmed. 目擊者的報告還未經確認。
(D) The plane is on fire. 飛機著火了。

> **解說**
>
> 由報導中第三句 ... high winds and rough seas are hindering the rescue efforts. 可知，正確答案為 (A)。注意，原文中 high winds and rough sea 改以 rough and stormy 來描述。

47. 正確答案：(C) ☆☆

What is the rescue team looking for?　　　　救難小組在找什麼？

(A) Witness of the accident　　　　　　　　事故的目擊者

(B) Airplane crew of the crashed plane　　　墜毀飛機上的機組人員

(C) Survivers and the flight recorder　　　生還者與飛航記錄器

(D) A telescope　　　　　　　　　　　　　望遠鏡

解說

由最後一句 The rescue team, while attempting to find ... anyone who may have survived, is also trying to locate the flight recorder. 可知，正確答案為 (C)。而因 witness 已出面陳述他用望遠鏡看到的事故狀況，所以 (A) 不是正確答案。另，(B) 提到 crashed plane，(D) 提到 telescope，目的就在於誘導，千萬不可誤選。

● 48 ~ 50 發言　　　　　　　　　　　　　🎧 35

Questions 48 through 50 refer to the following talk.

All right, everyone, may I have your attention for a moment? Okay, first comes the 100-meter dash, so those runners should go to the track now and get into position. After that will be the 5,000-meter run. About five minutes after that event begins, the 200-meter dash will start. That will be followed by the 200-meter hurdles, the 10,000-meter run, and the four-by 100-meter relay race. Runners, please remember the order and be in position a few minutes before your event begins. The marathon will be held tomorrow, so the four-by 100-meter relay will be the last event today. That's it! Good luck, everyone!

第 48 ~ 50 題與以下的發言內容有關。

好了，各位，可以請大家注意聽我說一下話嗎？好，首先要進行的是 100 公尺短跑，所以參加該項目的跑者現在請至跑道就位。接著是 5,000 公尺長跑。而在該項目開始後約 5 分鐘，200 公尺賽跑便會開始。再來是 200 公尺跨欄、10,000 公尺長跑，以及 4×100 公尺的接力賽。跑者們，請記得比賽順序，並於參加項目開始前的幾分鐘就定位。馬拉松將在明天舉行，因此 4×100 公尺接力賽會是今天的最後一項比賽。就這樣了！祝各位幸運！

48. 正確答案：(B) ☆☆

What is taking place today?　　　　　　　今天在舉辦的是什麼活動？

(A) A race　　　　賽跑　　　　　　　　　**(B) A track meet　　　　田徑比賽**

(C) A horse race　賽馬　　　　　　　　　(D) The 5,000-meter run　5,000 公尺賽跑

因為舉辦的不只是賽跑一項，還會進行跨欄等其他多種競賽，所以 (B) 為正確答案。注意，track meet 指「田徑比賽」，也可說成 track and field。

49. 正確答案：(A) ☆☆

What event follows the 100-meter dash?	排在 100 公尺短跑之後的是何種項目？

(A) The 5,000-meter run　　　　　　　　**5,000 公尺長跑**
(B) The 200-meter hurdles　　　　　　　　200 公尺跨欄
(C) The 10,000-meter run　　　　　　　　10,000 公尺長跑
(D) The four-by 100-meter relay race　　　4 x 100 公尺的接力賽

第二句提到首先進行的是 100 公尺短跑，而第三句則說 After that will be the 5,000-meter run.，所以正確答案為 (A)。

50. 正確答案：(D) ☆

Who is this talk being addressed to?	這段發言是對誰說的？

(A) The audience　　　　　　　　　　　　觀眾
(B) The organizer of the track meet　　　田徑比賽的主辦者
(C) Event staff members　　　　　　　　各比賽項目的工作人員
(D) The runners participating in the events　**參加各比賽項目的跑者**

由說話者提到的 Runners, please remember ...，以及最後一句 Good luck, everyone! 可知，答案為 (D)。而 (A)、(B)、(C) 選項所指的人也可能在聽這段話，但是這些話並不是針對他們說的。

☆470 分等級 ☆☆600 分等級 ☆☆☆730 分以上

51. 正確答案：(C) ☆☆☆

As far as we know, Comtrex Corporation does not have a local distributor for its products in Malaysia.

就我們所知，康妥勒斯公司的產品在馬來西亞當地並無經銷商。

> **解說** as ... as ⊃ Pre 58
>
> As far as we know 指 「據我們所知」，(C) 為正確選項。(A) As long as 是「只要……」的意思，(B) As soon as 是「一……就……」的意思，(D) As much as 則為「與……一樣多」的意思，皆與題意不符。

52. 正確答案：(A) ☆☆

If the results of the laboratory tests are satisfactory, the new drug is likely to win government approval.

如果實驗室的測試結果令人滿意，該新藥很可能會獲得政府核准。

> **解說** 詞性 ⊃ Pre 51
>
> 依前後文意，這題須選表「令人滿意」之意的形容詞，(A) 為正解。而 (B) 為名詞，(C) 為動詞，皆不可選。另外 (D) 為形容詞，意思是「（感到）滿意的」，主詞必須是「人」，故亦為錯誤。

53. 正確答案：(A) ☆☆

Use of the gym facilities during the weekend will be 30 percent up the normal rates.

週末期間健身房設備的使用率會比平常高 30%。

> **解說** 介系詞 ⊃ Pre 62
>
> 依句意，本題應選 (A) up 來表達比平常使用率「高」30%。而 (B) 的 than 若改成 higher than 的話就算是正確答案。

54. 正確答案：(D) ☆☆☆

The goods we ordered on November 22 have not yet arrived, and we are concerned that they may have gotten lost in the mail.

我們在 11 月 22 日訂購的商品還沒送到，而我們擔心這些商品可能已經寄丟了。

> **解說** 助動詞、時態 ⊃ Pre 56
>
> (B) may get lost 和 (C) might get lost 是「可能會弄丟」的意思，與句意不符。欲表達「可能已經」之意時，要用 may 或 might 加現在完成式。故本題應選 (D)。

Strategies

Pre Test

Half Test 1

Half Test 2

Full Test

55. 正確答案：(C) ☆☆

After <u>remaining</u> low for two weeks, stock prices are beginning to show signs of recovery.

在持續兩週的低迷之後，股價開始出現復甦跡象。

> **解說** 詞性 ➲ **Pre 51**
>
> **After** 為介系詞，其後須接名詞或名詞片語，只有動名詞形式的 (C) **remaining** 符合此條件。

56. 正確答案：(A) ☆☆

As head of the project team, Julia was responsible for <u>setting</u> standards for the other members.

身為專案小組的組長，茱莉亞須負責替其他成員訂定標準。

> **解說** 合適的片語（常用片語）➲ **Pre 52**
>
> **set standards for ...** 是「為……訂定標準」之意。（注意，與上題相同，由於 **for** 為介系詞，故將 **set** 改成動名詞形式。）

57. 正確答案：(B) ☆☆☆

Having <u>attended</u> the cram session for eight straight hours, the staff felt completely exhausted.

在連續開了八小時會議之後，員工們都筋疲力盡了。

> **解說** 詞性、語法（分詞構句）
>
> 本句是將完成式 have + attended 改成分詞形式的 having attended ...，做為副詞來修飾接下來的主要子句。這種語法稱之為分詞構句。注意，原 have attended 的主詞亦為 the staff，為避免重複，故應予省略。

58. 正確答案：(A) ☆☆

Diabetes used to be a disease that affected mainly adults, but nowadays it <u>is becoming</u> more and more common among children.

糖尿病過去通常是主要影響成年人的一種疾病，但是現在也越來越常發生於兒童身上。

> **解說** 詞性（現在進行式）➲ **Pre 51**
>
> 由於句中所包含的 more and more 是在描述一種「越來越多」的變化狀況，所以用現在進行式較適當。（就算不認識本題中的 diabetes「糖尿病」這個字，像這類文法問題，通常只要觀察空格前後部分就能答得出來。）

59. 正確答案：(D) ☆☆☆

The congressman complained to the magazine, asking it to <u>retract</u> a statement it published about his involvement with criminals.

那個國會議員向該雜誌投訴，要求他們收回一篇雜誌上刊登關於他與罪犯有牽連的陳述。

> **解說** 形式類似的單字（字首 re-）▶ Pre 52
>
> 依前後文意，本題應選擇表示「撤回、收回」之意的 (D) retract。(A) reject 有「拒絕、駁回之意」，(B) refuse 指「拒絕」，而 (C) recall 則為「回憶、召回」的意思。（本題四個選項都用了表示 back 的字首 re-。）

60. 正確答案：(B) ☆☆

I'd like to speak to the person <u>in charge of</u> customer relations for your company.

我想和貴公司負責客戶關係的人談談。

> **解說** 常用片語 ➲ Pre 52
>
> 依句意，本題應選有「負責……、主管……」之意的選項，(B) in charge of 為正確答案。注意，若要用 responsible 表達同樣意義時，必須使用「responsible for + 動名詞或名詞」的形式，所以 (C) responsible to 和 (D) responsible in 都非正確答案。

61. 正確答案：(D) ☆☆

Building costs in this area are at an all-time high, but rental prices have remained <u>relatively</u> steady.

此區的建築成本達到歷史新高，但是租賃價格仍維持相對穩定。

> **解說** 詞性、詞類 ➲ Pre 51
>
> steady 為形容詞，所以修飾它的字一定要是副詞，故選 (D) relatively「相對地」。

62. 正確答案：(A) ☆☆

Our retailers are reluctant to lower their prices, but I think we should try to <u>convince</u> them that this is actually a good idea.

我們的零售商都不願意降價，但是我認為我們應該要努力說服他們，讓他們相信這其實是個好主意。

> **Word List**
>
> ☐ reluctant [rɪˋlʌktənt] 形 不願意的

形式類似的單字（字首 con-） ➲ Pre 52

(A) convince 是「說服、使相信」的意思。(B) convict 與 (A) 看起來很像，但意義完全不同，它是「判決……有罪」之意。另外 (C) 的 conform 為「使遵照」之意，(D) 的 contact 則是「與……聯絡」的意思。（本題四個選項都用了表示 together 的字首 con-。）

63. 正確答案：(C) ☆☆

No matter <u>how</u> hard he tried, Brian could not seem to achieve his monthly sales targets.

不論多麼努力，布萊恩似乎都無法達成他的月銷售目標。

no matter ... ➲ Pre 60

「no matter how + 形容詞／副詞 + S + V」之句型可表達「不論怎麼……」這樣的強調意義。本題正確答案為 (C)。注意，本句也可說成 However hard he tried ...。

64. 正確答案：(B) ☆☆

The air conditioner needs <u>repairing</u> because it seems unable to maintain a constant temperature.

空調需要修理了，因為它似乎無法維持恆溫。

詞性 ➲ Pre 51

need + 動名詞就是「需要……了」的意思。本題正確答案為 (B)。注意，本句的 need 也可用 want 來替換。另外，the air conditioner needs to be repaired 這種講法容易給人太正式、艱澀的印象，所以一般並不常用。

65. 正確答案：(C) ☆☆

There is so little work between Christmas and New Year's that we <u>may</u> as well close the office for the entire period.

聖誕節和新年之間幾乎沒有工作要做，所以我們不妨整段期間都暫停營業。

助動詞 ➲ Pre 56

may as well ... 是「不妨……」之意，用來表達對情況的判斷。另外，也可使用 might as well ...，但語氣較為客氣、緩和一些。

66. 正確答案：(C) ☆☆

Consumer prices <u>have risen</u> for the first time in more than two years.

消費者物價指數在兩年多以來首度升高。

解說 時態、不及物動詞 ▶ 及物動詞 ────

raise 為及物動詞「提高」之意，rise 則為不及物動詞「上升」之意，兩者意義不同，請特別注意。另，依本句前後文意，應選現在完成式。(C) 為正確答案。

67. 正確答案：(C) ☆☆☆

Only when sales figures get worse <u>will the head office begin</u> to act.
只有在銷售數字惡化時，總公司才會開始採取行動。

解說 詞序（強調語法）+ 時態 ────

以 Only when 起頭的強調句型，主要句子必須使用倒裝形式。原句直述形式為：
The head office will begin to act only when sales figures get worse.

68. 正確答案：(A) ☆☆

A new state law prohibits people from using hand-held electronic communication devices <u>while</u> driving a car.
新的州法禁止人們在開車時使用手持的電子通訊裝置。

解說 while / during 的區別 ⊃ Pre 61 ────

while 為連接詞，其後可接子句或將主詞省略的分詞構句。(A) 為正確答案。另，注意不可選介系詞 (B) during，因為其後只能接名詞。（※其他介系詞 in, on ... 可加分詞構句）

69. 正確答案：(B) ☆☆☆

One great <u>incentive</u> for companies to set up in the new business zone is a lower tax rate.
將公司設立在該新商業區的一大誘因就是稅率較低。

解說 詞彙（意義近似） ⊃ Pre 52 ────

依本句文意，正確答案應為 (B) incentive 「誘因、激勵」。(A) increase 指「增加」，(C) reward 指「獎勵、報答」，(D) feature 則指「特徵」，在意義上都與本句不合。

70. 正確答案：(C) ☆☆

There are now high-speed plants that are <u>capable of</u> filling 300 bottles of juice per minute.
現在有每分鐘可填充 300 瓶果汁的高速工廠。

解說 常用片語 ────

be capable of 與 be able to 意思相仿，皆指「有能力……」，但 be capable of 可以人或物為主詞，而 be able to 則通常只以人為主詞，而且其後必須接著動詞原形。(B) possible to 「可能……」與 (D) suitable for 「適合……」則與句意不合。

Strategies / Pre Test / Half Test 1 / Half Test 2 / Full Test

● 71 ~ 73 文章（article）

第 71 ~ 73 題與以下的文章有關。

在英國享受美食

(71.) 就美食而言，英國已不再是世界的「窮親戚」[註1]了。平淡的調味、煮過頭的蔬菜和淡而無味的咖啡都已成歷史。尤其是倫敦，現已擁有許多世界最佳的餐廳，提供不少比任何其他地方都更創新又具創意的菜色。

不過，在倫敦的一流餐廳用餐可不便宜。如果你想用較低的預算好好吃上一餐，那麼英國移民社區的食物就很值得你探訪。例如印度咖哩在這二十年來變得非常受歡迎，使它幾乎成了英國人最愛的料理。大部分城鎮都有不錯的印度餐廳和中菜館，大城市裡還會有中東及加勒比海料理，而且價格都相當合理 (72.)。

在中高價格方面，則有很多的義大利與法國餐廳可選擇。西班牙小酒館[註2]現在如雨後春筍般在更時尚的都會區出現，而 (73.) 儘管價格仍高，如今也可以看到越來越多的日本料理店。

註1 poor relation「（討人厭的）窮親戚」：一種譬喻式的說法。在從前英國菜被大家公認為難吃料理的時代，此句被用來表示「在美食界被嫌棄」之意。

註2 tapas bar「小酒館」：西班牙式的酒吧。店面向著馬路呈開放狀，大家都可輕鬆入內吃喝，而店家以盤子盛裝各式各樣的小菜（tapas），讓客人能以小分量點購任何喜歡的菜色。

71. 正確答案：(B) ☆☆

> **解說** 固定說法 ➜ Pre 75
>
> as far as ... is concerned「就……而言」是一種固定句型。 (B) concerned 為正解。

72. 正確答案：(D) ☆☆

> **解說** 意思相近的單字 ➜ Pre 72
>
> 依前後文，本題應選 (D) reasonable「合理的、不貴的」作為形容詞，修飾其後的 prices。而若要用 (A)「平均的」，不應加 very，至於 (B) rational「理性的」和 (C) common「普通的」都不適用於此。

73. 正確答案：(C) ☆☆

> **解說** 連接詞 ➜ Pre 73
>
> (C) though 是表示「儘管……」之意的連接詞，用來引導表「讓步」的子句，文法與意思皆正確。(A) 的 even「甚至」為副詞，(B) despite。雖然意思與 though 相仿，但為介系詞，而 (D) however「然而」亦為副詞。

● 74 ~ 76 電子郵件 ⊃ Pre 88 ~ 90

第 74 ~ 76 題與以下的電子郵件有關。

2008 年 9 月 30 日
收件人：fhall@hallbrothers.com
寄件人：janice@treetop.com
主旨：屋頂修護

親愛的霍爾先生，

很遺憾必須通知你，我家屋頂又漏水了。原本 7 月份經過你修理之後已經沒問題了，但是你也知道，週六我們下了一場暴雨。(74.) 結果，水又開始漏進來了。不過，我很確定我的房東會負擔所有的修理費。這棟房子是他的，所以修理的責任當然也歸屬於他。但是他說，要先有修理工程的估價他才能下決定。因此如果你能 (75.) 儘快來看一下並讓我知道需要多少修理費，我將會非常感激。狀況沒有先前那麼糟，但是時間拖越久情況就會 (76.) 越惡化。請告訴我你何時能來看一下。

順頌商祺

珍妮絲‧史提波頓

---

74. 正確答案：(D) ☆

解說

因前一句 ... we had a very heavy rainstorm on Saturday. 而導致下一句 ... water has started coming in again.，所以選 (D)作為起承轉合最合理。(A) 是「另一方面」，(B) 是「附帶一提」，(C) 則是「儘管如此」之意，皆不符前後文意。

75. 正確答案：(C) ☆☆

解說

在 I would therefore be very grateful if you could take a look ... 之後接表示「儘快」之意的片語 as soon as possible 最為合理，故本題選 (C)。(A) 是「只要……」，(B) 是「與……相同」，(D) 則是「與……同樣多」之意。

76. 正確答案：(A) ☆☆

解說

the + 比較級 + 主詞 + 動詞，the + 比較級 + 主詞 + 動詞為雙重比較結構。用來表示「越……，就越……」，而依句意本題應選 (A) worse 而非 (C) better。

Memo:

Part 7 Reading Comprehension 文章理解題

☆470 分等級 ☆☆600 分等級 ☆☆☆730 分以上

● 77 ~ 78 通知（notice）

第 77 ~ 78 題與以下通知有關。

巴黎小酒館停業裝修通知

巴黎小酒館的全體員工要感謝所有顧客自我們開幕以來，在過去 5 年間的持續支持。事實上，也正因為各位的大力支持，使得我們的空間不再足夠容納所有人！為了確保您不必再忍受長時間的等待與窄小的餐桌，我們終於決定將餐廳擴大。真的非常抱歉，我們將在 8 月 4 日週一起至 8 月 17 日週日止的改裝期間停業兩週。我們不僅將建造一個新的、可容納 30 名顧客的戶外用餐露台，還將設置擁有最先進設備的全新廚房。而在改裝餐廳的同時，我們也將重新設計菜單。您最愛的經典好菜都將保留，但是我們新的得獎主廚馬賽爾‧羅素將會加入一些美味新作。很抱歉造成各位的不便，但是我們確信我們的餐廳將變得更好。

Word List

□ ensure [ɪn`ʃʊr] 動 保證、擔保　　□ install [ɪn`stɔl] 動 安裝、設置

---

77. 正確答案：(C) ☆

What is happening to the restaurant?　　這家餐廳發生了什麼事？

(A) It is moving to another location to improve its business.　　它正搬往他處好讓生意更好。

(B) It is reducing the number of employees.　　它正在裁減員工人數。

(C) It is expanding the restaurant space to accommodate more customers.　　**它正在擴充餐廳空間以容納更多顧客。**

(D) It is replacing its current menu with a completely new one.　　它正以全新菜單取代目前的菜單。

解說

由第二句的 ... we no longer have enough room for everyone! 與第三句後半的 ... we have finally decided to expand the restaurant. 可知，正確答案為 (C)。文中並無與裁減人員有關的描述，甚至從第七句的 our new awardwinning chef, Marcel Roussel 看來反而還雇用了新的主廚，所以 (B) 是錯的。另外，第七句提到 All your old favorites will still be available ...，表示菜單並非全部換新，因此 (D) 也是錯的。至於 (A) 則完全為無中生有。

78. 正確答案：(B) ☆☆ ⊃ Pre 95

The word "state-of-the-art" in line 8 is closest in meaning to

第 8 行中的 state-of-the-art 這個字的意義最相近

(A) down-to-earth　　　實際的　　　　　　　　　**(B) up-to-date**　　　**最新的**

(C) spacious　　　　　　寬敞的　　　　　　　　　(D) decorative　　　　裝飾性的

> **解說**
>
> state-of-the-art 是「最先進的」之意，所以正確答案為 (B)。其它選項的意思皆不符。

● 79 ~ 82 注意事項（notice）

第 79 ~ 82 題與以下的注意事項有關。

工作場所的安全

所有作業都必須詳加規畫以避免意外發生。請遵守以下規範：

(a) 所有員工都應向主管報告危險狀況或行為。如果主管沒有立即採取改善措施，員工就必須與風險管理部門聯繫。

(b) 工作區域必須盡可能隨時保持清潔整齊。

(c) 任何時候都必須穿著合適的服裝、帽子與鞋子。

(d) 所有員工都應參加一次由其主管主持的安全講習。

(e) 任何受了酒精或藥物（也包含醫師處方藥）影響的人，都不可進入工作區域。

(f) 員工應確保所有保護裝置都已正確配置並調整妥當。

(g) 舉起重物時，要利用腳部的大肌肉而非背部較小的肌肉。

(h) 不可把東西丟在地上。所有廢棄物都應妥善並謹慎地處理。

Word List

☐ corrective action [kəˈrɛktɪv ˈækʃən] 改善措施
☐ tidy [ˈtaɪdɪ] 形 整齊的
☐ prescription drug [prɪˈskrɪpʃən drʌg] 醫師處方藥
☐ protective device [prəˈtɛktɪv dɪˈvaɪs] 保護裝置
☐ dispose of [dɪˈspoz] 處理、丟棄（不需要的東西）

79. 正確答案：(B) ☆☆

What must employees do first if they find themselves in dangerous conditions?

如果員工發現自己身處危險狀況下，他們必須先做什麼？

(A) Contact the Risk Management Department.　　與風險管理部門聯繫。

(B) Inform their supervisor.　　**通知他們的主管。**

(C) Take corrective action.　　採取改善行動。

(D) Attend a safety meeting.　　參加安全講習。

解說

由項目 (a) 提到的 All employees must report unsafe conditions ... to their supervisors 可知，正確答案為 (A)。請注意，原文中的 unsafe conditions 在此被換成了同義的 dangerous conditions。

80. 正確答案：(B) ☆☆

In what instance should workers get in touch with the Risk Management Department?
員工在什麼情況下應聯繫風險管理部門？

(A) When directed by their supervisor to do so　　當其主管指示要這麼做時

(B) When the supervisor does not take rapid　　**當其主管並未採取迅速的改善措施時**
  corrective action

(C) When unsafe conditions are discovered　　發現不安全的狀況時

(D) When there is a safety meeting　　舉辦安全講習時

解說

由項目 (a) 的第二句 If your supervisor does not take a corrective action immediately, employees mus t contact the Risk Management Department. 可知，本題應選 (B)。注意，原文中的 contact 在此用同樣的 get in touch with 替換。

81. 正確答案：(A) ☆

How often do workers have to participate in safety meetings?
工作人員必須多常參加安全講習？

(A) At least once　　**至少一次**

(B) Whenever they think it is necessary　　只要覺得有需要時就參加

(C) Whenever a meeting is held　　只要有舉辦講習時就參加

(D) If the Risk Management Department tells them to 如果風險管理部門要求就參加

解說

項目 (d) 提到 All employees are expected to attend one safety meeting ...，因此 (A)「至少一次」為正確答案。

82. 正確答案：(C) ☆☆

What kind of workers are NOT prohibited from entering the workplace?

哪種工作人員不被禁止進入工作場所？

(A) Those who have drunk alcohol　　　　　　喝了酒的工作人員

(B) Those not wearing the correct clothing　　沒穿著正確服裝的工作人員

(C) Those who cannot drive　　　　　　　　**不會開車的工作人員**

(D) Those who have taken strong medication　吃了強效藥物的工作人員

> 解説
>
> 只要將包含 NOT 的疑問句先改成肯定句，便能輕易理解其意思。此題問的是「不被禁止」的人，亦即「可以進入工作場所」的人，而 (C)「不會開車的工作人員」並未被列入禁止事項中，也就是說這樣的人是可以進入該工作場所的，所以為正確答案。

● 83 ~ 86 廣告（advertisement） ⊃ Pre 77 ~ 78

第 83 ~ 86 題與以下廣告有關。

黃金婚禮套裝專案

（至少 100 名賓客起）

我們的黃金婚禮套裝專案提供最華麗的婚禮體驗，可說是除了新郎以外一應俱全。本專案能讓您從任何與規劃婚禮喜宴有關的壓力中解放出來。擁有 30 年以上經驗，我們專業的工作人員將協助並引導您規劃出一場令人永難忘懷的活動，以幫助您慶祝這最特別的一天！

此套裝專案包括：

樂團於現場連續演奏 5 小時的音樂

葡萄酒、香檳與並附贈巧克力

除了提供搭配晚餐用的葡萄酒及敬酒的香檳外，還附贈以緞帶裝飾的巧克力給全體賓客作為小禮物

豪華轎車接送

黑或白色的 8 人座豪華轎車

從府上至婚禮會場，提供香檳、紅毯及專屬司機共 3 小時的完整服務

男士晚禮服

每人 80 美元

新郎禮服免費，而參加婚禮者若需租借晚禮服，每件可享有 20 美元的折扣（至少租借 5 套）

喜帖

精選的全套喜帖，包含婚禮請帖、回函及感謝函

實際價格請來電洽詢。

Word List

☐ superb [su`pɝb] 形 一流的、華麗的　　☐ chauffeur [`ʃofɚ] 名 司機

83. 正確答案：(C) ☆☆

Who is the Golden Wedding Package designed for?　黃金婚禮套裝專案是為誰設計的？

(A) A couple 30 years old or above　　30 歲以上的情侶

(B) A couple celebrating their wedding anniversary　要慶祝結婚紀念日的夫妻

(C) A couple with 100 guests or more　**將招待 100 名以上賓客的情侶**

(D) A couple who do not want to spend a lot　不想花太多錢的情侶

解說

由廣告本文前置於括號中的說明 (Based on minimum 100 guests) 可知，(C) 為正解。

84. 正確答案：(D) ☆

What does the company stress about itself?　這家公司強調了本身的哪一項優點？

(A) It is cheaper than its competitors.　它比競爭對手便宜。

(B) It can arrange weddings for groups of any size.　它能安排任何人數規模的婚禮。

(C) It specializes in providing gourmet food.　它專門提供美食。

(D) It has a lot of experience.　**它經驗豐富。**

解說

由廣告本文的第三句提到 With more than 30 years of experience, ... 可知，(D) 為正確答案。而由廣告最後寫的 Call for pricing. 可知，(A) 並不正確。另外，廣告一開始就說了賓客最少需有一百個人，因此 (B) 也不對。至於 (C) 的內容則無法從這則廣告中判斷。

85. 正確答案：(B) ☆☆

What is the cost of tuxedos for the groom and three guests?
租借新郎和 3 名賓客的晚禮服需要多少錢？

(A) $180.　　180 美元。

(B) $240.　　**240 美元。**

(C) It depends on the season.　會依季節不同。

(D) The service is not available.　並未提供這種服務。

由於廣告中提到 Free tuxedo for the groom ...，所以新郎的部分免費，而 20 美元的折扣要 五人以上才有，僅三人時不適用，因此 80 美元 × 3 = 240 美元 (B) 為正確答案。

86. 正確答案：(A) ☆

What can guests enjoy throughout the party?　　賓客在婚禮中可以一直享受什麼服務？

(A) Live music　　　　　　　　　　　　　**現場音樂演奏**
(B) Limousine service　　　　　　　　　　豪華轎車服務
(C) Beautiful thank-you cards　　　　　　美麗的感謝卡
(D) Many different meal choices　　　　許多不同的餐點選擇

由廣告中 Five Hours of Continuous Music with Band 一項可知正解為 (A)。(B)、(C) 兩項並非發生在婚禮中的事，而文中並無與 (D)有任何相關的資訊。

● 87 ~ 90 指示（instructions） ⊃ Pre 85 ~ 87
第 87 ~ 90 題與以下的指示有關。

發生火災或爆炸時，所有員工都應遵循以下的消防應變程序。

當你發現火災或看見煙霧時：
1. 請讓所有訪客與員工離開有立即性危險的區域。
2. 啓動火災警報系統。
3. 撥 9999（控制中心）並回報以下狀況：
   (a) 火災發生的確實位置（建築物、樓層及房號）；
   (b) 火災類型（電氣、易燃液體、廢棄物等）；
   (c) 火勢（火的猛烈程度及／或煙霧量）；
   (d) 你的名字。

4. 如果可以，請試著用合適的滅火器滅火。
5. 關閉所有的門窗以阻擋火和煙。
6. 不要鎖門。不要關閉走道與房間的燈。
7. 如果可能，請關閉該區中所有不必要的瓦斯與電氣用品，並移除任何危險物品。
8. 若火勢與煙霧已無法控制，或你認為有必要時，請利用最近的內部疏散樓梯或地面出口將人員撤離建築物。

9. 只有在建築物警報系統發出重覆的間歇鳴響訊號，明示「所有危險均已排除」之後，才可再度進入該棟建築物。

建築物中的工作人員應發揮團隊合作精神以完成上述程序。

Word List

☐ activate [ˋæktəˏvet] 動 啟動

☐ extinguish the fire [ɪkˋstɪŋgwɪʃ] 撲滅火災

☐ flammable [ˋflæməbḷ] 形 易燃的

☐ evacuate [ɪˋvækjuˏet] 動 撤離

☐ intermittent sound [ˏɪntəˋmɪtṇt] 間歇鳴響

---

87. 正確答案：(B) ☆☆

In case of fire, what must employees do first?	發生火災時，員工首先必須做什麼？
(A) Call the nearest fire station.	打電話給最近的消防局。
(B) Evacuate guests and co-workers.	**撤離訪客與同事。**
(C) Try to bring the fire under control.	試著控制火勢。
(D) Sound an alarm.	鳴響警報。

解說

指示第一項提到 Remove all visitors and employees ... 故 (B) 為正解。注意，原句在 (B) 中換成同義的表達方式：Evacuate guests and co-workers.。

---

88. 正確答案：(A) ☆☆

Why do employees have to close all windows and doors?
員工為何必須關閉所有的門窗？

(A) **To stop the fire from spreading**	**為了阻止火勢擴散**
(B) To make it easy to extinguish the fire	為了讓火災更容易撲滅
(C) To determine the exact location of the fire	為了判定火災的確切位置
(D) To judge how severe the fire is	為了評斷火勢

解說

指示第五項提到的 Confine the fire and smoke 與 (A) 選項 To stop the fire from spreading 的意思相同，所以 (A) 即正確答案。

89. 正確答案：(D) ☆

What must employees do if they think the fire cannot be controlled?
當覺得火勢無法控制時，員工必須做什麼？

(A) Activate the fire alarm. 啓動火災警報。

(B) Make sure all doors are unlocked. 確定所有的門都未鎖上。

(C) Turn off unnecessary appliances. 關掉不必要的電器設備。

(D) Just leave the building from the closest exit. 從最近的出口離開建築物。

第八項指示的 Evacuate the building using the nearest enclosed stairway or ground exit 與 (D) Just leave the building from the closest exit. 為同義表達，故 (D) 為正解。

90. 正確答案：(B) ☆☆

When can employees reenter the building? 員工何時可重新進入建築物？

(A) When the alarm rings continuously 當警報聲持續響起時

(B) When the alarm rings on and off 當警報聲間歇鳴響起時

(C) When the fire department says it is safe to do so 當消防隊說已經安全可進入時

(D) When they can no longer see smoke 當他們已看不到煙時

第九項指示中的 repeated intermittent sounds on the building alarm system 與 (B) 選項中的 alarm rings on and off 屬同義表達，所以 (B) 為正確答案。

● 91～95 公告與備忘錄（announcement、memo）

第 91～95 題與以下的公告及備忘錄有關。

公告

格蘭特廣場會議中心

格蘭特廣場會議中心以其位於市內商業區的核心之便利位置而自豪。本會議中心的每人會議費率為 80 美元再加上使用稅。而基本方案包括以下內容：

I.　會議空間內建有最先進的視聽及會議設備

II.　會議室內備有主管級辦公椅及會議桌，且可依您的喜好安排設置

III.　提供早餐輕食、自助午餐，以及午後茶點

Part 7

Strategies

Pre Test

Half Test 1

Half Test 2

Full Test

IV. 提供鉛筆、筆記本、活動翻頁掛圖、圖釘與麥克筆等會議用品

V. 配有一名會議策劃員，可為您協調從會議室設置到晚餐服務等所有需求

VI. 商務中心還提供影印、傳真及秘書助理等附加服務

* 若您需要視訊會議、電話會議或同步口譯等服務，您的會議策劃員將告知您所需的額外費用。

備忘錄

辦公室備忘錄

收件人：布魯斯‧福爾曼
寄件人：賴瑞‧席爾曼
主旨：會議中心搜查

請看看我附加於此備忘錄的格蘭特廣場會議中心資訊。我想該中心應值得考慮作為今年研究會議可能的舉辦地點。

我知道我們已利用太平洋高地中心好些年了，但是老實說，我認為我們需要改變一下。太平洋高地中心的水準在持續下降。幾週前我到該中心參加另一場會議，而我並未留下什麼好印象。該中心看來開始看起來老舊且年久失修。更糟的是，投影系統竟然在簡報進行中故障了。大約花了半小時才修好，結果一切都因此而延誤。那裡的食物也沒什麼特別的。

反觀，格蘭特廣場會議中心才開始營運沒有多久，但是名氣越來越大。我知道它的價格高於太平洋高地中心，不過如果我們能以建立長期關係為由來說服他們，或許可以交涉出一個較優惠的費率。此外，我們今年的會議將有一些具影響力的重要賓客來參加，我們得努力讓他們留下好印象才行。

請讓我知道你的想法。

賴瑞

Word List

- occupancy tax [`ɑkjəpənsɪ tæks]（會場、飯店房間等）的使用稅
- secretarial assistance [sɛkrə`tɛrɪəl ə`sɪstəns] 秘書助理服務
- reputation [ˌrɛpjə`teʃən] 图 名聲、名氣
- state-of-the-art 形 最先進的
- built-in 形 內建的
- be impressed 留下深刻印象
- break down 故障

91. 正確答案：(B) ☆☆

What is NOT included in the basic price of the conference center?
該會議中心的基本費用中不包含以下哪項服務？

(A) Meal service 餐飲服務
(B) Simultaneous interpretation **同步口譯**
(C) Audiovisual equipment 視聽設備
(D) Stationery 文具

> **解說**
>
> 由公告最後的註腳中的 ... simultaneous interpretation ... additional cost. 可知， (B) 是正確答案。而 (A) 列在項目 III、(C) 列在項目 I、(D) 列在項目 IV 中皆包含於基本費用內。

92. 正確答案：(C) ☆☆

Why is Larry Thieleman suggesting a change of the place?
賴瑞・席爾曼為何建議改變開會地點？

(A) The Grant Plaza Conference Center has offered a discount. 格蘭特廣場會議中心已提供折扣。
(B) The Pacific Heights Conference Center has increased its rates. 太平洋高地會議中心漲價了。
(C) He is unhappy with the present conference center. **他對目前使用的會議中心不滿意。**
(D) The Grant Plaza Conference Center is in a more convenient location. 格蘭特廣場會議中心位於更方便的地點。

> **解說**
>
> 由備忘錄第二段的敘述可知，他們目前所使用的會議中心（太平洋高地中心）的水準在下降，(C) 為正確選項。文中並無任何與 (A)、(B)、(D) 相關的資訊。

93. 正確答案：(A) ☆

What must conference participants do if they want photocopies?
參與會議的人如果想影印，就必須做什麼？

(A) Go to the Business Center. **去商務中心。**
(B) Ask the Conference Planner. 請會議策劃員幫忙。
(C) Use the copy machine in the conference room. 使用會議室裡的影印機。
(D) Pay an additional fee. 支付額外費用。

解說

由公告之項目 VI 提到的 ... photocopying ... available at the Business Center 可知，正確答案為 (A)。而影印並非會議策劃員的工作（依據項目 V 所述），所以 (B) 不對；影印機並未列在會議室設備中（依據項目 I 所述），所以 (C) 也不對；最後，影印也未包含在註腳所列需額外費用的服務中，因此 (D) 亦非正確答案。

94. 正確答案：(D) ☆

What problem did Larry Thielemans recently experience at a conference?
賴瑞・席爾曼最近在一場會議中經歷到什麼問題？

(A) The computer system crashed.　　　電腦系統故障。

(B) There was not enough food.　　　食物不夠。

(C) The standards dropped.　　　水準下降。

(D) A projector stopped working.　　　**投影機無法運作。**

解說

由備忘錄第二段倒數第三句提到的 the projection system broke down「投影系統故障了」可知， (D) 為正確答案。文中並未提及「電腦系統故障」，所以 (A) 不對；而文中第二段最後一句提到那裡提供的食物沒什麼特別之處，但並沒有說是「食物不夠」，所以 (B) 也不對；至於「水準下降」一事，並非在會議中直接經歷到的問題，而是在問題發生後推導出的結論，所以 (C) 亦非正確答案。

95. 正確答案：(B) ☆☆

How would Larry Thielemans approach the new convention center for a cheaper rate?
賴瑞・席爾曼會如何向新的會議中心要到較便宜的價格？

(A) By mentioning its inconvenient access　　　提及其交通不便

(B) By mentioning his company's wish to keep using it for a long time　　　**提及他的公司希望長期合作**

(C) By mentioning the possibility of holding a big conference there　　　提及在該中心舉辦大型會議的可能性

(D) By mentioning the poor quality of the equipment　　　提及其設備品質不良

解說

由備忘錄第三段第二句中提到的 ... negotiate a better rate ... convince them we want a long-term relationship. 可知，正確答案為 (B) 。而公告的第一句就曾提到該會議中心的 convenient location，所以 (A) 是錯的；另，公告之項目 I 中提到該中心有 state-of-the-art, built-in audiovisual and conference equipment 等先進的視聽及會議設備，因此 (D) 也不對。

● 96 ~ 100 電子郵件（e-mail） ⊃ Pre 91 ~ 95

第 96 ~ 100 題與以下兩封電子郵件有關。

電子郵件

寄件人：fdavies@earth.com
收件人：rdarcy@link.com
主旨：新的創投事業？

嗨，露絲。近來好嗎？我知道我們好一陣子沒聯絡了，不過我想聽聽妳對我最近在考慮的一個新事業構想有何看法。

妳去過去年在卡爾頓開幕的新商務園區嗎？我上週有事去了一趟。當時我有些空檔，所以就決定開著車四處看看。現在那兒已經有許多公司進駐，也有一些餐廳，但是我卻連一間賣三明治的店都沒看到。我認為一家好的三明治店在那裡應該會很賺錢。我們只要找個可讓我們在早上製作三明治的廚房，然後建置好點菜與外送系統，以及一個小攤位就行了。

我過去一直很喜歡在餐飲業工作，現在孩子都大了，我很想有機會重返餐飲業。我覺得這正是個大好時機，但我無法單打獨鬥。我真的很需要一位可靠又有良好餐飲背景的夥伴，而妳正是不二人選。請讓我知道妳有沒有興趣。

祝好。
菲歐娜・戴維斯

電子郵件

寄件人：rdarcy@link.com
收件人：fdavies@earth.com
主旨：Re: 新的創投事業？

親愛的菲歐娜，

很高興收到妳的來信。我必須說，妳實在是太會掌握時機了！自從傑瑞和我賣掉餐廳後，我一直有點閒不下來，所以我非常樂意再次投身事業。我覺得妳的計畫聽起來很棒，我已經做了一些調查。

妳還記得我的朋友湯米‧戴維森嗎？他剛剛開了一家新餐廳，就在離卡爾頓新商務園區不遠的地方，他已經同意讓我們在早上使用他的廚房。我還與我們以前的一些供應商重新取得了聯繫，因此我知道我能以非常合理的價格取得高品質食材。另外還有很多事情需要考慮，像是點菜與外送系統、菜單及定價等。工作將會很辛苦，但是我很確定我們一定能建立起一個不必花太多錢，但是卻非常成功的小生意。

讓我們儘快見面討論吧。

露絲‧達西

Word List

☐ sound out 搜尋……的意見
☐ catering [ˋketərɪŋ] 名 外燴
☐ put ... in place 設置……
☐ set up 建立、創立（事業等）

96. 正確答案：(B) ☆

What do the two women want to do?　　　　這兩位女子想做什麼？

(A) Open a restaurant.　　　　　　　　　開一家餐廳。
(B) Open a sandwich business.　　　　　**開一家三明治店。**
(C) Move to Carlton.　　　　　　　　　　搬到卡爾頓。
(D) Sell their restaurant.　　　　　　　　賣掉她們的餐廳。

解說

由第一封郵件第二段第五句提到的 ... a good sandwich shop ... would do tremendous business「一家好的三明治店……應該會很賺錢」可知，正解為 (B)。

97. 正確答案：(A) ☆☆

Which statement best describes experience in their food business?
以下哪項陳述最能說明她們在餐飲業方面的經歷？

(A) They both have experience.　　　　　　　**她們兩個人都有經驗。**
(B) Neither of them has experience.　　　　　　她們兩個人都沒經驗。
(C) Fiona has experience, but Ruth does not.　　菲歐娜有經驗，但是露絲沒經驗。
(D) Ruth has experience, but Fiona does not.　　露絲有經驗，但是菲歐娜沒經驗。

解說

菲歐娜在她的電子郵件第三段的第一句提到 I used to love working in the catering business ...，而露絲則在她的電子郵件第一段第三句提到 ... since Jerry and I sold the restaurant，由此可知兩個人都有餐飲業經驗。

98. 正確答案：(A) ☆☆

Why does Fiona want Ruth for her business partner?
菲歐娜為何希望露絲成為她的生意夥伴？

(A) Ruth is trustworthy and experienced.　　　**露絲值得信賴又有經驗。**
(B) Ruth has no job at the moment.　　　　　　　露絲目前沒有工作。
(C) Ruth and her husband are her old friends.　　露絲和她先生是菲歐娜的老朋友。
(D) Ruth is hard-working and energetic.　　　　　露絲工作勤奮而且精力充沛。

解說

由第一封電子郵件第三段第三句提到的 I really need a reliable partner with a good background in food, and you're the obvious choice.「我真的很需要一位可靠又有良好餐飲相關背景的夥伴,而妳正是不二人選」可知,以同義表達的 (A) 為正解。 (B)、(C) 或許是事實,但是並不是菲歐娜選擇露絲的理由。另外,文中並無任何與 (D) 有關的資訊。

99. 正確答案:(C) ☆

Who is Tommy Davidson?   湯米・戴維森是誰?

(A) A sandwich shop owner   一家三明治店的老闆
(B) The women's business partner   這兩名女子的事業夥伴
(C) A restaurant owner   **一個餐廳老闆**
(D) Ruth's husband   露絲的先生

解說

由第二封電子郵件第二段第一、二句提到的 ... Tommy Davidson? He's just opened a new restaurant ... 可知,正確答案為 (C)。注意,湯米・戴維森雖然提供了廚房,但算不上是「事業夥伴」,所以不能選 (B)。

100. 正確答案:(D) ☆

What is Ruth's reaction to Fiona's plan for a new business?
露絲對菲歐娜的新事業構想有何反應?

(A) She thinks it will be easy.   她認為會很簡單。
(B) She does not think it will be successful.   她不認為會成功。
(C) She thinks it will be expensive but successful.   她認為會很花錢但是會成功。
(D) She thinks it will be difficult but successful.   **她認為會很艱鉅但是會成功。**

解說

第二封郵件第二段的最後一句提到 It will be hard work, but ... we could set up a very successful little business ...「工作將會很辛苦,但是……我們一定能建立起一個非常成功的小生意」,所以正確答案應為 (D)。而露絲同時還說她相信 ... without having to spend too much money.「不必花太多錢」,因此 (C) 是錯的。

Memo:

解答與解說

Half Test 2 （100 題）

Listening Section

Part	No.	正解	你的答案
Part 1	1	A	
	2	C	
	3	D	
	4	B	
	5	D	
Part 2	6	B	
	7	C	
	8	B	
	9	B	
	10	C	
	11	C	
	12	B	
	13	C	
	14	C	
	15	C	
	16	C	
	17	A	
	18	C	
	19	B	
	20	A	
Part 3	21	C	
	22	B	
	23	D	
	24	B	
	25	C	
	26	A	
	27	D	
	28	A	
	29	B	
	30	D	
	31	B	
	32	A	
	33	A	
	34	C	
	35	C	
Part 4	36	C	
	37	C	
	38	A	
	39	B	
	40	D	
	41	B	
	42	B	
	43	D	
	44	B	
	45	C	
	46	B	
	47	A	
	48	B	
	49	A	
	50	D	

Reading Section

Part	No.	正解	你的答案
Part 5	51	B	
	52	B	
	53	D	
	54	D	
	55	D	
	56	B	
	57	B	
	58	D	
	59	A	
	60	B	
	61	C	
	62	B	
	63	D	
	64	D	
	65	C	
	66	B	
	67	B	
	68	C	
	69	A	
	70	D	
Part 6	71	B	
	72	B	
	73	A	
	74	D	
	75	B	
	76	A	
Part 7	77	C	
	78	A	
	79	A	
	80	C	
	81	D	
	82	A	
	83	C	
	84	B	
	85	B	
	86	D	
	87	A	
	88	B	
	89	C	
	90	C	
	91	D	
	92	C	
	93	D	
	94	C	
	95	A	
	96	B	
	97	D	
	98	D	
	99	B	
	100	C	

請記下 Half Test 2 的成績。

	答對題數	答對率	目標答對率
Part 1	/ 5	%	90%
Part 2	/ 15	%	80%
Part 3	/ 15	%	70%
Part 4	/ 15	%	70%
合計	/ 50	%	75%

	答對題數	答對率	目標答對率
Part 5	/ 20	%	70%
Part 6	/ 6	%	70%
Part 7	/ 24	%	70%
合計	/ 50	%	70%

Part ① Photographs 圖片題

☆470 分等級 ☆☆600 分等級 ☆☆☆730 分以上

1. 正確答案：(A) ☆☆ 🔊 37

(A) The carpenters are working in the higher floor. 木工們正在較高樓層工作。

(B) The house looks ready to live in. 這間房子看來已可居住。

(C) The men are standing on the roof. 男子們站在屋頂上。

(D) The workers are taking a lunch break. 工人們正在午休。

> 解說 人的動作、狀態 ➲ Pre 1
>
> 照片中的工人明顯正在新建木造房屋的較高樓層工作，故本題應選 (A)。圖中的屋頂還沒蓋好，所以 (B)、(C) 皆不成立。

2. 正確答案：(C) ☆☆

(A) A laboratory technician is conducting an experiment. 實驗室的技術人員正在進行實驗。

(B) The patient is being X-rayed. 病人正在照 X 光。

(C) A patient is receiving a dental treatment. 病人正在接受牙科治療。

(D) The patient 's tooth is about to be extracted. 該名病人的牙齒即將被拔除。

> 解說 人的動作、狀態、進行式、被動式 ➲ Pre 1, 3
>
> 此題的重點在於要能聽出現在進行式及被動式的句子。照片顯示一名牙醫正在為病人做治療；反過來說也就是病人正在接受治療。(C) 為正解。選項 (B) 中的 is being X-rayed 為現在進行被動式，因病人並未照 X 光，故此為錯誤選項。另外，(D) 的 be about to ... 為「即將……」之意，但從照片中無法看出是否在拔牙，所以 (D) 亦非正確答案。

3. 正確答案：(D) ☆

(A) The cooking stove is in the middle of the room. 房間中央有個做菜用的爐子。

(B) A fire is burning brightly in the stove. 爐裡的火燒得正旺。

(C) There's a wooden floor directly under the stove. 爐子下方直接就是木板地。

(D) The woodburning stove is placed on the bricks. 燒木柴的火爐被架在磚塊上。

> 解說 物的狀態 ➲ Pre 2
>
> (A) 選項中的 cooking stove 指「煮飯做菜用的爐子」，照片中顯示的則是燒柴的「火爐」woodburning stove。可以看出在火爐下方墊著「磚塊」bricks，故選 (D)。

4. 正確答案：(B) ☆☆

(A) Two people's arms look bare. 兩人的手臂看來光溜溜的。

(B) Two people's arms barely reach around the tree. **兩人的手臂勉強能環抱樹幹。**

(C) The tree is about to be cut down. 此樹即將被砍斷。

(D) The forest is full of tall and old trees. 這森林充滿了又高又古老的樹。

> **解說** 人的狀態 ⊃ Pre 1
>
> 照片顯示此兩人將手臂張開環抱樹幹。(B) 為正解。注意，選項 (A) 中的 bare 指「裸露的」，不可與 (B) 中的 barely「勉強地」混淆。

5. 正確答案：(D) ☆☆

(A) All the seats are occupied. 所有座位都坐滿了。

(B) All the luggage bins are shut. 所有的行李置物箱都是關閉的。

(C) The plane will be landing soon. 飛機即將著陸。

(D) Most of the passengers have deplaned. **大部分乘客都已下機。**

> **解說** 人、物的狀態 ⊃ Pre 1, 2／不可自行想像 ⊃ Pre 5
>
> 雖然機艙內看來有些雜亂，但是放行李用的置物箱都是空的，也幾乎看不到什麼乘客。據此可推測，這應是飛機抵達目的地後，乘客已下機時的狀態，所以正確答案為 (D)。

Memo:

6. 正確答案：(B) ☆☆　　　　　　　　　　　　　　　　　　　　　　　　　🔊 39

What percentage of wheat is imported?　　　　　有多少百分比的麥子是進口的？

(A) About 30% is grown in this country.　　　　　約有 30% 是在國內栽種的。

(B) About 15% is imported from other countries.　　**約有 15% 是從其他國家輸入的。**

(C) About 20% is exported to other countries.　　約有 20% 輸出至其他國家。

> **解說** 使用 What (percentage of) 的疑問句 ➲ Pre 8
>
> 請務必聽清楚百分比數值及 import、export 等單字。因為 (A) 與 (C) 都沒有正面回答到問題，所以均非正確答案。

💣 小心陷阱

與百分比有關的題目在 Part 2 中通常會出現一題，在 Part 3、4、6、7 中也都可能出現。請務必將腦海中由中文直譯而來的 How many percent、How much percent 等講法抹除，記住 What percentage ... 這樣的句型。另外最好也一併熟記下列各種與比率有關的表達方式。

▶ 以不同說法來描述百分比值：

ratio / proportion 比例	by a ratio of 1 to 10（以 1 比 10 的比例）
	1 out of 10 （每十個中有一個）
fraction 分數	1/5　one fifth[註1]
	2/5　two fifths[註2]
multiple number 倍數	twice as much / many as　（2 倍份量的／數量的）
	4 x 6　four by six / four times six

註1 分子用基數表示，分母則用序數表示。
註2 分子為複數時，分母也要用複數形。（這是從 2/5 是由兩個 1/5 集合而成之概念得來的。）

7. 正確答案：(C) ☆☆

When and where would you like the meeting to take place?
你希望會議在何時、何地舉行？

(A) We'll be at the convention center.　　　　　我們將在會議中心。

(B) We should have a meeting soon.　　　　　我們應該儘快開個會。

(C) How about 9 a.m. in the conference room　　**明天早上 9 點在會議室如何？**
tomorrow?

解說 包含兩個疑問詞的疑問句 ⊃ Pre 14

確實針對 when、where 這兩個疑問詞回答的選項只有 (C)。由於疑問詞總是在句首，須小心別漏聽。另外，正確答案 (C) 使用了 How about ...? 的提議句型，關於此句型的詳細說明可參考 Pre Test 17。

8. 正確答案：(B) ☆☆☆

Could you tell me where I can get the document printed out?
能不能告訴我去哪裡可以把文件列印出來？

(A) The document is available at Counter 4. 　　文件可在 4 號櫃台取得。

(B) Use this laptop. It's connected to the printer. 用這台筆記型電腦。它有連接印表機。

(C) I always have my assistant copy them. 　　我總是叫我的助理去影印。

解說 表達拜託、請求之意（Could you tell me ... ?）⊃ Pre 20

由於此問句用的是 Could you ...? 這樣較有禮貌的說法，所以可理解發問的人應是在非自己熟悉的場所，面臨到必須印出文件的情況。get ... 可表達「使……、令……」之意，而 print out 是用來描述將電腦中的資料等印刷成紙本的動作。針對問題做出合理回應的只有 (B) 選項。

9. 正確答案：(B) ☆☆

The radio says there has been an accident ahead of us on Highway 3.
廣播說在我們前方的 3 號高速公路上發生了事故。

(A) Then let's take Highway 3. 　　那我們就走 3 號高速公路。

(B) Then let's take a local road. 那我們就走地方道路。

(C) Then let's talk to the tollgate attendant. 　　那我們和收費站服務員談談。

解說 陳述與反應 ⊃ Pre 6

問題中的 accident ahead of us on Highway 3 為關鍵之所在，由於已知三號高速公路上有事故，所以就該 take a local road。正解為 (B)。

10. 正確答案：(C) ☆☆　　　　　　　　　　　　　　🔊 40

What are your expectations for the coming year, Prime Minister?
首相，您對未來一年的期望是什麼？

(A) Well, last year was certainly a difficult one. 　　嗯，去年確實是很艱困的一年。

(B) I really need to think about it. 　　我真的需要好好想一想。

(C) I'm certain our economy will improve. 我確信我們的經濟狀況會改善。

解說 使用 What 的疑問句 ⊃ Pre 8

此題詢問了一國的首相對明年的期望（expectation）為何，(C) 選項中提到的 economy will improve 即為正確答案的關鍵字詞。注意，(B) 的回答太含糊，作為一國首相的回並不合理。(A) 則完全牛頭 (last year) 不對馬嘴 (the coming year)。

11. 正確答案：(C) ☆☆

Did you remember to send out the package to Max Corporation?
你有記得把包裹寄給麥克斯公司嗎？

(A) Yes, I remember the small package.　　　　有，我記得那個小包裹。

(B) Yes, a small package was delivered to me.　有，有個小包裹送到了我這兒。

(C) Yes, of course I did.　　　　　　　　**有，我當然記得。**

解說 Yes-No 疑問句 ⊃ Pre 7

Did you remember to ...? 表示「有記得做……？」之意，(A) 與 (B) 皆答非所問。只有 (C) 針對 Did you remember to ...? 做了合理回應。

12. 正確答案：(B) ☆☆

Why are cars banned from 5th Avenue today?　今天第 5 大道為何禁止汽車通行？

(A) The traffic is congested.　　　　　　　　交通壅塞。

(B) There's going to be a parade.　　　　**即將有個遊行。**

(C) Take a detour that goes uptown.　　　　請繞道至通往上城區的路。

解說 使用 Why 的疑問句 ⊃ Pre 13

本題問為何車子 are banned 「被禁止通行」只有 (B) 提出合理的理由。一般而言，沒有理由因為「交通壅塞」而禁止汽車通行，故 (A) 為誤。而 (C) 並未直接回答到問題。

13. 正確答案：(C) ☆☆☆

Ernie, we're still waiting for your reply to our wedding invitation.
厄尼，我們還在等你回覆我們的婚禮邀請。

(A) How nice! Congratulations!　　　　　　太好了！恭喜！

(B) We'll send you an invitation soon.　　　我們很快就會把邀請函寄給你。

(C) Sorry, it just slipped my mind.　　　**對不起，我不小心忘了這件事。**

解說 陳述與反應 ⊃ Pre 6

本題考的是針對陳述句的回應。說話者的意思其實是 You haven't replied yet. Why? 而最直接的回應就是 I forgot.，不過為了不傷到對方，所以用 It slipped my mind.「我不小心忘了這件事」這樣較委婉的方式表達。(C) 為正解。

14. 正確答案：(C) ☆☆

How much do you estimate our firm's profit will be this year?

依你估計我們公司今年的利潤會是多少？

(A) Your estimation is always correct.   你的估算總是對的。

(B) We earned over 15 million last year.   我們去年賺了超過 1,500 萬。

(C) It will be over 2 billion dollars.   **會超過 20 億美元。**

> **解說** 用 How (much) 的疑問句 ⊃ Pre 16
>
> How much ...？疑問句應以數字回答，而選項 (B) 和 (C) 都有數字，但是 (B) 說的是 last year「去年」，所以正確答案是 (C)。

15. 正確答案：(C) ☆

How stupid I am to forget my passport at home!

我真是愚蠢，竟把護照忘在家裡了！

(A) I got mine 10 days ago.   我 10 天前拿到我的。

(B) You can borrow mine.   你可以借用我的。

(C) Go home and get it!   **回家去拿！**

> **解說** 感嘆句 ⊃ Pre 19
>
> 說話者忘了帶護照，建議他「回去拿」的選項 (C) 為最佳回應。(A) 說的是自己的護照、(B) 則行不通，因此都非正確答案。

16. 正確答案：(C) ☆☆

Where shall we meet to go to the ballgame together?

我們該在哪裡會合然後一起去看球賽？

(A) I'm all for going to a ballgame.   我完全贊成去看球賽。

(B) I can meet anytime you want.   我可配合任何你希望的時間。

(C) How about in front of the stadium?   **在體育館前如何？**

> **解說** 使用 Where 的疑問句 ⊃ Pre 12
>
> 三個選項中只有 (C) 針對問題的 Where 做出回應：in front of the stadium。不過由於此回答是以 How about 起頭，所以可能會令人有些猶豫。How about ...? 是常用於會話中表達「……如何？」的提議說法，請熟記。

17. 正確答案：(A) ☆☆

The new employees will all receive intensive on-the-job training for 3 months.

新進員工都將接受三個月密集的在職訓練。

(A) The training will be hard. 這訓練會很辛苦。

(B) They are training for the marathon. 他們在進行馬拉松訓練。

(C) They took the train to headquarters. 他們坐火車去總公司。

解說 陳述與反應、同音異字 ➲ Pre 6

(A) 選項針對說話者提到的 intensive ... training 做出了回應，故為正解。(B) 提到的馬拉松訓練和題目裡的在職訓練是兩回事，而 (C) 則用同音不同義的 train（火車）來混淆視聽。

💡 **奪分祕笈**

擁有多種意義的詞彙即，多義詞，在 TOEIC 中經常做為陷阱題。請熟記以下常見的多義詞彙。

mean	表示……的意思；平均值；手段（使用複數形）；壞心的；卑賤的
run	跑、逃跑；經營；開動（機器）；競選；執行
train	火車；（婚紗等的）長裙襬；訓練
work	工作；成果；作品；能正常運作；有效、起作用

18. 正確答案：(C) ☆☆ 🔊 42

Who is the management going to assign the Brazilian project to?

管理階層打算把該巴西專案指派給誰負責？

(A) The job is in Brazil. 該工作在巴西。

(B) They will begin the project in May. 他們將於 5 月展開該專案。

(C) They are going to send Mr. Roberts. 他們將派任羅伯茲先生去。

解說 Who ... for?／Who ... to? ➲ Pre 10

三個選項中只有 (C) 的 Mr. Roberts 回應了問題問的 Who，故為正解。(A) 選項用 Brazil 混淆視聽，(B) 選項回的是 When，皆不可選。

19. 正確答案：(B) ☆☆

You aren't going to cancel your wedding now, are you?

你不會打算現在要取消婚禮吧，是嗎？

(A) Yes, they are. 是的，他們會。

(B) No, of course not. 不，當然不會。

(C) No, you aren't. 不，你不會。

否定型的附加疑問句很容易讓人搞混。(A) 與 (C) 的主詞皆不對，而 (B) 雖然沒有使用主詞，但是其實是 No, of course I am not. 的省略式，故為正確選項。

20. 正確答案：(A) ☆☆

How's your brand-new computer working?　你的新電腦運作得如何？

(A) It was working fine until I dropped it.　**被我摔到之前一直運作得很好。**

(B) This is the latest laptop.　這是最新型的筆記型電腦。

(C) It was a gift on my birthday.　它是我的生日禮物。

本題問的是電腦運作的狀況如何，只有 (A) 的 working fine 回應了問題，(B) 和 (C) 皆答非所問。

Word List

☐ import [ɪm`port] 動 輸入、進口 (No. 6)

☐ export [ɪks`port] 動 輸出、出口

☐ take place 舉行 (No. 7)

☐ expectation [ˌɛkspɛk`teʃən] 名 期待、期望 (No. 10)

☐ prime minister 首相

☐ certain [`sɜtən] 形 確信的

☐ ban [bæn] 動 禁止 (No. 12)

☐ congested [kən`dʒɛstɪd] 形 壅塞的

☐ detour [`ditur] 名 繞道

☐ slip one's mind （事物）被遺忘 (No. 13)

☐ estimate [`ɛstəˌmet] 動 估計、估價 (No. 14)

☐ estimation [ˌɛstə`meʃən] 名 估算

☐ be all for ... 完全贊成……(No. 16)

☐ headquarters [`hɛd`kwɔrtəz] 名 總公司 (No. 17)

☐ brand-new [`brænd`nu] 形 全新的、嶄新的 (No. 20)

Part ③ Short Conversation 簡短對話題

☆470 分等級 ☆☆600 分等級 ☆☆☆730 分以上

●21 ~ 23 電腦方面的問題 ➲ Pre 21 ~ 23 🔊 44

Man: Hello. I just subscribed to your Internet service, but I can't seem to make it work properly.

Woman: Perhaps I can help. Can you tell me what you've done so far?

Man: I've inserted the CD-ROM, followed the instructions for installation, and restarted the computer. But for some reason, the browser won't open.

Woman: Okay. If you have diagnostic software, please use it and see if you can locate the problem. If you don't have the software, restart your computer and try to open the browser one more time.

男：　　喂，我剛剛申請使用貴公司的網路服務，但是我似乎無法讓它正確運作。

女：　　或許我能幫上忙。可以告訴我你目前為止做了哪些動作嗎？

男：　　我已插入唯讀光碟，並遵照指示安裝，也重新啟動電腦了。但是不知什麼原因無法開啟瀏覽器。

女：　　好。如果你有診斷軟體，請使用該軟體看看能否找出問題。如果你沒有那個軟體的話，就請你重新啟動電腦，再次試著開啟瀏覽器看看。

Word List

☐ installation [ˌɪnstəˋleʃən] 图 安裝

---

21. 正確答案：(C) ☆☆

Who does the man call?　　　　　　　　　這名男子打電話給誰？

(A) An Internet subscriber　　　　　　　一名網路服務用戶

(B) An electronic appliance store　　　　電器用品店

(C) An Internet service provider　　　**網路服務業者**

(D) A CD rental shop　　　　　　　　　CD 出租店

解說

由男子一開始所說的 I just subscribed to your Internet service, ...「我剛剛使用申請貴公司的網路服務」可知，對方應為網路服務業者，所以正確答案為 (C)。請注意，(A) 中的 subscriber 指申請用戶，請小心別弄混。

22. 正確答案：(B) ☆☆

What does the woman ask the man? 女子問了男子什麼？

(A) If she can help him 她是否能幫助他
(B) What steps he has taken **他已進行了哪些步驟**
(C) To tell her what he is doing 告訴她他正在做什麼
(D) To tell her what is wrong 告訴她出了什麼錯

解說

由女子說的 Can you tell me what you've done so far?「可以告訴我你目前為止做了哪些動作嗎？」可知，正解為 (B)。注意，不可誤選 (D)，因為男子一開始就已做了說明。

23. 正確答案：(D) ☆☆

What has the man NOT done before calling the woman?
男子在打電話給女子之前，沒做過以下哪件事？

(A) Followed installation instructions 遵循安裝指示
(B) Restarted the computer 重新啟動電腦
(C) Put the CD-ROM in 插入唯讀光碟
(D) Sent an e-mail requesting help **寄出請求協助的電子郵件**

解說

(A)、(B)、(C) 在男生的第二次發言中都有提到，而他並沒有寄電子郵件，所以 (D) 為正確答案。

● **24 ~ 26 投訴、抱怨** ⊃ Pre 33 ~ 35

Man: Excuse me. I just came through this checkout line a few minutes ago, and I think there may have been a mistake. I may have paid for an item that wasn't even in my cart.

Woman: I'm sorry, but I can't help you. If you have a question about your receipt, you'll have to go to the service counter. It's right over there, near the entrance.

Man: But I don't see how they can help me. You're the person who was at the register when I came through.

Woman: That's true, sir, but once you pay, and you receive your change and the receipt, it's no longer my responsibility.

Man: All right, fine, I don't have all day. Where exactly is the service counter?

男： 對不起。我幾分鐘前才在這個收銀台結過帳，我想可能出了個錯。我可能多付了一項根本不在我購物車裡的商品的錢。

女： 很抱歉，我幫不上忙。如果您對您的收據有疑問，必須去服務台處理。就在那兒，在入口旁。

男： 但是我不懂他們能怎麼幫我處理。我結帳時站在收銀台的就是妳啊。

女： 沒錯，先生，不過一旦您付了帳，拿到收據和找錢後，就不再是我的責任了。

男： 好吧，好，我也沒一整天時間跟你耗。服務台到底在哪兒？

24. 正確答案：(B) ☆☆

What is the man's problem?	這名男子有何問題？
(A) The cashier did not give him a receipt.	收銀員沒給他收據。
(B) He was charged for something he did not buy.	**他被收取了某項他並未購買的商品的費用。**
(C) He is angry with the cashier.	他在生收銀員的氣。
(D) An item was missing from his cart.	他的購物車裡有一樣商品不見了。

解說

男子第一次發言時所說的 I may have paid for an item that wasn't even in my cart.「我可能多付了一項根本不在我購物車裡的商品的錢」就指向正確答案 (B)。另外，(C) 提到的「男子在生氣」或許是事實，但是並沒有針對此問題回答，所以非正確選項。

25. 正確答案：(C) ☆

What does the cashier recommend?	收銀員建議什麼？
(A) Going over to the entrance	去入口處
(B) Asking about his receipt	詢問與收據相關的問題
(C) Checking with the service counter	**與服務台確認**
(D) Leaving her alone	不要打擾她

解說 以物為主題 ⊃ Pre 2

由女子第一次發言的第二句 ...You'll have to go to the service counter. 可知，正確答案是 (C)。(A) 的 entrance 是服務台的所在地；(B) Asking about his receipt 為誤導選項，因為和原對話前半部分中的 question about your receipt 容易產生混淆。至於 (D) Leave her alone 則是「別打擾她」的意思，這或許是忙碌收銀員的心聲，不過在會話中並未實際說出口。

26. 正確答案：(A) ☆☆

According to the man, who is responsible for the problem?

這名男子認為誰該為此問題負責？

(A) The cashier	**收銀員**
(B) The owner of the store	商店老闆
(C) The service counter	服務台
(D) The salesperson	銷售人員

解說

由男子在第二次發言時說的 You're the person who was at the register when I came through. 來推論，他認為應該負責的是 (A) 收銀員。最終或許還是要 (B) 商店老闆負責，但這是題外話，答題時應從會話中來找答案。

● **27 ~ 29 餐廳訂位** ⊃ Pre 27   🎧 45

Man: We'd like a table for dinner for 6—by a window if possible. We don't have a reservation, but we don't mind waiting.

Woman: No reservation? It'll be about 30 minutes. We can't guarantee a table by the window, but we'll do our best. Would you care to order drinks at the bar while you wait?

Man: Yes, that would be perfect. It would be nice to unwind with a drink before dinner.

Woman: Wonderful! By the way, the last order is 11 o'clock. We'll be closing at 12:00.

男：   我們要六人坐的桌子吃晚餐，如果有可能，請給我們靠窗的位置。我們沒訂位，但是願意等。

女：   沒訂位嗎？大概要等 30 分鐘喔。我們無法保證有靠窗的位子，但是會盡量安排。你們等位子的時候要不要到吧台那邊點些飲料？

男：   好啊，那太好不過了。晚餐前來杯飲料放鬆一下很不錯呢。

女：   太好了！順便說一下，點菜最後的時間是 11 點。我們 12 點打烊。

Word List

□ unwind [ʌnˋwaɪnd] 勔 放鬆

27. 正確答案：(D) ☆

Where does this conversation take place?   這段對話發生在何處？

(A) At a home improvement center	在家居裝修中心
(B) At a hotel lobby	在旅館大廳
(C) At an airport	在機場
(D) At a restaurant	**在餐廳**

解說

男子一開始說的 dinner for 6 就是指向正確答案 (D)。注意，(A) 的 home inprovement center 指「家居裝修中心」（類似台灣特力屋賣場）。而飯店大廳不會有 seating service （帶位服務），所以 (B) 不對。另外也請小心別被男生說的 by the window 誤導，以為是在說飛機上的座位而選 (C)。

28. 正確答案：(A) ☆☆

How long will the customers have to wait?	這幾位客人必須等多久？
(A) For half an hour	**半小時**
(B) About 6 minutes	大約 6 分鐘
(C) Until 11:00	到 11 點為止
(D) Until 12:00	到 12 點為止

解說

由女子所說的 It'll be about 30 minutes. 可知，正確答案為 (A)。而 (B) 為顧客人數，(C) 為最後的點菜時間，(D) 是打烊時間，這些數字都是 distracter（陷阱選項）小心不要誤選。

29. 正確答案：(B) ☆

What are they going to do after this conversation?	在這段對話結束後，他們打算做什麼？
(A) Board the plane	登機
(B) Have drinks at the bar	**到吧台喝點飲料**
(C) Get in line	去排隊
(D) Reserve a window seat	預訂靠窗的座位

解說

在對話中女子問 Would you care to order drinks at the bar while you wait?，而男子答 Yes, that would be perfect.，由此可知正確答案為 (B)。(A) 是利用 reservation、window seat 等關鍵詞所設計的 distracter（陷阱選項）。而雖然會話中完全沒有與 (C) 有關的資訊，但是仍可能一個不小心就誤以為它是正確答案。另外，由於女子說的是 We can't guarantee a table by the window but will do our best.，並沒有要他們預約，因此 (D) 也不對。

● **30 ~ 32 投訴、抱怨** ⊃ Pre 33 ~ 35

Man 1: Mr. Thomas, I called the supplier again, and they said the soonest they can deliver our order is the 23rd of this month. However, they can deliver one half of the order by the 16th.

Man 2: No, that won't do. We need the entire order here by the 18th, or it won't be in time for the trade show. Thanks, John. I'm going to call them myself and tell them that if they can't fill our order in full as we originally requested, we're going to contact another supplier.

Man 1: That might work, Mr. Thomas. With the trade show coming up on the 21st, we do need the entire order. Good luck.

男 1: 湯瑪斯先生，我又打了一次電話給供應商，他們說我們訂的貨他們最快本月 23 日可以送來。不過他們可以在 16 號前先送一半的貨。

男 2: 不，那是行不通的。我們需要整批貨在 18 日之前就送到這兒，否則就會趕不上貿易展。謝了，約翰。我會親自打電話給他們，並告訴他們如果他們無法依據我們原本的要求完整出貨，我們就要聯絡另一家供應商。

男 1: 那樣或許可行，湯瑪斯先生。貿易展 21 日就要開始，我們確實需要整批貨才行。祝你好運囉。

Word List

□ supplier [sə`plaɪə] 图 供應商　　　□ fill the order 完整且準時地出貨、完成訂單要求

30. 正確答案：(D) ☆☆

What's the soonest the supplier can ship the entire order?
供應商最快何時能送達整批貨？

(A) The 16th	16 日	(B) The 18th	18 日
(C) The 21st	21 日	**(D) The 23rd**	**23 日**

解說

由男子 1 說的 ... the soonest they can deliver our order is the 23rd of this month 可知，正確答案為 (D) 的關鍵。而 (A) 是部分貨品的送達日，(B) 是為了趕上貿易展的必要到貨日，(C) 則為貿易展的開始日期。

31. 正確答案：(B) ☆☆

What is Mr. Thomas going to tell the supplier?　　湯瑪斯先生打算對供應商說什麼？

(A) Have the entire order shipped by the 23rd.　　讓整批貨於 23 日前送達。

(B) Ship on time or they will lose the order.　　**準時出貨，不然他們就會失去訂單。**

(C) Ship what they have in stock. 　　　　　將他們有的庫存送過來。

(D) That he wants to cancel the order. 　　　他們要取消訂單。

解說

由湯瑪斯先生（男子2）說的 ... if they can't fill our order in full ... we're going to contact another supplier. 可知，正確答案為 (B)。而 23 日送達會趕不上貿易展，所以 (A) 不對；對話裡曾提到只送一半（庫存）來是行不通的，因此 (C) 也不對；最後，湯瑪斯先生的意思是「沒有全部準時送到才要取消」，而不是「現在就要取消」，所以 (D) 亦非正確答案。

32. 正確答案：(A) ☆

Why do they need the entire shipment by the 18th?

他們為何需要整批貨於 18 日前送到？

(A) For the trade show on the 21st 　　　　　**為了 21 日的貿易展**

(B) So Mr. Thomas won't get angry 　　　　　這樣湯瑪斯先生才不會生氣

(C) Because the trade show will be over by then 　因為那時貿易展就結束了

(D) Because they are going to contact another supplier 　因為他們將與另一家供應商聯繫

解說

由湯瑪斯先生（男子2）說的 We need the entire order here by the 18th, or it won't be in time for the trade show. 可知，正解為 (A)。而對話中並未提及湯瑪斯先生是否在生氣，所以 (B) 不對；而對話中沒有提到貿易展的結束日，所以 (C) 也不對；最後，對話裡並沒說到已經決定聯絡其他供應商，所以也不能選 (D)。

● **33 ~ 35 尋求協助** ⟹ Pre 30 ~ 32 　　　　　🔊 46

Woman: Good morning. My name is Lorraine Smith, and I have a 9:30 appointment. Will I have to wait long?

Man: Yes, I'm afraid so, Ms. Smith. The doctor had an emergency operation last night and arrived late this morning. You'll have to wait for about 20 to 30 minutes.

Woman: Oh, that's a problem. Actually, all I need is my usual allergy pills. Do you think you could give me some?

Man: I'm very sorry, Ms. Smith, but I'm not allowed to give prescribed medicine to a patient.

女： 早安。我叫蘿倫・史密斯，我預約了 9 點 30 分。我必須等很久嗎？

男： 是的，恐怕是如此，史密斯小姐。醫生昨晚有個緊急手術，所以今天早上遲到了。您必須等個 20 到 30 分鐘。

女： 噢，糟糕。其實我只是需要平常吃的過敏藥丸。你想你可以給我一些嗎？

男： 很抱歉，史密斯小姐，我是不能提供醫師處方藥給病人的。

Word List

☐ prescribed medicine [prɪˈskraɪbd ˈmɛdəsn̩] 醫師處方藥

33. 正確答案：(A) ☆

What is Ms. Smith worried about? 史密斯小姐擔心的是什麼？

(A) When she can see the doctor **她何時能給醫生看診**

(B) Being late for her doctor's appointment 預約門診卻遲到

(C) Having an operation 接受手術治療

(D) The date of a new appointment 下一次預約的日期

解說

根據女子問的 Will I have to wait long?「我必須等很久嗎？」這句話可判斷，她希望盡快給醫生看診，所以正確答案為 (A)。這位女子說她約的是 9 點 30 分，表示她並未遲到，因此 (B) 不對；而接受手術的並不是這名女子，所以 (C) 也不對；最後，下一次預約尚未發生，根本沒有擔心的理由，所以 (D) 亦非正確答案。

34. 正確答案：(C) ☆

How long will Ms. Smith have to wait? 史密斯小姐必須等多久？

(A) Until 9:30 等到 9 點 30 分

(B) Until the doctor arrives 等到醫師抵達

(C) Twenty or thirty minutes **20 或 30 分鐘**

(D) An hour 1 小時

解說

由男子說的 You'll have to wait for about 20 to 30 minutes. 可知，正確答案為 (C)。(A) 為女子預約的時間；而男子說「醫生今天早上遲到了」，表示醫生已經到了，所以 (B) 不對；至於 (D)「1 小時」這項資訊則完全不曾出現在對話中。

35. 正確答案：(C) ☆☆

Who is Ms. Smith speaking to? 史密斯小姐在跟誰說話？

(A) A doctor 醫生 (B) A patient 病人

(C) A nurse **護士** (D) A pharmacist 藥劑師

解說

由男子告訴史密斯小姐需等多久，及他不能擅自提供處方藥等可推測，他應是 (C) 護士。

Part 4 Short Talks 簡短獨白題

☆470 分等級 ☆☆600 分等級 ☆☆☆730 分以上

● 36 ~ 38 廣告文宣 ➲ Pre 45 ~ 47 🔊 48

Questions 36 through 38 refer to the following advertisement.

E-mail has made communication easy and even enjoyable. Except, of course, for spam. It seems there's no escape from the offensive and misleading ads and various scams. If you haven't used a spam filter before, give SpamBlaster a try. You can download it from www.ihatespam.org and use it for two weeks at no cost. It's easy to install, and we guarantee that, if properly used, it will reduce your spam volume by 75% or more. If you aren't satisfied, you can stop using SpamBlaster with no further obligation. We're confident, though, that you'll be amazed at the results. If you like SpamBlaster, it's yours for the unbelievably low price of $39.99. Spam getting you down? Blast it into cyberspace with SpamBlaster.

第 36 ~ 38 題與以下廣告有關。

電子郵件已使得通訊更輕鬆，甚至更有樂趣。當然，除了垃圾郵件以外。我們似乎總是無法逃脫那些討人厭的、誤導人的廣告，以及各式各樣的詐騙手法。如果您先前從未使用過垃圾郵件過濾軟體，請試試 SpamBlaster。您可上 www.ihatespam.org 網站下載，並免費試用 2 週。本軟體很容易安裝，而且我們保證，只要使用方式正確，它就能替您減少 75% 以上的垃圾郵件。如果試用不滿意，您可停止使用 SpamBlaster，不必進一步負擔任何義務。不過我們很有信心，您一定會發現它的驚人效果。如果您喜歡 SpamBlaster，只要不可思議的超低價格 39.99 美元，即可擁有。垃圾郵件令您不堪其擾嗎？用 SpamBlaster 把它們都轟到網路的虛擬空間去吧。

Word List

□ spam [spæm] 图 垃圾郵件
（也可稱為 junk mail）
□ blast [blæst] 動 炸毀、爆破

□ scam [`skæm] 图 詐欺、詐騙
□ get ... down 使……覺得討厭
□ cyberspce [`saɪbə‚spes] 图 網路的虛擬空間

36. 正確答案：(C) ☆☆

How does spam affect e-mail use?	垃圾郵件如何影響電子郵件的使用？
(A) It makes communication more efficient.	它使通訊更有效率。
(B) It makes communication easier.	它使通訊更容易。
(C) Lots of junk mail annoys the users.	**大量的垃圾郵件會困擾使用者。**
(D) Lots of junk mail destroys the computer system.	大量的垃圾郵件會破壞電腦系統。

解說

由廣告中第三句提到的 ... no escape from the offensive and misleading ads and various scams. 可知，(C) 為正確答案。

37. 正確答案：(C) ☆☆

What benefits does SpamBlaster offer?   SpamBlaster 提供什麼好處？

(A) It is free of charge.   它不收費。

(B) It gets rid of spam 100%.   它能 100% 除去垃圾郵件。

(C) It is free for two weeks and easy to install.   **它可免費試用 2 週而且容易安裝。**

(D) The price is reduced to 75%.   它打七五折。

> 【解說】
>
> 由廣告中第五句提到的 use it for two weeks at no cost 和第六句提到的 easy to install 可知，正確答案為 (C)。而廣告中說的是可免費試用二週並不收費，所以 (A) 不對。另，廣告中提到的 75% 是垃圾信件的減少量，所以 (B)、(D) 也都不對。

38. 正確答案：(A) ☆☆

What can the user do if not satisfied with the product after the trial period?
在試用期間過後如果對該產品不滿意，使用者可以怎麼做？

(A) Simply stop using it.   **直接停止使用即可。**

(B) Send it back to the company.   把它寄回該公司。

(C) Write to the company.   寫信給該公司。

(D) Get the money back.   可以退錢。

> 【解說】
>
> 廣告中第七句說 If you aren't satisfied, you can stop using SpamBlaster with no further obligation.，所以正確答案為 (A)。而由於是免費試用，所以 (D) 是錯的。另，廣告中並無與 (B)、(C) 相關的資訊。

●39 ~ 41 發言 ➲ Pre 45 ~ 47

Questions 39 through 41 refer to the following talk.

Hi, this is Jane Levy of Something Buoyant. To spread some holiday cheer and spice up the wardrobe of the man in your life, Something Buoyant is the place to go. This week, we're offering 20% off all cashmere V-necks, crew necks, cardigans and vests. We also have a selection of very stylish men's overcoats, in camel, navy blue, black and charcoal gray. And, with every coat purchased, we're giving away a $25 gift certificate good until next March 31st. It's the season of giving, so stop by any of our six locations and give that special guy a super special surprise! We're open from 9:00 to 9:00 during the holidays. Something Buoyant—your first and last stop for variety, service and price!

第 39 ~ 41 題與以下發言有關。

嗨，我是 Something Buoyant 的珍‧利維。為了散播一些節慶的歡樂並為您生命中的男人增添衣櫃裡的樂趣，來 Something Buoyant 準沒錯。本週我們所有喀什米爾的 V 領、圓領、開襟衫與背心都打八折。我們還有一系列非常時髦有型的男性外套，有駝色、海軍藍、黑色與木炭灰等不同色款。此外，每買一件外套，我們還會送您一張期限至 3 月 31 為止的 25 美元禮券。現在正是送禮的季節，所以請到我們 6 家分店的任一間逛逛，好給您那位特別的人一份超級特別的驚喜！假日期間，我們從早上 9 點營業至晚上 9 點。不論就種類、服務還是價格，Something Buoyant 都是您的第一站，也是最後一站。

Word List

☐ buoyant [`bɔɪənt] 形 樂天的、活潑的　　☐ give away 免費贈送

☐ gift certificate [gɪft sə`tɪfəkɪt] 禮券

39. 正確答案：(B) ☆☆

What kind of store is Something Buoyant?　　Something Buoyant 是哪種商店？

(A) A gift shop　　禮品店

(B) A men's clothing store　　**男性服飾店**

(C) A sporting goods store　　運動用品店

(D) A discount outlet　　折扣商店

解說

由發言中第二句提到的 wardrobe of the man in your life 即可知，正確答案為 (B)。而出現在此文中的全是男性服飾，所以 (A) 與 (C) 都不對。另，文中雖提及 20% off、$25 gift certificate 等，但並不意味此為折扣商店，因此 (D) 也不正確。

40. 正確答案：(D) ☆☆

What kind of benefit comes with the purchase of an overcoat?

每買一件外套就會附帶哪種好處？

(A) A free gift　　一件贈品

(B) A 20% discount　　打八折

(C) An invitation to a show　　一張表演招待券

(D) A gift certificate　　**一張禮券**

解說

由第五句中提到的 ... every coat purchased ... a $25 gift certificate ... 可知，這段敘述可知正確答案是 (D)。注意，(B) 的打八折指的是喀什米爾毛衣類。

41. 正確答案：(B) ☆☆☆

What kind of shoppers does the advertisement target?

這篇廣告以哪種購物者為目標？

(A) Easter shoppers　　　　　　　　　　復活節的購物者

(B) Christmas shoppers　　　　　　　**聖誕節的購物者**

(C) Annual-sale shoppers　　　　　　　年度特賣的購物者

(D) Back-to-school shoppers　　　　　　開學特賣的購物者

解說

由第二句 To spread some holiday cheer ... 可知，這是聖誕節期間所做的促銷活動，所以正解為 (B)。請記住，holiday cheer、holiday season、seasons of giving 等都屬於聖誕節時期用的詞彙。

● 42 ~ 44 新聞報導 ⊃ Pre 42 ~ 44　　　　　　　　　🎧 49

Questions 42 through 44 refer to the following news item.

Governor Gonzalez gave a speech in the Tall Valley town square today in an attempt to gain support for his reelection bid. The large turnout was expected. The explosion that turned the gathering into confusion, however, was not. The blast sent people running for safety, and there were some minor injuries resulting from the panic, but no one was seriously hurt. Police and fire department personnel quickly arrived at the scene and began investigating. The governor, visibly shaken yet determined, said to reporters that this act was undoubtedly the work of a small, poorly organized opposition group. He went on to say that nothing would stop him in his quest to continue serving the state.

第 42 ~ 44 題與以下新聞報導有關。

岡薩雷斯州長今日在大河谷市鎮廣場發表了一篇演說，試圖為競選連任一事爭取支持。事前已預期會有大批群眾出席。然而沒預料到的是，爆炸事件讓聚集活動變得一片混亂。爆炸使得群眾四處逃命，恐慌造成了一些輕傷，不過並沒有人受到嚴重傷害。警察與消防人員快速抵達現場並開始調查。州長明顯受到驚嚇，但是仍然表現出堅決態度，他告訴記者此次行動無疑是一個小型、組織拙劣的反對派團體所為。他還表示，沒有任何事情能阻止他繼續為本州服務。

Word List

☐ attempt to... 試圖……　　　　　　　☐ quest [kwɛst] 图 追求、請求

42. 正確答案：(B) ☆☆☆

What disrupted the governor's speech? 　是什麼打斷了州長的演說？

(A) A large turnout 　大批出席群眾

(B) An explosion 　**爆炸**

(C) Police department officials 　警局的官員

(D) People running for safety 　四處逃命的人們

> **解說**
>
> 由報導第三句 The explosion that turned the gathering into confusion ...可知，正確答案為 (B)。注意，(D) 是因爆炸造成演說中斷之後，才產生的行動。

43. 正確答案：(D) ☆☆☆

Who was responsible for the explosion? 　誰該為這場爆炸負責？

(A) The gas company. 　瓦斯公司。

(B) High-school kids. 　高中生們。

(C) A group opposing his reelection. 　反對他競選連任的一個團體。

(D) No one knows for certain. 　**沒有人確切知道。**

> **解說**
>
> 報導中提到 Police and fire department personnel ... began investigating，依此判斷，正確答案應為 (D)。注意，(C) 是州長個人的說法，尚未獲得證實。

44. 正確答案：(B) ☆☆

What did the governor say after the explosion? 　州長在爆炸後說了什麼？

(A) He is planning to retire. 　他計劃要引退。

(B) He will not stop campaigning. 　**他不會停止競選。**

(C) He was shaken and terrified. 　他很震驚而且被嚇壞了。

(D) He didn't comment a word. 　他沒發表任何意見。

> **解說**
>
> 報導最後一句提到 ... nothing would stop him ... to continue serving the state.，因此正確答案為 (B)。注意，(C) 州長的感受，並不是他所說的話，不可誤選。

●45 ~ 47 廣告 ⊃ Pre 45 ~ 47

Questions 45 through 47 refer to the following advertisement.

Are you unsatisfied with your current Internet provider? Have they not offered the quality of service you feel you deserve? Or have you simply outgrown them? If the answer to any of these questions is "Yes," consider FiberViper. Communications technology is constantly changing, and we're on top of the latest developments. Our 10Mbps standard service and 100Mbps high-speed service are rapidly gaining in popularity. We recently welcomed our one-millionth subscriber. FiberViper promises and delivers fast connection speed, high-volume transmission capability, a fixed monthly rate with unlimited access, and initial setup that couldn't be any easier. Call or e-mail us for details on our various services. We're FiberViper, a provider in the truest sense of the word.

第 45 ~ 47 題與以下廣告有關。
您對您目前的網路服務供應商不滿意嗎？他們是否沒能提供您覺得您應得的服務品質呢？又或者您對他們已毫無期待？如果您對這些問題中任何一題的回答為「是」，那麼請考慮 FiberViper。通訊技術日新月異，而我們始終站在最新發展之巔峰。我們的 10Mbps 標準服務與 100Mbps 高速服務都在迅速普及。我們最近才剛剛迎接了第一百萬個用戶。FiberViper 承諾並提供極快的連線速度、高容量的傳輸能力、每月固定費率無限上網吃到飽，以及簡單到不行的初期設定。請來電或以電子郵件詢問我們的各類服務細節。我們是 FiberViper，一家名符其實的供應商。

Word List
- outgrow [`aʊt`gro] 動 因長大成熟而不再……
- Mbps （Mega bits per second）表示每秒鐘所傳輸資料量的單位

45. 正確答案：(C) ☆

Who is this advertisement targeted specifically towards?　這篇廣告特別以誰為對象？

(A) Internet providers　網路服務供應商
(B) Computer engineers　電腦工程師
(C) People who are not happy with their Internet providers　**對自己的網路服務供應商**不滿意的人
(D) People with technical experience　有技術經驗的人

解說
廣告一開頭就問 Are you unsatisfied with your current Internet provider?，很明顯地訴求的對象就是「對網路服務供應商感到不滿意的人」，因此 (C) 為正確答案。

46. 正確答案：(B) ☆☆

How many customers does the provider serve?　　該供應商服務多少客戶？

(A) Nearly one million　　　　　　　　　　　　　接近 100 萬

(B) Over one million　　　　　　　　　　　**超過 100 萬**

(C) One hundred million　　　　　　　　　　　1 億

(D) One hundred　　　　　　　　　　　　　　　100

> **解說**
>
> 廣告中提到 We recently welcomed our one-millionth subscriber. 由此可知現在應已超過 100 萬用戶。

47. 正確答案：(A) ☆☆

What does the FiberViper offer?　　　　　　　FiberViper 公司提供什麼？

(A) Fast connection service　　　　　　　　**高速連線服務**

(B) A big discount on the monthly fee　　　　在月租費上的大幅折扣

(C) Free update information　　　　　　　　　免費的更新資訊

(D) Free trial period　　　　　　　　　　　　免費的試用期

> **解說** 以物為主題 ⊃ Pre 2
>
> 廣告後半部提到該公司提供的服務，其中包括了 fast connection speed，所以正確答案為 (A)。而廣告中雖提到了 a fixed monthly rate with unlimited access，但是並未提及任何折扣資訊，所以 (B) 不對，另外，廣告中並無與 (C)、(D) 相關的資訊。

●48 ~ 50 致詞（人物介紹） 50

Questions 48 through 50 refer to the following speech.

Dear Fellow Workers,

Sorry to interrupt the merrymaking, but I'd like to ask for your attention for a moment. As you're all aware, this has been a trying but very successful year for our organization. Credit goes to everyone for giving all your effort and doing such a fantastic job. And as we do every year, we've chosen one person this year. Without the person's efforts, support and sacrifice, our fabulous performance wouldn't have been possible. The person clearly stood out of several others in a very difficult selection process, and certainly deserves the prize. However, that could be said for so many of you as well. Without further ado, it gives me tremendous pleasure to present the year's Most Valuable Employee award to the head of product development, Ms. Lorraine DuPont!

第 48 ~ 50 題與以下的致詞內容有關。

親愛的同仁們，

很抱歉打斷各位的歡樂，在此想請各位注意聽我說幾句話。誠如大家所知，今年對我們公司來說是充滿試煉的一年，但也是極為成功的一年。這都要歸功於各位的努力和優秀的工作表現。而一如往年，我們今年也選出了一位員工。若是沒有這位同仁的努力、支持及犧牲，我們就不可能有如此好的成績。這位同仁在經過難以抉擇的過程，從其他數名候選人中脫穎而出，她的獲獎可說是實至名歸。然而，你們當中的許多人其實也都是如此。廢話不多說，我非常榮幸將本年度的「最有價值員工獎」頒發給產品開發部門的負責人羅琳‧杜邦女士！

Word List

☐ credit [`krɛdɪt] 名 功勞　　　　☐ fabulous [`fæbjələs] 形 極好的、絕妙的

☐ without further ado [ə`du] 不再多囉唆

48. 正確答案：(B) ☆☆

Where is this speech being made?　　　　這段致詞發表於何處？

(A) At a sport event　　　　　　　　　　在一場體育活動中

(B) At a company party　　　　　　　　**在一場公司的宴會中**

(C) At someone's office　　　　　　　　在某人的辦公室裡

(D) At an award presentation ceremony　在一場頒獎典禮上

解說

致詞人一開始就說 Sorry to interrupt the merrymaking, 最後則宣布將 present the year's Most Valuable Employee award，由此可推測這應是在公司宴會中頒獎給員工，故選 (B)。

 奪分祕笈

請熟記如下這些經常出現在 TOEIC 測驗中的致詞起頭用語。

一開始的呼喚可用 Dear Fellow workers「親愛的同仁們」、Attention, everyone.「各位，請注意」、Hello, everyone.「大家好」等講法，接著便可說出該段致詞或聚會的主旨。而演說、致詞時經常會以如下這類問句起頭：

a. May I interrupt for a few minutes?　　　可以打擾幾分鐘時間嗎？

b. May I say something on behalf of our　　可否讓我代表本公司總裁說幾句
　 President?　　　　　　　　　　　　　　 話嗎？

c. Can I have a few minutes of your precious time?　能耽誤您寶貴的幾分鐘時間嗎？

d. Could you just listen to me for a few seconds?　能否請各位聽我說一下話？

49. 正確答案：(A) ☆

How did the company do this year? 　　　　這家公司今年的業績如何？

(A) It was very successful. 　　　　**公司非常成功。**

(B) It tried very hard. 　　　　公司非常努力。

(C) It was presented with an award. 　　　　公司獲頒一個獎。

(D) Its income doubled. 　　　　公司收入倍增。

解說

由致詞第二句中提到的 very successful year 即可知正確答案為 (A)。注意，(B) 中的 tried hard 是過程而非結果，所以不對；而得獎的不是公司而是員工，所以 (C) 也不對；最後，雖然第二句提到 successful year，但並沒有說 income doubled，所以 (D) 亦非正確答案。

50. 正確答案：(D) ☆

What kind of person is the speaker most likely? 　　這位致詞者最有可能是什麼人物？

(A) A celebrity 　　　　一位名人

(B) A senior employee 　　　　一位資深員工

(C) An award winner 　　　　一位得獎者

(D) A high-level executive 　　　　**一位高階主管**

解說

由致詞者也是頒獎人，以及致詞中不斷提及公司、同仁等來推斷，本題正確答案應為 (D) 一位高階主管。

Memo:

51. 正確答案：(B) ☆☆

Applicants for this assignment must be aged between 22 and 30, and <u>physically fit</u>.

此項工作的申請者年齡必須在 22 到 30 歲之間，而且身體健壯。

> **解説** 詞性 ⊃ Pre 51
>
> be fit 是「健康的、（肉體上）強健」之意，而由於 fit 為形容詞，所以修飾它的必須為副詞 physically。

52. 正確答案：(B) ☆☆

The problem <u>would be</u> easier to solve if damage caused by pollution were restricted to only this area.

假如汙染所造成的損害僅限於此區的話，那這個問題就會比較容易解決了。

> **解説** 過去假設式 ⊃ Pre 68
>
> If 子句為與現在事實相反的過去假設式，所以主要子句也應用表非事實的 (B) would be。

53. 正確答案：(D) ☆☆

Using e-mail instead of writing letters by hand is becoming more common, but it is <u>unlikely</u> that all future communications will be electronic.

以電子郵件取代手寫信件的情況越來越普遍，但是未來不可能所有的通訊都電子化。

> **解説** 詞彙類問題 ⊃ Pre 52
>
> 依前後句意，本題應選表「不可能」之意的 (D)。注意，unlikely 雖以 -ly 結尾，但其實是個形容詞。

54. 正確答案：(D) ☆☆

It was so <u>inconsiderate</u> of Meg to tell Ian that she would never go out with him no matter what.

梅格對伊恩說無論如何她永遠都不可能和他出去約會，實在是很不顧別人的感受。

> **解説** 形式類似的單字（字首 in-） ⊃ Pre 52
>
> 依前後句意，本題正確答案應為 (D) inconsiderate「不替別人著想的、不體貼的」。其他選項的 (A) inconsistent 指「不一致的」，(B) inappropriate 指「不恰當的」，(C) insufficient 指「不充分的」。（本題四個選項都用了表 not 的字首 in-。）

Word List

☐ no matter what 無論如何

55. 正確答案：(D) ☆☆

Business customs in the United States differ significantly from <u>those</u> in Japan.

美國的商務習慣和日本的明顯不同。

> **解說** 代名詞、數量形容詞 ⊃ Pre 57
>
> 在句子中為了避免同樣名詞重複出現，應使用代名詞 that（單數）和 those（複數）來代替。此空格要填的就是相當於前面提到的 business customs 的代名詞，因為 customs 為複數形，所以對應的代名詞要用複數形的 those。

56. 正確答案：(B) ☆☆

The company is likely to face <u>bankruptcy</u> if it fails to win the new government contract.

如果不能贏得新的政府合約，該公司很可能就要面臨破產了。

> **解說** 詞性 ⊃ Pre 51
>
> 由於 face「面對」為及物動詞，其後必須接名詞作為其受詞，故應選 (B) bankruptcy。

57. 正確答案：(B) ☆☆

Advertising products is most <u>effective</u> when it is approached as multi-media activity.

以多媒體的活動方式進行商品宣傳是最有效的。

> **解說** 詞性 ⊃ Pre 51
>
> 主要子句的動詞為 be 動詞，其後須接主詞補語，而主詞補語可為名詞或形容詞，但因空格前後有最高級的 most，故應選形容詞 (B) effective。

58. 正確答案：(D) ☆☆

Oil inventories are well above normal, yet prices are almost twice as <u>high</u> as they were in the 1980s.

原油庫存量遠高於常態水平，但是價格卻幾乎是 1980 年代的兩倍。

> **解說** 比較（twice as ... as）▶Pre 58
>
> 英文裡價格的高低應用 high 和 low 來表示，不可用 expensive（昂貴）或 inexpensive（不昂貴）來修飾，這一點請注意。Twice as high as ... 指「是……的兩倍高」。

59. 正確答案：(A) ☆☆☆

The company decided to <u>reward</u> its workers by giving an across-the-board pay raise.

該公司決定以全面加薪的方式來獎勵員工。

解說 詞彙 ⊃ Pre 52

依前後句意，公司加薪的目的應該是為了「獎勵」員工，故正確答案為 (A)。而 (B) approve「贊同、認可」、(C) refund「退款」、(D) lay off「解雇」皆與句意不符。

Word List

☐ across-the-board 形 全面的　　　☐ pay raise 加薪

60. 正確答案：(B) ☆☆☆

Jake Cornford always attributed his success in life to <u>dropping</u> out of college to pursue his dream.

傑克・康福德總是將他人生的成功歸因於大學時為了追求夢想而中途輟學一事。

解說 合適的片語（動詞＋介系詞）⊃ Pre 70

drop out of「輟學、休學」是唯一符合句意的片語，而因接在介系詞 to 之後；故為動名詞形式。另外，fall out of 是「戒掉（癖好或習慣等）、從⋯⋯掉出來」，run out of 是「用完⋯⋯、耗盡⋯⋯」，fly out of 則指「從⋯⋯飛出來」，皆與本句意不符。

61. 正確答案：(C) ☆☆

The standard <u>warranty</u> period on this product is one year, but this can be extended up to five years with an additional payment.

此產品的標準保固期為一年，但是只要支付額外費用便能延長為五年。

Word List

☐ extend [ɪkˋstɛnd] 動 延長、擴展

解說 類似的單字 ⊃ Pre 52

(A) 的 security 容易令人困惑，其正確意思應該為「安全（保障）」，而產品或服務的「保固、保證」則要用 (C) warranty 表示。(B) discount「折扣」與 (D) trail「嘗試、試用」不適用此句。

62. 正確答案：(B) ☆☆

One attractive feature of the apartment block is that it has a handyman <u>on</u> call 24 hours a day.

這個公寓大樓區吸引人的特色之一，就是有二十四小時待命的雜務工。

解說 常用介系詞片語 ⊃ Pre 62

on call 為表示「待命」之意的特殊片語，(B) 為正確答案。而 (A)、(C)、(D) 用於此句意思都說不通。注意，句中的 handyman 指住宅社區裡專門負責修繕維護等雜務的人員，這類人員也經常兼任 superintendent「管理人」。

63. 正確答案：(D) ☆☆

Our new series of basic tools is essential <u>for doing</u> small jobs around the house.
我們公司新的基礎工具系列對於與房屋相關的簡易處理工作來說非常重要。

> **解說** 詞性（介系詞 + 動名詞）▶ Pre 51
> 欲表達「對……來說不可或缺、對……來說至關重大」之意時，便可用 be essential for + 動名詞（doing）形式來表達。另外， (C) 指「被做」，不可選 (C)。

64. 正確答案：(D) ☆☆☆

We are proud of our reputation as being the benchmark <u>against</u> which all other facilities are measured.
我們很自豪擁有做為其他設施之評估基準的名氣。

> **Word List**
> ☐ benchmark [`bɛntʃ.mark] 图 基準、標準

> **解說** 意義適切的詞彙（介系詞） ⊃ Pre 52
> 因為 the benchmark 為「相對於……」其他事物之基準，故介系詞應選 (D) against。

65. 正確答案：(C) ☆☆☆

<u>Whether</u> the upward trend continues depends largely on the nation's economy and unemployment rate.
上升趨勢的持續與否，主要取決於該國的經濟狀況和失業率。

> **解說** 引導名詞子句的連接詞 ⊃ Pre 52
> 本句的主詞為名詞子句，而四個選項皆可引導名詞子句，但依句意來看，應選 (C) Whether「是否……」。

66. 正確答案：(B) ☆☆

The recent survey we conducted shows that people who invest in our company stock <u>earn</u> salaries of between $50,000 and $100,000 annually.
依據我們最近進行的調查顯示，投資我們公司股票的人年薪約在 5 萬至 10 萬美元間。

> **解說** 意思相近的單字 ⊃ Pre 52
> 因為受詞是 salaries「薪水」，所以動詞應選 (B) earn「賺得」。(A) 的 gain 是「獲得」之意，並非正確答案。

Strategies Pre Test Half Test 1 Half Test 2 Full Test

67. 正確答案：(B) ☆☆

The newly constructed port is located <u>within</u> a 90-minute drive of the region's two major airports.

新建設的港口位於距離該區兩個主要機場 90 分鐘以內車程的地方。

> **解說** 介系詞與連接詞 ➲ Pre 61
>
> 依句意，本題空格應填入表「……以內」的介系詞，(B) within 為正確答案。注意，(A) inside 通常指「在……裡面」，與句意不符。

68. 正確答案：(C) ☆

We had better leave the door <u>unlocked</u> in case Jane and Tom do not have a key.

我們最好別鎖門，以防萬一珍與湯姆沒有鑰匙。

> **解說** 詞性 ➲ Pre 51
>
> 這是 leave + 受詞 + 過去分詞的句型，(C) unlocked 為「沒上鎖的」之意，為正解。

69. 正確答案：(A) ☆

The Euro has recently declined in value <u>against</u> the yen.

最近歐元相對於日圓貶值了。

> **解說** 選擇意義適切的詞彙（介系詞）➲ Pre 52
>
> 因為歐元是「相對於」日圓貶值，故選 (A) against。

70. 正確答案：(D) ☆☆

A drop in temperature of <u>as little as</u> 3 degrees Celsius would have a dramatic effect on life on Earth.

氣溫只要稍微降個攝氏三度，便會對地球上的生物產生巨大影響。

> **解說** as ... as ➲ Pre 58
>
> 依句意，雖然只降了 3 度這麼「少」，還是會產生很大的影響，故應選 (D) as little as。注意，句中的 dramatic 原意為「戲劇性的」，在此可作「巨大」解。

Part ⑥ Text Completion 短文填空題

☆470 分等級 ☆☆600 分等級 ☆☆☆730 分以上

● 71 ~ 73 信件（letter）

第 71 ~ 73 題與以下的信件內容有關。

來自「越過國境之手」的地震救災呼籲

針對最近地震的無數倖存者的大規模救援工作，仍持續 (71.) 進行中。

我們預估提供避難所、食物、緊急經濟援助及醫療服務將花費超過 10 億美元。只靠政府援助是不夠的。還得 (72.) 仰賴「跨越國境之手」這類組織及個人的協助。有數以千計的人們 (73.) 亟需援助，而重建將是個漫長又艱辛的工作。您的捐款對於幫助我們持續提供這迫切需要之援助來說非常重要。

截至目前為止，我們已經以食物和避難所的形式提供了 5 億美元以上的直接經濟援助給許多家庭。但是接下來還必須進行好幾週、好幾個月的救災工作。請您盡力提供援助。

---

71. 正確答案：(B) ☆☆

解說 詞彙類問題 ─

依前後文意，(B) underway「進行中」為正確答案。(A) undergo 指「忍受、經歷」，(C) underweight 是「體重過輕」之意，(D) underground 則指「地下的」，皆與文意不合。

72. 正確答案：(B) ☆

解說 常用片語 ─

片語 be up to ... 可指「仰賴……」，(B) 為唯一符合前後文意的選項。be up to sb. 則指「由某人決定」，如 It's up to you.「由你決定。」

73. 正確答案：(A) ☆☆

解說 固定說法 ─

in need of ... 為固定說法，in desperate need of 指「極需」。

● 74 ~ 76 報導文章

第 74 ~ 76 題與以下的報導文章有關。

「公平貿易，一種商業新趨勢」

現今，許多已開發國家的企業紛紛開始熱衷於奉行貿易原則。(74.) 也就是說，他們試圖盡可能做到讓商務運作對於人類及環境的傷害降至最低，同時更加關切改善世界各地生活水準所必須做的事之關切。

所謂的公平貿易包括以下這些規則：

規則 1　不投資政府 (75.) 罔顧人民人權的國家。
規則 2　不投資營業活動會破壞環境的公司。
規則 3　不投資用動物進行產品 (76.) 實驗的公司。

---

74. 正確答案：(D) ☆☆

解說 連接表達 ⊃ Pre 76

由於第二句的內容解釋了第一句的意思，所以用 (D) In other words「換言之」作為起承轉合最合理。至於 (A)、(B)、(C)，則皆為逆接詞，所以都不對。

75. 正確答案：(B) ☆☆

解說 詞彙類問題

此處的三項規則列出的都是不投資的對象，規則 1 的對象應為「罔顧國民人權」之政府，故應選 (B) deny。而其他選項 (A) stop「停止」、(C) quit「放棄」、(D) prohibit「禁止」，在意思上都說不通。

76. 正確答案：(A) ☆☆

解說 詞彙

規則 3 中不投資對象應該是「用動物進行產品實驗」的公司，故選 (A) test。(B) examine「檢查」、(C) exercise「運用」、(D) experience「經歷」皆與句意不符。

Part 7 Reading Comprehension 文章理解題

☆470 分等級 ☆☆600 分等級 ☆☆☆730 分以上

● **77 ~ 80 介紹性文章**

第 77 ~ 80 題與以下的介紹性文章有關。

派崔克‧J‧芬利
創辦人兼首席執行長

派崔克‧芬利在娛樂產業中的多方面背景包括超過 15 年在授權業務、製作、契約法及財務等方面的經驗。他在 2001 年時創立了天使娛樂公司，在他的帶領下，該公司已成為具影響力以年輕人為導向的娛樂領導品牌。芬利先生不僅是一位熟練的製作人，還因 16 歲之前都住在橫濱，所以能說一口流利的日語。他經常以主講嘉賓的身分出現在國際會議中。此外，他也在美國和日本的大學擔任客座講師。

身為天使娛樂公司的執行長和總裁，芬利先生募集到的股值，超過了 1,500 萬美元，他還親自洽談並和許多國際的出版、電玩遊戲、動畫和電影公司簽訂了授權協議。

在創辦天使娛樂公司之前，芬利先生曾積極參與多個創新數位娛樂專案的創作及製作工作。芬利先生擁有西雅圖大學的經濟學學士學位。在從米德蘭大學法律中心畢業後，他以律師身分展開了他的事業，同時為華盛頓州律師協會的會員。

Word List

- □ founder [`faʊndə] 名 創辦人
- □ equity [`ɛkwətɪ] 名 股票價值
- □ multifaceted [`mʌltɪˌfæsɪtɪd] 形 多方面的
- □ attorney [ə`tɜnɪ] 名 律師

---

77. 正確答案：(C) ☆

What is Patrick J. Finley's main area of professional activity?

派崔克‧J‧芬利先生的主要專業領域為何？

(A) He is a lawyer.	他是個律師。
(B) He is an entertainer.	他是個藝人。
(C) He is a company boss.	**他是個公司老闆。**
(D) He is a university lecturer.	他是個大學講師。

解說

由一開始列在芬利先生名字之下的頭銜以及第二段的第一句提到的 CEO and president of Angel Entertainment 可知，(C) 為正確選項。注意，律師和大學講師並非芬利先生的主要領域（main area），所以 (A) 與 (D) 皆不對。

78. 正確答案：(A) ☆☆

Which market does Angel Entertainment focus on?　　天使娛樂公司主攻於哪個市場？

(A) Young people　　　　　　　　　　　　　**年輕人**
(B) The United States　　　　　　　　　　　　美國
(C) Japan　　　　　　　　　　　　　　　　　日本
(D) International events　　　　　　　　　　　國際活動

> **解說**
>
> 由第一段第二句提到的 ... the company has become an influential youth-oriented entertainment brand. 可知，正確答案為 (A)。

79. 正確答案：(A) ☆☆

As CEO, what has Mr. Finley done for his company?
身為首席執行長，芬利先生為他的公司做了什麼？

(A) Issued stocks worth over $15 million　　**發行了價值超過 1,500 萬美元的股票**
(B) Signed contracts worth over $15 million　　簽署了價值超過 1,500 萬美元的合約
(C) Set up branch offices in Japan　　　　　在日本設立了分公司
(D) Collaborated with universities　　　　　與大學合作

> **解說**
>
> 由第二段第一句有提到的 As CEO ... Mr. Finley has raised over $15 million in equity ... 可知，正確答案為 (A)。注意，提到相同數字的 (B)、提到日本的 (C) 以及提到大學的 (D) 皆為誤導選項，千萬不要上當。

80. 正確答案：(C) ☆☆☆

When did Mr. Finley become involved in digital entertainment?
芬利先生何時開始參與數位娛樂產業？

(A) While he was a university student　　　　在他還是大學生的時候
(B) Since going to Japan　　　　　　　　　自從去了日本之後
(C) Before setting up Angel Entertainment　**在創辦天使娛樂公司之前**
(D) After negotiating licensing deals　　　　在洽談授權協議之後

> **解說**
>
> 最後一段第一句明確提到 Prior to founding Angel Entertainment, Mr. Finley was active in ... digital entertainment projects.，所以正確答案為 (C)。注意，原文中的 prior to 就是答案中 before 之意，而原文用的 founding 在答案中則用同義的 setting up 表示。

● **81 ~ 84 廣告**

第 81 ~ 84 題與以下廣告有關。

購買 TMR 3G 手機——最高可獲得 50 美元回饋

現在，若您於限定期間內直接來 TMR.com 購買一支 TMR 3G 手機，並簽訂 2 年的服務合約，就能獲得 50 美元的郵寄退款。或者您也可以簽 1 年的服務合約，以獲得 20 美元的郵寄退款。這表示您現在只要花區區 99 美元，就能買到最新最熱門的 3G 手機。

若要利用此優惠，只需：

1. 在 2005 年 10 月 1 日至 2005 年 12 月 31 日期間至 TMR.com 購買新手機並啟用新服務門號。

   請注意：購買價格必須在 149 美元以上才可享有此優惠。

2. 在選取合約方案時，請選 2 年服務合約以獲得 50 美元的郵寄退款，或選 1 年的服務合約以獲得 20 美元的郵寄退款。

3. 待您的 TMR 3G 手機送達後，請將下列資料郵寄至申請表所列地址：

   填寫完成的退款申請表

   售貨收據或確認訂單之電子郵件影本

   從您的 TMR 3G 手機包裝盒剪下的原始條碼（不接受影本）

4. 好好享受您的新 TMR 3G 手機！您的郵寄退款應會在 8 至 10 週以內寄達。退款支票必須在開出日算起 90 天內兌現。

Word List

☐ take advantage of 利用……

☐ mail-in rebate [`ribet] 以郵寄優惠券或支票的方式提供之折扣服務

---

81. 正確答案：(D) ☆☆

What is this passage telling people about?　　　　這篇文章要告訴人們什麼？

(A) A low-priced brand item　　　　低價名牌商品

(B) A clearance sale　　　　清倉大拍賣

(C) A trade-in discount　　　　舊換新折扣

(D) A money-back offer for a limited time　　　　**期間限定的現金回饋優惠**

由廣告的標題 Buy a TMR mobile phone—get up to $50 banck 即可知正解為 (D)。

82. 正確答案：(A) ☆☆

What should people do to get a $50 cash-back bonus?

要怎麼做才能獲得 50 美元的現金回饋優惠？

(A) **Buy a TMR 3G and apply for a two-year service period**　　**購買一支 TMR 3G 手機並申請 2 年的服務合約**

(B) Use a credit card to buy a TMR 3G　　使用信用卡購買一支 TMR 3G 手機

(C) Cash a check within 90 days　　在 90 天內兌現支票

(D) Spend up to $149 on a TMR 3G　　最多花 149 美元購買 TMR 3G 手機

解說

廣告第一段及條件第二項都提到簽兩年的服務合約 (a two-year service contract) 就可獲得 50 美元的郵寄退款 ($50 mail-in rebate)，所以正確答案為 (A)。而支票只是回饋金的形式，並非回饋條件，所以 (C) 不對。另外，149 美元是金額下限（最少要花 149 美元）不是上限，所以 (D) 也不對。(B) 選項的資訊則屬無中生有。

83. 正確答案：(C) ☆☆

What items do people have to send to take advantage of this offer?

人們必須寄出哪些資料才能利用此項優惠？

(A) A completed rebate form, an original sales slip and barcode cut out from the box　　填寫完成的退款申請表、收據正本和從包裝盒剪下的條碼

(B) A completed rebate form, copies of the sales slip and the barcode　　填寫完成的退款申請表、收據和條碼影本

(C) **A completed rebate form, a copy of the sales slip and an original barcode**　　**填寫完成的退款申請表、收據影本和條碼正本**

(D) A completed rebate form, copies of the sales slip and the order confirmation e-mail　　填寫完成的退款申請表、收據和確認訂單之電子郵件的影本

解說

第三項條件清楚列出 completed rebate form、copy of sales receipt、original barcode，所以正確答案為 (C)。而收據寄影本即可，所以 (A) 不對；條碼必須是剪下的原始條碼，所以 (B) 也不對；最後，(D) 選項沒列出原始條碼，因此亦非正確答案。

84. 正確答案：(B) ☆☆

Under what conditions does the rebate offer apply? 在什麼條件下此退款優惠才適用？

(A) On 2-year service contracts only　　　　　　僅限簽訂 2 年服務合約者

(B) On 1-year and 2-year service contracts　　**簽訂 1 年或 2 年服務合約者**

(C) On any phone costing more than $99　　　手機價格在 99 美元以上者

(D) On any phone purchased in 2005　　　　　任何於 2005 年購買的手機

> 解說
>
> 廣告第一段就提到 ... you can get a $50 ... for a two-year service contract. Or get a $20 ... with a one-year service contract.，而條件第 2 項也列出相同的資訊，所以正確答案為 (B)。而購買金額方面的限制應該是 149 美元以上，所以 (C) 不對；至於日期限制方面，則是 2005 年 10 月 1 日到 12 月 31 日為止所購買的手機才能享有優惠，故 (D) 為非。

● 85 ~ 87 公告通知

第 85 ~ 87 題與以下的公告通知有關。

雷德班克市
廢棄物與資源回收

為了支付增加了 **32%** 的垃圾掩埋費用，市政府必須提高廢棄物回收費。然而只要有以下的廢棄物清理許可證，雷德班克市居民便可將特定家庭廢棄物免費丟棄於市立垃圾場。

該許可證僅限雷德班克市居民使用。

廢棄物傾倒開放時間：上午 7 點 30 分 ~ 下午 4 點，每週 7 天，國定假日除外。

營利單位不可使用家庭廢棄物許可證來丟棄營業廢棄物。

遺失或弄丟廢棄物許可證（如下所示）的居民，將須支付 30 美元現金。此筆現金費用不可退還。

　廢棄物清理許可證
　雷德班克市
　地產：雷德班克市，325格雷森街

　此證可供市區住戶在雷德班克市
　垃圾場丟棄花園廢棄物或塑膠廢棄
　物時使用
　（此證不可轉讓）

＊持有者可能會被要求出示與此證所記載地址相符的居住證明。

---

85. 正確答案：(B) ☆☆

What information does the City of Redbank want to convey to residents?
雷德班克市要向居民傳達什麼資訊？

(A) Details of new waste disposal charges　　新的廢棄物處理費用細節

(B) How to dispose of some waste free of charge　　**如何免費丟棄某些廢棄物**

(C) The location of a new waste disposal facility　　新廢棄物處理設施的所在位置

(D) How to pay for waste disposal　　如何支付廢棄物處理費

> **解說**
>
> 由公告第一段第二句提到的 ... entitles residents ... to dispose of specified domestic waste at the city dump free of charge. 可知，正確答案為 (B)。

86. 正確答案：(D) ☆☆

Who can use the pass?　　誰能使用該許可證？

(A) Any resident of the City of Redbank　　任何雷德班克市的居民

(B) Any business located in the City of Redbank　　所有位於雷德班克市的公司行號

(C) City waste disposal employees　　市立廢棄物處理設施的員工

(D) The resident whose address is on the pass　　**其地址記載於該許可證上的居民**

> **解說**
>
> 由廢棄物清理許可證反面下方標註的 This pass is not transferable「此許可證不可轉讓」可知，並非「任何」居民皆可使用此證。而由許可證正面必須記載持證者的地址是否屬實，及公告最下方必須出示居住證明的規定來看，(D) 為最佳答案。

87. 正確答案：(A) ☆

What must a resident do if he or she does not have a pass when dumping waste?
在丟棄廢棄物時未持有許可證的居民必須做什麼？

(A) Pay a fee

(B) Apply for a new pass

(C) Pay a fee and ask for a refund later

(D) Register his or her name and address

支付費用

申請新的許可證

先付費，稍後再要求退費

登錄其姓名與地址

解說

第五段第一句提到 Residents who misplace or lose their Waste passes ... pay $30 in cash，也就是說，沒許可證就要付費，所以正確答案為 (A)。而第五段則寫明了 This cash patment is non-refundable，所以不能選 (C)。

● 88 ~ 90 宣傳公告

第 88 ~ 90 題與以下的宣傳公告有關。

一項針對油電混合車所設立的新法律已經生效。若您在 2009 年 12 月 31 日前購買新的油電混合車，就有資格獲得最高可達 2,000 美元的聯邦所得稅減免一次。

而該扣除額將依據該車輛的燃料經濟效益、預估省油量及其他因素而定。

有資格獲得課稅減免優惠的車輛，還必須符合以下條件：

a 你必須購買新車，而且必須是自用，不能轉賣。

b 你必須主要行駛美國地區。

c 該車輛必須符合所有聯邦與州的廢棄排放要求。

d 政府相關部門、免稅機構及外國機構都不具資格。

其它條件亦可申請。請上我們的網站了解與扣抵稅額有關的最新資訊。

Word List

☐ effective [ɪˋfɛktɪv] 形 （法律等）生效的、起作用的

☐ eligible for ... [ˋɛlɪdʒəbl] 有……的資格

☐ deduction [dɪˋdʌkʃən] 名 扣除、減免

☐ tax-exempt organizations [ˋtæksɪgˋzɛmpt ͵ɔrgənəˋzeʃən] 不必繳稅的團體、免稅機構

☐ foreign entitiy [ˋfɔrɪn ˋɛntətɪ] 外國機構

88. 正確答案：(B) ☆☆

What benefit can people get if they buy a new hybrid car on December 15, 2009?

在 2009 年 12 月 15 日購買新油電混合車的人可享有何種好處？

(A) They can get $2,000 cash back. 可獲得 2,000 美元的現金回饋。

(B) They can have a maximum of $2,000 deducted from their taxable income. **所得課稅最多可扣除 2,000 美元。**

(C) They have until December 31 to pay the tax. 稅款的繳納期限至 12 月 31 日為止。

(D) They can apply for a tax deduction at any time. 可隨時申請課稅減免優惠。

> **解說**
>
> 第一段第二句中提到的 income tax deduction of up to $2,000 與 (B) 中的 maximum of $2,000 deducted from their taxable income 為同義表達，故選 (B)。

89. 正確答案：(C) ☆☆

How will the amount of tax deduction be decided? 扣除額將如何決定？

(A) It will depend on the size of the car. 將依據車輛大小而定。

(B) It will depend on the cost of the car. 將依據車輛價格而定。

(C) It will depend on the gas mileage and energy savings. **將依據汽油的里程數油耗和節省能源的程度而定。**

(D) It will be up to the tax office to decide. 將由稅務機關決定。

> **解說**
>
> 第二段提到的 the vehicle's fuel economy, estimated fuel savings, ... 與 (C) 中的 gas mileage and energy savings 為同義表達，故選 (C)。

90. 正確答案：(C) ☆☆

What kind of hybrid car qualifies for a tax deduction? 哪種油電混合車才具備課稅減免資格？

(A) One used by a foreign company 外商公司所用的車

(B) One imported from Japan 從日本進口的車

(C) One bought new for personal use **新購入的自用車**

(D) One that is intended to be resold 以轉賣為目的而購入的車

> **解說**
>
> 由條件項目 a 所寫的 You must purchase the vehicle new and for your own use, not for sale. 可知，(C) 為正確答案，(D) 則錯誤。而項目 d 寫明了 Government agencies, taxexempt organizations, and foreign entities are not eligible.，所以 (A) 的外商公司資格不符。另外，文中並無與 (B) 相關的敘述。

● 91 ~ 95 電子郵件

第 91 ~ 95 題與以下的電子郵件有關。

電子郵件

收件人：法蘭西斯·戴爾摩
寄件人：羅傑·克勞福德
主旨：要出租的房子

親愛的戴爾摩小姐，

我很有興趣於今年夏天在法國南部租一間房子，我看到了您在該區的房屋出租廣告。依據您的簡短描述，它似乎非常合適，但是在明確出價之前我想再確認幾點。我想在整個七和八月份承租一間房子。我正在寫一本書，所以需要一個可讓我專心寫作的安靜房子。我太太是一位畫家，因此她會需要一間有窗戶面向南邊的大房間，以便她可以盡可能獲得最充足的陽光。我們還有一對雙胞胎男孩，他們將共用一間房間。他們很喜歡游泳，所以我們希望能離海近些（最好頂多 30 分鐘車程的距離）。由於房子位於鄉間，因此我希望我們帶著狗兒過去也不會有問題。如果您能儘快以電子郵件答覆我，我將非常感激，因為我們希望在為時太晚之前確定能租到一間房子。

羅傑·克勞福德
祝好

電子郵件

收件人：羅傑・克勞福德
寄件人：法蘭西斯・戴爾摩
主旨：回覆：要出租的房子

親愛的克勞福德先生，

非常感謝您來信詢問我在法國南部的房子。那是一間美麗的老農舍，有一個大廚房、一個客廳、一個餐廳、四間臥房和兩間衛浴。還有一個大花園。讓我回答一下您所提出的幾個問題。房子和周圍環境都非常安寧幽靜。事實上，房屋本身座落在村莊邊緣一條車流量極少的鄉間道路旁。主臥室是最大的，而且向南，應該最適合您的夫人做為工作室使用。而這表示您和您的夫人就必須睡在第二臥室，不過別擔心，因為這間臥室也相當大。唯一的問題是，最近的海灘距離約 1 小時車程。不過，在離房子步行只要 10 分鐘的地方有一個湖。這個湖很乾淨、安全，非常受到當地家庭的歡迎。

當然，狗兒不是問題。不過，我曾經有過幾個房客帶了貓來。那些貓造成了相當多的損壞，因此我恐怕無法再接受貓那些動物了！如果您仍有興趣租屋，請盡快和我聯繫。

法蘭西斯・戴爾摩
謹啓

Word List

- [ ] description [dɪ`skrɪpʃən] 說明、描述
- [ ] definite offer [`dɛfənɪt `ɔfə] 明確出價
- [ ] rental property [`rɛntl `prɑpətɪ] 租賃房地產

91. 正確答案：(D) ☆☆

What is the relationship between Frances Delmore and Roger Crawford?

法蘭西斯‧戴爾摩和羅傑‧克勞福德之間是什麼關係？

(A) Frances Delmore owns the house Roger Crawford lives in.	法蘭西斯‧戴爾摩擁有羅傑‧克勞福德所住的房子。
(B) Roger Crawford wants to buy Frances Delmore's house.	羅傑‧克勞福德想購買法蘭西斯‧戴爾摩的房子。
(C) They are old friends.	他們是老朋友。
(D) They have never met each other.	**他們從沒見過面。**

解說

由第一封電子郵件第一句中的 I saw your advertisement for a house ... 可知，這兩人彼此並不認識，所以正確答案是 (D)。

小心陷阱

由第一句提到的 I'm very interested in renting a house ... in summer ... 可知克勞福德應不是要「買」房子，因此請小心別被 (B) 選項所騙。

92. 正確答案：(C) ☆

What does Roger Crawford want to do in the summer?

羅傑‧克勞福德想在這個夏天做些什麼？

(A) Spend three months in the south of France.	在南法度過三個月。
(B) Paint a picture of his wife.	畫一張他太太的畫像。
(C) Find a quiet place to write.	**找個安靜的地方寫作。**
(D) Have a vacation at the beach.	在沙灘度假。

解說

由第一封電子郵件的第四句所提到的 I am in the process of writing a book and so I need a quiet house ... 可知，正確答案為 (C)。

小心陷阱

第三句清楚寫道 I would like to rent a house for the whole of July and August.，所以 (A) 選項說的三個月是錯的。

93. 正確答案：(D) ☆☆

What problem does Frances Delmore mention?　　法蘭西斯・戴爾摩提到了什麼問題？

(A) There is nowhere for the boys to swim.　　男孩們沒地方可游泳。

(B) No room faces south.　　沒有面向南的房間。

(C) The house is far away from the village.　　該房屋離村莊很遠。

(D) Some pets are not allowed.　　**有些寵物不被允許帶入。**

> **解說**
>
> 第二封電子郵件第二段的第一句提到 Dogs ... are no problem.，而第三句說 The cats caused ... a lot of damage ... those animals are no longer welcome!，這表示可以帶狗但是不能帶貓，因此正確答案為 (D)。而第一段最後提到 ... there's a beautiful lake ... It's clean, safe and very popular with local families，所以 (A) 不對；第一段的第六句提到 The master bedroom ... faces south ...，所以 (B) 也不對；第一段第五句提到 The house actually stands at the edge of the village ...，因此 (C) 亦非正確答案。

💣 **小心陷阱**

由於第七句提到 The only problem is that the closest beach is about one-hour's drive away.，所以可能有人會誤選 (A)。但是接下來有步行可到、很受當地人歡迎的湖」，因此選項 (A)「沒地方可游泳」的說法是不對的。

94. 正確答案：(C) ☆☆

How many bedrooms will Roger Crawford's family likely use?

羅傑・克勞福德一家可能會使用幾間房間？

(A) One 1　　　　　(B) Two 2　　　　　(C) Three 3　　　　　**(D) Four 4**

> **解說**
>
> 第二封電子郵件中提到 master bedroom 可作為 studio，克勞福德和他太太則可以睡 the second bedroom，加上第一封電子郵件中提到的 ... twin boys ... will share a bedroom，所以一共會用到 3 個房間。

💣 **小心陷阱**

請注意，雖然第二封電子郵件的第二句提到 It's a beautifl old farmhouse with ... four bedrooms. 但並未提到羅傑・克勞福德一家會用到所有房間，因此不可誤選 (D)。

95. 正確答案：(A) ☆

In the first e-mail, the phrase "in the process of" in line 4, is closest in meaning to

第一封電子郵件第四行裡的片語「in the process of」意義最相近

(A) in the middle of   **正在……當中**

(B) about to finish   即將完成

(C) doing research for   調查……

(D) having problems with   有問題

> **解說**
>
> 該句提到 I am in the process of writing a book ... I need a quiet house ...，依前後文意來判斷，其意思應是因為「正在」寫書，所以需要一間安靜的房子，故正確答案為 (A)。若是即將完成書，那就不用租房子了，所以 (B) 不對，而 (C) 與 (D) 的意思都無法與租屋連在一起，因此也非正確答案。

● 96～100 廣告與電子郵件

第 96～100 題與以下的廣告和電子郵件有關。

廣告

請試試效果驚人的 Permawarm 發熱墊！

Permawarm 發熱墊

·持續發熱 12 小時　　　　·超輕巧　　　　·無臭味

Permawarm 發熱墊是您需要穩定熱源的最佳選擇。Permawarm 發熱墊輕薄、可攜帶。只要將發熱墊放在您身體需要熱敷的位置上即可。這樣發熱墊便會自然發熱，提供最長可達 12 小時的持續溫熱。除了用於緩解運動傷害與肌肉痠痛外，也可帶到戶外任何你覺得寒冷的地方。

足部專用 Permawarm 發熱墊

·持續發熱 5 小時　　　　·輕薄舒適

·貼合足部形狀　　　　·抗菌除臭

足部專用 Permawarm 發熱墊採取貼合男鞋及女鞋形狀之設計，可在您想維持腳趾的溫暖舒適時發揮功效。當您在戶外觀賞運動競賽、參加在室外舉辦的如婚禮或賽跑等活動，或進行滑雪及釣魚等戶外活動時，都可使用足部專用的 Permawarm 發熱墊。足部專用 Permawarm 發熱墊有防滑設計，能固定在您的鞋內，而且還能抗菌除臭。

若想獲得更多資訊，請來信至 info@permawarm.com 與我們聯繫。

☐ odorless [ˋodəlɪs] 形 無臭的

電子郵件

收件人：info@permawarm.com
寄件人：hnielsen@sol.com
主旨：詢問關於 Permawarm 發熱墊

今天稍早我在瀏覽網路時偶然發現了貴公司的網站。我先生和我在哥本哈根經營一家小公司。我們已經營業了大約 2 年左右，而本公司目前在丹麥、挪威、瑞典及芬蘭都有穩定的客源。我們主要經手女性服飾配件，我認為對我們的產品線來說，加入貴公司的發熱墊將如虎添翼。

本公司為網路銷售商——我們只透過我們的網站販賣。我非常有興趣想了解貴公司更多的產品細節。此外，如果銷售結果很成功，我們也建立了良好的合作關係的話，是否能討論未來讓我們成為貴公司在斯堪地納維亞地區之之獨家代理的可能性？

非常期待您的回應。若您有興趣，可以到我們公司的網站 www.allegria.co.dk 去看看我們目前的產品線。

順頌商祺
希爾達‧尼爾森
總裁

☐ stable [ˋstebl] 形 穩定的

☐ vendor [ˋvɛndə] 名 小販、銷售商

☐ exclusive distributor [ɪkˋsklusɪv dɪˋstrɪbjətə] 獨家代理商

96. 正確答案：(B) ☆☆

How many different products does Permawarm offer?　　Permawarm 提供幾種不同的商品？

(A) One 1 種　　　**(B) Two 2 種**　　　(C) Five 5 種　　　(D) Twelve 12 種

> **解說**
>
> 廣告中宣傳的是 Permawarm Heat Pads「Permawarm 發熱墊」與 Permawarm Heat Pads for Feet「足部專用 Permawarm 發熱墊」兩種產品，所以正確答案為 (B)。而 (C) 的數字 5 是「足部專用」產品持續發熱的時數，(D) 的數字 12 則是「身體用」產品的持續發熱時數。與數字有關的問題，一定要快速掃瞄過以爭取時間，但是由於這種題目一定都包含陷阱選項，須小心別弄錯各數字所代表的意義。

97. 正確答案：(D) ☆☆☆

What is NOT included in the features of Permawarm Heat Pads for Feet?
足部專用的 Permawarm 發熱墊不包含以下哪項功能？

(A) They keep your feet free of germs and bad smells. 它們能避免足部產生細菌或難聞的氣味。

(B) They do not move around in your shoes.　　它們不會在你的鞋子裡滑來滑去。

(C) They last for five hours.　　它們能維持 5 小時。

(D) They are waterproof.　　**它們可防水。**

> **解說**
>
> 在列出的四個特點中就提到 Anti-bacterial and deodorizing「抗菌除臭」而內文部分的最後一句又再次提到 antibacterial and deodorizing，也提到 designed not to slip when inside your shoes「有防滑設計，能固定在您的鞋內」，所以 (A)、(B) 皆不能選。另外，列出的四個特點亦包括 Last for five hours，因此 (C) 亦不可選。廣告中唯一沒提到的只有 waterproof，因此正確答案為 (D)。

98. 正確答案：(D) ☆☆

What does Hilde Nielsen's company do?　　希爾達‧尼爾森的公司是做什麼的？

(A) It provides Internet service.　　提供網路連線服務。

(B) It sells goods in fashion stores.　　在服飾店販賣商品。

(C) It is a wholesale supplier.　　是批發商。

(D) It sells goods online.　　**是在網路上販賣商品。**

> **解說**
>
> 由電子郵件第二段第一句提到的 The company is an Internet-based vendor ...「本公司為網路銷售商」可知，正確答案為 (D)，因為 Internet-based vendor 做的就是 sells goods online。

99. 正確答案：(B) ☆☆

Why is Hilde Nielsen interested in Permawarm's products?

希爾達‧尼爾森為何對 Permawarm 的產品有興趣？

(A) They are cheap. 因為它們便宜。

(B) They go with her company's other products. 因為它們能搭配她公司的其他商品。

(C) Scandinavia has cold winters. 因為北歐的冬天很冷。

(D) Her husband recommended them. 因為她先生推薦它們。

解說

由電子郵件第一段的最後一句提到的 ... I think your headed pads would be a very useful addition to our range of products.「我認為對我們的產品線來說，加入貴公司的發熱墊將會如虎添翼」，換句話說，尼爾森認為 Permawarm 的產品可以用來搭配她公司的其他商品，因此本題選 (B)。

100. 正確答案：(C) ☆☆

What does Hilde Nielsen want her company to do in the future?

希爾達‧尼爾森希望她的公司將來做什麼？

(A) Start to manufacture heat pads. 開始製造發熱墊。

(B) Set up branches all over Scandinavia. 在北歐各地開分店。

(C) Become Permawarm's only Scandinavian importer. 成為 Permawarm 公司在北歐地區唯一的進口商。

(D) Give up its current business and become a wholesaler. 放棄其目前業務，成為批發商。

解說

電子郵件第二段最後一句所提到的 ... becoming your exclusive distributor in Scandinavia ...「成為斯地納維亞地區之獨家代理」就指向正確答案 (C)。注意，在 (C) 選項裡原文的 exclusive distributor 用了同義的 only importer「唯一進口商」來取代。

解答與解說

Full Test（200 題）

解答一覽表

Listening Section

Part	No.	正解	你的答案		Part	No.	正解	你的答案
Part 1	1	C				51	C	
	2	A				52	D	
	3	B				53	B	
	4	D				54	C	
	5	C				55	D	
	6	D				56	A	
	7	C				57	C	
	8	C				58	B	
	9	D				59	B	
	10	A				60	B	
Part 2	11	B				61	A	
	12	A				62	C	
	13	B				63	A	
	14	C				64	D	
	15	C				65	B	
	16	C				66	C	
	17	B				67	C	
	18	B				68	D	
	19	B				69	A	
	20	A				70	D	
	21	A			Part 4	71	C	
	22	C				72	D	
	23	A				73	B	
	24	C				74	B	
	25	A				75	A	
	26	B				76	D	
	27	A				77	D	
	28	A				78	C	
	29	C				79	A	
	30	B				80	B	
	31	B				81	B	
	32	C				82	A	
	33	A				83	C	
	34	A				84	A	
	35	C				85	C	
	36	C				86	D	
	37	A				87	C	
	38	B				88	A	
	39	A				89	D	
	40	B				90	C	
Part 3	41	D				91	B	
	42	C				92	B	
	43	A				93	A	
	44	B				94	D	
	45	C				95	B	
	46	C				96	B	
	47	B				97	C	
	48	C				98	B	
	49	D				99	A	
	50	B				100	C	

Reading Section

Part	No.	正解	你的答案
Part 5	101	A	
	102	A	
	103	D	
	104	D	
	105	A	
	106	B	
	107	B	
	108	A	
	109	B	
	110	B	
	111	A	
	112	D	
	113	C	
	114	B	
	115	A	
	116	A	
	117	D	
	118	C	
	119	A	
	120	B	
	121	C	
	122	C	
	123	A	
	124	B	
	125	C	
	126	D	
	127	D	
	128	D	
	129	A	
	130	B	
	131	A	
	132	C	
	133	A	
	134	D	
	135	C	
	136	D	
	137	D	
	138	D	
	139	C	
	140	B	
Part 6	141	D	
	142	D	
	143	C	
	144	D	
	145	B	
	146	A	
	147	C	
	148	C	
	149	B	
	150	B	

Part	No.	正解	你的答案
	151	B	
	152	B	
Part 7	153	C	
	154	D	
	155	A	
	156	C	
	157	B	
	158	C	
	159	C	
	160	A	
	161	B	
	162	D	
	163	B	
	164	A	
	165	C	
	166	B	
	167	B	
	168	D	
	169	B	
	170	D	
	171	B	
	172	C	
	173	D	
	174	B	
	175	C	
	176	D	
	177	C	
	178	B	
	179	D	
	180	A	
	181	B	
	182	C	
	183	B	
	184	B	
	185	D	
	186	C	
	187	B	
	188	B	
	189	D	
	190	D	
	191	A	
	192	C	
	193	B	
	194	C	
	195	A	
	196	C	
	197	A	
	198	D	
	199	B	
	200	B	

請記下 Full Test 的成績。

	答對題數	答對率	目標答對率
Part 1	/ 10	%	90%
Part 2	/ 30	%	80%
Part 3	/ 30	%	70%
Part 4	/ 30	%	70%
合計	/ 100	%	75%

	答對題數	答對率	目標答對率
Part 5	/ 40	%	70%
Part 6	/ 12	%	70%
Part 7	/ 48	%	70%
合計	/ 100	%	70%

1. 正確答案：(C) ☆　　　　　　　　　　　　　　　　　🔊 52

(A) The house is being built.　　　　　　　這房屋正在建造中。

(B) The house looks hardly livable.　　　　這房屋看來幾乎不能住。

(C) The house is made of wood.　　　　**這房屋是木造的。**

(D) The house is made of plastic material.　這房屋是塑膠製的。

> **解説** 被動式 ⊃ Pre 4
>
> 圖片顯示的是間小木屋，(C)「這房屋是木造的」為正確答案。由於房屋看來狀況還不錯，因此 (B) 的 hardly livable「幾乎不能住」，並非正解。

2. 正確答案：(A) ☆☆

(A) Some people are waiting in line.　　**有一些人在排隊。**

(B) The lobby is deserted.　　　　　　　大廳空無一人。

(C) People are in a hurry.　　　　　　　人們都在趕時間。

(D) Passengers have just arrived.　　　乘客們剛剛抵達。

> **解説** 人的動作、狀態、不依臆測作答 ⊃ Pre1, 5
>
> 由照片可以看到的確「有一些人在排隊」，故 (A) 為正確選項。請注意此選項中的 some people 指「幾個人」，和 (C) 選項的 people「所有的人」兩者意思的差異。另外，(D) 以現在完成式描述「乘客們剛剛抵達」只是種臆測，非正確答案。

3. 正確答案：(B) ☆☆

(A) The dogs are the same size.　　　　　狗兒們的體型一樣大。

(B) The dogs are on leashes.　　　　　**狗兒們都被皮帶拴著。**

(C) The dogs are barking at each other.　狗兒們正在對彼此吠叫。

(D) The dogs are facing away from each other.　狗兒們沒有面對面。

> **解説** 物的狀態 ⊃ Pre 1, 2
>
> 照片顯示兩隻狗都 on leashes「被皮帶拴著」，故 (B) 為正確選項。而這隻狗大小不同，雖然面對面，但是並沒有在吠叫，因此 (A)、(C)、(D) 皆誤。

4. 正確答案：(D) ☆☆

(A) The beautician is having her hair tied.　　　美容師正在接受綁頭髮的服務。

(B) The beautician is spraying the customer's hair.　美容師正對著客人的頭髮噴東西。

(C) The customer is having his hair trimmed.　　客人正在接受剪髮服務。

(D) The customer is having his hair washed.　**客人正在接受洗髮服務。**

解說 人的動作 ➔ Pre 1

照片顯示美容師 (beautician) 正在為客人 (customer) 洗頭。反之，就是客人在接受洗髮的服務，(D) 為正解。注意，本句使役動詞 have 的受詞之後用過去分詞來表示「被動」。

5. 正確答案：(C) ☆☆

(A) A picture hangs on the wall.	牆上掛著一張畫。
(B) The armchair is facing the wall.	有扶手的椅子面向牆壁。
(C) There are table lamps on each side of the sofa.	**沙發兩側都有檯燈。**
(D) The lamps are on.	檯燈是點亮的。

解說 物的狀態 ➔ Pre 1, 2

此題測試考生是否能聽出物體之數量與位置。牆上掛了三張畫，並非單數的 "a picture"，故 (A) 為誤。而椅子並非朝向牆壁，(B) 不正確。照片中也看不出檯燈是亮的，(D) 不能選。唯一吻合的敘述為 (C)。另外，(C) 選項與 (D) 選項的介系詞 on 差異在於其後是否接受詞；(C) 選項 "on each side of ..." 指在……兩側，(D) 選項的 on 之後沒接受詞，作形容詞用，表示「點亮的、（機器）開著的」。

6. 正確答案：(D) ☆   ⏺ 53

(A) Only hardcover books are sold here.	這裡只賣精裝書。
(B) Train tickets are sold here.	這裡賣火車票。
(C) Medicine and liquor are sold here.	這裡賣藥品和酒類。
(D) Magazines and newspapers are sold here.	**這裡賣雜誌與報紙。**

解說 多個物體的狀態、被動式 ➔ Pre 2, 4

圖片清楚顯示此處陳列的是雜誌、報紙和書籍等商品而非精裝圖書及藥品、酒類，因此 (A)、(C) 都不對，(D) 為正解。注意，此處雖陳列書籍，但看不出為精裝書（hardcover），況且還擺放了雜誌等其他物品，故不可選 (A)。

7. 正確答案：(C) ☆☆

(A) The ocean looks stormy.	海面看來有狂風暴雨。
(B) The beach is covered with white sand.	海灘上覆蓋著白沙。
(C) The beach is bumpy and rocky.	**海灘崎嶇不平又充滿岩石。**
(D) Birds are flying over the ocean.	鳥兒正飛過海上。

解說 物的狀態 ➔ Pre 2, 4

由照片中看不出有暴風雨，海灘上沒有白沙，鳥兒也沒有在飛，所以 (A)、(B)、(D) 皆不對。而海灘的確是 bumpy「崎嶇不平」且 rocky「充滿岩石」，故 (C) 為正解。此題的重點就在於要聽出與海邊風景有關的 ocean、beach、sand、stormy、bumpy、rocky 等詞彙。

8. 正確答案：(C) ☆☆

(A) The woman is working on this floor. 這名女子正在此樓層工作。

(B) The woman is carrying a suitcase. 這名女子帶著一個行李箱。

(C) The window on the left is open for business. 左邊的窗口是打開的，正在營業中。

(D) All the windows are closed for the day. 所有窗口都已結束當天的營業。

> **解說** 人、物的狀態 ⊃ Pre 1, 2
>
> 照片中左邊窗戶上方寫著的 CURRENCY EXCHANGE 可知，這裡應該是銀行。而此窗戶是開的，也就表示為營業中，故選 (C)。請記住 (C) 的 open for business「營業中」，以及 (D) 的 closed for the day「本日營業時間結束」等商業相關表達方式。

9. 正確答案：(D) ☆☆

(A) The shovel is lying on the ground. 圖中的鏟子平放在地面上。

(B) The umbrella is used on rainy days. 圖中的傘是雨天用的。

(C) The man is putting on a T-shirt. 這名男子正在穿 T 恤。

(D) A man is smiling and posing for a picture. 這名男子正在微笑並擺姿勢拍照。

> **解說** 人的狀態 ⊃ Pre 1, 5
>
> 照片中的男子正對鏡頭微笑拍照，(D) 為正確選項。請注意 put on 和 wear 的不同處。可能有很多人會以為 (C) 也是正解，但是 is putting on 是「正在穿」的意思，因此非正解。若要表達「穿著」，則應說成 He is wearing a T-shirt.。另，照片中的傘應該是遮陽用的大傘，而不是雨傘，故不可選 (B)。而照片中的鏟子是豎立著放的，故 (A) 也不對。

10. 正確答案：(A) ☆☆

(A) Shoes are neatly put away in a shoe rack. 鞋子都整齊地收在鞋架裡。

(B) Shoes are stacked up on the floor. 鞋子都堆在地板上。

(C) The shoe rack is completely full. 鞋架已全滿。

(D) All of the shoes are brand-new. 所有鞋子都是全新的。

> **解說** 物的狀態、被動式 ⊃ Pre 1, 4
>
> 照片中所有的鞋子都已經收好放在架子裡，(A) 為正確答案。注意，(A) 選項裡的 put away 指「收拾、放好」，(B) 選項中的 stack up 則指「堆起」，(D) 選項 brand-new 指「全新的、嶄新的」。

Word List

☐ deserted [`dɛzət] 形 廢棄的、冷清無人的 (No. 2)

☐ face away from ... 不正面朝向…… (No. 3)

☐ beautician [bjuˋtɪʃən] 名 美容師 (No. 4)

☐ neatly [`nitlɪ] 副 整潔地 (No. 10)

11. 正確答案：(B) ☆   🔊 55

How do you travel to work, Paula?   寶拉，妳如何去上班？

(A) I tripped over the bicycle.   我被腳踏車絆倒了。

(B) I usually take the subway.   **我通常搭地鐵。**

(C) The roads are usually jammed.   道路通常都很壅塞。

> **解說** 使用 How 的疑問句 ➲ Pre 14
>
> travel 除了一般指 「旅行」 之外，還可如本句作「去某處」解，而 (B) 中的 take the subway 就是指向正確答案之關鍵字詞。另外，請注意 (A) 的動詞 trip 在這裡不是指「旅遊」，而是指「絆倒」，因此請小心別因題目中的 travel 一詞而選擇 (A)。

12. 正確答案：(A) ☆☆

My boss just told me I didn't get the promotion this time.
我老闆剛剛才告訴我，我這次沒能獲得升遷。

(A) I'm so sorry to hear that.   **我很遺憾聽到這個消息。**

(B) He should be promoted.   他應該獲得升遷。

(C) I don't want a promotion.   我不想升遷。

> **解說** 陳述與反應 ➲ Pre 6
>
> 解答此題的關鍵就在於要正確聽出問題裡的兩個主詞 my boss 和 I。沒獲得升遷的是說話者本人，因此應以 (A)「我很遺憾聽到這個消息」作為回應。

13. 正確答案：(B) ☆☆

How would you like your steak, sir?   先生，您的牛排要幾分熟？

(A) It's a bit tough.   有點硬。

(B) Medium rare, please.   **三分熟，麻煩你。**

(C) I think it's cheap.   我覺得很便宜。

> **解說** 使用 How 的疑問句 ➲ Pre 14
>
> How would you like your steak? 是到餐廳吃牛排一定會被問到的話，意思就是「您的牛排要幾分熟？」，只有 (B) 針對問題做回應。而 (A) 是針對 How do you like your steak? 「你覺得您的牛排（味道）如何？」問句的回答。這題考的就是分辨這兩種問句的能力。雖然兩者都常用於日常生活，但卻很容易答錯。

14. 正確答案：(C) ☆☆

Who is in charge of reporting the monthly statements?   負責報告月報表的是誰？

(A) The monthly statements are ready.   月報表已完成。

Strategies | Pre Test | Half Test 1 | Half Test 2 | Full Test

(B) It will be reported at the meeting this afternoon. 它將在今天下午的會議中被報告出來。

(C) Peter Rankin is. **是彼得‧蘭金。**

> **解說** 使用 **Who** 的疑問句 ➲ Pre 9
> 由於問句問的是 Who，所以應答人名。(C) 為正解。

---

15. 正確答案：(C) ☆☆　　　　　　　　　　　　　　　　　　　🔊 56

How long have you been working for this laboratory? 你在此實驗室工作了多久？

(A) I work 40 hours per week. 我每週工作四十小時。

(B) I worked out for two hours. 我運動了兩小時。

(C) I've been here since 2001. **我從 2001 年起就在這兒了。**

> **解說** 使用 **How** 的疑問句（How long） ➲ Pre 14
> 以 How long ... 起頭的問句可以用 for 加時間長度（如：for five years）或 since 加過去時間（如：(C) 選項）回答。(A) 說的是每週工作時間，(B) 中的 work out 則指「運動、健身」，所以兩者都答非所問。

---

16. 正確答案：(C) ☆☆

Hello, Caesar's Pizza? This is Ed Brown and I ordered 5 mixed pizzas one hour ago.
喂，凱薩比薩嗎？我叫艾德‧布朗，我 1 小時前訂了五個什錦比薩。

(A) The call has been received. 該通電話已接到。

(B) The pizza is getting cold. 比薩漸漸冷掉了。

(C) They're on their way, sir. **它們已經在路上了，先生。**

> **解說** 陳述與反應 ➲ Pre 6
> 這是與比薩外送有關的問題，表面上雖為普通的直述句，但是卻是隱含著「為什麼訂的披薩還沒有送來？」的疑問，(C) 為正解。會話中並未提到與 (B) 有關的資訊，須小心別被發音和 called 相似的 cold 所騙。

---

17. 正確答案：(B) ☆☆☆

Do you happen to have the time? 你會不會剛好知道現在幾點？

(A) Sure, what do you want? 當然。有什麼事嗎？

(B) It's a quarter past ten. **10 點 15 分。**

(C) Sorry, I'm too busy to talk now. 抱歉，我現在忙得沒空講話。

> **解說** Yes-No 疑問句 ➲ Pre 7
> Do you have the time? 是「現在幾點了？」的意思，因此本題選 (B)。注意，(A) 和 (C) 都是針對 Do you have time?「你現在有空嗎？」的回答，故為誤。

18. 正確答案：(B) ☆☆

I think Renee took the noon flight to Chicago. | 我想芮妮搭中午的飛機去芝加哥了。

(A) She arrived in Chicago at noon. | 她中午抵達了芝加哥。

(B) She should be in Chicago by now. | **她現在應該已經到芝加哥了。**

(C) She's leaving Chicago in a few hours. | 她幾小時後將離開芝加哥。

解說 陳述與反應 ➲ Pre 6

針對芮妮以搭機前往芝加哥的陳述，以「她現在應該已經到了」作為回應最合理，故選 (B)。而 (A) 說她「中午」抵達芝加哥不合理，(C) 則雖可能在未來發生，但並未針對問題做回答，所以兩者都不能選。

19. 正確答案：(B) ☆ 🎧 57

It's getting late. Shall we close up for the day? | 已經很晚了。我們是不是該打烊了？

(A) Yes, it is. | 是的，沒錯。

(B) Yes, let's. | **好，咱們就這麼做吧。**

(C) Yes, you will. | 是的，你會的。

解說 Shall we ... ? ➲ Pre 18

以 Shall we 起頭的問句可能用 Yes, let's.（let us do that）或 No, let's not（let us not do that）來回答，本題用的是前者。(A) 與 (C) 的回應則牛頭不對馬嘴。

20. 正確答案：(A) ☆☆

You haven't met my younger brother Ted yet, have you?
你還沒有見過我弟弟泰德吧，有嗎？

(A) No, I haven't. | **沒有，我還沒見過。**

(B) Yes, I haven't. | 是啊，我還沒見過。

(C) I like him very much. | 我很喜歡他。

解說 附加疑問句（否定句） ➲ Pre 16

不論問題或附加問句為肯定或否定，若答案為肯定就用 Yes，若為否定就用 No，例如本題，如果見過，就說 Yes, I have.，如果沒見過，就說 No, I haven't.（選項(C)）。(B) 的 Yes, I haven't. 剛好對應成中文的「是啊，我還沒見過」，很容易讓人一不小心就上當，但別忘了這種講法在英文裡是不成立的。

21. 正確答案：(A) ☆

Your yellow tie really goes well with your blue shirt.
你的黃領帶和藍襯衫真的很搭。

(A) Thanks. This is my favorite tie.　　　　謝了。這是我最愛的領帶。

(B) The suit is very old.　　　　　　　　　　這西裝非常舊了。

(C) The tie cost 50 dollars.　　　　　　　　這條領帶價值 50 美元。

> **解説** 陳述與反應 ➲ Pre 6 ────
> 只有 (A) 針對對方的讚美「你的黃領帶和藍襯衫真的很搭」做出回應，為正解。

22. 正確答案：(C) ☆☆

What should I wear to the welcome dinner for our new CEO?

去參加我們新執行長的歡迎晚宴時，我該穿什麼？

(A) It's going to be at the Rainbow Room.　　　該晚宴將在彩虹廳舉辦。

(B) It's going to start at 7:00 p.m.　　　　　　晚宴將於晚上 7 點開始。

(C) The invitation says 'informal.'　　　　邀請卡上寫著「非正式」。

> **解説** 使用 What 的疑問句 ➲ Pre 8 ────
> 此題的回答方式不那麼直接，而答案關鍵就在於 (C) 的 informal 這個字，間接告訴對方不需要穿得太正式。另外，(A) 說的是地點，(B) 說的是時間，兩者都沒針對問題回答，所以都不對。

23. 正確答案：(A) ☆☆　　　　　　　　　　　　　　　　　　　🔊 58

We've got to cut down on our monthly living cost or we'll go broke.

我們必須削減每個月的生活費，否則就要破產了。

(A) Maybe we can cancel some of the pay-TV　或許我們可以取消一些付費電視頻道。
channels.

(B) We should cut down the huge tree in our yard.　我們應該要砍掉院子裡的那棵大樹。

(C) They should pay us for our car that broke down.　他們應該付給我們那台拋錨車的錢。

> **解説** 陳述與反應 ➲ Pre 6 ────
> 三個選項中只有 (A) 的 cancel pay-TV channel針對了statement 中的 cut down on「削減……」做回應，因此 (A) 為正解。另外，(B) 的 cut down「砍伐木頭」與「削減」無關，而問題裡的 go broke 在 (C) 中則被換成 broke down「拋錨」以設計成誘餌選項，所以兩者都非正確答案。

24. 正確答案：(C) ☆

Who are those men and women dressed in dark suits?

穿著深色西裝的那些男女是什麼人？

(A) I don't like dark suits. 　　　　　　　　我不喜歡深色西裝。

(B) I think they are efficient. 　　　　　　　我覺得他們很有效率。

(C) I don't know who they are. 　　　　**我不知道他們是誰。**

> **解說** 使用 Who 的疑問句 ⊃ Pre 9 ─────
> 以 who 開頭的問句通常問的都是身分，(A) 與 (B) 皆牛頭不對馬嘴。而此題答案 (C) I don't know who they are. 較特別，只要切合提意，答「不知道」也可以是合理回應。

25. 正確答案：(A) ☆☆

Carter, if you're late one more time, I have no choice but to let you go.
卡特，如果你再遲到一次，我別無選擇，只能解雇你了。

(A) I'm sorry, boss. My alarm didn't go off. 　**我很抱歉，老闆。我的鬧鐘沒響。**

(B) You should feel sorry yourself, ma'am. 　女士，你自己應該感到歉疚。

(C) You should try to be punctual, ma'am. 　女士，你應該要試著盡量準時的。

> **解說** 陳述與反應 ⊃ Pre 6 ─────
> 老闆以相當強烈的責備語氣，提出了「如果妳再遲到，只能解雇你了」這樣的警告，而先道歉再提出解釋的 (A) 為合理回應。(B) 和 (C) 都是被罵的男子反過來責怪上司，均非正確答案。

26. 正確答案：(B) ☆

What's the fastest way to the airport from here?
從這裡到機場最快的方式是什麼？

(A) The traffic is jammed due to heavy snow. 　由於大雪而造成了交通堵塞。

(B) Take the Long Island Expressway and get off 　**走長島高速公路然後下 8 號出口。**
at Exit 8.

(C) This plane will land in a few minutes. 　本班機將於幾分鐘後降落。

> **解說** 使用 What 的疑問句 ⊃ Pre 8 ─────
> 問題問哪一條為 fastest way，因此說明路線的 (B) Take the Long Island Expressway ... 為正確答案。

27. 正確答案：(A) ☆☆☆ 　　　　　　　　　　　　　　　🔊 59

I don't care to spend a lot of money on luxurious hotels when I travel.
旅行時我不喜歡花大把鈔票在豪華的旅館上。

(A) I don't, either. 我也不喜歡。　　　(B) So am I. 我也是。　　　(C) I do, too. 我也這麼做。

英文中當對方以否定句敘述時，若你贊同，一定要用否定形式回答，例如：I don't either / I am not either，或 neither do I / neither am I，這一點與中文不同，請特別注意。本題三個選項中，只有 (A) 針對否定敘述回應，(B)、(C) 皆為針對肯定句的回應。

28. 正確答案：(A) ☆☆

Wasn't that an inspiring speech?	那場演說不是很激勵人心嗎？
(A) I was really impressed.	**我真的印象深刻。**
(B) I couldn't help laughing.	我忍不住笑了。
(C) I couldn't keep my eyes open.	我無法一直睜開眼睛。

解說 Yes-No 疑問句（否定疑問句的回答） ⊃ Pre 7

本題以否定型問句的形式來表達肯定的陳述。說話者的意思是「那場演說很激勵人心」，故以表贊同對方看法的 (A) 為合理回應。注意，(B) 選項中的 couldn't help V-ing 是「不由得……、忍不住……」的意思。

29. 正確答案：(C) ☆☆

Have you heard anything about the contract for the new city gymnasium?
你有聽說任何關於新市立體育館的合約狀況嗎？

(A) Not very often.	不常。
(B) No, I haven't told them.	沒有，我還沒告訴他們。
(C) We're still waiting.	**我們還在等。**

解說 Yes-No 疑問句 ⊃ Pre 7

問話者想知道對方有沒有聽到有關合約的消息，以 (C) We're still waiting.「我們還在等」回應，表示「還沒有消息」。(C) 為最佳選項。

30. 正確答案：(B) ☆☆

Do you have something planned for Friday night?	你週五晚上有什麼計畫嗎？
(A) No. I always plan something.	不。我總是會做些計畫。
(B) No. What did you have in mind?	**沒有。你有什麼想法了嗎？**
(C) Sure, I can go with you.	當然，我可以和你一起去。

解說 Yes-No 疑問句 ⊃ Pre 7

問話者想知道對方星期五晚上有沒有什麼節目，先回應「沒有」，再反問對方「你有什麼想法了嗎？」為合理回應。(B) 為正解。這是邀請他人時經常使用的問法之一，而若要回答沒有計畫，則可用 No. Nothing particular.（沒有。沒什麼特別計畫。）或 No, what do you want to do?（沒有，你想做些什麼？）等講法。

31. 正確答案：(B) ☆☆☆　　　　　　　　　　　　　　　　　　　　🌐 60

Hello, I'm calling about the maintenance position you advertised in the paper.
喂，我是為了貴公司在報紙上刊登的維修職缺而打電話來的。

(A) Oh sorry, it was already advertised.　　　喔，抱歉，那個已經刊登了。

(B) Oh sorry, it's already been filled.　　　**喔，抱歉，那個職缺已經找到人了。**

(C) Oh sorry, the maintenance person just quit.　喔，抱歉，那名維修人員剛辭職。

> **解說** 陳述與反應 ➲ Pre 6
>
> 打電話來的人想應徵 maintenance position「維修職務」，因此以「該職務已經找到人」為回應的 (B) 為正解。注意，這裡的 fill 指「填補職缺」。而 maintenance 是指「維護管理、大樓的維護、清掃保養」等工作，和 administration「經營管理」不同。

32. 正確答案：(C) ☆☆

Could you tell Mr. Gonzalez that we'll be on our way?
能否請你告訴岡薩雷斯先生我們即將上路？

(A) Yes, I was just about to leave.　　　是，我正要離開了。

(B) Yes, I'll let you know.　　　好，我會讓你知道的。

(C) Yes, I'll give your message to Mr. Gonzalez. 好的，我會把你的話傳達給岡薩雷斯先生。

> **解說** 表達拜託、請求之意（Could you ...?）➲ Pre 20
>
> 說話者請對方幫忙轉告岡薩雷斯先生他們即將上路，只有 (C) 針對這個要求做回應，故為正解。這類句子常見於辦公室留言方面。請反覆讀出以熟記此種較有禮貌的請求句型「Could you tell A that ...」。另外 (A)、(B) 說的都是接受留言者的事情，和岡薩雷斯先生無關，所以不對。

33. 正確答案：(A) ☆☆

Who do you work for, Liz?　　　麗茲，你為誰工作（在哪兒高就）？

(A) I'm self-employed.　　　**我做的是自營業。**

(B) I work 5 days a week.　　　我每週工作五天。

(C) I'm a foreman.　　　我是工廠領班。

> **解說** Who ... for? 形式的問句 ➲ Pre 10
>
> Who do you work for? 為「你在誰的手下做事、工作？」之意，(A) 中的 self-employed「自營業」指麗茲不替他人工作，她自己是老闆，此為合理回應。(C) 中的 foreman 為「工頭、領班」之一，指的是職務階級，並未針對問題回答，故為誤。

34. 正確答案：(A) ☆☆

You look familiar. We've met before, haven't we?

你看起來好眼熟。我們以前見過吧，不是嗎？

(A) Yes, at the Rice Growers Convention in Seattle. 是的，在西雅圖的稻農大會上。

(B) Yes, I saw your picture in the album. 是的，我在相簿裡看過你的照片。

(C) Yes, you look like my younger sister. 是的，你看起來很像我妹妹。

> **解說** 附加疑問句 ⊃ Pre 16
>
> 雖然三個選項都答 Yes，但是只有 (A) 中的 at the Rice Growers Conventiob in Seattle 為回應。 (B) 中的 I saw your picture ... 是「我看過你的照片」，並非「見到面」。另外，題目中的 look familiar「看起來好眼熟」與 (C) 中的 look like my younger sister「看起來像我妹妹」無關。

35. 正確答案：(C) ☆☆　　　　　　　　　　　　　　　　　　　　　　🔘 61

Does your cell phone work in the mountain areas? 你的手機在山區能用嗎？

(A) The mountain is very high. 那座山非常高。

(B) My cell phone is very simple to use. 我的手機非常容易操作。

(C) The reception is not the best. 收訊狀況不是最理想的。

> **解說** Yes-No 疑問句 ⊃ Pre 7
>
> 問題中的 work 在此表示「可通訊、能運作」之意，因此， (C) The reception is not the best. 為正確答案。

36. 正確答案：(C) ☆☆

What's Tom's itinerary like in Bangkok? 湯姆在曼谷的行程如何安排？

(A) It's already been decided. 已經決定好了。

(B) He's looking forward to visiting Bangkok. 他很期待曼谷之行。

(C) He has a very tight schedule. 他的時程相當緊迫。

> **解說** 使用 What 的疑問句 ⊃ Pre 8
>
> What is ... like? 是指「……是怎樣的狀態？」之意，說話者想知道湯姆的 itinerary「行程」怎麼樣。只有 (C) 的 tight schedule 回答了問題。

37. 正確答案：(A) ☆☆

Excuse me, where might I catch the bus for Homet Plaza?

對不起，請問哪裡可搭乘開往霍梅特廣場的公車？

(A) Why, Homet Plaza is just around the corner. 為什麼呢？霍梅特廣場就在那個轉角處啊。

(B) Buses around here are not very reliable.　　這一帶的公車不是很可靠。

(C) The next bus leaves at 12:15.　　下一班公車 12 點 15 分發車。

> **解說** 使用 Where 的疑問句 ➲ Pre 12 ─
> 這題問的是該到哪裡搭開往 Homet Plaza的公車，(B) 和 (C) 的內容雖然都與公車有關，卻與Homet Plaza毫不相干，因此都不正確。而 (A) 選項中明白表示 Homet Plaza 就在轉角，因此不用搭車，為正解。注意，(A) 中的 Why 有「很驚訝為什麼對方想要搭公車去」之意。

38. 正確答案：(B) ☆☆

I need information on the new influenza.　　我需要新型流行性感冒有關的資訊。

(A) Go ask at the police station.　　請至警察局詢問。

(B) Go check on the Internet.　　請上網搜尋。

(C) Go get a vaccination shot.　　**請去接種疫苗。**

> **解說** 陳述與反應 ➲ Pre 6 ─
> 說話者需要新型流感相關的資訊，建議他上網搜尋為合理回應。 故 (B) 為正解。而 (A)、提到的警察局並非可取得相關資訊的地方；(C) 則是接種疫苗預防疾病的方式，不是取得資訊的方式。注意，「go + 動詞」的形式經常用於口語表達，意思等同於「go ahead and do...。」

39. 正確答案：(A) ☆☆　　　　🔊 62

Why are you working so late?　　你為何工作到這麼晚？

(A) I have to work overtime to make up for the delay. 我必須加班好趕延誤進度。

(B) I'm completely overworked.　　我徹底過勞了。

(C) I seldom work after five.　　我很少工作超過 5 點。

> **解說** 使用 Why 的疑問句 ➲ Pre 13 ─
> 題目問為何加班，(A) 的 make up for the delay 「彌補延誤」是說明了原因。請特別注意，work overtime 是「加班」，(B) 的 overwork 則指「工作過度」，誤將兩者混淆。

40. 正確答案：(B) ☆

Did you listen to the weather forecast this morning?
你今天早上有聽氣象預報嗎？

(A) Yes, the weather person is always right.　　有，氣象預報員永遠是對的。

(B) Yes, Hurricane Paul is approaching Key West.　　**有，颶風保羅正逼近基韋斯特。**

(C) Yes, the snow last week did lots of damage to our garden.　　有，上週的大雪對我們的花園造成了很多損壞。

說話者問對方早上有沒有收聽氣象預報，雖然三個選項都答 Yes，但是 (A) 並未針對氣象回答，(C) 提到的大雪則是上週的事，皆非正確答案。(B) 提到了最新氣象狀況，表示回話者有聽預報，故為合理回應。

Word List

- [ ] trip over [trɪp] 絆倒 (No. 11)
- [ ] jammed [dʒæmd] 形 堵塞的
- [ ] promotion [prə`moʃən] 名 升遷 (No. 12)
- [ ] be promoted [prə`motɪd] 被升遷
- [ ] in charge of [tʃɑrdʒ] 負責…… (No. 14)
- [ ] have the time 有錶（知道現在幾點）
- [ ] monthly statement [`mʌnθlɪ `stetmənt] 月報表（「月報表、銀行帳戶月結單、信用卡的每月帳單明細」）
- [ ] CEO（Chief Executive Officer）名 執行長 (No. 22)
- [ ] do you happen to ... 你會不會剛好…… (No. 17)
- [ ] cut down on ... 削減……（經費等）(No. 23)
- [ ] living cost 生活費
- [ ] go broke 破產
- [ ] pay-TV 付費電視
- [ ] go off 響起
- [ ] efficient [ɪ`fɪʃənt] 形 有效率的 (No. 24)
- [ ] let someone go 解雇某人、讓某人離開 (No. 25)
- [ ] punctual [`pʌŋktʃuəl] 形 準時的
- [ ] due to 由於…… (No. 26)
- [ ] care to ... 喜歡……、願意…… (No. 27)

- [ ] contract [`kɑntrækt] 名 合約 (No. 29)
- [ ] impressed [ɪm`prɛst] 形 印象深刻的 (No. 28)
- [ ] gymnasium [dʒɪm`nezɪəm] 名 體育館、健身房（= gym）
- [ ] maintenance person [`mentənəns `pɜsn] 名 維修人員 (No. 31)
- [ ] quit [kwɪt] 動 辭職
- [ ] reception [rɪ`sɛpʃən] 名 收訊狀況
- [ ] forman [`fɔrmæn] 名 工頭、領班 (No. 33)
- [ ] tight schedule [taɪt `skɛdʒʊl] 緊迫的時程
- [ ] itinerary [aɪ`tɪnə.rɛrɪ] 名 行程、旅行計畫 (No. 36)
- [ ] cell phone 名 行動電話 (No. 35)
- [ ] reliable [rɪ`laɪəbl] 形 可信賴的、可靠的 (No. 37)
- [ ] vaccination shot [.væksn̩`eʃən ʃɑt] 接種疫苗 (No. 38)
- [ ] work overtime 加班 (No. 39)
- [ ] overworked [.ovə`wɜkt] 形 過勞的
- [ ] weather forecast [`wɛðə `fɔrkæst] 名 氣象預報 (No. 40)

Short Conversation 簡短對話題

☆470 分等級 ☆☆600 分等級 ☆☆☆730 分以上

● **41 ~ 43 與機械、汽車故障有關的問題** ➲ Pre 21 ~ 23　　🕓 64

Man:　　I need to have the oil changed. Can you finish by 5:00 today?

Woman:　That won't be a problem. Could I have your home phone number so we can contact you when we finish?

Man:　　I'll be at the office—you can call me there at 555-3869.

Woman:　Okay. By the way, it's going to cost you about 45 dollars, including labor.

男：　　我需要更換機油。妳可以在今天 5 點以前完成嗎？

女：　　沒問題。能否請你給我你的家用電話號碼，以便我們完成時通知你？

男：　　我會在辦公室——妳可以打我辦公室的電話 555-3869。

女：　　好的。順便說明一下，這大約要花你 45 美元，包括工錢。

Word List

☐ labor [`lebə] 图 勞動力、勞工

41. 正確答案：(D) ☆

What is wrong with the man's car?	這名男子的車有什麼問題？
(A) He needs to have a tire changed.	他需要換輪胎。
(B) It's out of gas.	沒油了。
(C) It's not running very well.	跑得不是很順。
(D) The oil needs to be changed.	**機油該換了。**

解說

由對話中的第一句話 I need to have the oil changed. 可知，正確答案是 (D)。

42. 正確答案：(C) ☆☆

When does he need the car?	他何時需要用車？
(A) Tomorrow	明天
(B) Until 5:00	直到 5 點為止
(C) By 5:00	**5 點之前**
(D) When it's finished	（作業）完成時

解說

由第二句 Can you finish by 5:00 可推知，正確答案為 (C)。請注意，(B) Until 5:00 指的是「直到 5 點為止都需要車」，並不正確。

265

43. 正確答案：(A) ☆

What number did he give to the woman? 他把什麼號碼給了這名女子？

(A) His work number **他工作處的電話號碼**
(B) His home number 他家的電話號碼
(C) His mobile number 他的手機號碼
(D) His license plate number 他的車牌號碼

> 解說
>
> 男子第二次發言時說的 I'll be at the office you can call me at ... 可知，他要女子打到工作處，故正確答案為 (A)。

● 44 ~ 46 與請求、訂購有關的問題

Woman: Don't forget, George. We need six boxes of letter-size paper for the printer, four toner cartridges for the color printers, and two new batteries for our laptops.
Man: Yes, Ms. Barrymore. By the way, are these orders urgent?
Woman: Well, we need the laptop batteries as quickly as we can get them. There's no particular hurry for the other two items.

女： 別忘了，喬治。我們需要六盒信紙尺寸的印表機用紙、四個彩色印表機用的碳粉匣，還有兩個給我們筆記型電腦用的新電池。
男： 好的，巴里摩爾小姐。順便問一下，這些訂單很急嗎？
女： 嗯，我們需要儘快取得筆記型電腦的電池。另外兩項並不特別急。

44. 正確答案：(B) ☆☆

How many different items does the man have to order?
該名男子必須訂購幾種不同的商品？

(A) Two 2 **(B) Three 3** (C) Four 4 (D) Six 6

> 解說
>
> 必須訂購的是 paper for the printer、toner cartridges、batteries「印表機用紙、碳粉匣、電池」三項，所以答案是 (B)。

> 💡 奪分祕笈
>
> 與商品的訂購、處理手續及麻煩爭議有關的問題也常出現在 TOEIC 測驗中。

> ▶ **較大範圍的問題，例如：**

What kind of merchandise are they discussing?

他們在討論哪種商品？

What seems to be the problem?

問題似乎是什麼？

> ▶ **較小範圍的問題，例如：**

When can they deliver the merchandise?

他們何時可遞送商品？

What is causing the delay?

是什麼造成了出貨延誤？

When was the order placed?

是何時下的訂單？

How many dining tables have been ordered?

下單訂了多少張餐桌？

How are they going to send the shipment?

他們將如何運送貨品？

> ▶ **請牢記以下各種相關用語：**

☐ place an order 下訂單

☐ cancel the order 取消訂單

☐ put it on the credit card 以信用卡付款

☐ handling charge 图 手續費

☐ bill 图 帳單

☐ surface mail [`sɜfɪs mel] 图 普通郵件、平信

☐ special delivery [`spɛʃəl dɪ`lɪvərɪ] 图 限時專送

☐ fill the order 依訂單出貨

☐ charge 動 收費、索價

☐ shipping cost 運費

☐ estimate [`ɛstəˌmet] 图 動 估價

☐ invoice [`ɪnvɔɪs] 图 動 發票、發貨單

☐ sea mail 图 海運

☐ air parcel [ɛr `pɑrsl] 图 航空包裹

☐ express [ɪk`sprɛs] 動 图 快遞、快運

---

45. 正確答案：(C) ☆☆

Which item do they need the soonest?　　　　　他們需要最快取得哪項物品？

(A) Paper　　　　　　　　　　　　　　　　紙張

(B) Salespeople　　　　　　　　　　　　　業務員

(C) Batteries for their laptops　　　　**他們筆記型電腦用的電池**

(D) Toner cartridges　　　　　　　　　　　碳粉匣

由女子第二次發言時所說的 ... we need the laptop batteries as quickly as we can get them.「我們需要儘快取得筆記型電腦的電池」便可知，正確答案為 (C)。

46. 正確答案：(C) ☆☆

What does the woman say about the paper order?

對於用紙的訂購，女子說了些什麼？

(A) It is okay to accept any size paper. 　　　任何尺寸的紙都行。

(B) They need it as quickly as possible. 　　他們需要儘快取得紙張。

(C) There is no rush. 　　　　　　　　　　**不急。**

(D) They do not need paper for the copier. 　他們不需要紙張。

女子在最後一句說 There's no particular hurry for the other two items.，而印表機用紙為其中之一，所以正確答案為 (C)。原句的 no particnlar hurry 在此用同意的 (C) 選項 no rush 來表達。

● 47 ~ 49 與訂購有關的問題 　　　　　　　　　　　　　　🔊 65

Woman: (On the Phone) Yes, I'd like to order a birthday cake, please. Would it be possible to have the cake delivered to my home?

Man: 　　We do deliver, but only within the city limits. Where do you live?

Woman: I live out in the suburbs. That's okay. I'll go to your bakery and pick up the cake myself.

Man: 　　Fine. Now, what name would you like on the cake?

Woman: Einstein, E-I-N-S-T-E-I-N. Actually we're celebrating his 23rd birthday. He's the longest-lived cat in the neighborhood, and he's like a son to us.

女： 　　（電話中）是的，我想訂一個生日蛋糕，麻煩你。有可能把蛋糕送到我家嗎？

男： 　　我們有外送服務，但是僅限市區範圍内。您住在哪兒？

女： 　　我住在郊區。沒關係。我會自己過去你們的麵包店拿蛋糕。

男： 　　好的。那，您希望在蛋糕上寫什麼名字？

女： 　　愛因斯坦，E-I-N-S-T-E-I-N。事實上我們是要替他慶祝 23 歲生日。他是這一帶最長壽的貓，而對我們來說他就像是我們的兒子般。

47. 正確答案：(B) ☆

What does the woman ask about?

這名女子問的是有關什麼的問題？

(A) Sending a cake as a gift

將蛋糕做為禮物贈送的事

(B) Having a cake delivered

外送蛋糕的事

(C) Delivering a cake herself

她要自己外送蛋糕一事

(D) Baking a cake herself

她要自己烤蛋糕一事

解說

由女子所說的 Would it be possible to have the cake delivered ...? 就指向正確答案 (B)。

48. 正確答案：(C) ☆☆

How will the woman get the cake?

這名女子將如何取得蛋糕？

(A) She will deliver it.

她會負責外送。

(B) She will have it delivered.

她會請人外送過來。

(C) She will pick it up.

她會自己去拿。

(D) She will go to the suburbs.

她會到郊區去。

解說

由於女子住在郊區，無法享受宅配服務，因此第二次談話時說 I'll go to your bakery and pick up the cake myself.，由此可知本題的正確答案為 (C)。

49. 正確答案：(D) ☆☆

Who is Einstein?

愛因斯坦是誰？

(A) The woman

該女子

(B) The man

該男子

(C) The woman's son

該女子的兒子

(D) The woman's cat

該女子的貓

解說

由對話最後女子所說的 Einstein ... he's the longest-lived cat ... 可知，正確答案為 (D)。注意，對話中女子提到 He's like a son ...，是說「他像兒子般……」，但是並非真正的兒子，所以 (C) 不可選。

Man 1:　　Welcome to the Wyatt Hotel, Mr. Jameson. You've reserved a single room for three nights. Is that correct?

Man 2:　　Yes, that's right. I'd like to pay using my credit card.

Man 1:　　That's fine, sir. Just a moment, please. Oh, I'm sorry, but it appears this card has expired. I'm afraid I can't accept it.

Man 2:　　What? Oh, no, I must have brought the old card and left the new one at home.

男 1:　　歡迎光臨惠悅酒店，詹姆森先生。您預約了三晚的單人房。正確嗎？

男 2:　　是的，沒錯。我想用信用卡付款。

男 1:　　沒問題。請稍等。喔，很抱歉，看來這張卡已過期了。我恐怕無法接受這張卡。

男 2:　　什麼？噢，不，我一定是帶了舊卡來，把新卡給留在家裡了。

50. 正確答案：(B) ☆☆

What does the front desk ask Mr. Jameson about?

櫃台問了詹姆森先生什麼問題？

(A) When he made a reservation　　　　　　他是何時預約的

(B) How long he will stay　　　　　　　**他要住多久**

(C) If his name is correct　　　　　　　　他的名字是否正確

(D) If he has a credit card　　　　　　　　他是否有信用卡

> **解說**
> 由男子 1 說的第二、三句話 You've reserved ... for three nights. Is that correct? 可知，正確答案為 (B)。本題是剛抵達飯店時很常見的確認對話內容，請務必聽熟。

51. 正確答案：(C) ☆

What does Mr. Jameson want to do?　　　　詹姆森先生想做什麼？

(A) Change the room.　　　　　　　　　換房間。

(B) Stay for the night.　　　　　　　　　當晚住下來。

(C) Pay with his credit card.　　　　　　**用信用卡付款。**

(D) Cancel the reservation.　　　　　　　取消預約。

> **解說**
> 由男子 2 說的第二句話 I'd like to pay using my credit card. 可知，正確答案為 (C)。而 (B) Stay for the night 指的是「只有當晚住下來」之意，所以並不正確。

52. 正確答案：(D) ☆☆

What did the clerk tell Mr. Jameson about his credit card?

櫃台人員告訴了詹姆森先生有關他信用卡的什麼問題？

(A) The hotel does not accept credit cards.　該飯店不接受信用卡。

(B) The hotel accepts only bank credit cards.　該飯店只接受銀行信用卡。

(C) The card has been accepted.　該信用卡已被接受。

(D) The card is no longer valid.　**該信用卡已失效。**

解說

男子 1 在第二次發言中提到 ... this card has expired.，換句話說，該信用卡已失效 (no longer valid)。 (D)為正解。

● 53 ~ 55 尋求協助或建議的問題 ⊃ Pre30 ~ 32　　66

Woman: Excuse me, I'm trying to find the office of a Mr. Belmont. Would you happen to know where it is?

Man: Yes, he's my supervisor. Go straight back down the hallway, then turn right when you reach the end. His office is the fifth door on the left. And please make sure you knock first. He gets angry when people don't knock.

Woman: Okay, thank you very much for the directions and the advice. Sounds like Mr. Belmont is not such an easy person to get along with.

女： 對不起，我在找一位叫貝爾蒙特的先生的辦公室。你會不會碰巧知道在哪兒？

男： 知道，他是我的上司。請回頭沿走廊直走，到底後右轉。他的辦公室是左邊第五個門。請務必先敲門。如果不敲門，他就會生氣。

女： 好，非常謝謝你的指示與建議。聽起來貝爾蒙特先生似乎不是個好相處的人。

Word List

☐ supervisor [ˌsupəˋvaɪzə] 名上司、主管　☐ get along with ... 和……相處

53. 正確答案：(B) ☆

What is the woman looking for?　這位女子在找什麼？

(A) Her supervisor　她的上司

(B) Mr. Belmont's office　**貝爾蒙特先生的辦公室**

(C) Advice about Mr. Belmont　有關貝爾蒙特先生的建議

(D) The way to get to the fifth floor　去 5 樓的方法

女子一開始就說 ... I'm trying to find the office of a Mr. Belmont. 故正確答案為 (B)。注意人名前加上冠詞 a 可表達「一個叫……的人」之意。

54. 正確答案：(C) ☆☆

What advice does the man give the woman? 這名男子給了這名女子什麼建議？

(A) To go straight down the hallway　　　沿著走廊直走
(B) Not to get angry　　　不要生氣
(C) To knock on Mr. Belmont's door　　　**要敲貝爾蒙特先生的門**
(D) To go to Mr. Belmont's office　　　去貝爾蒙特先生的辦公室

解說

男子在發言最後提到的 ... make sure you knock first. 就指向正確答案 (C)。注意，選項 (A) To go straight down the hallway 是「路線指示」，並非建議，因此不可選。

55. 正確答案：(D) ☆☆

What information does the man NOT give to the woman?
這名男子沒有提供給這名女子什麼資訊？

(A) Directions to Mr. Belmont's office　　　去貝爾蒙特先生辦公室的路線指示
(B) Advice about knocking on Mr. Belmont's door　　　關於敲貝爾蒙特先生的門的建議
(C) His relationship with Mr. Belmont　　　貝爾蒙特先生與他的關係
(D) Where to take the elevator　　　**該去哪裡搭電梯**

解說

注意，本題問的是對話中沒有的資訊。由對話中 Go straight back down the hallway、make sure you knock、he's my supervisor 等部分可確定 (A)、(B)、(C) 皆非答案。為了能確實答對此題，你最好在聽會話前先瀏覽過問題。由於這題問的是對話「不」包含的資訊，所以聽會話時最好也能同時瀏覽一下選項。

● **56～58 與投訴、抱怨有關的問題** ⊃ Pre 33～35

Man:　　Joan, everyone's starting to complain about the temperature in here. I know you called maintenance this morning. When did they say they could come by and look into the problem?

Woman:　Yes, I called them before lunch. They told me that they had to find the cause of a wiring problem on the third floor. After that, they would come up here and check our air conditioning system.

Man:　　Well, Joan, it's already four. They may have entirely forgotten about us. Please call them again and tell them we need them here as soon as possible.

男：　　瓊，每個人都開始抱怨這裡的溫度了。我知道妳今早打了電話給維護管理部門。他們說何時能過來並看是哪裡有問題呢？

女：　　是的，我在午餐前打了電話給他們。他們告訴我，他們必須找出 3 樓一個線路問題的原因。之後，他們就會上來檢查我們的空調系統。

男：　　嗯，不過瓊，現在已經四點了。他們可能已經徹底忘了我們。請再打給他們一次，告訴他們我們需要他們儘快過來。

Word List

☐ maintenance [`mentənəns] 名 維護管理部門　　　☐ look into 調查、檢查原因

56. 正確答案：(A) ☆☆

What are the two people discussing?　　　這兩個人在討論什麼？

(A) A problem with the air conditioner　　**空調的問題**
(B) The maintenance department　　　維護修部門
(C) The weather condition　　　天氣狀況
(D) Complaints from clients　　　客戶的抱怨

解說

由男子在第一句提到的 complain about the temperature 以及女子第三句提到的 check our air conditioning system 可知，正確答案為 (A)。

57. 正確答案：(C) ☆☆

When are the maintenance people supposed to come?　維修人員應該會何時來？

(A) Right away　　　立刻
(B) At 4 o'clock　　　4 點
(C) After they finish the work on the 3rd floor　　**等他們完成 3 樓的工作後**
(D) Not within today　　　今天之內來不了

58. 正確答案：(B) ☆

What does the man suggest?　　　　　　該名男子提出了什麼建議？

(A) Forgetting about the problem　　　　忘了那問題

(B) Calling maintenance again　　　　**再打一次電話給維修部門**

(C) Calling another company　　　　　　打給另一家公司

(D) Fixing the air conditioning by themselves　　自己修空調

● 59～61 與投訴、抱怨有關的問題 ⊃ Pre 33～35　　　　● 67

Woman: Usher, excuse me. There's a rather large man who's taken my seat. He insists that it's his seat, even though I've shown him my ticket. Here it is. My ticket says seat H18, right? But he wouldn't give up the seat or show me his ticket. He just sat there and completely ignored me.

Man: I see. Let me talk with him. I've had to deal with such people before.

Woman: Yes, I suppose you meet a lot of people who aren't very pleasant. Thank you for your help.

Man: Not at all, ma'am. It may take a couple of minutes, but you'll soon have your seat back.

女：　不好意思，帶位的先生。有位相當高大的男子坐了我的位子。即使我已把我的票拿給他看，他仍然堅稱那是他的座位。你看，我的票上寫的座位是 H18，對吧？但是他不願意放棄那個座位，也不給我看他的票。他就只是坐在那兒，完全忽視我的存在。

男：　我知道了。讓我和他談談。我以前也曾經得應付這種人。

女：　是啊，我想你一定遇過很多不太親切的人。謝謝你的幫忙。

男：　不客氣，女士。這可能需要幾分鐘，但是您很快就會要回您的座位。

Word List

☐ usher [`ʌʃɚ] 名 帶位員　　　　　　☐ insist ... 動 堅持……

59. 正確答案：(B) ☆☆

What is the woman's problem?　　　　　　這名女子的問題是什麼？

(A) The usher is very rude to her.　　　　　帶位人員對她非常沒禮貌。

(B) Someone is sitting in her seat.　　　　**有人坐在她的座位上。**

(C) A large man stole her ticket.　　　　　有個高大的男子偷了她的票。

(D) The woman lost her ticket.　　　　　　這名女子弄丟了她的票。

解說

女子第二句說的 There's a man who's taken my seat. 就指向正確答案 (B)。

60. 正確答案：(B) ☆☆

How did the man react when the woman showed him her ticket?

當女子拿出她的票時，該男子有何反應？

(A) He apologized and moved to the next seat.　　他道歉並移到旁邊的座位。

(B) He didn't care what the woman said to him.　**他完全不理會女子對他說了什麼。**

(C) He showed his own ticket to prove he was right.　他拿出了他的票以證明他是對的。

(D) He yelled at her and told her to go away.　　他對她大吼並叫她走開。

解說

由女子第一次說話的最後一句 He just sat there and completely ignored me. 可知，正確答案為 (B)。注意，原文中的 completely ignored 的意思就是「完全不理會」。

61. 正確答案：(A) ☆☆

How is the usher probably going to help the woman?

這位帶位人員可能會怎麼幫這名女子？

(A) He will persuade the big man to give up　**他會說服那名高大男子放棄該座位。**
the seat.

(B) He will call the police and report the incident.　他會打電話給警察舉報這個事件。

(C) He will give the big man a free ticket.　　他會給那名高大男子一張免費的票。

(D) He will go to the big man and throw him out.　他會走向那名高大男子並把他趕出去。

解說

由帶位員先說的 Let me talk with him. 和最後說的 ... you'll soon have your seat back. 來推斷，他應該會說服該名男子放棄那個女子的座位，因此選 (B)。

● 62 ~ 64 尋求協助或建議的問題 ⊃ Pre 30 ~ 32

Man: That's odd. This elevator apparently only goes as high as the 24th floor. I need to go to the 37th floor.

Woman: The elevators that service floors 25 through 52 are the ones across the hall from this elevator. Go back to the 1st floor again and if you can't find them, you can ask security personnel for help.

Man: I appreciate your kindness. This is the first time I've ever been in this building.

Woman: You're welcome. Just don't forget to cross the hall when you get to the 1st floor.

男： 真奇怪。這台電梯顯然最高只到 24 樓。我得去 37 樓。

女： 可達 25 到 52 樓的電梯在這個電梯對面，就是大廳另一側的那幾台。你先回到 1 樓，要是找不到那些電梯的話，可以問警衛。

男： 很感謝你好心告訴我。這是我第一次進到這棟大樓。

女： 不客氣。回到 1 樓之後別忘了要穿過大廳到另一側。

Word List

☐ security personnel [sɪ`kjʊrətɪ ˌpɜsn̩`ɛl] 图 保全人員

62. 正確答案：(C) ☆☆

What does the man need to do next?	這位男子接下來該做什麼？
(A) To get off the elevator at the 37th floor	在 37 樓下電梯
(B) To press the button for 37	按下 37 樓的按鈕
(C) To go downstairs and find the correct elevator	**下樓，然後找到正確的電梯**
(D) To go as high as the 24th floor	到 24 樓那麼高的地方

解說

女子告訴男子若他要搭到更高樓層的電梯必須 Go back to the 1st floor again，所以正確答案為 (C)。

63. 正確答案：(A) ☆

What does the woman tell him?　　　　　女子告訴了他什麼？

(A) How to find the elevator he needs to use　　**如何找到他需要使用的電梯**

(B) How to find a security guard　　　　如何找到警衛

(C) How many floors there are in the building　　該棟大樓有幾層樓

(D) How to get to the first floor　　　　去 1 樓的辦法

解說

女子所說的 The elevators ... are ... across the hall from this elevator. 等都是在告訴男子
如何找到正確的電梯，Go back to the 1st floor again 因此本題選 (A)。

64. 正確答案：(D) ☆☆

What should he do if he can't find the correct elevators?
如果找不到正確的電梯，他該怎麼辦？

(A) Look at the map on the wall　　　　看牆上的地圖

(B) Ask another passenger on the elevator　　問電梯裡的其他乘客

(C) Go to the 37th floor　　　　去 37 樓

(D) Ask someone who works in the building　　**問某個在該大樓裡工作的人**

解說

女子說 ... if you can find them, you can ask security personnel for help.，而 security
personnel 當然是在大樓工作的人員，因此本題選 (D)。

● **65 ～ 67 與投訴、抱怨有關的問題** ⊃ **Pre 33 ～ 35**　　　　🔊 68

Man 1: Hello, I bought this sweater here about a week ago, and I'd like to exchange it for a
　　　　larger size. I thought I could fit in a medium, but obviously this manufacturer's size
　　　　comes smaller than others. Here's my receipt.

Man 2: I'm sorry, but I'm afraid this item is not exchangeable. It was on sale, and we have
　　　　a no-return policy on reduced-price merchandise.

Man 1: But it doesn't fit! If you won't let me exchange it, what can I do with it? I wish you'd
　　　　told me about the policy before I bought it.

Man 2: I wish I could help you, but I don't make the rules here.

男 1： 你好，我大約 1 週前在這裡買了這件毛衣，我想換成較大尺寸的。我原以為我穿得下中號尺寸，但是顯然這家製造商的尺寸比別家的小。這是我的收據。

男 2： 很抱歉，恐怕這項商品是不能退換的。它是特價品，而我們的折價商品規定不可退換。

男 1： 但是尺寸不合啊！如果你不讓我換，我留著它幹嘛？我希望你們能在我購買前就告訴我這項規定。

男 2： 我很想幫您，但是這兒的規矩不是我訂的。

Word List

□ merchandise [`mɜtʃən.daɪz] 图 商品

65. 正確答案：(B) ☆

What are they discussing?　　　　　　他們在討論什麼？

(A) Merchandise on sale　　　　　　特價商品
(B) Exchanging an item　　　　　　**更換一項商品**
(C) A lost receipt　　　　　　弄丟了的收據
(D) A sweater returned a week ago　　一週前退回的毛衣

解說

男子 1 一開始就說 ... I bought this here ... I'd lke to exchange it ...，因此 (B) 為正解。注意，(D) 選項中的 returned a week ago 是指「於 1 週前退貨」，和對話中說的「在 1 週前購買」是兩回事，千萬不要誤選。

66. 正確答案：(C) ☆☆

Why can't the customer exchange the sweater?　客人為何不能換毛衣？

(A) He does not have proof of purchase.　他沒有購買證明。
(B) He bought it a week ago.　　　　他一週前購買的。
(C) He bought it on sale.　　　　　**他是以特價購買的。**
(D) He already wore it.　　　　　　他已經穿過了。

解說

依據男子 2 的說明，他們公司有「折價商品不退貨規定」(no-return policy on reduced-price merchandise)，而因為男子的毛衣是特價時買的，所以不能換。正確答案為 (C)。

67. 正確答案：(C) ☆☆

How does the customer feel about the store policy?

這位客人對於店家的規定有何感覺？

(A) They should have tried it on. 　　　　　他們當時應該要試穿。

(B) They should give back the money. 　　　他們應該要退錢。

(C) They should have told him about the policy. 他們當時應該要告訴他這項規定。

(D) They should have warned about the size. 　他們當時應該警告他尺寸的問題。

> 解說
>
> 由男子 1 第二次發言時說的 I wish you'd told me about the policy before I bought it.「我希望你們能在我購買之前就告訴我這項政策」可知，正確答案為 (C)。注意，原句的 you'd told 指 you had told。

● 68 ~ 70 尋求協助或建議的問題 ⊃ Pre 32 ~ 35

Woman: Oh dear, one of my contact lenses has fallen out. How am I going to find it on this white carpet? George, would you help me look for it?

Man: Yes, of course. Where do you think it would be? Right around here?

Woman: Most likely. And George, don't step on it. I can't drive without my contact lenses.

Man: There's an optical shop downstairs in the shopping complex. I think they're still open. Do you want to try them?

Woman: Let's look for a few more minutes and if we still can't find it, we'll go to that shop.

女： 噢，糟糕，我的一只隱形眼鏡掉出來了。我要怎麼在這白地毯上找到它啊？喬治，你能不能幫我找找？

男： 好的，當然。妳覺得會在哪兒？就在這附近嗎？

女： 很有可能。喬治，千萬別踩到它。沒有隱形眼鏡我就沒辦法開車了。

男： 在樓下購物商場就有間眼鏡行。我想他們還開著。妳想去看看嗎？

女： 我們再找幾分鐘吧，如果還是找不到，我們就去那間店。

Word List

☐ optical shop [`ɑptɪkl̩ ʃɑp] 图 眼鏡行

68. 正確答案：(D) ☆

What happened to the woman's contact lens?   該名女子的隱形眼鏡怎麼了？

(A) It rolled off the desk.   從桌上掉了下來。

(B) It fell out of her purse.   從她的手提包裡掉了出來。

(C) She took it out and dropped it.   她把它拿出之後掉了。

(D) It came out of her eye.   **從她的眼睛掉了出來。**

> 解說
>
> 女子一開始就說 ... one of my contact lenses has fallen out.「我的一只隱形眼鏡掉了出來」。注意，最可能是從眼睛戴著時脫落了。故最佳的選項為 (D)。

69. 正確答案：(A) ☆☆

Why does she think it will be difficult to find?   她為何認為會很難找隱形眼鏡？

(A) The color of the carpet is very light.   **地毯的顏色非常淺。**

(B) George won't help her find it.   喬治不幫她找。

(C) She cannot drive without her contact lenses.   她沒有隱形眼鏡就無法開車。

(D) She could have dropped it somewhere else.   她可能掉在別的地方了。

> 解說
>
> 女子第二句話中提到的 How am I going to find it on this white carpet? 中的 white carpet 就是關鍵，因為白色就是淺色，所以 (B) 為正確答案。

70. 正確答案：(D) ☆☆

What does the woman tell George?   這名女子對喬治說了什麼？

(A) To go down and find an optical shop   下樓去找一家眼鏡行

(B) To tell her where the lens is   告訴她隱形眼鏡在哪裡

(C) To look for the white carpet   去找白色地毯

(D) To be careful where he steps   **要小心腳步**

> 解說
>
> 女子第二次發言時說的 ... George, don't step on it. 為關鍵詞句，女子要喬治小心不要踩到隱形眼鏡，(D) 為正確選項。

Part 4 Short Talks 簡短獨白題

☆470 分等級 ☆☆600 分等級 ☆☆☆730 分以上

● 71 ~ 73 錄音訊息 ⊃ Pre 36 ~ 38

🔵 70

Questions 71 through 73 refer to the following recorded message.

Thank you for calling Worldwide Airlines. For your convenience, you may utilize our automated assistance system by pressing the appropriate number. For general information on Worldwide Airlines and our destinations, press 1. For specific flight schedules and seasonal specials, press 2. To confirm the status of a flight reservation you've already made, press 3. If you have questions or need information about our World Trotter mileage program, press 4. To change or to cancel a reservation, press 5. If you need to speak with our representative, stay on the line and your call will be answered by the first available operator.

第 71 ~ 73 題與以下的錄音訊息有關。

感謝您致電全球航空公司。為了您的方便，只要您按下對應的數字鍵就可使用我們的自動協助系統。想知道關於全球航空公司的一般資訊及航點，請按 1。特定航班時刻表及季節性促銷，請按 2。想確認已預約的班機狀態，請按 3。若您對於我們的世界環遊者里程計劃有疑問或需要相關資訊，請按 4。若要變更或取消預約，請按 5。如果您需要和我們的業務人員對話，請別掛斷，第一位有空的接線人員將會與您通話。

Word List

☐ utilize [`jutḷ.aɪz] 動 使用、利用

---

71. 正確答案：(C) ☆☆

How can the caller speak with an airline representative?
打電話來的人如何能和航空公司的業務人員對話？

(A) By pressing 4 　　　　　　　　　　按 4
(B) By pressing 5 　　　　　　　　　　按 5
(C) By holding the line 　　　　　　**不掛斷電話等候**
(D) By calling a different number 　　　打另一個號碼

解說

由訊息最後一句中的 stay on the line 可知，正確答案為 (D)。 注意，stay on the line 或 hold on the line 皆為「不掛斷電話等候」之意，為電話對會中的常用語，一定要記起來。

281

72. 正確答案：(D) ☆☆

What number should the caller press to learn about the World Trotter mileage program?
想了解世界環遊者里程計劃的人應按下幾號鍵？

(A) 1　　　(B) 2　　　(C) 3　　　**(D) 4**

> **解説**
>
> 由訊息第五句中的 ... about our World Trotter mileage program, press 4. 可知，正確答案為 (D)。

73. 正確答案：(B) ☆☆

How does the automated assistance system help the caller?

自動協助系統能夠如何幫助打電話來的人？

(A) It is more pleasant than talking to the operator.

它比和接線人員對話更愉快。

(B) It helps the caller to get what they need quickly.

它幫助打電話來的人快速取得所需資訊。

(C) The operator answers each call politely.

接線人員會有禮貌地回應每通電話。

(D) Callers are given special discounts on tickets.

打電話來的人能獲得特別的機票折扣。

> **解説**
>
> 由訊息第二句中提到的 pressing the appropriate number 以及之後各號碼的功能說明可知，只要來電者按數字鍵就能利用自動協助系統，也就是說，這個系統能幫助來電者get what they need quickly，(B) 為正確選項。而 (D) 的 special discounts 對應到訊息中的 seasonal specials「季節性促銷」，只要按 2 就能獲得相關資訊，非正解。

● 74 ～ 76 與天氣狀況有關的通告 ⊃ Pre 39 ～ 41

Questions 74 through 76 refer to the following public announcement.

The overnight snowstorm has made roads nearly impassable in certain areas, and as of this time the following schools have announced that they are closed for today: Wesley Smith Junior High School, Jefferson City Junior and Senior High Schools, Taft Brentwood Middle School, and all schools in the Fairbright school district. If your school was not mentioned, then classes will be conducted as scheduled.

There may be a 10-to-15-minute delay in the arrival of your school bus, but for safety's sake we ask that parents not drive their children to school. Again, if your school was not among those mentioned, then you do have regular classes today.

第 74 ~ 76 題與以下公告有關。

整夜的暴風雪已造成某些地區的道路幾乎無法通行，而目前下列各學校都已宣布今日停課：韋斯利・史密斯國中、傑佛遜市國中與高中、塔夫脫・布倫特伍德中學，還有菲爾伯萊特學區內的所有學校。如果你的學校未在上列名單中，那就表示將照常上課。

你的校車可能會延遲 10 到 15 分鐘到達，但是為了安全起見，我們請求各位父母不要開車送孩子去學校。再提醒一次，如果你的學校不在上列名單中，那就表示你今天要照常上課。

Word List

☐ snowstorm [`sno.stɔrm] 名 暴風雪　　☐ impassable [ɪm`pæsəbl] 形 無法通行的
☐ school district [skul `dɪstrɪkt] 學區　　☐ for safety's sake 為了安全起見

74. 正確答案：(B) ☆☆

Why are some schools closing for the day?　　為何今日有些學校停課？

(A) A storm is coming.　　有暴風雨要來。

(B) A snowstorm came last night.　　**昨晚有暴風雪。**

(C) The school bus is not running.　　校車不開。

(D) All the roads are closed.　　所有道路都封閉了。

解說

由通告一開始提到的 the overnight snowstorm「整夜的暴風雪」可知，昨晚有暴風雪，故正確答案為 (B)。而由 roads「nearly」impassable in certain areas 可知，並非所有道路都被封閉，因此 (D) 不正確。

75. 正確答案：(A) ☆☆☆

Which district is closing all of its schools?　　哪個區域的學校全都停課？

(A) Fairbright　　**菲爾伯萊特**

(B) Wesley Smith　　韋斯利・史密斯

(C) Jefferson City　　傑佛遜市

(D) Taft Brentwood　　塔夫脫・布倫特伍德

解說

由通告第一句最後明確指出的 all schools in the Fairbright school district 可知，(D) 為正解。再次提醒，請記得要先瀏覽問題再聽語音，以提高答對率。

76. 正確答案：(D) ☆☆

What are parents expected to do?

(A) Have their children leave home earlier.

(B) Have their children stay home from school.

(C) Drive their children to school.

(D) Wait for the school bus to arrive.

父母親們該怎麼做？

讓他們的孩子早點出門。

讓他們的孩子待在家，不去上課。

開車送他們的孩子去上學。

等校車到。

解說

由通告第三句提到的校車會有 10-to-15-minute delay「10到15分鐘的延誤」但是請父母 not drive their children to school「不要開車送孩子去學校。」可知，(A) 和 (C) 都不對，正確答案為 (D)。

● 77 ~ 79 通知（節目）　　　🔊 71

Questions 77 through 79 refer to the following announcement.

Stay tuned for Channel 7's lineup of hit shows tonight, starting at 8:00 with the season finale of the most loved family drama "*Empty Pages*." Tonight we'll find out if Bill will finally propose to May or leave her forever. Then at 8:30, join us for the top-rated comedy show "*Strike Two*." Enjoy the Dan and Stan Brothers and their silly mistakes and failures. Finally, to finish off a hot Thursday night at 9:00 is the exciting courtroom drama, "*Innocent Until Proven Guilty*." This week lawyers Phil Blane and Sandra Fry take on the most challenging case of "The Robbery at the White House." Channel 7 has it all tonight! Find a comfortable place to sit, toss the remote control aside, and enjoy a great night of TV right here!

第 77 ~ 79 題與以下通知有關。

敬請鎖定今晚第 7 頻道的眾多熱門節目，首先在 8 點開場的是最受歡迎家庭倫理劇「空白頁」的本季大結局。今晚我們將知道比爾最終是會向梅伊求婚，還是永遠離開她。接著在 8 點 30 分的時候，請準時收看收視率最高的喜劇節目「走運二人組」。享受觀賞丹與史丹兄弟，及他們所製造的愚蠢錯誤和失敗的樂趣。最後，為了讓熱力四射的週二夜晚有個完美句點，9 點我們將為您獻上最精采的法庭戲「無罪推定」。本週，律師菲爾‧布雷恩與珊卓‧佛萊將面對最具挑戰性的案件「白宮劫盜」。今晚的第 7 頻道應有盡有！請找個舒適的位子坐好，把遙控器丟在一邊，在本頻道盡情享受一個美好的電視之夜！

Word List

☐ **courtroom drama** [`kort͵rum `drɑmə] 图 法庭劇

☐ **innocent** [`ɪnəsn̩t] 形 無罪的、清白的

☐ **guilty** [`gɪltɪ] 形 有罪的

☐ **robbery** [`rɑbərɪ] 图 搶劫

77. 正確答案：(D) ☆

What kind of program is "*Empty Pages*"? 「空白頁」是哪一種節目？

(A) A comedy 喜劇

(B) A mystery 懸疑推理

(C) A documentary 紀錄片

(D) A family drama **家庭倫理劇**

解説

由此通知第一句中的 the most loved family drama「最受歡迎家庭倫理劇」即可知，正確答案是 (D)。

78. 正確答案：(C) ☆☆

What makes the comedy show featuring Dan and Stan so popular?

以丹和史丹為主角的喜劇節目為何如此受歡迎？

(A) They have funny faces. 他們長得很滑稽。

(B) They are inventive. 他們很有創造力。

(C) They make stupid mistakes. **他們會犯愚蠢的錯誤。**

(D) They always succeed in life. 他們在生活中總是很成功。

解説

由通知中有關該節目的敘述 ... the Dan and Stan Brothers and their silly mistakes and failures 即可知，正確答案為 (C)。

79. 正確答案：(A) ☆☆

What kind of people will we probably see if we watch Channel 7 at 9:00?

如果我們在晚上 9 點看第 7 頻道，很可能會看見哪種人？

(A) Lawyers **律師**

(B) Librarian 圖書館員

(C) Teachers 教師

(D) Businessperson 商人

解説

根據節目通知，9 點時上演的是法庭戲「無罪推論」，而其主角就是 lawyers Phil Blane and Sandra Fry，故正確答案為 (A)。

● 80 ~ 82 新聞 ⊃ Pre 42 ~ 44

Questions 80 through 82 refer to the following news item.

Tonight, a four-year-old boy who had been trapped in an old well ten-feet underground for two nights was rescued. Billy Thompson, son of Mr. and Mrs. Tom Thompson of South Parkville, was playing in the yard when the ground under him suddenly gave way. He fell about ten feet and got stuck, unable to move at all. His parents had had the well removed and filled when they bought the house, but the job was obviously done poorly. Tonight rescuers were finally able to tunnel their way to Billy and pull him out. The boy, terrified and exhausted from the cold and lack of food and water, was not seriously injured. He was seen in the arms of his overjoyed parents, sipping cocoa.

第 80 ~ 82 題與以下的新聞有關。
今晚，一名被困在深達地底 10 英尺的古井兩個晚上的四歲男童終於獲救。當時住南帕克維爾的湯姆‧湯普森夫婦之子——比利‧湯普森正在庭院裡玩耍，他腳下的地面竟突然崩落。他跌落約 10 英尺後被卡住，動彈不得。他的父母早在購買該間房屋時，就已經請人拆除那個古井並將之填平，但是這工程顯然做得非常粗糙。今晚，救援人員終於挖出了一條通道找到比利，並把他拉出來。男童嚇壞了，而且因為寒冷又缺乏食物與飲水而筋疲力竭，但是並未嚴重受傷。我們看到他在興喜萬分的雙親懷抱中啜飲著可可。

Word List

- trap [træp] 動 困住
- get stuck 被卡住
- terrified [ˋtɛrəˌfaɪd] 形 被嚇壞的
- overjoyed [ˌovəˋdʒɔɪd] 形 狂喜的
- yard [jɑrd] 名 庭院
- obviously [ˋɑbvɪəslɪ] 副 顯然地
- exhausted [ɪgˋzɔstɪd] 形 筋疲力竭的

80. 正確答案：(B) ☆☆

How long was the boy trapped underground?　　男童被困在地底多久？

(A) Two days　　兩天
(B) Three days　　**三天**
(C) Three nights　　三個晚上
(D) Overnight　　過了一夜

解說

由新聞報導第一句的 ... trapped ... underground for two nights ... 可知，該男童已受困了兩晚，而兩晚湊整數算起來就是三天，因此正確答案為 (B)。

81. 正確答案：(B) ☆

What was the boy doing when he fell into the well?

(A) He was cycling in the street.

(B) He was playing in the garden.

(C) He was walking in the tunnel.

(D) He was working in the garage.

男童跌落古井時正在做什麼？

他正在街道上騎腳踏車。

他正在花園裡玩耍。

他正在隧道中散步。

他正在車庫裡工作。

> **解說**
>
> 報導第二句提到 Bill Thompson ... was playing in the yard ...，這裡的 yard 與 (B) 選項中的 garden 同義，故 (B) 為正確答案。

82. 正確答案：(A) ☆☆

How was the boy's condition when he was rescued?

(A) He was very tired but not hurt badly.

(B) He was terrified and injured badly.

(C) He was unconscious.

(D) He was lively and talkative.

被救出時，男童的情況如何？

他非常疲累，但是沒有嚴重受傷。

他嚇壞了，而且嚴重受傷。

他失去了意識。

他很活潑話太多。

> **解說**
>
> 由倒數第二句 The boy, terrified and exhausted from the cold and lack of food and water, was not seriously injured. 可知，男童雖然受到驚嚇、很疲累，但是並未受到嚴重傷害，所以 (A) 為正確答案，而 (B) 不正確。另外，新聞最後提到「男童在啜飲可可」，可見是有意識的，所以 (C) 也不對。最後，男童既然被「嚇壞了而且筋疲力竭」，就不會「很活潑又多話」，因此 (D) 亦不正確。

● 83 ~ 85 發言（菜色說明） ⊃ Pre 45 ~ 47   ⊛ 72

Questions 83 through 85 refer to the following talk.

Good evening. My name's Frederick, and I'll be your waiter this evening. We have three wonderful specials for you tonight. First, there's a batter-fried swordfish filet with a creamy garlic and lemon sauce, served with wild rice and vegetables. We also have a 16-ounce sirloin steak that's cooked-to-order and served with grilled onions and your choice of potatoes or rice. Lastly, the pasta special is a spinach fettuccine with flaked salmon in a white cream sauce and comes with a Caesar salad. Dessert and coffee or tea is included in all dinners. Last order is 11 o'clock, just one hour before closing time. So you still have plenty of time to enjoy your dinner. Would you care to order now?

第 83 ~ 85 題與以下的發言內容有關。

晚安。我叫弗雷德里克，是您今晚的服務生。今晚我們提供 3 道絕妙的特別料理。首先是油炸酥皮旗魚排佐奶油大蒜檸檬醬，再搭配菰米與蔬菜。我們還有 16 盎司的沙朗牛排，可依您的偏好烹煮，並搭配烤洋蔥，您還可選擇要馬鈴薯還是米飯。最後的特製義大利麵是鮭魚片波菜寬麵佐奶油白醬，並搭配凱薩沙拉。每道晚餐都附有甜點和咖啡或茶。最後點菜時間為 11 點鐘，也就是打烊前 1 小時。您還有很多時間可享受晚餐。您現在要點餐了嗎？

Word List

□ batter-fried [ˋbætə] 形 裹粉油炸的   □ swordfish [ˋsord.fɪʃ] 图 旗魚

83. 正確答案：(C) ☆☆

What are the three specials they offer?   他們提供的 3 道特別料理為何？

(A) Fish, pork and chicken   魚、豬和雞
(B) Fish, pasta and chicken   魚、義大利麵和雞
(C) Fish, meat and pasta   **魚、肉和義大利麵**
(D) Fish, salad and pasta   魚、沙拉和義大利麵

解說

依據菜色的說明，三道特別料理為 （1）swordfish filet、（2）sirloin steak、（3）pasta special，因此正解為 (C)。由於服務生在做介紹時將做法和食材等都一併提出說明，所以聽起來會有些複雜難懂，建議讀者多聽幾遍以熟悉西方料理的說法。

84. 正確答案：(A) ☆

What kind of meat dish is offered on the special menu?
特別料理所提供的肉類餐點是什麼？

(A) Beefsteak   **牛排**
(B) Pork cutlet   豬排
(C) Roast chicken   烤雞
(D) Lamb roast   烤羔羊肉

解說

依據菜色說明，第二道菜是 a 16-ounce sirloin steak 故正確答案為 (A)。

85. 正確答案：(C) ☆☆

How late is the restaurant open?   該餐廳營業到多晚？

(A) As long as there are customers   只要還有客人就一直開著
(B) As long as the food lasts   只要還有食物就一直開著
(C) Until 12:00   **到 12 點為止**
(D) Until 11:00   到 11 點為止

> **解說**
>
> 依服務生說的，倒數第三句 Last order is 11 o'clock, just one hour before closing time. 可知，打烊時間是 (C) 12 點。

● 86 ~ 88 公告、宣布 ➲ Pre 48 ~ 50

Questions 86 through 88 refer to the following announcement.

Okay, listen up, people. There appears to be a dangerous computer virus that may have infiltrated our company's network. Two employees have already lost all of the data on their hard disks. In order to avoid any further damage, we must all exercise proper safety precautions. First and foremost, never give anyone but the systems administrator your computer password. Secondly, do not open any suspiciously titled e-mail. If you don't recognize the sender's name, delete the mail. Don't download any data or programs from websites that are not secure. Lastly, be sure to log out if you leave your computer for more than a minute or so. Let's be sensible and careful, and protect ourselves from this virus.

第 86 ~ 88 題與以下的宣布內容有關。

好，各位，聽好了。似乎有個危險的電腦病毒已經滲透了我們公司的網路。有兩位員工失去了他們硬碟裡的所有資料。為了避免任何進一步的損失，我們都必須採取適當的安全防範措施。首先，也是最重要的，就是除了系統管理人員外，絕不能告訴任何其他人你的電腦密碼。其次，不要打開任何標題看來可疑的電子郵件。如果你不認得寄件者的姓名，就刪除該信件。不要從不安全的網站下載任何資料或程式。最後，如果你要離開電腦一分鐘以上，請務必先登出。讓我們更警覺且小心，以保護自己免於此病毒的侵害。

Word List

- □ infiltrate [ɪnˋfɪltret] 動 進入、滲透
- □ first and foremost [ˋfor͵most]
  形 首先而且是最重要的
- □ sensible [ˋsɛnsəbl] 形 警覺的、注意的
- □ precaution [prɪˋkɔʃən] 名 預防措施
- □ suspiciously [səˋspɪʃəslɪ] 副 可疑地
- □ secure [sɪˋkjur] 形 安全的

86. 正確答案：(D) ☆

Where is this talk being given? 這段發言發生在何處？

(A) At a school 在某學校

(B) At a restaurant 在某餐廳

(C) At a hospital 在某醫院

(D) At a company office **在某公司的辦公室**

> **解說**
>
> 由第兩句裡的 our company's network 即可知，本題應選 (D)。

87. 正確答案：(C) ☆☆

What happened to two employees? 有兩名員工發生了什麼事？

(A) They caught a virus. 他們感染了病毒。

(B) Their data was stolen. 他們的資料被偷了。

(C) Their data was lost. **他們的資料不見了。**

(D) Their hard disks were replaced. 他們的硬碟被換掉了。

> **解說**
>
> 由第三句話 Two employees have already lost all of the data on their hard disks. 可知，正確答案為 (C)。而由於資料並不是被偷走，所以 (B) 是錯的。另外 (A) 的 caught a virus 中的 virus 是指「感染感冒之類的病毒」，因此也不正確。

88. 正確答案：(A) ☆☆☆

What should the employees NOT do? 員工不應該做什麼？

(A) Share their personal passwords. **將個人密碼告訴他人。**

(B) Open e-mail. 打開電子郵件。

(C) Leave their desks. 離開他們的辦公桌。

(D) Visit websites. 瀏覽網站。

> **解說**
>
> 請注意本題問的是員工「不」應該做什麼。發言中特別強調 never give anyone ... your computer password，因此本題正解為 (A)。注意，這裡的 share 是「告訴他人讓他人知道」的意思。至於 (B)、(C)、(D) 選項中提到的事件並非「不」可做的事，指示須小心行事罷了，故並非正解。

● 89 ～ 91 指示說明 ➲ Half 1 39 ～ 41 ⚡ 73

Questions 89 through 91 refer to the following instructions.

Before you enter the stadium grounds, you must present all belongings for inspection by stadium personnel. As you reach the inspectors, please place handbags, shoulder bags, knapsacks and other such items on the table and open or unzip them. Please note that no cameras will be allowed in the stadium today. If you have a camera on your person, it will be confiscated, and will be returned to you after the concert. Also, alcoholic beverages are available for purchase in the stadium and may not be brought in. As is clearly noted on your tickets, any alcohol you are carrying will be confiscated and not returned. Once your belongings have been inspected, please present your ticket and you may enter the grounds. Thank you for your cooperation.

第 89 ～ 91 題與以下的指示說明有關。
在您進入體育館的場地前，必須交出您所有的隨身物品，讓體育館的工作人員檢查。當您到達檢查人員面前時，請將手提袋、側肩背包、背包以及其他類似物品放在桌上，然後打開袋口或拉開拉鍊。請注意，今天禁止攜帶相機進入體育館。如果您帶了相機，則相機將被沒收，演唱會結束後才會歸還給您。此外，含酒精飲料可在體育館內購買，但不可自行帶入會場。正如您門票上所載明的，您所帶來的任何酒精性飲料都將被沒收，而且不會歸還。在您的隨身物品都檢查完畢後，請出示您的門票，接著便可進入會場。謝謝您的合作。

Word List

- □ belongings [bə`lɔŋɪŋz] 图 所有物
- □ unzip [ʌn`zɪp] 動 拉開拉鍊
- □ inspection [ɪn`spɛkʃən] 图 檢查
- □ confiscate [`kɑnfɪsˌket] 動 沒收

89. 正確答案：(D) ☆☆

What type of event is taking place?	在進行的是哪類活動？
(A) A security inspection	安全檢查
(B) A play	戲劇
(C) A baseball game	棒球比賽
(D) A concert	**演唱會**

解說

由指示中提到的 camera ... will be returned to you after the concert 可知，正確答案為 (D)。而要小心的是，由於不斷出現體育館這個字，所以很容易讓人以為答案就是 (C) 的棒球比賽。另外，安全檢查本身不是活動，因此 (A) 非正確答案。

90. 正確答案：(C) ☆☆☆

What items cannot be brought into the stadium?　　哪些物品不能帶進體育館？

(A) Knapsacks and alcoholic beverages　　背包與酒精性飲料

(B) Cameras and shoulder bags　　相機與側肩背包

(C) Cameras and alcoholic beverages　　**相機與酒精性飲料**

(D) Alcoholic beverages and tickets　　酒精性飲料與門票

指示中提到 no cameras will be allowed 和 alcoholic beverages ... may not be brought in，故正確答案為 (C)。

91. 正確答案：(B) ☆☆

What will happen to cameras if they are found during inspection?　　若在檢查時發現相機，相機會被怎麼處理？

(A) The inspector will take the person's picture.　　檢查人員會替那個人照張相。

(B) The inspector will take the camera, and return it after the event.　　**檢查人員會拿走相機，在活動結束後再歸還。**

(C) The inspector will take the camera and not return it.　　檢查人員會拿走相機，而且不會歸還。

(D) The inspector will take out the film and　　檢查人員會拿出底片並保管起來。

指示中明確表明 ... camera ... will be confiscated, and will be returned to you after the concert. 也就是說照相機會先被沒收，在演唱會之後再歸還。(B) 為正確答案。

● 92 ~ 94 指示說明 ⊃ Half 1 39 ~ 41

Questions 92 through 94 refer to the following instructions.

Thank you for purchasing the Zx100 component stereo system. This compact disc provides a brief explanation on how to connect your system. First, the basic Zx100 system. Remove all components and accessories from the box and confirm that no parts are missing. Next, stack the components on a level, sturdy surface, placing the control amplifier on the bottom. Connect them using the cables and illustrated instruction sheet provided. Position and connect your speakers, recheck all other connections, and turn on the power first to the amplifier and then to the other components. You are now ready to begin enjoying your new stereo system. If you purchased a system that includes the subwoofer, do not stop this compact disc but continue to listen for special guidelines on setting up your system.

第 92 ~ 94 題與以下的指示說明有關。

感謝您購買 Zx100 型組合立體音響系統。本光碟提供簡要系統連接說明。首先從基礎 Zx100 系統開始。請將所有組件及配件從箱子中取出,並確認沒有缺少任何部分。接著將組件堆疊在水平、堅固的平面上,將控制擴大機置於最下方。使用連接線及所提供的圖示說明書將它們連接起來。配置並連接喇叭,再次檢查所有其他的連接部分,然後先開啟擴大機的電源,再開啟其他組件的電源。這樣您就可開始享受全新的立體音響系統了。如果您購買的系統包括重低音喇叭,那麼不要停止播放此光碟,請繼續聽取有關您系統設定的特別指引。

92. 正確答案:(B) ☆

What is the purpose of the compact disc?　　光碟的目的何在?

(A) To thank the customer　　為了感謝顧客

(B) To tell the customer how to set up the stereo　　**為了告訴顧客該如何組裝立體音響**

(C) To sell the customer a subwoofer　　為了賣重低音喇叭給顧客

(D) To make sure no parts are missing　　為了確保沒有缺少組件

由第二句 This compact disc provides a brief explanation on how to connect your system. 可知,(B)「為了告訴顧客該如何組裝立體音響」為正確答案。

93. 正確答案:(A) ☆☆☆

Where must the control amplifier be positioned?　　控制擴大機應置於何處?

(A) On the bottom　　**最下方**

(B) In a stack　　在堆疊中

(C) On top of the other components　　在其他組件之上

(D) In the box　　在箱子裡

說明中提到的 placing the control amplifier on the bottom 就指向正確答案 (A)。

94. 正確答案：(D) ☆☆

Who should continue to listen to the compact disc?

誰應該繼續聽取光碟內容？

(A) People who didn't understand the instructions

   沒聽懂指示的人

(B) People who like to listen to music

   喜歡聽音樂的人

(C) People who have stereo systems

   擁有立體音響系統的人

(D) People who bought the system with the subwoofer

   購買了該系統以及重低音喇叭的人

解說

依據說明最後提到的 If you purchased a system that includes the subwoofer, do not stop this compact disc but continue to listen ... 可知，正確答案為 (D)。

● 95 ~ 97 廣告 ⊃ Pre 45 ~ 47   ● 74

Questions 95 through 97 refer to the following advertisement.

Good morning, shoppers. Numerous items are on sale this morning. First, everything in the frozen foods section with a blue tag is available at half the regular price. There's a limit of six items per customer. Next, in the dairy section, if you buy two quarts of milk, you can get a third one for free. That's buy two, get one free! Also, canned goods are on sale. There's a limit of six items per customer for canned goods at half price. Finally, don't forget to show your member's card at the register for an additional 5% off your entire purchase. These specials are only good until noon, so hurry and take advantage of these great bargains!

第 95 ~ 97 題與以下廣告有關。

早安，各位購物來賓。今天早上有眾多商品特價優惠。首先，冷凍食品區的藍標商品統統半價。每位顧客限購 6 項。接著，要是您在乳製品區購買 2 夸脫牛奶，就能免費獲得第 3 夸脫。也就是買二送一！另外罐頭食品也有特價。每位顧客限購 6 件罐裝食品，以半價優惠。最後，別忘了在收銀台示出您的會員卡，這樣整體購物金額還可享有額外的 5% 折扣。這些優惠都只到中午為止，所以請把握機會享受這些大特價！

95. 正確答案：(B) ☆

What is on sale with blue tags?	有藍標的特價商品是什麼？
(A) Canned goods	罐頭食品
(B) Frozen foods	**冷凍食品**
(C) All the dairy products	所有乳製品
(D) Fruits and vegetables	水果與蔬菜

解說

由廣告第二句提到的 ... everything in the frozen foods section with a blue tag ... at half the regular price. 可知，正確答案為 (B)。

96. 正確答案：(B) ☆☆

How many canned products on sale can a customer buy?
每位顧客可購買幾個特價罐裝產品？

(A) As many as they want	想買幾個就買幾個
(B) Up to six per customer	**每位顧客最多六個**
(C) Up to five per customer	每位顧客最多五個
(D) One can for every two cans	每買兩罐就特價一罐

解說

廣告中明白提到 There's a limit of six items per customer for canned food ...，因此正確答案為 (B)。注意，(B) 中的 up to 就相當於原句的 a limit of。

97. 正確答案：(C) ☆

How can customers get a 5% discount at the cash register?
顧客如何能在收銀台獲得 5% 的折扣？

(A) By showing the discount items they bought	展示他們所購買的折價商品
(B) By showing identification	示出身分證明
(C) By showing their member's card	**示出會員卡**
(D) By shopping before noon	在中午前購物

解說

倒數第二句提到 ... show your member's card at the register for an additional 5% off ...，故正確答案為 (C)。

● 98 ~ 100 致詞

Questions 98 through 100 refer to the following speech.

It was a great game, and I applaud our opponent team, Westmore State. They were clearly prepared, and in the end they showed they wanted the game more than we did. We were optimistic going in, having great players like seniors Johnny Baker and Wayne Phillips healthy and playing better than ever. And, though we were without our top defensive player, Simon Fields, we did have several chances to win this game. We're a very good team, but they were better tonight and are very worthy national champions. Our guys are very disappointed in the locker room right now, but we were simply outplayed by a hungrier team, and that's the bottom line. Congratulations again to Westmore State on winning the championship. That's all.

第 98 ~ 100 題與以下的致詞內容有關。

這真是一場很棒的比賽，我為我們的對手球隊魏斯特摩州立大學喝采。他們顯然準備周全，而且最終展示出比我們更旺盛的獲勝決心。因為擁有像大四的強尼・貝克及韋恩・飛利浦等健康、表現得比以往任何時候都好的優秀球員，我們持樂觀的態度參賽。而雖然少了我們的頂尖防守員西蒙・菲爾茲，我們仍取得了好幾次的獲勝機會。我們是支很好的隊伍，但是他們今晚表現得更好，成為全國冠軍可說是當之無愧。我們的球員們現在在更衣室裡，他們都很沮喪，不過重點是，我們只是被一個更渴望勝利的隊伍擊敗罷了。再次恭喜魏斯特摩州立大學贏得冠軍。完畢。

98. 正確答案：(B) ☆☆☆

Who is the speaker?	致詞者是誰？
(A) The coach of Westmore State	魏斯特摩州立大學的教練
(B) The coach of the losing team	**輸球隊伍的教練**
(C) A reporter	一名記者
(D) A player on the winning team	一名贏球隊伍的球員

 解說

請注意致詞最後提到的 Congratulations again。 依據第一句提到的 ... I applaud our opponent team, Westmore State. 和倒數第三句提到的 Our guys are very disappointed ... 等來推斷，(A)、(C)、(D) 都不可能，只有 (B) 為合理選項。

99. 正確答案：(A) ☆☆

Why does the speaker think the team lost?　　該致詞者認為這支球隊為何會輸？

(A) They didn't want to win the game badly　他們想贏球的慾望不夠強烈。
enough.

(B) They were better than the other team.　　他們比另一隊更強。

(C) Their best players were injured.　　　　他們的主力球員受傷了。

(D) Their best players were healthy.　　　　他們的主力球員很健康。

解說

這段致詞第二句提到 ... they wanted the game more than we did.，倒數第三句又提到 ...
we were simply outplayed by a hungrier team ...；換句話說，他顯然認為他的球隊「贏
球的慾望不夠強烈」。因此，(A) 為正解。

100. 正確答案：(C) ☆☆

What did the speaker say about Westmore State?
該致詞者對魏斯特摩州立大學有何評論？

(A) They looked hungry.　　　　　　　　　他們看起來很餓。

(B) They were in the locker room.　　　　　他們在更衣室裡。

(C) They were worthy champions.　　　　他們成為冠軍可說是當之無愧。

(D) They were playing better than ever　　　他們的表現是前所未有的優秀。

解說

致詞者第五句提到的 ... they ... are very worthy national champions.「他們成為全國冠軍
可說是當之無愧」，因此本題選 (C)。注意，致詞中提到的 playing better than ever 指的
是他們自己的隊員 Johnny Baker 和 Wayne Philips，而不是魏斯特州立大學隊伍，故 (D)
不可選。

101. 正確答案：(A) ☆☆

Could you make _room_ for me? I'd like to sit down.

可以挪點空間給我嗎？我想坐下。

> **解說** 詞性（可數名詞、不可數名詞） ⊃ **Pre 51, 57**
>
> make room 是指「騰出空間」，而表此意時，room 為不可數名詞，所以不可加 a 或用複數形。

102. 正確答案：(A) ☆☆

The order _placed_ yesterday will be shipped by global priority mail.

昨天下的訂單將以全球優先郵件送出。

> **解說** 意思相近的單字 ⊃ **Pre 52**
>
> 「下訂單」說成 place an order，此處用過去分詞表示被動之意。

103. 正確答案：(D) ☆☆☆

I _should have known_ better than to invest all my money in the new start-up business last year.

我早該知道不該把所有的錢都投資在去年才剛創立的那家新公司上。

> **解說** 助動詞、時態 ⊃ **Pre 56**
>
> 依句意，本題應用「should + 完成式」來表示「過去該做而沒做……」的事。正確答案為 (D)。

104. 正確答案：(D) ☆☆

The only problem with my new camera is that it does not have _rechargeable_ batteries.

我的新相機唯一的問題就在於它沒有可充電電池。

> **解說** 詞性（詞類、V-ing 形等） ⊃ **Pre 51**
>
> 空格後為名詞，故應選形容詞，(C) recharging 雖可做形容詞用，但意思為「正充電的」，不符句意。rechargeable batteries 指「可以充電的電池」，(D) 為正確選項。

105. 正確答案：(A) ☆☆

Fortunately, Monday's earthquake did not _do_ any significant damage.

很幸運地，週一的地震並未造成任何重大災害。

解說 使用 do 的常用片語 ➲ Pre 69

do damage「造成損害」為慣用語。雖然英文裡有 (C) suffer damage「遭受損害」這種說法,但是必須以受害的物或人等為主詞。

106. 正確答案：(B) ☆☆

Applicants must be 18 years old or above to take _part_ in the competition.
參加此項競賽的申請人必須在 18 歲以上。

解說 動詞片語 ➲ Pre 70

take part in 為固定片語,意思是「參加」。

107. 正確答案：(B) ☆☆☆

In _contrast_ to the downsizing trend in the market, the firm recruited extra staff.
相對於市場上的人力縮編趨勢,該公司卻雇用了更多額外工作人員。

解說 具有副詞功能的介系詞片語 ➲ Pre 62

in contrast to 是「相對於……」之意。若要用 (A),則應說成 contrary to「與……相反」,前面不可加介系詞 in。

108. 正確答案：(A) ☆☆

With the sudden increase in customers, we may achieve our goal much earlier than we expected.
由於顧客人數急遽增加,我們可能會比預期更快達成目標。

解說 介系詞

一前後句意,本題應選可表達「由於……」之意的 (A) With。

109. 正確答案：(B) ☆☆☆

The downturn in the economy is making it much harder for new graduates to _secure_ jobs.
經濟衰退使得新的畢業生更難找到工作。

解說 詞性（不定詞）➲ Pre 51

句中的代名詞 it 指 to 不定詞之後的內容,而 to 之後必須用動詞原形,故選 (B)。

110. 正確答案：(B) ☆☆

This software application is _complicated_ for the average user.

此應用軟體對一般使用者來說是複雜的。

> **解說** 詞性、詞類 ⊃ Pre 51
>
> Be 動詞之後需要主詞補語，雖然 (A) complication（名詞） 和 (D) complicating（現在分詞）皆可做補語，但是在意思上都說不通。只有 (B) complicated「複雜的」（形容詞）為正解。

111. 正確答案：(A) ☆☆

The survey showed that fewer than half the employees were in _favor_ of adopting flextime working hours.

調查結果顯示，只有不到一半的員工贊成採取彈性工時。

> **解說** 介系詞片語
>
> 空格前為介系詞，因此只能填入名詞 (A) favor，而 in favor of ... 是「贊成……」的意思。注意，雖然 (D) favoring（動名詞）也合文法，但是意思不通。

112. 正確答案：(D) ☆☆

The new filing system will _save_ us a lot of time and trouble in finding the right folder.

新的歸檔系統將替我們省下許多尋找正確資料夾的時間及麻煩。

> **解說** 意思相近的單字 ⊃ Pre 52
>
> (D) save 是「節省、節約」之意，是唯一合理的選項。(A) stop「停止」、(B) prevent「防止」、(C) end「結束」的意思都不通。

113. 正確答案：(C) ☆

The CEO will make _an announcement_ about the new models at the conference in San Diego next week.

執行長將於下週在聖地牙哥舉辦的會議上發表新機型。

> **解說** 詞性 ⊃ Pre 51
>
> make an announcement 是「宣布」之意。(A) announce（動詞）、(B) announcing（動名詞）文法不通，不適合置於動詞 make 之後；(D) an announcer「一名宣告者」不符合句意。

114. 正確答案：(B) ☆☆☆

The information provided in these reports is _intended_ for in-house use only.

這些報告所提供的資訊僅供公司內部使用。

> **解說** 詞性 ⊃ Pre 51 ——
>
> be intended for ... 是「供……之用、為了……而準備」之意。

115. 正確答案：(A) ☆☆☆

Rival firms have grown _so alarmed_ at our activities in this area that they have united against us.

競爭公司對於我們在此區域的活動已變得非常緊張，所以已聯合起來對抗我們。

> **解說** so ... that ... 、too ... to ——
>
> 句中有由 that 引導、表結果的子句，因此應選擇 (A) 或 (B) 等有 so 的選項。而 (A) 的 alarmed「驚恐的、憂慮的」表被動，(B) 的 alarming「令人感到驚恐的、令人感到憂慮的」表主動。本題的主詞 rival firms「競爭公司」因為「我們（舉辦的）的活動」而感到緊張，所以「競爭公司」是「被動」的感到緊張，本題應選 (A)。

💡 奪分祕笈：分詞的用法

分詞是由動詞轉變而來的，目的是讓動詞變成形容詞。分詞可分為現在分詞 (V-ing) 跟過去分詞 (-ed)。兩者區別在於：

▶ **當受到形容的主體是主動的／作為工具、媒介等等的時候，選擇現在分詞：**

ex: a. crying baby	在哭的娃娃	（娃娃自己哭）
b. smiling girl	在微笑的女孩	（女孩自己微笑， 不是別人幫她微笑）
c. smoking room	吸煙室	（用來吸煙的房間， 屬於工具或媒介）
d. Tom is an interesting person.	湯姆是個有趣的人。	（湯姆本身有趣）
e. Jeff is annoying.	傑夫很讓人生氣。	（主動讓人不高興）

▶ 當被形容的主體是被動的，使用過去分詞：

ex:
a. the stolen money 贓款 （錢是被人偷的）
b. a broken heart 破碎的心 （心不是自己破碎的）
c. she is disappointed. 她感到失望。 （有人事物讓她產生
情緒）

d. Tom is interested in the book. 湯姆對那本書有興趣。 （被書吸引）
e. Jeff is annoyed. 傑夫生氣了。 （被某人事物應想而
生氣了）

116. 正確答案：(A) ☆☆

This area has a less humid climate than <u>any</u> other in the country, and is perfect for growing grapes.

這個區域的氣候比該國任何其他區域都要乾燥，很適合種植葡萄。

> **解說** less than any other... ⟲ Pre 65
>
> area「區域」為可數名詞，而空格後的 other 代表的是 other area，為單數，因此 (B)、(C)、(D) 皆為不可能的選項。本題以「比較級 + than any other + 單數形」的形式便可表達「比其它任何地方都更……」這樣最高級的意思。

117. 正確答案：(D) ☆☆

The key to <u>making</u> good decisions for your business is to know all available options.

為你的事業做出良好決策之關鍵，就是要知道所有可能的選擇。

> **解說** 詞性（介系詞 + 動名詞） ⟲ Pre 51
>
> the key to ... 的 to 是介系詞而非不定詞，因此其後須接名詞或動名詞。本題應選 (D) making。

118. 正確答案：(C) ☆☆

This DVD player is so hard to operate that I have spent twice <u>as much</u> time reading the manual as using the machine itself.

這台 DVD 播放器是如此地難操作，以至於我必須花費相當於使用該機器本身的兩倍時間閱讀使用手冊。

> **解說** 比較（twice as much / many as）
>
> 由句中後方的 as 可知，此句要表達的是「同等比較」，故 (A) 與 (B) 不予考慮。而因為空格前後為不可數名詞 time，所以本題選 (C) as much。注意，句中的 twice 指「兩倍」，置於比較式前並不影響其結構。

119. 正確答案：(A) ☆☆

 Most of the customers seem to be very pleased with the company's level of service.
大部分顧客似乎都非常滿意該公司的服務水準。

> **解說** most、almost 和 mostly
>
> 空格前後為名詞，因此副詞 (B) Almost 和 (C) Mostly 可立即排除。而本句為肯定句，不定代名詞沒有理由用 any，故本題應選 (A)。注意，most 與 any 同為不定代名詞，而 most of 指「大部分的⋯⋯」。

120. 正確答案：(B) ☆☆

Every candidate must have a good knowledge of electronics and a valid work visa.
每個應徵者都必須具備豐富的電子學知識以及有效的工作簽證。

> **解說** 使用 have 的片語
>
> have 為及物動詞，其後須接名詞作為受詞，因此 (C) 與 (D) 可先排除。而 (A) 中的 enough 雖可置於名詞後，但其後應接不定詞結構。本題應選 (B) a good knowledge。

121. 正確答案：(C) ☆

Who do you think the best soccer player was this year?
你覺得誰是今年最好的足球選手？

> **解說** 間接疑問句 ⊃ Pre 67
>
> 本句原為簡單的 WH- 問句，在插入 do you think 之後，原來的直接問句必須改成間接問句形式。本題空格中應填入原本的動詞，(A)、(B) 形式不對，(D) 時態不符，故本題選 (C)。注意，句中的 this year 可以解釋成「過去的這一年」。

122. 正確答案：(C) ☆☆

The old manual typewriter in the display case reminds me of the early days of the company.
展示櫃裡的老式手動打字機，讓我想起了公司成立初期的日子。

remind someone of something 是「使某人想起某事物」的意思。(A) remembers 「記得」、(B) memorize(s)「熟記」、(D) recall (s)「回憶」句意皆不符。

💡 **奪分祕笈：remind、remember、memorize及recalls的差異**

▶ remember 記得、記住

Do you remember his telephone number?　　你記得他的電話號碼嗎？

▶ memorize 記住、背熟

memorize a poem　　　　　　　　　　　背熟一首詩

▶ remind 提醒、使想起（remind sb. of + sth. / doing sth.）

The story reminds me of an experience
I once had.　　　　　　　　　　　　這個故事使我想起我的一次親身經歷。

▶ recalls 回憶、回想（sb. recall that + 從屬子句）

He recalled that she always came home late
on Wednesdays.　　　　　　　　　　他回想起她星期三總是晚歸。

---

123. 正確答案：(A) ☆☆☆

If it **had not been** for your advice, we could never have met the deadline.

要不是有你的建議，我們可能永遠也趕不上截止期限。

解說 假設式 ⊃ Pre 68

由主要子句的 could have not met 可知此為與過去事實相反的過去完成假設式。而「若沒有⋯⋯」的過去假設式為 if it were not for ...，轉換成過去完成假設式就是 if it had not been for ...。

---

124. 正確答案：(B) ☆☆

The Stark Foundation's new residential development **consists of** five units of single-parent family homes.

斯塔克基金會新的住宅開發案，是由五個單親家庭住宅所構成。

解說 動詞片語 ⊃ Pre 70

「由⋯⋯構成、由⋯⋯組成」必須用主動形式的 consist of ... 表達。(A) consisting of 為動名詞非動詞，不可選。(C) is consisted by、(D) was consisted 為被動式，不可選。

125. 正確答案：(C) ☆☆

Avoid incorrect punctuation and <u>wrongly</u> used capital letters because this may confuse readers.

避免使用不正確的標點符號和誤用大寫字母，因為這可能會混淆讀者。

> **解說** 詞性、意思相近的單字 ⊃ Pre 51, 52
>
> 各選項的意義為 (A) inadequate 形「不充分的」、(B) bad 形「不好的」、(C) wrongly 副「錯誤地」、(D) properly 副「恰當地」；而題目中 used 為過去分詞當形容詞，用來修飾名詞 capital letters，修飾形容詞的必須是副詞，因此首先排除 (A)、(B)。而句意提到「誤將字大寫而混淆讀者」可知，(C) 符合題意。

126. 正確答案：(D) ☆☆

I have arranged a meeting <u>over</u> lunch with our design director.

我已安排了和我們的設計總監進行午餐會議。

> **解說** 介系詞
>
> 介系詞 over 用來表達「一邊吃……（一邊做……）」之意，而所謂 a meeting over lunch「邊吃午餐邊開會」也可說成 a lunch meeting「午餐會議」。

127. 正確答案：(D) ☆☆

Before the 19th century, almost all countries had to concentrate <u>on</u> the task of feeding their people.

在 19 世紀以前，幾乎所有國家都必須專注於餵飽人民肚子的工作。

> **解說** 動詞片語 ⊃ Pre 70
>
> concentrate on ... 為固定用法，指「專注於……、集中精力在……」。

128. 正確答案：(D) ☆☆☆

James, Katherine and Terry are going to play the parts of the husband, the wife and her lover <u>respectively</u> in the next musical.

詹姆士、凱薩琳與泰瑞在下一齣音樂劇中，將分別扮演丈夫、妻子和其情人的角色。

> **解說** 詞性 ⊃ Pre 51
>
> 依句意，三個人應該是「分別」扮演不同的角色，也就是說，本題應選出適合修飾動詞 play 的副詞。(A) respestfully「恭敬地」雖是副詞但意思不合題意，(B) respectable「值得尊敬的」，與 (C) respective「分別的」同為形容詞，不可選，故本題選 (D) respectivly 副「分別地」。

Strategies　Pre Test　Half Test 1　Half Test 2　Full Test

129. 正確答案：(A) ☆☆

The company's range of products includes semiconductors, heavy equipment and petrochemicals.

該公司的產品範圍包括了半導體、重機械設備及石油化學製品。

> **解說** 詞性、可數名詞、不可數名詞 ➲ Pre 51, 57 ─────
>
> equipment 為不可數名詞，一般不用複數形。(B)、(D) 可先排除。而名詞應用形容詞修飾，故 (C) 亦為誤。

130. 正確答案：(B) ☆

Ms. Schultz will be leaving for London tomorrow morning, but she can be reached at this number.

舒爾茨小姐明早將動身前往倫敦，但是透過此電話號碼可以聯繫到她。

> **解說**
>
> 句中所述時間為 tomorrow morning，因此動詞應選未來式動詞，而由於空格後為現在分詞，故形成未來進行式。

131. 正確答案：(A) ☆☆

The latest report shows that these books published last month are selling very well.

最新報告顯示，上個月出版的這些書賣得非常好。

> **解說** 主動式、被動式 ➲ Pre 55 ─────
>
> 表達「書賣好不好」之意時，sell 必須用主動式表示，而因空格前有 are，所以選 (A) selling，構成現在進行式。

132. 正確答案：(C) ☆☆☆

In the U.S. you are eligible for a tax deduction if you donate to a charity organization certified by the government.

在美國，如果捐款給政府認證的慈善團體，就有資格獲得課稅減免。

> **解說** 意思相近的單字 ➲ Pre 52 ─────
>
> be eligible for ... 是「有……的資格」之意，(C) 為唯一合理的選項。(A) liable 形 「有義務的」、(B) credible 形 「可信的」、(D) reliable 形 「可靠的」皆與句意不符。

133. 正確答案：(A) ☆☆

Their new office was completely refurnished at _great_ cost.

他們的新辦公室是花了大錢徹底重新整修的。

> **解說** 詞性、詞類 ⊃ Pre 51 ——
>
> cost 是不可數名詞，應以形容詞 great 來修飾。而 (C) most 形 「大多數的」與 (D) a few 形 「幾個」雖然可作形容詞用，但皆與句意不符，而且只能用來修飾可數名詞。

134. 正確答案：(D) ☆☆

The customer service department _told_ the client that he had to show in what way the product was defective.

客服部門告訴那位顧客他必須出示該產品有怎樣的瑕疵。

> **解說** 詞性 ⊃ Pre 51 ——
>
> tell 不必加介系詞，即可直接接受詞，而 (A) 的 say 必須加介系詞 to，(B) 的 speak 和 (C) 的 talk 則須加 to 或 with 才能接說話對象。

135. 正確答案：(C) ☆

All employees who want to use these facilities must attend an orientation session.

所有想使用這些設施的員工都必須出席說明會。

> **解說** 數量形容詞 all / some / every ⊃ Pre 57 ——
>
> 由於句中出現了must，依語意應是針對所有或每一位員工所做的規定，但是因為空格後的 employees 為複數，所以只能選 (C) All，而不可選 (D) Every。

136. 正確答案：(D) ☆☆

Temporary staff _looking_ after in-patients at our hospital are usually paid 15 dollars an hour plus transportation expenses.

在我們醫院照顧住院病患的臨時雇員的薪資通常是每小時 15 美元再加上交通費。

> **解說** 現在分詞的形容詞用法 ——
>
> 照顧病患為主動行為，因此應選擇現在分詞 (V-ing) 作為形容詞。

小心陷阱

請注意，一個句子內只能有一個動詞，若選 (C) was looking，則再加上 are paid，此句就會有兩個動詞，故 (C) 為錯誤選項。

137. 正確答案：(D) ☆☆

There were many inquiries about when operations at the plant _would resume_ .

很多人詢問該工廠何時會恢復作業。

> **解說** 詞性、時態 ⊃ **Pre 51**─────
> 本句主要子句的動詞為過去式（were），因此從屬子句的助動詞也必須使用過去式，故
> 應從 will 改為 would。四個選項中只有 (D) 屬過去式，故為正確選項。

138. 正確答案：(D) ☆☆

Imprecise use of language can _lead to_ confusion and misinterpretation in business deals.

不精確的言詞運用可能造成商業交易上的混亂和誤解。

> **解說** 動詞片語 ⊃ **Pre 70** ─────
> (D) lead to 指「導致……、造成……」，為唯一符合句意的選項。(A) result from 指
> 「因……而產生」意思完全相反。另外，(B) come across 是「偶然遇見」，(C) take up
> 則是「拿起、占用」之意，皆與句意不符。

139. 正確答案：(C) ☆

By law, all employees and visitors _must_ wear hard hats when entering the construction site.

依據法律規定，所有員工與訪客在進入工地時都必須戴上安全帽。

> **解說** 助動詞 ⊃ **Pre 56** ─────
> 由於是「法律」規定，因此必須搭配表示義務的助動詞 (C) must。

140. 正確答案：(B) ☆☆

Full-time _employees_ who have worked for the company for 12 months are entitled to two weeks' paid vacation.

在該公司任職滿十二個月的全職員工可享有兩週的帶薪休假。

> **解說** 關係代名詞 ⊃ **Pre 66** ─────
> 空格前後有關係代名詞 who，所以前面一定得是表「人」的先行詞。而 (C) employer 图
> 「雇主」與 (B) employee 图「員工」皆為「人」，但依句意應選後者。

Part 6 Text Completion 短文填空題

☆470 分等級 ☆☆600 分等級 ☆☆☆730 分以上

● 141 ~ 143 公告訊息

第 141 ~ 143 題與以下的公告訊息有關。

致顧客們之重要訊息

近來網路詐騙案件大幅增加，許多人都被誘騙而 (141.) 洩露了個人資訊，如銀行帳號及密碼等。

如果您登入了敝公司的網站卻進入您從未看過的頁面時，請在輸入任何資訊前，先仔細 (142.) 閱讀該頁面。如果您被要求重新確認您的帳號、密碼或任何其他個人資訊，(143.) 那麼在您確認該頁面為真之前，請勿進行這些動作。

若您有任何疑慮，請上敝公司網站，或撥打 1-800-754-0011 給我們的客服部門。

Word List

☐ fraud [frɔd] 图 詐騙　　　　　　　☐ genuine [ˋdʒɛnjʊɪn] 形 真正的

141. 正確答案：(D) ☆☆

解說

be tricked into V-ing 指「被誘騙而做……」，其後接 (D) revealing「洩漏」最為合理。(A) creating「創造」、(B) 的 opening「打開」、(C) stealing「偷竊」的意思皆與題目的前後文不符。

142. 正確答案：(D) ☆

解說

修飾動詞 read「閱讀」的應用副詞，(D) carefully 副「謹慎地」為正確答案。

143. 正確答案：(C) ☆☆☆

解說

按前後文義，這部分要表達的應該是「直到確定該頁面為真之前」，因此應選 (C) until。其它選項皆不合邏輯。

Strategies　Pre Test　Half Test 1　Half Test 2　Full Test

第 144 ~ 146 題與以下的信件內容有關。

傑拉德・芬頓先生
357 號，馬力歐街
哈里斯堡，賓州 17101

親愛的芬頓先生，

感謝您近日申請 (144.) 房屋貸款。不過，在我們處理您的申請之前，我們需要一些與您目前收入有關的資訊。

我們希望您能寄來 2 份最近的薪資單，以及 1 封由您目前的雇主 (145.) 提供的信函，而其中必須包含您的年薪細節。

該房屋物件的支付期限為 7 月 31 日，因此若要趕上截止期限，我們就得動作快些。如果您有任何疑問，請儘管 (146.) 與我聯繫。您可透過電子郵件（karenb@ghsbanking.com）跟我聯絡，或直接打電話（6539-7001）給我。期待很快就能獲得您的回覆。

凱倫・伯格
顧客關係經理
謹啓

Word List

☐ look forward to ... 期待著……

---

144. 正確答案：(D) ☆☆

解說

形容詞 recent「最近的」之後應接名詞。(B)、(C) 雖與 (D) 雖皆為名詞，但是 (B) applicant指「申請人」，(C) appliance指「用具、器具」，意思都不通。正確答案應為 (D) application「申請」。

145. 正確答案：(B) ☆

解說

與上一題相同，在形容詞 current「目前的」之後應接名詞。 (B) employer、(C) employee、(D) employment 皆為名詞，但只有 a letter from your current employer「由您不前的雇主提供的信函」才說得通。

146. 正確答案：(A) ☆☆

解說

get in touch with ...「與……聯繫」為固定片語，(A) in 為正解。

● **147 ~ 149 廣告** ➲ Pre 71 ~ 73

第 147 ~ 149 題與以下的徵才廣告有關。

音樂產業招募實習生

阿古斯音樂，一間信譽卓著的藝人經紀公司，正在尋找充滿熱情的年輕人來擔任實習工作。職責 (147.) 將包括一般辦公室事務、接電話，以及更新產品資訊等。

你偶爾也會需要代表 (148.) 公司陪伴藝人至錄音室，以處理任何可能發生的問題。

這對充滿活力且積極進取的年輕人來說是個絕佳的機會，可以藉此培養未來在娛樂產業職涯中所需極具價值的 (149.) 技術和知識。在六個月的實習之後，如果實習生的表現優異，我們便可能考慮提供一份有給職成為正式員工。

如果你是個條理分明的人，具備良好人際能力，而且正在尋找一個通往刺激、充滿活力之行業界的跳板的話，請與我們聯繫以預約面試時間。

---

147. 正確答案：(C) ☆☆

解說

空格後為動詞 will include，因此必須填入名詞作為主詞，而因動詞之後列出的是工作內容，因此 (C) Responsibilities 图「職責」應為正確答案。(A) Response「回應」雖然也是名詞但是在意思上都說不通，所以不對。

148. 正確答案：(C) ☆

解說

根據前後文意，「代表」處理問題最為合理，故本題選 (C)。(A) show 動「展示」、(B) illustrate 動「說明」、(C) demonstrate 動「示範」皆與句意不符。

149. 正確答案：(B) ☆☆☆

invaluable 是「無價的、極具價值的」之意，與其前提到的 skills 和 knowledge 相呼應。而 (A) worthless 指 形 「沒價值的」、(C) inexpensive 指 形 「便宜的」、(D) pointless 指 形 「沒意義的」，在意思上都說不通。

● 150 ~ 152 公告、通知

第 150 ~ 152 題與以下的公告通知有關。

奧爾巴尼古董及藝術品博覽會：取消通知

我們很遺憾地宣布，奧爾巴尼古董及藝術品博覽會，本國最著名的藝術與古董博覽會之一今年將取消展覽。本年度活動原本計畫於 9 月 3 日至 8 日於哈羅德・雅各布森會議中心舉行。遺憾的是，由於（150）一場嚴重的大火，使得該場地已無法再用。其損壞極為嚴重，現在完全不可能使用。

當然，我們也已盡力尋找替代場地，但是現在已經是 7 月份，此區域所有其他合適的場地都已被預約一空。對於所有已預訂了會場空間的業者們，我們致上誠摯的歉意。

我們將全額退還您已支付的租借費，再加上（152）明年度費用的 10% 優惠折扣。我們很期待您光臨明年的博覽會。若需要進一步的詳細資訊，請透過 jbenson@aafaf.com 電子郵件信箱與我們的客服經理，珍妮佛・班森聯繫。

Word List

☐ antique [æn`tik] 名 古董　　　　☐ alternative site [ɔl`tɜnətɪv saɪt] 名 替代場地
☐ full refund [rɪ`fʌnd] 全額退還

150. 正確答案：(B) ☆☆☆

「因為一場大火，場地已無法使用」，能用來表達這種「因果」關係的只有 (A) because 「因為」和 (B) resulting from 「起因於……」，但是因為空格後為名詞片語而非子句，所以正解應為 (B)。至於 (A) 選項，只須將 because 改為 because of，即可符合本題文法。

151. 正確答案：(B) ☆☆

解說

由於場地「嚴重損壞」，故已「不可能」使用，本題應選 (B)。out of the question 為固定片語，意思即「不可能」。而各選項的意思分別為 (A) picture 图 「圖片」，(B) question 图 「問題」，(C) possibility 图 「可能性」，(D) planning 图 「制訂計畫」。

小心陷阱

out of the question 為固定片語，意思即「不可能」。請注意，英文中並沒有 out of the pcssibility 這種說法。(C) 不可選。

152. 正確答案：(B) ☆☆

解說

along with 為固定片語，意思是「與……一起」，在本句中指除了退款外「再加上」10% 的折扣，正確答案是 (B)。

小心陷阱

注意，不可誤選 (D)，along together 為錯誤組合。

Memo:

☆470 分等級 ☆☆600 分等級 ☆☆☆730 分以上

● **153 ~ 154 電子郵件** ⊃ Pre 88 ~ 90

第 153 ~ 154 題與以下的電子郵件有關。

日期：2009 年 4 月 24 日
收件人：全體員工
寄件人：湯姆‧諾蘭，資訊部經理
主旨：病毒防護

誠如各位都知道的，我們最近遇到了病毒感染某些辦公室電腦的問題。這已造成一些嚴重的資料遺失問題，而且由於移除這些病毒花了很長的時間，使得公司損失了大量工時。去年 12 月，資訊部曾發送關於如何避免讓電腦中毒的說明給所有員工。我誠摯地請求各位再閱讀一次該說明，並確保你採取了所有的必要防護措施。有項建議我必須再次提出，那就是：絕不要打開任何電子郵件附件，除非你對於它是什麼東西，以及是誰寄來的有完全的把握。此外，為了強化保護，我們最近購買了最新的病毒防護軟體。從下週一至週五，資訊部門人員會把該軟體安裝在公司的每一部電腦上。安裝時間表張貼於公司布告欄上，請參閱。在安裝該新軟體時，你將無法使用自己的電腦。所以請務必將你所有的重要資料複製到外接式硬碟中，這樣一來如果有需要，你才能在另一台電腦上使用這些資料。

湯姆‧諾蘭
資訊部門經理

Word List

☐ IT (information technology) 資訊科技
☐ infect [ɪnˋfɛkt] 動 感染
☐ e-mail attachment [iˋmel əˋtætʃmənt] 電子郵件附件
☐ bulletin board [ˋbʊlətɪn bord] 布告欄
☐ external hard drive [ɪkˋstɜnəl] 電腦用的外接式硬碟

153. 正確答案：(C) ☆☆☆

What is the purpose of this message?

(A) To warn staff about a new kind of computer virus

(B) To give detailed instructions on how to get rid of computer virus

(C) To inform staff about installing new software

(D) To inform staff about installing new computers

這封電子郵件的目的為何？

為了警告員工有關新型電腦病毒的事

為了提供如何去除電腦病毒的詳細說明

為了通知員工關於安裝新軟體的事

為了通知員工關於安裝新電腦的事

解說

由電子郵件第八句提到的 ... the most up-to-date virus protection software. 和第九句提到的 From Monday through Friday next week, members of the IT department will be installing it ... 可知，正確答案應為 (C)。

小心陷阱

注意，本電子郵件一開始就說 As you all know, we have had some problems recently with viruses infecting some of our office computers.，換言之，員工已經知道有病毒之事，故 (A) 並不正確。

154. 正確答案：(D) ☆☆

What problem will staff have in the following week?

(A) They will not be able to open e-mail attachments.

(B) They will have to search for computer viruses.

(C) Their computers will be replaced with new ones.

(D) Their computers will not be available temporarily.

下週員工將會遇上什麼問題？

他們將無法開啟電子郵件附件。

他們將必須搜尋電腦病毒。

他們的電腦將換成新的。

他們的電腦將暫時無法使用。

解說

由電子郵件倒數第三句 While this new software is being installed, you will not be able to use your own computer. 可知，正確答案為 (D)。注意，被安裝的是 new software，不是 new computers，千萬不要誤選 (C)。

1. 首先一定要讀過「收件人姓名與職稱」、「寄件人與其職稱」還有「主旨」。
2. 此類問題可能會以單篇文章形式，也可能做為雙篇文章組合來出題。內容不是那麼複雜，通常與「事務及集體會議」、「由主管發出的佈達事項、指令」還有「與公司內設備有關的公告」等有關。
3. 偶爾也會出現私人電子郵件，其內容主要為「為活動而進行的溝通協調」、「路線指引」、「約定時間」、「有關商品的申訴、抱怨」等。並不會出現與私人感情及流言八卦有關的內容。
4. 電子郵件也是一種書信，只不過其寫法較輕鬆、不正式。
   a. 一般在簡單的稱謂之後就會立刻進入主題。因此通常電子郵件的第一個關鍵詞就出現在 Dear ... 之後的第一個句子中。
   b. 而由於電子郵件寫好後就馬上寄出，所以通常不分 paragraph。
   c. 最後的 closing compliment（結尾敬語），一般對上司會使用 Sincerely / Best Regards，對同事平輩可用 Regards / Best Regards，而對朋友、家人則用 Love / Hugs / Kisses 等。

● 155 ~ 157 廣告 ⊃ Pre 77 ~ 78

第 155 ~ 157 題與以下廣告有關。

這個夏天到特羅品康納飯店進行海外打工！

・住宿費全免
・包三餐
・工作種類繁多

資格：
應徵者必須持有合適的簽證、具備良好英語溝通能力。有飯店工作經驗尤佳，但非必要。

工作條件：
・員工每週可休息一天，除了週六和週日外的任一天皆可。
・員工應時時保持外表乾淨整潔。飯店會負責清洗由飯店所提供的員工制服。
・員工可於非上班時間使用飯店的所有設施，例如網球場、健身房、游泳池及美容沙龍等。使用費為原價的六折。

Word List

☐ full board [fʊl bord] 包三餐（board 指「伙食」）

☐ qualification [ˌkwɑləfə`keʃən] 图 資格

☐ advantage [əd`væntɪdʒ] 图 有利條件、優勢

☐ neat and tidy [`taɪdɪ] 形 整齊的

155. 正確答案：(A) ☆☆

What is one of the benefits for workers at the hotel?

此飯店工作人員的福利之一是什麼？

(A) They do not have to pay for meals.	**他們不必付餐費。**
(B) They are allowed free use of all the facilities.	他們可免費使用所有設施。
(C) They can choose any work they like.	他們可選擇任何自己喜歡的工作。
(D) They have to buy their own work clothes.	他們必須購買自己的工作服。

解說

廣告副標的第二項明白列出 Full board「包三餐」，因此正解是 (A)。員工使用飯店設施必須付 60 percent of normal fees，並非免費，故 (B) 為誤。而廣告中副標只提到工作種類繁多 (Varied work)，並未說可以自己選工作，因此 (C) 也不對。最後，廣告工作條件 Conditions 第二點最後提到員工制服由飯店提供 (which [= employee uniforms] the hotel provides)，所以亦不可選 (D)。

156. 正確答案：(C) ☆

What is one requirement for job applicants?

對應徵工作者的資格要求之一為何？

(A) They should speak English and one other language.	他們應該要能說英語和另一國語言。
(B) They should have experience in hotel work.	他們應該要有飯店工作經驗。
(C) They must have a work visa.	**他們必須持有工作簽證。**
(D) They must be in their early 20s.	他們的年齡必須是 20 出頭。

解說

在資格 (Qualifications) 部分的一開頭就提到 Applicants must possess proper visas ...，而 proper visas 指的就是「工作簽證」。(C) work visa 為正解。

Strategies

Pre Test

Half Test 1

Half Test 2

Full Test

157. 正確答案：(B) ☆☆

Which of the following does NOT apply to the employees?

下列哪一項不適用於員工？

(A) They can take a day off on any day but　　他們可在週末以外的任一天休假。
　　 weekends.

(B) They can use the gym free of charge.　　**他們可以免費使用健身房。**

(C) They are not expected to clean their uniforms.　他們不必清洗自己的制服。

(D) They must be careful about their appearance.　他們必須注意自己的外表儀容。

> **解說**
>
> 注意，本題問的是何者「不」適用 (does Not apply) 於員工。依據文中最後項目所說的 All facilities ... are available to employees ... Charges for use will be 60 percent of normal fees. 可知，(B) 並「不」適用於員工。由於與此題相關的資訊遍布於文章各段落，因此不要忘了先掃描過題目。

● **158 ～ 161 商務信函** ➲ Pre 96 ～ 100

第 158 ～ 161 題與以下的信件內容有關。

安全標準處

321 號，柳橙街，西拉法葉，印第安納州 47695

法蘭西斯・格蘭傑先生
438 號，西碧斯黛爾街
普渡，印第安納州 47597

2009 年 6 月 3 日

親愛的格蘭傑先生：

安全標準處（SSD）進行了一次人行道檢查，依其標準他們發現您房子前的人行道並不安全。這些損壞可能會造成人們絆倒或跌倒。依據州法，所有土地持有人都有責任確保其住宅範圍內的人行道維持在良好的狀態下。有些人行道可透過打磨受損部分來修復，但是在某些情況下則可能需要更整體性的修補。

每一位因人行道須修繕而收到此通知的土地持有人，都必須在今年的 11 月 30 日前完成修繕。您必須先取得許可後才能動工。而許可證可免費於柳橙街 321 號的安全標準處總部取得。在修繕工程完成後，請致電離您最近的 SSD 辦公室以安排檢查。

您若有任何疑問，或想取得更多資訊，請撥打 217-236-8659 至安全標準部總部。

祝安好

路易斯 · D · 史卡利

安全標準處處長

謹啓

Word List

☐ inspection [ɪn`spɛkʃən] 名 檢查

☐ in good repair [rɪ`pɛr] 修理完善

☐ defect [dɪ`fɛkt] 名 缺陷、損壞

☐ permit [pə`mɪt] 名 許可

158. 正確答案：(C) ☆☆☆

What does the Safety Standards Division tell Mr. Grainger?

安全標準處通知格蘭傑先生什麼事？

(A) It plans to arrange a sidewalk inspection.　　該處計畫安排一次人行道檢查。

(B) It wants him to come to the office for an interview.　　該處要他來辦公室面試。

(C) It wants him to repair his sidewalks.　　**該處要他修繕他的人行道。**

(D) It will repair defective sidewalks.　　該處將修補有損壞的人行道。

解說

由信函第一段第三句中的 ... every landowner is responsible for keeping his or her sidewalks in good repair. 可知，正確答案為 (C)。

159. 正確答案：(C) ☆☆

What does Mr. Grainger have to do?　　格蘭傑先生必須做什麼？

(A) Obtain a permit for the SSD to repair the sidewalks.　　替安全標準處取得修補人行道的許可。

(B) Start to repair his sidewalks by November 30.　　在 11 月 30 日前開始修繕其人行道。

(C) Finish his sidewalk repairs by November 30.　　**在 11 月 30 日前完成人行道的修補。**

(D) Begin sidewalk repairs before getting a permit.　　在取得許可前就開始修補人行道。

依據信函第二段第一句提到的 Every owner ... must complete the work by November 30 可知，正確答案為 (C)。而 (A) 選項的意思是「為了讓 SSD 進行修繕，須由格蘭傑先生取得許可」，邏輯不通。(C) 選項說在 11 月 30 日前「開始修繕」，是誤導選項。另外，第二段第二句說 You must obtain a permit before the repairs can begin.，表示在開始修補工程前須先取得許可，所以 (D) 也不對。

160. 正確答案：(A) ☆☆

Where does the SSD issue permits for sidewalk repairs?

安全標準處於何處發給人行道修繕許可？

(A) At its main office	**在其總部**
(B) On West Beasdale Street	在西碧斯黛爾街
(C) At the landowner's nearest SSD office	在離土地持有人最近的安全標準處辦公室
(D) At the inspection site	在檢查現場

依第二段第三句提到的 Permits are available ... at the headquarters of the Safety Standards Division 可知，正確答案為 (A)。（注意，原文中的 headquarters 被以同義的 main office 代替。）而 (B) 是格蘭傑先生的地址，(C) 是申請安排檢查的地點，(D) 則是無中生有。

161. 正確答案：(B) ☆☆

What does Mr. Grainger have to do after repairs are completed?

在修繕完成後，格蘭傑先生必須做什麼？

(A) Apply for a permit every year.	每年都申請許可。
(B) Have his sidewalk repair inspected.	**請人來檢查他的人行道修繕結果。**
(C) Pay for the repair at the SSD office.	到安全標準處的辦公室支付維修費。
(D) Inspect the sidewalk himself.	自行檢查人行道。

由第二段的最後一句 After the work has been completed, ... arrange for an inspection.可知，修繕完畢之後格蘭傑先生必須請人來檢查，故 (B) 為正解。而其中的 after the work 就等同於 after repairs，只要搜尋問題中的關鍵詞，便能找出答案。

● 162 ~ 165 投訴信 ⊃ Pre 79 ~ 80

第 162 ~ 165 題與以下的信件內容有關。

多蘿西‧嘉蘭德女士
業務部經理
CE 工程
425 號，德文工業園區
西艾德蒙斯，華盛頓州 98026-6509

2008 年 8 月 15 日

親愛的嘉蘭德女士，

自 1995 年起，我們就從貴公司購入了數台印刷機及其他必要的周邊配備，我們對這些產品的效能都很滿意。不過，最近貴公司的售後服務品質已開始變差。

我們在 2005 年設置了 2 台貴公司的 550B 型印刷機，而你們標準的每年 2 次服務讓這些機器維持著良好的運作狀態。每當有故障發生，貴公司的維修工程師就會在 24 小時內到達我們工廠。

然而，上週其中一台印刷機突然停止運作，所以我們打電話要求貴公司的一家代理商來看看。我們以為他會馬上到，但是他卻說他最快只能安排大約七天後才過來！

更糟的是，該維修工程師本來應該在早上 11 點到，但是他卻到了下午 4 點後才現身。這使得我們的某些工程師不得不留到較晚，直到貴公司的代理商修好機器為止。

我知道您一定能理解我們的不滿。我們已向該服務代理商投訴此一事件，但是還沒有收到任何回應。

我們很期待您的回覆，並希望您能承諾會立即改善貴公司的售後服務。

丹‧愛德華茲
產品部經理
特羅特印刷服務公司
謹啟

Strategies ‧ Pre Test ‧ Half Test 1 ‧ Half Test 2 ‧ Full Test

162. 正確答案：(D) ☆☆☆

Why is the printing company dissatisfied with CE Engineering?

此印刷公司為何對 CE 工程不滿？

(A) The quality of its machines is going down.　　他們機器的品質不斷下降。

(B) It cannot provide suitable machines.　　他們無法提供合適的機器。

(C) Its engineers are not as skillful as before.　　他們工程師的技術沒有以前好。

(D) Its level of service has declined.　　**他們的服務水準已下降。**

> **解說**
>
> 由信函第一段第二句的 ... the quality of your after-sales service has become worse. 即可知，正確答案為 (D)。而文中並無任何與 (A)、(B)、(C) 選項有關的資訊。

163. 正確答案：(B) ☆

How often did a CE service engineer visit Trot Printing Service, Inc. in the past?

以前 CE 的維修工程師拜訪特羅特印刷服務公司的頻率為何？

(A) Once a year　　每年一次

(B) Twice a year　　**每年兩次**

(C) Six times a year　　每年六次

(D) Every month　　每個月

> **解說**
>
> 由信函第二段第一句提到的 your regular twice-yearly service 可知，正確答案是 (B)。

164. 正確答案：(A) ☆☆

What happened last week?　　上週發生了什麼事？

(A) A machine broke down.　　**有台機器故障了。**

(B) A machine was not delivered on time.　　有台機器並未準時送到。

(C) An engineer failed to repair a machine.　　有個工程師沒能成功修好機器。

(D) An engineer came a day late.　　有個工程師遲到了一天。

解說

第三段第一句提到的 ... last week, one of the printers stopped suddenly ... ，也就是說，有一台機器壞掉了，故本題選 **(A)**。

165. 正確答案：(C) ☆☆

Why did Mr. Edwards write to Ms. Garland?　　愛德華茲先生為何要寫信給嘉蘭德女士？

(A) To sign a contract with her company　　為了和她的公司簽訂一份合約

(B) To build a better relationship with her　　為了和她建立更好的關係

(C) To ask for better service　　**為了要求更好的服務**

(D) To arrange a meeting　　為了安排一場會議

解說

由信尾提到的 We ... hope that you can promise an immediate improvement in your after-sales service 可知，正確答案為 **(C)**。

● **166 ~ 168 指示** ⊃ Pre 85 ~ 87

第 166 ~ 168 題與以下的指示有關。

被蛇咬傷時的處理方法

毒蛇咬傷屬於緊急醫療事件，而且有致命危機。但是如果能妥善處理，或許就不會造成嚴重影響。因此，首要任務就是儘速將傷患送到急診室。然而，在此之前，你還能進行其他動作來幫助傷患。

務必遵守以下準則：

1. 讓傷患保持平靜。移動會使得毒性擴散。試著將受傷的部位保持在低於心臟的位置，以減低毒性的流動量。

2. 在被咬部分上方用東西（例如手帕）綁緊，以避免毒性擴散。如果你有可吸出毒液的裝置，應依循製造商的用法說明使用。
   注意：千萬不可用口吸出毒液。

3. 請小心死後的毒蛇，因為毒蛇死後 1 小時內仍可能有咬人的反射動作出現。

- □ top priority [tɑp praɪˋɔrətɪ] 最優先的事
- □ victim [ˋvɪktɪm] 图 犧牲者、受害者（在此指傷患）
- □ keep ... calm 讓……保持冷靜
- □ affected area [əˋfɛktɪd ˋɛrɪə] 受傷部位

166. 正確答案：(B) ☆☆

How should people be treated if they have been bitten by a poisonous snake?
如果被毒蛇咬傷應該如何處理？

(A) They should be moved to a bed or a chair. 　應將他們移到床上或椅子上。

(B) They should be taken to an emergency 　**應儘速將他們送往急診室。**
**　　room as soon as possible.**

(C) The bite must be cleaned. 　必須清潔咬傷處。

(D) The bite should be bandaged. 　必須用繃帶包紮咬傷處。

> **解說**
>
> 由指示第一段第三句 So, the top priority is getting the victim to an emergency room as quickly as possible. 可知，正確答案為 (B)。

167. 正確答案：(B) ☆☆

Why is it important to keep the bite below heart level?
為何必須將被咬部位保持在低於心臟的位置？

(A) To keep the person calm 　為了讓傷患保持冷靜。

(B) To stop the poison from spreading 　**為了阻止毒性擴散**

(C) To increase the flow of poison 　為了增加毒性的流動量

(D) To affect the area that was bitten 　為了感染被咬部位

> **解說**
>
> 指示中的準則 1 提到的 Try to keep the affected area below heart level to reduce the flow of poison. ，因此本題應選 (B)。注意，原文中的 affected area 指的就是被咬到的部位。另，選項中 (D) 中的 affect 指「影響」，與 affected area 的 affect 同字但不同義。

168. 正確答案：(D) ☆

What should people do if they find a dead poisonous snake?

(A) Take it to the doctor within an hour.
(B) Check its reflexes.
(C) Put it in a box.
(D) Make sure not to touch it.

如果發現死掉的毒蛇時該怎麼做？

在 1 小時內把牠帶去給醫生。
檢查其反射動作。
放進箱子裡。
絕對不要碰牠。

 解說

由準則 3 的 Be careful of the dead snake because it can bite as a reflex action for up to an hour. 可知，正確答案為 (D)。

● 169 ~ 172 廣告 ⊃ Pre 77 ~ 78

第 169 ~ 172 題與以下廣告有關。

清潔大師
地毯與布面家具的清潔專家

主要製造商都建議，為了維持外觀，地毯每隔十二到十八個月，家具每隔十八至二十四個月應接受一次專業清洗。透過我們的定期維護服務，便能讓您的地毯與家具呈現最佳狀態。

布面家具的清潔

布面家具可使用蒸氣、泡沫洗潔劑或乾洗等方式清潔。而清潔布面家具時必須特別小心。用於清潔地毯的產品不可用在布面家具上，因為布面類家具可能包含必須使用不同種類清潔劑的纖維。有了正確的定期維護，布面家具就能持續使用多年。

東方地毯的清潔

手洗

我們會先去除表面乾鬆的泥土，然後用特殊的清潔劑讓髒汙與油垢鬆脫。我們使用特殊的清潔溶液，以手輕柔、徹底地搓揉與沖洗您嬌貴的地毯。您地毯上的任何污漬，都會以污漬清除劑小心地清除。接著地毯會再進行一次沖洗，好徹底去除任何殘餘的污漬清除劑。

乾洗

我們採用自己獨特的乾洗產品，這是專為清理東方地毯中的天然纖維而配製的。此產品能使泥土鬆脫，同時維持纖維的柔軟，又不損害染料。地毯上的任何污漬都會以污漬清除劑仔細清除。

＊我們將到府取毯並送回，不加任何額外費用。

169. 正確答案：(B) ☆

How often do manufacturers recommend furnishing be cleaned at least?
製造商建議家具至少應以怎樣的頻率清潔？

(A) Twice a year 每年 2 次
(B) Every two years **每 2 年 1 次**
(C) Every two and a half years 每 2 年半 1 次
(D) Every three years 每 3 年 1 次

解說

廣告副標題下方的引言提到 ... professionally cleaned ... furnishings every 18 to 24 months ...，換句話說，至少每兩年要清潔一次，因此正解為 (B)。請注意別漏看問題最後的 at least。

170. 正確答案：(D) ☆☆

Why can upholstery furniture not be cleaned in the same way as carpets?
布面家具為何不能採用和地毯一樣的清潔方式？

(A) Carpet cleaners are too strong. 地毯清潔劑的效果太強烈了。
(B) Carpet cleaners are too weak. 地毯清潔劑的效果太弱了。
(C) Upholstery may contain the same fibers as carpets. 布面家具可能包含和地毯一樣的纖維。
(D) Upholstery may contain different fibers than carpets. **布面家具所包含的纖維可能和地毯不同。**

解說

由 Upholstery Cleaning「布面家具的清潔」說明第三句提到的 ... as it may contain fibers that require a different type of cleaner. 來推斷，布面家具可能包含與地毯不同的纖維，正確答案是 (D)。

171. 正確答案：(B) ☆

What is done first if an oriental rug is washed by hand?

手洗東方地毯時的第一個步驟為何？

(A) It is steam cleaned.　　　　　　　　　以蒸氣洗淨。

(B) It is cleaned of dry soil.　　　　　　**清除乾泥土。**

(C) Dirt and oil are loosened.　　　　　　讓髒汙與油垢鬆脫。

(D) Spots are removed　　　　　　　　　去除污漬。

> **解說**
>
> 依據東方地毯 Hand-Washing 說明第一句 We will remove dry loose soil and then ... 可知
> 正確答案就是 (B)。而以蒸氣洗淨的是布料家具，所以 (A) 不對；(C)、(D) 則是接在 (B)
> 之後的步驟，所以都不對。

172. 正確答案：(C) ☆☆

What should NOT be done to the carpet in the dry cleaning process?

在乾洗程序中不該對地毯進行哪項處理？

(A) Loosen dirt.　　　　　　　　　　　讓泥土鬆脫。

(B) Remove spots.　　　　　　　　　　去除污漬。

(C) Change the colors.　　　　　　　**改變顏色。**

(D) Make the fibers soft.　　　　　　　軟化纖維。

> **解說**
>
> Dry Cleaning 下方說明中的第二句提到 without harming the dyes，意思就是不會讓地毯
> 變色，因此 (C) 為正確答案。而 (A)、(B)、(D) 都包含在清洗程序中。（注意，此句為問
> Not 的問題。）

● 173 ~ 176 觀光導覽

第 173 ~ 176 題與以下的城市觀光導覽有關。

探索洛杉磯

對遊客來說，洛杉磯並非最便利的城市。這個城市幅員廣大寬闊，以至於許多遊客在去過好萊塢大道及環球影城之後，就覺得他們看夠了。但是這「天使之城」還有更多東西可以提供給那些願意多花一點力氣的人——博物館、音樂，以及可能算得上是世上最多樣化的美食。最大的問題是如何四處移動。最好的辦法是雇用一個司機整天，或事先預約計程車。要在街上攔到計程車並不容易，穿梭於 LA 複雜的高速公路系統的任務，還是交給已經熟悉該城市的專業司機為上。

或許，最知名的 LA 文化地標的好萊塢露天碗形劇場，是體驗絕妙音樂的最佳去處，不論你喜歡古典、搖滾、拉丁美洲或任何其他類型的音樂都不成問題。在這個擁有 18,000 個座位的場館中，您可選擇靠前面的高檔座位（通常需要事前預約），或是後方只需要幾美元、在最後一刻仍可取得的座位。另一個欣賞好音樂的地方，則是華特迪士尼音樂廳，洛杉磯愛樂管弦樂團的發源地。此音樂廳號稱是世界上聽覺效果絕佳的音樂廳之一。

兩個最棒的博物館分別是 J．保羅．蓋蒂博物館和洛杉磯郡立美術館。俗稱「蓋蒂」的這間博物館擁有令人印象深刻的建築物及景觀，使得其建築物本身甚至比裡面的藝術收藏更有名。而郡立美術館則擁有非常棒的美洲、亞洲及伊斯蘭教藝術品收藏，也經常舉辦電影及音樂系列活動和巡迴展。下午五點後以及每個月的第二個星期二，都可免費入場參觀。

Word List

- □ vast [væst] 形 巨大的、廣大的
- □ landmark [`lænd.mark] 名 地標
- □ cuisine [kwɪ`zin] 名 菜餚
- □ ongoing [`ɑn.goɪŋ] 形 進行中的、不間斷的

173. 正確答案：(D) ☆☆

Why is Los Angeles a difficult city for tourists?
對遊客來說，洛杉磯為何是個困難的城市？

(A) It is not easy to catch a taxi.　　　　　不容易招到計程車。
(B) It has a high level of crime.　　　　　這裡的犯罪率高。
(C) Transportation is very expensive.　　　交通費非常昂貴。
(D) It is hard to get from one place to another.　難從一個地方到另一個地方。

解說

由導覽第一段第四句 The biggest problem is getting around. 可知，正確答案為 (D)。

174. 正確答案：(B) ☆

What is the best way to see the sights of Los Angeles?
遊覽洛杉磯的最佳辦法為何？

(A) Take a bus tour. 　參加巴士旅行團。
(B) Hire an experienced driver. 　**雇用經驗豐富的司機。**
(C) Get a good map of the freeway system. 　拿張詳盡的高速公路系統地圖。
(D) Plan the tour very carefully. 　非常仔細地規劃旅遊行程。

解說

導覽第一段的最後一句提到的 a driver already familiar with the city 意思就是選項裡的 an experienced driver。

175. 正確答案：(C) ☆☆

Which of the followings can be best appreciated from the outside?
以下哪個景點最適合從外部欣賞？

(A) The Hollywood Bowl 　好萊塢碗形劇場
(B) The Walt Disney Concert Hall 　華特迪士尼音樂廳
(C) The J. Paul Getty Museum 　**J・保羅・蓋蒂博物館**
(D) The Los Angeles County Museum of Art 　洛杉磯縣立美術館

解說

由第三段的第二句提到的 "The Getty," ... has such impressive buildings and views ... 推斷，正確答案應為 (C)。

176. 正確答案：(D) ☆☆☆

What is NOT a feature of the Hollywood Bowl?
何者不是好萊塢碗形劇場的特色之一？

(A) It presents various styles of music. 　它提供各式各樣的音樂。
(B) Seats can be reserved at short notice. 　可臨時預約座位。
(C) The arena is uncovered. 　該場館沒有屋頂。
(D) It sometimes puts on free concerts 　**有時會舉辦免費的演唱會。**

在第二段關於費用的說明中提到 as little as a couple of dollars，但並非「免費」，因此正解是 (D)。而由該段中的 any other kind of music、last-minute seats、the open-air Hollywood Bowl 可知， (A)、(B)、(C) 皆為該場地的特色。（注意，本題為問 NOT 的問題。）

● 177 ~ 180 申請表 ⊃ Pre 81 ~ 84

第 177 ~ 180 題與以下的申請表有關。

別做井底蛙！
讓《全球商業雜誌》打開您的眼界，看見充滿機會的世界

只要 4.75 美元，就能獲得一期《全球商業雜誌》直接送到府上！
只需填寫下列表格，並利用隨附信封將表格和費用一同寄回即可。
僅需 47 美元就能獲得整年份十二期的雜誌。

請勾選以下合適的項目：
☐ 我要訂閱《全球商業雜誌》。除非我通知貴公司取消，否則我將每年續訂。我了解我每年
　　將持續被收取現行費率。
姓名：
住址：

☐ 訂閱一份雜誌作為賀禮，寄送給下方這個姓名的人。
姓名：
住址：

付款方式：
☐ 個人支票 或 ☐ 隨信附上 $ _____ 的美元國際匯票
☐ 以信用卡支付 ☐ VISA ☐ MasterCard ☐ 大來卡（Diners Club）
☐ 美國運通卡（American Express）
＊信用卡將依據交易日適用匯率，以當地貨幣扣款。

Word List

☐ prevailing rate [prɪ`velɪŋ ret] 現行費率、一般行情
☐ transaction [træn`zækʃən] 图 交易

177. 正確答案：(C) ☆

What is Global Business Journal?	「全球商業雜誌」是什麼？

(A) A daily paper　　　　　　　　　　　　一份日報
(B) A weekly magazine　　　　　　　　　　一份週刊
(C) A monthly magazine　　　　　　　　**一份月刊**
(D) An annual journal　　　　　　　　　　　一份年刊

解說

由前言第三句裡 Get 12 issues annually for only $47.00! 可知，該雜誌一年有 12 期，因此 (C) 為正解。

178. 正確答案：(B) ☆☆

What will happen if people do not inform the office they want to cancel their subscription?
如果人們不通知該雜誌社想取消訂閱的話，會發生什麼事？

(A) No more copies will be delivered. 雜誌將不再寄來。
(B) They will continue to receive issues. **他們會持續收到雜誌。**
(C) They will be asked if they want to continue. 他們會被詢問是否想繼續訂閱。
(D) They will be notified that their subscription has expired. 他們會收到訂閱過期的通知。

解說

在訂購申請表中 I WISH TO SUBSCRIBE to Global Business Journal 之後的 I will continue my subscription each year unless I notify you otherwise. 意思就是，如果未通知取消訂閱就是為繼續訂閱，因此 (B) continue to receive issues 為正解。

179. 正確答案：(D) ☆

What must people do to buy a subscription for a friend?
如果要替朋友付款訂購，該怎麼做？

(A) Get a gift card and send it to the friend directly. 取得一張禮物卡並直接寄給朋友。
(B) Write the friend's name and address on the form. 將朋友的姓名和地址填入表格中。
(C) Write their own name and address on the form. 將自己的姓名和地址填入表格中。
(D) Write the friend's name and address as well as their own. 將朋友和自己的姓名及地址都填入表格中。

由 SEND A GIFT SUBSCRIPTION to the person named below. 可知，須將寫受贈者的姓名和地址填在下方空格中。 (C) 為正解。

180. 正確答案：(A) ☆

What kind of payment is NOT accepted? 哪種付款方式不被接受？

(A) Cash | **現金**
(B) Credit card | 信用卡
(C) Personal check | 個人支票
(D) International money order | 國際匯票

在 Payment Method 部分，未列出的方式為 (A) Cash「現金」。（注意，本題為問 NOT 的題目。）

● 181 ~ 185 電子郵件 ⊃ Pre 91 ~ 95

第 181 ~ 185 題與以下的公告及電子郵件有關。

公告
每年兩次的慈善晚宴
「國際助童組織」

國際助童組織很高興地宣布即將舉辦慈善晚宴。我們所募集的善款，將用來協助提供庇護所和教育給世界各國無家可歸的孩童。晚宴將於 11 月 15 日晚上，從晚上 7 點到 11 點在城堡酒店舉辦。入場券為每人 75 美元。如果您希望出席，請依下列程序辦理申請。

預約方法：
1. 預約請透過傳真（756-9584-9955）或電子郵件（nspicer@htci.org），與尼古拉・史派賽聯繫。很抱歉我們不接受電話預約。
2. 預約截止日：10 月 31 日（星期四）
3. 請以銀行轉帳方式付款至：
   商業銀行，主街分行
   帳號：1409383
   帳戶名稱：HTCI

4. 在付款完成之前，預約將不被接受。

5. 每桌將坐 10 人。如果你們的團體較小，我們將做必要安排，讓你們與其他人併桌。

6. 若要預約整桌，請以團體方式預約付款、指定一位桌代表，並提供團體成員名單。

電子郵件

收件人：nspicer@htci.org
寄件人：jholland@iol.com
主旨：慈善晚宴的預約

親愛的尼古拉，

我想預約慈善晚宴。很抱歉我錯過了預約的截止期限，因為我出國了一陣子，現在才剛回來。如果你仍能幫我們安排出席事宜的話，我真的會很感激。

我們一共有六個人，所以我希望能預約六人的桌子。

只要一知道是否還能預約，我就會立刻透過銀行轉帳付款，並將付款單據傳真給你。

傑瑞·霍蘭
團體代表
祝好

Word List

☐ biannual [baɪˋænjʊəl] 形 一年兩次的

☐ raise money 募款

☐ share a table 併桌

☐ miss the deadline [ˋdɛdˏlaɪn] 錯過截止期限

☐ bank transfer [trænsˋfɝ] 銀行轉帳

181. 正確答案：(B) ☆

How often is the dinner held? 該晚宴的舉辦頻率如何？

(A) Every month 每月一次

(B) Every six months **每六個月一次**

(C) Every year 每年一次

(D) Every other year 每兩年 一次

> 解說
>
> 標題一開頭的 Biannual「每年兩次」就是「每半年一次」，亦即 (B)「每六個月一次」。

182. 正確答案：(C) ☆☆☆

When will the organization officially accept a reservation?

該組織何時會正式接受預約（視為預約完成）？

(A) When it receives cash from an applicant 從申請者那兒收到現金時

(B) When it receives a reservation form 收到預約表格時

(C) When it receives payment into the bank **收到匯入銀行帳戶之款項時**
   account

(D) When it receives an e-mail message 收到電子郵件時

> 解說
>
> 由公告中之項目 3 提到的 Send payment by bank transfer ... 和項目 4 的 Reservations are not considered accepted until payment is made. 可知，正確答案為 (C)。

183. 正確答案：(B) ☆☆

What kind of information is necessary to complete Jerry Holland's reservation?

傑瑞・霍蘭的預約還需要哪種資料才能完成？

(A) The ages of the people in his group 他的團體成員年齡

(B) The names of the people in his group **他的團體成員姓名**

(C) The name of his bank 他的銀行名稱

(D) His occupation 他的職業

> 解說
>
> 由公告中之項目 6 提到 When reserving a table, ... providing a list of members in the party.「若要預約一整桌時，……提供團體成員名單。」可知，正確答案為 (B)。(A)、(C)、(D) 則都非預約時必須提供的資料。

184. 正確答案：(B) ☆☆

Which part of the instructions has Jerry Holland NOT understood?

傑瑞・霍蘭並未理解公告說明中的哪個部分？

(A) The deadline for reservations   預約截止期限

**(B) The number of people who can sit   一桌可坐的人數
at one table**

(C) How to send confirmation of payment   如何傳送付款確認資訊

(D) The date of the charity dinner   慈善晚宴的日期

解說

公告中之項目 5 明白指出 Tables will seat 10 people，但是他在信中卻說 I'd like to reserve a six-person table.「我希望能預約 6 人的桌子」，因此 (B) 為正解。而由於在他的信中提到 I apologize for missing the deadline ...「很抱歉我錯過了截止期限」，可見他知道 (A)。另外，他還提到 I'll send the money by bank transfer and fax you the receipt.「我會透過銀行轉帳付款，並將付款單據傳真給你」，所以也證明了他知道 (C)。最後，他既然要參加晚宴，理當知道 (D)。

185. 正確答案：(D) ☆

How will the charity money be spent?   募得的慈善款項將被如何使用？

(A) To train group leaders   訓練團體代表

(B) To send volunteers to different countries   派遣義工到不同的國家

(C) To provide children with food   提供孩童食物

(D) To provide children with homes and schools 提供孩童住處以及學校

解說

由公告第二句提到的 The money we raise will provide homeless children with shelter and education ...「我們所募集的善款將用來協助提供庇護所，和教育給無家可歸的孩童」可知，正確答案為 (D)。

Strategies   Pre Test   Half Test 1   Half Test 2   Full Test

第 186 ~ 190 題與以下的兩封信件有關。

信函 1

詹姆士・庫柏先生
庫柏投顧
4 室，布羅德本特大廈
獨立大街
匹茲堡，賓州 15204

親愛的詹姆士，
你好嗎？希望你的事業順利。如你所知，我們認識多年以來，我一直非常感謝你給我的投資建議，而我在想，不知道你是否能夠再幫我一次忙。

就和很多其他人一樣，我對於過去幾年股市的表現相當失望，所以想試著轉移到一個不同的領域。我看到最近有許多報紙和雜誌報導說現在是投資澳洲房地產的好時機。你是否知道有任何好機會呢？如果你知道，那麼請寄些相關資訊給我，我會非常感激。
期待你的回覆。

凱文・米勒
敬上

信函 2

凱文・米勒先生
437 號，綠樹大道
哈里斯堡，賓州 17101

親愛的凱文，

隔了這麼久又再聽到你的消息，真是令人高興。我很樂意幫助你尋找理想的不動產投資機會。目前確實有許多人對澳洲市場很感興趣，而新建案也不少。我們公司已對新建案做了廣泛調查，而且終於決定出我們認為最理想的標的。詳細資訊請見下方。請讓我知道你是否對此有興趣，而如果有任何疑問，儘管與我聯繫。

詹姆士・庫柏
謹啓

日出之城（布里斯本）：提供一或兩房豪華格局，一棟品質精品綜合公寓，每間皆有大露台或花園。價格從 300,000 美元起。日出之城為高檔公寓大樓，鄰近布里斯本商業區，但是周圍卻有景觀綠地圍繞。日出之城還擁有一個健康俱樂部、一個奧運規格的泳池，以及兒童托育和寵物照顧設施。租賃市場極為理想，資本成長前景也十分看好。

Word List

- [ ] performance of the stock market [pəˋfɔməns] [stɑk ˋmɑrkɪt] 股市表現
- [ ] investment [ɪnˋvɛstmənt] 名 投資
- [ ] opportunity [ˌɑpəˋtjnətɪ] 名 機會
- [ ] extensive research [ɪkˋstɛnsɪv rɪˋsɝtʃ] 廣泛的調查
- [ ] boutique [buˋtik] 名 精品
- [ ] apartment complex [əˋpɑrtmənt ˋkɑmplɛks] 綜合公寓
- [ ] high-end condominium [haɪɛnd ˋkɑndəˌmɪnɪəm] 高檔公寓大樓
- [ ] landscaped [ˋlændˌskept] 形 經庭園造景的、經景觀美化的

186. 正確答案：(C) ☆☆

What is the relationship between James Cooper and Kevin Miller?

詹姆士·庫柏和凱文·米勒兩人是什麼關係？

(A) Friends 朋友

(B) Colleagues 同事

(C) Advisor and client **顧問與客戶**

(D) Superior and subordinate 上司與下屬

解說

由信函 1 第一段第三句提到的 ... I'm very grateful for the investment advice you've given me「我一直非常感謝你給我的投資建議」推斷，凱文應該是詹姆士的客戶。

187. 正確答案：(B) ☆

Why did Kevin Miller write to James Cooper? 凱文·米勒為何寫信給詹姆士·庫柏？

(A) To sell some real estate 為了賣不動產

(B) To get advice on an investment **為了獲得投資建議**

(C) To apply for a job 為了應徵工作

(D) To carry out research 為了進行調查

解說

由信函 1 第一段第三句提到的 ... I was wondering if you might be able to help me again. 和第二段最後兩句 Do you know of any good opportunities? If you do, I'd greatly appreciate your sending me some information. 即可確定，(B) 為本題正解。

188. 正確答案：(B) ☆☆

What is one benefit of buying an apartment in Sunrise City?

購買日出之城公寓的好處之一為何？

(A) The price is very low. 價格很低。

(B) The value is likely to rise. **很可能增值。**

(C) Sunrise City is close to the beach. 日出之城離海灘很近。

(D) The apartments have many bedrooms. 該公寓房間數眾多。

解說

由信函 2 日出之城簡介部分最後一句提到的 ... there are very good prospects for capital growth.「資本成長前景十分看好」這句介紹可知，正確答案是 (B)。而該公寓價格算不上低，所以 (A) 不對；文中有提到鄰近 business district（商業區），但沒說靠近海灘，所以 (C) 不對；由於是 one-or two-bedroom luxury units，可見房間數不多，所以 (D) 也不對。

189. 正確答案：(D) ☆

How long have Kevin Miller and James Cooper known each other?
凱文・米勒和詹姆士・庫柏認識了多久？

(A) This is their first communication.　　　　　這是他們第一次通信。

(B) A few weeks.　　　　　數週。

(C) A few months.　　　　　數個月。

(D) A few years.　　　　　**好幾年。**

解說

由信函 1 第一段第三句提到的 ... the investment advice you've given me over the years we've known each other ...「自相識多年以來，我一直非常感謝你給我的投資建議」可知，正確答案就是 (D)。

190. 正確答案：(D) ☆☆☆

Who might be most interested in purchasing a condominium in Sunrise City?
誰可能會對購買日出之城的公寓最有興趣？

(A) A single person with low income　　　　　低所得的單身人士

(B) A retired senior citizen　　　　　已退休的老年人

(C) A family with many children　　　　　有很多小孩的家庭

(D) A young working couple with a child　　　　　**有一個小孩的年輕雙薪家庭**

解說

由信函 2 日出之城簡介中提到的 one- or two-bedroom「一或兩房」和 child-care facility「兒童托育設施」來判斷，正確答案應為 (D)。簡介中有提到 luxury units，可見對低所得者來說此物件太貴了，所以 (A) 不對；文中亦提到 very close to business district「鄰近商業區」，因此並不適合退休老人，所以 (B) 不對；而該公寓雖有兒童托育設施，但為一到兩房格局的公寓，顯然不適合小孩多的家庭，所以 (C) 也不對。

第 191 ~ 195 題與以下的 2 封信件有關。

信函 1

顧客服務經理
FRB 電器
376 號，弗林德斯廣場
布里斯本，昆士蘭州 4000

10 月 19 日

敬啟者：

8 月 10 日，我用 85 美元的價格購買了貴公司產品之一的 MW2000 型烤麵包機。該價格包含 30 天退款試用期。這 85 美元當時已經以信用卡付款。可是當我第 1 次嘗試使用該烤麵包機時，卻發現計時器有問題，然後在 9 月 10 日那天，我決定將它退還給貴公司。貴公司的某位職員以電話通知我運費、手續費及 MW2000 的價錢都將存入我的帳戶。於是我把烤麵包機寄回貴公司，而貴公司也通知我你們已於 9 月 15 日收到。可是今天我卻收到信用卡帳單，貴公司不但收取了烤麵包機的錢，也收了運費和手續費。

過去我常使用貴公司產品，而且對其品質非常滿意。但是我很遺憾必須說，貴公司的售後服務實在有待改進。若貴公司能儘快將欠我的所有金額存入我的帳號，我會非常感激。

埃德加 · 邁克羅夫特
謹啟

信函 2

埃德加‧邁克羅夫特先生
148 號，木蘭巷
庫倫加塔，昆士蘭州 4225

10 月 25 日

親愛的邁克羅夫特先生，

非常感謝您來信提到有關購買 MW2000 及退款方面的問題。首先要對延誤退款至您帳戶的疏失表達歉意。我向您保證這只是個例外，因為我們一向很努力實現對尊貴顧客的承諾。

我已經親自指示我們的一位員工要採取必要行動，以確保全部金額能存入您的帳戶。此外，為了彌補我們的錯誤，我想提供 20% 的折扣給今年內您所購買的任何一項敝公司產品。

再一次，關於造成您的不便一事，請您接受我誠摯的歉意。我們很重視老主顧，而且願意盡一切努力，讓他們對我們的產品和雙方面的服務品質都感到滿意。

凱莉‧特雷弗
顧客服務經理
敬上

Word List

- [ ] defective [dɪ`fɛktɪv] 形 有瑕疵的
- [ ] shipping and handling charges 運費與手續費
- [ ] credit [`krɛdɪt] 動 存入銀行帳戶
- [ ] notify [`notə‚faɪ] 動 通知
- [ ] much to be desired [dɪ`zaɪrd] 有許多地方尚待改進、有許多不足之處
- [ ] oversight [`ovə‚saɪt] 名 疏失
- [ ] valued [`væljud] 形 寶貴的、看重的
- [ ] make up for ... 彌補……

191. 正確答案：(A) ☆☆

Why did the customer experience a problem? 這位顧客為何遇上問題？

(A) **The company was careless.** 　　該公司有所疏失。

(B) There was a computer error. 　　電腦出了錯。

(C) His letter did not reach the company. 　　他的信沒寄到該公司。

(D) His credit card company made an error. 　　他的信用卡公司出錯。

解說

由信函 1 第一段中提到的 money-back trail offer（第二句）、I shipped the toaster to you（第六句），及 charging me both the price and the shipping and handling charges（第七句）可知，正確答案應為 (A)。而 (D) 說的是「信用卡公司的錯」，請小心別誤解。

192. 正確答案：(C) ☆☆

What did the customer expect the company to do? 這位顧客希望該公司怎麼做？

(A) Replace the defective product. 　　更換瑕疵商品。

(B) Send him a check. 　　寄給他支票。

(C) **Refund all of his costs.** 　　退還給他所有費用。

(D) Give him a discount on future purchases. 　　在未來購買商品時給他折扣。

解說

由信函 1 第二段最後一句 I would be very grateful if you could credit my account with the full amount owed to me as soon as possible.「若貴公司能儘快將欠我的所有金額存入我的帳號，我會非常感激」可知，正確答案是 (C)。而顧客並未依求換貨，所以 (A) 不對；另，文中並無與 check「支票」有關的資訊，所以 (B) 也不對；最後，說要「在購買商品時提供折扣」的是客服經理不是顧客，因次 (D) 亦不對。

193. 正確答案：(B) ☆☆

What did the customer do after finding the product did not work properly?
在發現產品無法正常運作後，這位顧客做了什麼事？

(A) He threw it away. 　　他把該產品丟了。

(B) **He returned it to the manufacturer.** 　　他把產品退還給廠商。

(C) He tried to repair it by himself. 　　他試圖自行修理。

(D) He called on the manufacturer. 　　他去拜訪了製造商。

解說

由信函 1 第一段、第六句提到的 I shipped the toaster to you 即可知，正確答案為 (B)。而 (A)、(C)、(D) 中所提的狀況皆未發生，故不可選。

---

194. 正確答案：(C) ☆☆

What action did Kylie Trevor take in response to the customer's letter?

(A) She called the customer's credit card company.

(B) She sent the customer a new product at a lower cost.

(C) She told one of her staff to deal with the problem.

(D) She offered the customer a discount on all his future purchases.

凱莉・特雷弗針對顧客的信採取了什麼行動做為回應？

她打電話給顧客的信用卡公司。

她以較低的價格寄送新產品給該顧客。

她要求她的一名員工處理該問題。

她提供折扣給該顧客日後購買的所有商品。

解說

由信函 2 第二段第一句提到的 I have personally instructed one of our staff members to take the necessary action ...「我已經親自指示我們的一位員工要採取必要行動」可知，正確答案為 (C)。而 (D) 選項中的 all his future purchases 是指「此後購買的所有商品」，但是原文中所說的折扣期間只限今年內，而且僅限一項產品，所以 (D) 是錯的。

---

195. 正確答案：(A) ☆☆☆

What will be included in the refund from the company?

(A) The costs of merchandise, handling and shipping

(B) The cost of merchandise minus handling and shipping charges

(C) The cost of merchandise minus 20%

(D) The cost of merchandise plus 20%

該公司提供的退款將包含哪些款項？

商品價錢、手續費和運費

商品價錢減去手續費和運費

商品價錢減去 20%

商品價錢加上 20%

● 196 ~ 200 廣告與信函

第 196 ~ 200 題與以下的求才廣告及信函有關。

廣告

一流國際企業誠徵德語私人助理

協助資深主管在芝加哥開拓新營運據點,進行協助及事務管理等工作。

薪資約 40,000 美元　　工作地點:芝加哥市中心

工作地點為芝加哥市中心為據點,此新職務將協助 2 位石油及天然氣產業方面的德國企業開發主管。工作內容以安排行程、書信聯繫處理以及安排國外出差為主。理想的應徵者應為具高度組織能力與經驗的行政人員,擅長聽打且德語說寫流利。最重要的是,必須擁有人際關係技巧,能有效率地與高階主管一同工作。意者請將履歷與求職信寄給「戴維斯與查爾斯公司」的法蘭西斯・奧哈拉,地址為 60608 伊利諾州,芝加哥,里亞托廣場,4 室。

信函

法蘭西斯・奧哈拉女士
戴維斯與查爾斯公司
4 室,里亞托廣場 47
芝加哥,伊利諾州 60608

親愛的奧哈拉小姐,

我寫此信來應徵貴公司求才廣告上的德語私人助理一職。我對該職務非常有興趣,同時相信我充分具備擔任該職務的資格。我精通英語及德語。事實上我父親是德國人,我的童年是在德國度過的。在我 14 歲時,我們舉家搬到美國,我在美國唸的高中和大學是。我的法文和

義大利文的口語能力也很好。

正如您將在我的履歷中看到的，我過去 5 年擔任的都是行政管理職。雖然這項資歷主要是在金融服務業領域，但是我覺得我曾經花費 2 年時間協助一家德國銀行設立它在美國的辦公室的經驗，還是與此工作有相關性。

我相信我能成為貴公司的重要人才，而且非常期待能獲得面試的機會。

瑪格麗特・赫希
敬上

Word List

- □ executive [ɪg`zɛkjʊtɪv] 图 高階主管
- □ correspondence [ˌkɔrə`spɑndəns]
  图 書信聯繫
- □ administrator [əd`mɪnəˌstretɚ]
  图 行政人員
- □ résumé [rɪ`zjum] 图 履歷、簡歷
- □ well-qualified for [wɛl `kwɑləˌfaɪd]
  充分具備……的資格
- □ administrative position
  [əd`mɪnəˌstretɪv pə`zɪʃən] 行政管理職

- □ itinerary [aɪ`tɪnəˌrɛrɪ] 图 行程
- □ candidate [`kændədet] 图 應徵者
- □ audio typing [`ɔdɪo taɪpɪŋ] 聽口述打字
- □ relevant [`rɛləvənt] 形 相關的
- □ nevertheless [ˌnɛvəðə`lɛs]
  副 雖然如此、但是
- □ asset [`æsɛt] 图 資產、人才

---

196. 正確答案：(C) ☆

Where will the job be based?　　　　　此工作將以何處為據點？

(A) Germany　　　　　　　　　　　　德國
(B) Italy　　　　　　　　　　　　　　義大利
(C) The United States　　　　　　**美國**
(D) France　　　　　　　　　　　　　法國

解說

依據求才廣告引言中的 a new location in Chicago 及其下方的 Work place: Central Chicago，還有內文一開頭的 Based in central Chicago「以芝加哥市中心為據點」等可確定，正解為 (C)。而 (A) 是兩位高階主管的國籍，非正解。另外請小心別因應徵者會的外語種類而誤選了 (B) 或 (D)。

197. 正確答案：**(A)** ☆☆

What kind of person should apply for this position? 哪種人該應徵此職務？

(A) Someone who is good at human relations　　擅長人際關係的人

(B) Someone who is willing to learn　　**願意學習的人**

(C) Someone who can type well　　很會打字的人

(D) Someone who is quick in decision making　　能夠迅速做出決策的人

> **解說**
>
> 廣告內文中第四句提到的 interpersonal skills「人際關係技巧」與正確答案 (A) 中的 human relations 的意思相同。而依據第三句中的要求 experienced administrators「有經驗的行政人員」可知，(B) 不對；另外，應徵者必須會聽打而非一般的打字，所以 (C) 也不對；至於 (D) 的 decision making 在文中並沒有相關資訊，因此亦非正確答案。

198. 正確答案：**(D)** ☆☆

Why does Margarete Hirsh think she is well-qualified for the job? 瑪格麗特・赫希為何認為自己充分具備擔任該職務的資格？

(A) Because of her experience in the oil and gas industry　　因為她在石油及天然氣產業方面的經驗

(B) Because of her command of English　　因為她的英語能力

(C) Because of her banking experience in Germany　　因為她在德國時的銀行業相關資歷

(D) Because of her command of German　　**因為她的德語能力**

> **解說**
>
> 求才廣告的標題明白提到徵的是 GERMAN-SPEAKING PERSONAL ASSISTANT「德語私人助理」，而赫希小姐在求職信中則提到（信函第一段的第三句）I am completely bilingual in English and German「我精通英語及德語」，因此可知正確答案應為 (D)。

199. 正確答案：**(B)** ☆

How did Margarete Hirsh learn German? 瑪格麗特・赫希是如何學會德語的？

(A) She studied it at university.　　她在大學時學的。

(B) She lived in Germany as a child.　　**她小時候住在德國。**

(C) She worked in a German company.　　她曾在德國公司工作。

(D) She traveled to Germany for a few times.　　她去德國旅行了數次。

解說

由信函第一段第四句 In fact my father is German, and I spent my childhood in Germany，「事實上我父親是德國人，我的童年在德國度過的」可知，這是她會德語的原因之一，因此正確答案應為 (B)。而她沒提過在大學曾修德語，所以 (A) 不對；另外，她並未把 (C) 列為會德語的原因，所以 (C) 也不對；最後，信中完全沒提到與旅遊有關的事，所以 (D) 亦非正確答案。

200. 正確答案：(B) ☆☆

In the want ad, the word "interpersonal" in line 6, is closest in meaning to	與求才廣告第六行中的 interpersonal 意思最接近？
(A) International	國際的
(B) Person-to-person	**人與人之間的**
(C) Tactful and kind	圓融而親切的
(D) Clever and thoughtful	聰明且深思熟慮的

解說

interpersonal 是由字首 inter- 加上 personal 而來，而 inter- 是 between 之意，故 interpersonal 即為 between persons 之意，(B) 的意思顯然最接近。另，也可由接在 interpersonal skills 之後的 to work effectively with senior executives 判斷出其意義。（遇到考詞彙意義的題目時，便可像這樣觀察前後文以尋找相關的同義說法。）

Pre Test

題號	講述者國籍	音軌編號
Part 1		
Directions		2
1	美	
2	美	
3	加	3
4	英	
5	澳	
Part 2		
Directions		4
6	美→加	
7	加→美	5
8	美→加	
9	澳→英	
10	加→澳	
11	英→澳	6
12	英→加	
13	美→英	
14	英→美	
15	美→加	7
16	美→加	
17	英→澳	
18	澳→加	
19	加→英	8
20	加→澳	
Part 3		
Directions		9
223	女：美／男：加	10
24-26	男：加／女：澳	11
27-29	男：英／女：美	12
30-32	男：加／女：美	13
33-35	女：澳／男：英	14
Part 4		
Directions		15
36-38	美	16
39-41	美	17
444	英	18
45-47	加	19
48-50	澳	20

Half Test 1

題號	講述者國籍	音軌編號
Part 1		
Directions		21
1	加	
2	美	
3	澳	22
4	英	
5	美	
Part 2		
Directions		23
6	美→英	
7	加→英	24
8	英→美	
9	英→美	
10	澳→加	
11	加→英	25
12	英→澳	
13	加→英	
14	美→加	
15	美→加	26
16	加→澳	
17	澳→加	
18	加→美	
19	美→英	27
20	英→澳	
Part 3		
Directions		28
223	女：澳／男：加	29
24-26	男：英／女：美	
27-29	男1：加／男2：英	30
30-32	男：加／女：澳	
33-35	女：美／男：加	31
Part 4		
Directions		32
36-38	英	33
39-41	澳	
444	加	34
45-47	美	
48-50	美	35

Half Test 2

題號	講述者國籍	音軌編號
Part 1		
Directions		36
1	美	
2	加	
3	英	37
4	加	
5	澳	
Part 2		
Directions		38
6	美→英	
7	英→美	39
8	美→加	
9	加→英	
10	美→英	
11	英→加	40
12	美→英	
13	美→英	
14	澳→美	
15	美→加	41
16	英→美	
17	加→澳	
18	澳→加	
19	加→澳	42
20	加→英	
Part 3		
Directions		43
223	男：英／女：加	44
24-26	男：英／女：美	
27-29	男：加／女：美	45
30-32	男1：英／男2：加	
33-35	女：澳／男：加	46
Part 4		
Directions		47
36-38	英	48
39-41	澳	
444	英	49
45-47	美	
48-50	美	50

Full Test

題號	講述者國籍	音軌編號	題號	講述者國籍	音軌編號
Part 1			Part 3		
Directions		51	Directions		63
1	美	52	443	男：英 / 女：加	64
2	美		44-46	女：英 / 男：美	
3	英		47-49	女：澳 / 男：加	65
4	美		50-52	男1：美 / 男2：英	
5	美		53-55	女：加 / 男：英	66
6	澳	53	56-58	男：美 / 女：澳	
7	英		59-61	女：加 / 男：英	67
8	美		664	男：美 / 女：澳	
9	美		65-67	男1：英 / 男2：加	68
10	美		68-70	女：加 / 男：英	
Part 2			Part 4		
Directions		54	Directions		69
11	英→澳	55	773	加	70
12	美→英		74-76	澳	
13	加→英		77-79	美	71
14	加→英		80-82	澳	
15	澳→加	56	83-85	美	72
16	英→加		86-88	英	
17	美→英		89-91	澳	73
18	英→加		994	美	
19	英→美	57	95-97	加	74
20	加→英		98-100	美	
21	英→美				
22	美→英				
23	加→澳	58			
24	英→澳				
25	加→英				
26	英→加				
27	美→英	59			
28	澳→英				
29	英→美				
30	加→英				
31	加→英	60			
32	澳→加				
33	英→加				
34	加→英				
35	加→英	61			
36	英→加				
37	澳→加				
38	澳→英				
39	英→加	62			
40	英→美				

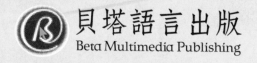

國家圖書館出版品預行編目資料

多益新鮮人一定要有的奪分筆記：輕鬆超越 650 分,熱門職缺搶著
要你! /大賀理惠等作；陳亦苓譯. -- 初版. -- 臺北市：貝塔, 2013. 01
　　面；　公分
　　ISBN 978-957-729-909-3（平裝附光碟片）
　　1.多益測驗
805.1895　　　　　　　　　　　　　　　　　　101024069

多益新鮮人一定要有的奪分筆記
—輕鬆超越 650 分，熱門職缺搶著要你！

作　　者 / 大賀理惠、Bill Benfield、Ann Gleason、Terry Browning
譯　　者 / 陳亦苓
執行編輯 / 范雅禎

出　　版 / 貝塔出版有限公司
地　　址 / 台北市 100 館前路 12 號 11 樓
電　　話 / (02) 2314-2525
傳　　真 / (02) 2312-3535
客服專線 / (02) 2314-3535
客服信箱 / btservice@betamedia.com.tw
郵撥帳號 / 19493777
帳戶名稱 / 貝塔出版有限公司

總 經 銷 / 時報文化出版企業股份有限公司
地　　址 / 桃園縣龜山鄉萬壽路二段 351 號
電　　話 / (02) 2306-6842

出版日期 / 2013年1月初版一刷
定　　價 / 560 元
ISBN：978-957-729-909-3

喚醒**你**的英文語感！

請對折後釘好，直接寄回即可！

100 台北市中正區館前路12號11樓

 貝塔語言出版 收
Beta Multimedia Publishing

寄件者住址 □□□

貝塔語言出版
Beta Multimedia Publishing

讀者服務專線（02）2314-3535　　讀者服務傳真（02）2312-3535
客戶服務信箱　btservice@betamedia.com.tw

www.betamedia.com.tw

謝謝您購買本書！！

貝塔語言擁有最優良之英文學習書籍，為提供您最佳的英語學習資訊，您可填妥此表後寄回（免貼郵票）將可不定期收到本公司最新發行書訊及活動訊息！

姓名：＿＿＿＿＿＿＿＿＿＿＿　性別：□男 □女　生日：＿＿＿年＿＿＿月＿＿＿日

電話：(公)＿＿＿＿＿＿＿＿＿(宅)＿＿＿＿＿＿＿＿＿(手機)＿＿＿＿＿＿＿＿＿

電子信箱：＿＿＿＿＿＿＿＿＿＿＿＿＿＿＿＿＿＿＿＿＿＿＿＿＿

學歷：□高中職含以下　□專科　□大學　□研究所含以上

職業：□金融　□服務　□傳播　□製造　□資訊　□軍公教　□出版

　　　□自由　□教育　□學生　□其他

職級：□企業負責人　□高階主管　□中階主管　□職員　□專業人士

1. 您購買的書籍是？＿＿＿＿＿＿＿＿＿＿＿＿＿＿＿＿＿＿＿＿

2. 您從何處得知本產品？(可複選)

　　　□書店 □網路 □書展 □校園活動 □廣告信函 □他人推薦 □新聞報導 □其他

3. 您覺得本產品價格：

　　　□偏高 □合理 □偏低

4. 請問目前您每週花了多少時間學英語？

　　　□ 不到十分鐘 □ 十分鐘以上，但不到半小時 □ 半小時以上，但不到一小時

　　　□ 一小時以上，但不到兩小時 □ 兩個小時以上 □ 不一定

5. 通常在選擇語言學習書時，哪些因素是您會考慮的？

　　　□ 封面 □ 內容、實用性 □ 品牌 □ 媒體、朋友推薦 □ 價格□ 其他＿＿＿＿＿

6. 市面上您最需要的語言書種類為？

　　　□ 聽力 □ 閱讀 □ 文法 □ 口說 □ 寫作 □ 其他＿＿＿＿＿＿

7. 通常您會透過何種方式選購語言學習書籍？

　　　□ 書店門市 □ 網路書店 □ 郵購 □ 直接找出版社 □ 學校或公司團購

　　　□ 其他＿＿＿＿＿＿＿

8. 給我們的建議：＿＿＿＿＿＿＿＿＿＿＿＿＿＿＿＿＿＿＿＿＿＿＿＿＿＿

＿＿＿＿＿＿＿＿＿＿＿＿＿＿＿＿＿＿＿＿＿＿＿＿＿＿＿＿＿＿＿＿＿＿＿

Get a Feel for English !

喚醒你的英文語感！